SISTERS OF THE HARROW

Printed in Australia

Book cover by Vladimir Shvachko

Title text art by Radovan Zivkovic

Interior illustrations by Vanessa Novak, @ImShyka

Internal design by Book Burrow www.bookburrow.com.au

Images in this book are copyright approved for the author.

First printing: March 2025

Paperback ISBN 978-0-6484-2415-4

eBook ISBN 978-0-6484-24146-1

 A catalogue record for this work is available from the National Library of Australia

For believing in me and my work before anyone else did,
as well as putting up with me when I became distant,
I dedicate this story to my sisters,
Rebecca and Karlie

Contents

One: A Great Regret

Tau

10 cycles ago

The Elysian Mountains

The compartment ramp slowly lowered with an unsettling whine, revealing a surreal, white forest. It touched down on the soft powder with a muffled thump. The nearby dark tree branches shook loose their burden of snow, letting it fall to the forest floor and form little frosty mounds.

Our squad's den mother was the first down the ramp, her grey armour blending into the blinding, snowy wonderland. 'Come on!' Corporal Tallu yelled over the droning aircraft engines.

We sixteen similarly dressed little sisters obeyed, rushing down the ramp one after another. I was last, hesitantly snatching my pistol from the rack and following the others in a line.

No sooner had I jumped off the ramp than it began to rise and seal. The craft's engines whirred again. It took off up and over the trees and into the sky.

We all moved into formation around the corporal. Some of the kids were shaking in the cold. It was the coldest I had ever felt.

Although we knew we were supposed to stand to attention, we couldn't help but be mesmerised by our surroundings. The others emitted gasps and squeals of awe as we had never seen snow before. Some crunched their armoured boots into the compacted snow over and over, just to hear the sound. I bent down and scooped up a clump to feel it with my gloved fingertips.

Ever since our squad heard the next training manoeuvre was scouting the world-famous icy mountains of Esprit, they had been over-the-moon excited. I'd usually be terrified after disembarking, but this place was truly breathtaking.

'Everyone, attention!' the corporal yelled with her arms behind her back.

We suddenly remembered we were on a mission. Those out of place quickly rejoined the line. I dropped my handful of snow, brushed my hand on my leg, and grasped my weapon with both hands. Together we stood up straight and waited in silence.

Tallu paced along the line, towering over us children. She held out her hand, caught a snowflake, and examined it as it melted in her glove. 'Our mission is to hunt down a small group of nomads that have been spotted in the area, and we can't do that if we're distracted by our environment.' She strode right up to me and smiled. 'And that is why… I want you to get your fill of it now.'

The rest of us glanced at one another in surprise.

'Ma'am?' Tarsus interrupted. 'What about the mission?'

The corporal nodded and paced over to her. 'It can wait. They don't know we're here yet. Their settlement's somewhere to the west, and it's not going anywhere. This snow on the other hand… you might never see anything like it again.'

Amiki, my closest friend, was by my side as usual. We both grinned at each other. She was no doubt thinking the same thing as me. Yesterday we talked about making a snowwoman and even having a snowball fight.

Tallu wandered to a nearby log, placed her weapon upon it, and took a seat, facing us. 'We leave here in twenty.' She raised her hands and flicked her fingers as if to shoo us away. 'Play.'

We little sisters had all been not-so-secretly hoping for this. The entire squad ran in different directions at the same time, smiling and giggling. We carelessly dropped our weapons before scooping some snow up, patting them into balls, and hurling them at our closest squad-sisters.

I felt a cold blast against my neck. Another hit me in the face, covering my normally transparent faceplate in white. I brushed it clear and took off the helmet.

Amiki was already preparing another ball for me, grinning gleefully. She juggled it around and launched it with pinpoint accuracy.

Three more snowballs hit me in quick succession, so I raised my hands to shield myself. 'I surrender!' I could barely feel the hits through my thick armour. I imagined it would feel a lot colder without it.

The corporal shook her head and laughed. 'Oh, Tau, you *really* aren't made for war, are you?'

'No surrendering, coward!' Amiki called, before ducking behind a tree.

I bent down and moulded some ammunition of my own, and once I had three I threw them at her fortified position. She took cover, but each missed anyway, hitting the tree trunk.

She laughed at my embarrassing attempts before receiving a barrage of snowballs from behind. Coleo had ambushed her from the brush.

Amiki smirked back at Coleo, bent down, hastily made another snowball and then gave chase. 'You're dead!'

I turned back to the corporal, who was still laughing just as much as the kids running around the forest. Tallu normally had a professional manner, which meant keeping us in line and making sure we were ready for battle, but I loved it when she showed kindness like this.

'Thank you, Ma'am,' I called to her.

She smiled warmly before gesturing to the others. 'Stop wasting your time talking to me. Go get them!'

I nodded appreciatively, turned and ran into the forest. 'Yes, Ma'am!'

We had been marching through the snowy forest most of the morning, a task made more difficult with every sinking step. We were forbidden from talking while marching; we wouldn't want to give our position away to the enemy. Even so, we all had permanent smiles plastered on our faces. I had never felt so happy.

I was getting tired, but the mission was far from over. We still had to kill or capture our targets. I'd give anything to not be a part of what was to come. I hated the nomads who killed my original squad-sisters, but these nomads weren't related to them at all, as far as I knew.

'You okay?' Amiki whispered, trying not to alert the corporal.

She had been marching beside me. Was I that easy to read? I forced a smile back and nodded.

Amiki, my best friend, was so different from all the other little sisters. While we mostly had pale skin, hers was bronzed. Her eyes were slightly upturned, and her black hair was glossier and smoother than my reddish, auburn hair. The most important difference, however, was that she thought all this killing was wrong, too. At least, that's the way she *used* to think, I wasn't sure now.

On our last mission, she killed a man for the first time. Granted, he was charging us with a knife, and if she hadn't fired, *I* certainly wouldn't have. After shooting, her face turned stone-cold, neutral, like killing a man meant nothing to her anymore.

Corporal Tallu was way ahead, leading us up the snowdrift. I made sure she wasn't looking and then brushed Amiki's shoulder. 'Hey, um. About that man you killed?'

What little warmth her face had faded. 'Yeah?'

It was hard for me to raise the question without also getting judged by the others within earshot, some of whom had already made a couple of kills themselves.

'How… did you feel afterwards?' I asked.

The two soldiers in front of me, Coleo and Tarsus, glanced back and sniggered. Among our squad, they had been bullying me the most over my lack of kills.

Amiki took her time with her answer, perhaps also aware of the others listening in. She stared ahead at the marching track. 'I did what was needed for you and me to live. It was him or us.'

'So, you didn't *feel* anything else?' I pressed.

She shook her head. 'Nothing. I... felt nothing for him.'

Coleo smirked back. 'Nervous, Tau? Don't worry, you'll make your first kill soon.'

Tarsus pointed into the forest. 'Maybe we'll find a baby animal for you to step on?'

'That's enough chatter back there,' the corporal's voice crackled through my helmet's receiver. 'We're getting close now.'

Tallu stopped the squad at the top of an icy ridge. She gave us a stern frown before facing ahead and crouching. Her faceplate lit up with green graphics, probably the map to make sure we were still on track.

There was a loud creak, perhaps from the trees. My eyes darted, searching for the source. Amiki was staring at my feet, so I followed her gaze. I was on a patch of ice, and small white cracks formed right beneath where I was standing.

'Don't... move,' Amiki said, before slowly reaching out.

A snap echoed, like breaking glass, and another, then several more. My gut lurched as the window-like ice shattered. I flailed my arms, hoping to latch onto the sharp ledge. I missed and plummeted into darkness.

I helplessly screamed and went rigid. The stale air whipped up as I fell. A sharp force in my back bent me at a painful angle. Another snap. My body slid off an outcropping. Pain shot through me like a thousand needles.

A second rocky thorn came out of nowhere, smashing my faceplate and sprinkling pieces everywhere. The glass ripped into my cheeks. My head snapped back as I continued to fall.

Thwomp!

Finally, a flat surface. My back was on the crevasse's ice floor. Now limp, I didn't feel anything.

My gaze was locked on the sky above. Stones and clumps of snow were still tumbling down after me. A couple of heads peered down into the hole. Their faces were too blurry to make out. I noticed occasional red splatters on the crevasse walls where I had hit. Vision fading.

'Tau? Are you alright?' an echoing voice said. 'Tau?'

'Please answer us!'

My whole body tingled. It was a strange feeling, like if my arm fell asleep, but all over. Little strands of white flicked near my eyes.

'What's that light?' someone said from above. 'I think I can see her torch.'

I came to, opening my eyes and slowly sitting up on the now snow-covered cave floor.

'She's moving!' someone said. It sounded like Coleo.

How was I moving? How was that possible? I thought those hits I took, let alone the fall…

'I'm… okay,' I called up, my voice echoing off the crystalline icicles.

Tallu's face appeared at the top of the unclimbable crag. 'Don't move, Tau!' She turned away. 'Set up the rope and winch. There, the tree, around that.'

I stood and brushed myself off. I pulled my helmet off for a moment to inspect it. The entire faceplate was gone, smashed in. Glass shards were lying about in random places, stained red with my blood. I put the helmet back on and stretched my back.

The armour plates where the rocks had hit me were warped. I didn't feel injured in those places though. I brushed my cheeks to check for wounds, but my skin was smooth. The fall hurt so much on the way down, but I somehow felt fine now.

There was a tunnel to my side, and a faint, flickering light coming through it. I was supposed to stay put, but what could possibly be creating that light down here? No one was watching from above; they were busy with the rope. My pistol was on the ground nearby, so I rushed over, picked it up, and made for the tunnel.

'Tau, stay calm,' a voice echoed down. 'We're going to get you out of there.'

I paused and glanced back up. 'Uh, okay.' I pressed forward and climbed through the narrow tunnel.

After a quick bend, the tunnel opened into a larger area. Giant stone columns were supporting a wide chamber that stretched into the darkness. Braziers lit with fire were interspersed throughout. The light flickered on the tiled stone floor.

Ruins. I had stumbled upon underground ruins. I froze in amazement.

How did this place even exist? Did the corporal know about this? Was this what we were trying to find?

I took several steps into the chamber to bask in its magnificence. I knew virtually nothing about the ruins and the people before the war. What stories did this place hold? Who lived here and why?

I heard a noise: scuttling and a pebble bouncing along the stone tiles.

I spun and raised my pistol. 'Who's there?'

Nothing, no response. I quickly fiddled with my weapon; it had a torch function somewhere. My hands shook. Which button was it again? Did one of those shadows just move? Was it just the flames playing tricks? Who lit the flames anyway?

'I'm... I'm warning you,' I mumbled, unable to mask the trembling fear in my voice.

I should turn around and run. But what if they strike when my back is turned? Why me? I hadn't hurt anyone before. Was I about to die? I can't die here.

Another shadow moved next to a pillar. I fired a round into the darkness, producing a distorted, ear-splitting zap. The red energy projectile lit the chamber but was gone in an instant.

There was a wooden clatter, a stick, no... a spear tumbled out of the dark. It rolled towards me and came to a stop. I waited with my pistol raised, panting.

A murmur, a gasp, and a moan. A person. I finally figured out the torch on my gun and immediately shone it on the pillar. A pair of legs were sticking out from behind it. I circled, keeping my distance.

The figure was propped up against the pillar, an unmoving teenage girl. My projectile had hit its mark; her rib cage was exposed through the nomad's tattered coat. Blood was everywhere and staining everything.

Kneeling over her was a small boy, unharmed and staring at her body. He appeared the same age as me. He squinted at the blinding light I was shining in his face.

'You *killed* her...'

She was dead. What had I done? I froze again.

'I... I...' I stammered.

Tears were forming in his eyes, but he did not cry out. He

continued to stare at me, perhaps thinking I was about to fire on *him*, too. I slowly lowered my gun. He hugged the dead girl, burying his face in her coat.

I shook my head repeatedly. 'I didn't mean to; I didn't know you were…'

He glanced back, tears now streaming. 'We were *hiding* from you! Why couldn't you just leave us alone?'

I slowly edged away. 'I…'

'I hate you,' he continued, blubbering as he spoke, '*every* one of you monsters. I hope you all *die*, that's all you deserve!'

My own tears trickled out as I turned and ran for the tunnel. 'I'm s-sorry.' I didn't stop. I couldn't. 'I'm sorry, I'm sorry!' When I reached the tunnel, I clambered through, around the bend, and suddenly stopped.

In front of me was Amiki. She had a rope expertly tied around her waist, groin, and shoulders.

Amiki pointed her pistol at the tunnel with one hand and grabbed my shoulder with the other. 'I heard a shot. Is everything okay?'

'Yeah, no, it was…' I began.

What would she do if she knew the boy was through the tunnel? Would she cut him down as easily as the other nomad?

I tried to steady my breath. 'I… thought I saw something, so I fired, but it was just my imagination.'

She stared into my eyes, noticing my tears. The silence was crushing.

A sound broke it. Crying, we could hear the boy's cries from here, bouncing along the tunnel. Amiki looked over my shoulder and tried to brush past me.

I placed my hand on her chest and shook my head pleadingly. 'Please, there's nothing there.'

She focused on the tunnel, but after another extended silence, she nodded and gave me a small smile. 'Okay. You're right, there's nothing there.'

'What's going on down there?' Tallu called out from above. 'Why did Tau fire?'

Amiki looked up. 'It's nothing, she's fine.'

'I got scared,' I yelled up, too.

'Alright,' Tallu replied, 'tell us when to pull.'

Amiki faced me and held out the extra rope. 'You asked me before how I felt when I killed?'

It was as if she knew exactly what had happened through the tunnel. She started tying me into a harness.

I wiped away my tears. 'What did you feel?'

She finished tying me in and stood, before shying away. 'What you're feeling now. Regret.'

We stared at each other, not saying a word.

'Just stay with me,' she finally said, before gently grabbing my wrist and pulling me back towards the light. 'I'll make sure you'll never have to kill again.'

Our squad above heaved us up until we were both safely out of the crevasse. Tallu met me at the hole's lip with a helping hand and a relieved smile. Once my harness was disconnected, she pulled me in for a hug.

The other girls crowded around as well, each offering reassuring smiles and words, even Tarsus and Coleo. I couldn't hear any of them, though, only the boy's wails echoing off the chamber walls.

Two: Choke

Sacet

The present

New Elysia's Commercial Quad

Colony was staring out the restaurant window, not noticing the clatter of plates and the loud discussions around him. What was he thinking about? Why did Tau even invite him? It had been almost an entire cycle since the coup, and one of my biggest regrets was involving him in all of this.

Everyone else at the elegantly decorated ring-shaped table was enjoying their mostly leafy foods and speaking freely. The staff at Alai's had really outdone themselves. Our private room on the top floor was perfect. A long balcony overlooked the crowded streets far below. This was both Tau's and my favourite restaurant in the city.

As usual, the titular Alai herself was silently waiting our table, her muteness never hindering her attentiveness. She was tall, pale, and thin, with long dark hair tied in a bun with cross-shaped decorative sticks. She and all her staff wore the same sheer, elegant red dress.

They replaced the polished-off plates with sizzling meats and steaming vegetables.

It was nice to just sit and socialise. After almost an entire cycle of getting the former FD territories under our Concordite control, managing our dwindling food supply, and countering constant Male Dominion incursions across half the planet, we barely had any time to ourselves.

Pilgrim and the rest of the nomadic delegation were sitting across from Tau and I. He had become a sort of bodyguard for the chieftains: Hati, Orrik, and Tamil. It was good to see him again after so much time apart.

Hati cleaned his white beard with his sleeve. 'Thank you, Alai. Each course was delicious.'

Alai gave a courteous bow before heading back to the kitchen.

Tau smiled. 'Can anyone else taste the difference now that we've gotten rid of all those additives?'

After we recently audited our farms, we discovered that all our food still contained hormone-controlling additives.

'Ah, that's what that aftertaste was?' Pilgrim said while chewing. 'Well, I'd still take those additives over prison food.'

'Damn right,' Noor said while cutting into a hunk of meat on his plate. 'That prison stuff was the worst, and I've eaten raw craterleech before. Uh, not like this place, though. This place is great.'

Noticing Tau's raised eyebrow, Tetsu stuck out his tongue. 'Craterleech is like… liquified fish, but stringy and… and… gooey.'

Colony seethed at them both but remained silent. Noor and Tetsu didn't even notice or possibly didn't care.

'I actually have a theory about that prison gruel,' Tetsu continued. 'I bet they were feeding us the prisoners who didn't make it.' Most around the table scrunched up our faces and groaned in disgust. Tetsu unapologetically shrugged, firm in his belief. 'If no one else wants to look into it, I will.'

Formerly known as the King's Wrath, the boys were sitting to our right, representing the ex-MD delegation and oblivious to proper dinner table discussion.

Noor occasionally brushed his long, brown fringe out of his eyes. He had slimmed down a lot since the rebellion. I remembered him having much more muscle tone. Tetsu was slimmer as well. I supposed we all were because of the food shortages.

It was a shame that so many ex-MD acolytes fled after the rebellion. Noor and Tetsu, on the other hand, had shown great loyalty to our new society, having gone on many missions with our troops. I smirked to myself, realising how much I'd come to depend on them.

Sitting to my left was Malu, still slumped in her arms. 'Give the prison talk a rest,' she mumbled. 'We get it, the FD was bad. Concordites good.'

Malu seemed gloomier than usual. The empty chair next to her was for her mother, who yet again hadn't accepted her invitation. They hadn't been on speaking terms since the coup. I admired Malu's stubbornness, constantly trying to reconnect with her estranged family, but somehow I didn't see it happening.

I never knew what to say to her because every discussion always seemed to circle back to how bad her side was, how she had killed her father, and how Tau couldn't resurrect a puddle of water. I went to grab her hand reassuringly, but she pulled away.

Pilgrim pointed behind Tau and I. 'I have to admit when your messenger told me you wanted to meet with all the delegations for lunch, I thought we'd be at each other's throats again.'

The "messenger" he was referring to, Amiki, became flustered. 'I'm the queen's personal guard!'

Amiki was wearing her Royal Guard dress uniform, which was mostly white with golden edges. Like all Royal Guards, she held a golden spear, its ceremonial design concealing a heavy-laser weapon.

Through my discussions with her I had learned that, like Malu, she wasn't born in the Female Dominion like Tau and I. I didn't know much else about her, other than she was a childhood friend of Tau, and that was good enough for me.

Pilgrim looked up and snapped his fingers in confusion. 'Ah, yes, Am... Amuki?'

Amiki's grip tightened around her weapon as she practically snarled. 'It's Amiki.'

Pilgrim raised his hands in apology. 'Alright, alright... *Amiki*. I'm just saying, it's good that we're not all bickering. We can finally sit and just eat.'

Colony scoffed loudly. 'Well, I hope you all *choke* on it.' All eyes watched as he got up from the table and, without saying another word, made his way to the door.

A few at the table raised their eyebrows, but the rest ignored him, used to Colony's outbursts.

Tau sighed and looked down.

Tamil, who hadn't said a word since she arrived, pointed her knife at the boys. 'If you don't pull your friend's head in soon, I'll remove it myself.'

Noor firmly shook his head. 'He is most definitely *not* our friend.'

I raised a hand to them and stood. 'I'll speak to him.' As I followed Colony out, I spotted him already at the end of the corridor. 'Colony, wait!'

He reached the elevator and pressed the call button, before glancing back with contempt, refusing to turn around fully. 'I came to her little celebration, as asked. I'm *glad* everything is going so well that you elites can afford to scoff your faces while my family starves under your feet.'

I reached him and gestured back to the table. 'Please come back. None of this was meant to insult you. There'll be time to talk politics again soon.' I had lost count of the number of times I had said something like this to him.

He reached out and flicked my black-tipped, purple streaks. 'Aren't you supposed to be a Matriarch now? All you do is make excuses for everyone.'

'We call it commander now,' I explained. 'Now that we let both women and—'

'I don't care about your stupid hierarchy!' He shook his head. 'It's been days since the last food drop. Do you have *any* idea how hard my swarm is to influence when they're dying of starvation?'

I sighed, looking around to make sure no one was eavesdropping. 'I... acknowledge that, but there are food shortages everywhere. You're not alone in this.'

The clear elevator whirred as it reached our floor, and its doors slid open.

'Just make sure you send food to the mines as we agreed,' he snapped back as he got in and turned around. The doors closed and muffled his last words. 'Maybe your queen should be organising it if you're not up to the task, *Commander*?'

I locked eyes with him as the elevator descended out of sight. What am I going to do about him?

I turned and rejoined the others back in the dining room. The delegations were now on the topic of how much they disliked Colony.

I sat next to Tau and leaned over to her. 'The necrolisk delegation is *not* happy.'

Tau sighed once more. 'I guess I'll go and heal those things again.' She looked back at Amiki. 'Tomorrow?'

Amiki nodded back. 'I'll find a place for it in the schedule, my Queen.'

Tau winced, still hating being referred to by her royal title.

'I'm telling you, every soldier hated him,' Noor said, not hearing our conversation. 'He'd get one of us killed and not even care.'

Pilgrim was hanging on the boys' every word, stroking his scruffy black beard. 'That bad, huh?'

Tetsu rapped Noor's chest. 'He was like Mycol's pet, wasn't he? And he comes here, has the opportunity to start over and be normal, and—'

'And he screws that up, too!' Noor finished for Tetsu.

'I know! Back to his freak family.'

'Unbelievable.'

A sudden rumbling rocked the building. Outside, the usual city noise was replaced with screams and sirens. Everyone at the table went silent and stood.

'We're under attack,' Pilgrim said.

Amiki rushed Tau away from the table. 'Stay back, my Queen.'

The rest ran to the balcony and looked down into the streets.

An explosion had ripped through the causeways between the buildings of the commercial quad. Citizens, male and female alike, were running away from the spreading flames. The once gleaming and untouched skyscrapers above us were ablaze, too. One of the towers was teetering in the other direction, currently in mid-fall.

'Everyone, get down!' I shouted, and our group huddled back inside under the table.

The resulting shockwave was tremendous. It rippled past with such force that all the nearby windows smashed and everything on the table flew off. A random glass shard punctured my arm.

As we got to our feet, a giant cloud of dust rushed up from the streets below, cloaking the sky brown. The haze obscured our view of the other side of the street.

Pilgrim assisted Hati up. 'Are you all right, Elder?'

My second perception flew down into the street like a glider, analysing the chaos. My vision wasn't limited like normal eyes; it sensed shapes, movement, and the lay of the land.

The others were frozen, staring into the dust. Debris was everywhere. Countless people were in the streets now, running every which way in the pandemonium.

Then I sensed them. A squad of dark, masked figures marched through the mess below, firing on the citizens.

'Male Dominion soldiers,' I said, turning back to the others.

'How'd they get through our defences?' Hati asked.

Amiki brushed past Tau and up to me. 'The queen cannot be here. Open a portal to her chambers, now.'

'No,' Tau interrupted, also approaching. 'I'm staying. What's the plan?'

Amiki glared back but quickly conceded. 'Wherever she goes, I go,' she said, stamping her spear into the carpet.

The others all stared at me expectantly, since I was the highest-ranked military member here. First things first: I had to send away the non-acolytes. I opened a portal to the Danger Room in the Military Quad, before pointing at the nomad delegation and gesturing them in. 'Get everyone on alert and send reinforcements.'

The three chieftains hurried through to the large auditorium on the other side.

Pilgrim stopped shy of the portal and shot me a look. 'Let me help you.'

Malu curled her lip. 'You don't even have a weapon.'

I clenched my fists. 'We don't have time for this, go!'

Pilgrim gave a solemn head shake but obeyed, stepping through the portal. I closed it, then gestured for those remaining to huddle up. Tau, Malu, Noor, Tetsu, and Amiki did so, and I put a new portal under the six of us. I flicked it up and sent us all to the streets below. The civilian screams were much louder here.

'I can't see a thing!' Noor yelled through the choking dust and smoke.

'Tetsu, shield,' I instructed.

Tetsu raised his arms and summoned a glowing, white shield around us. Its shell consisted of small hexagons no bigger than my head. As we walked, his shield followed.

'Alright, move as one.'

'I can't shoot what I can't see,' Noor countered.

Malu shrugged, too. 'And what am I supposed to do?'

'Just work with me here!' I shouted. 'Tau? You know what to do.'

Tau nodded, closed her eyes, and held her breath. Her shoulder-length, auburn hair gradually turned a dazzling light blue, almost white. An aura of cyan flames coated her body. I could feel the energy coursing into me. I, no doubt like the others, felt invigorated, like I was indestructible.

Amiki stood in front of Tau, aiming her spear into the dust.

My second perception sensed the soldiers marching this way. Each was clad in heavy, black armour. Their helmets had white, necrolisk-like features painted on their faces, with exaggerated, impossibly sharp teeth jutting from mandibles, and long, misshapen eyes streaking across their crowns.

They fired laser projectiles aimlessly into the smoke, each red burst briefly parting it with blazing tunnels that quickly swallowed back in. Some collided with the shield, but they loudly ricocheted and fizzled away to nothing.

'There!' I directed to Noor.

Noor flung his arms forward and produced a red-hot laser of his own, which exited the shield in a constant stream. But like our enemies, no one but me knew whether or not they were hitting their targets. Luckily his laser sliced through numerous enemy soldiers, completely disintegrating limbs, heads and torsos.

Amiki fired her spear into the dust too, and although she wasn't as destructive as Noor, thanks to her visor's readouts she was far more accurate, as though she could see through the dust like me.

'It's Havoc Division!' Tetsu called after having spotted one of the enemies.

I had never fought these guys up close before, but I had heard about them through the boys. Havoc Division were shock troops that specialised in deepstriking and hit-and-run tactics.

The soldiers that survived our barrage took cover behind fallen steel beams and concrete blocks.

This was going to be too easy. I brought my hands up, closed my eyes, and concentrated on each man. Soon after, a portal to the empty vacuum of space opened behind them. One after another they dropped their weapons and flailed about trying to grab onto something, before being sucked through the void doorway.

Far behind the other troops, an enormous lone soldier in the same armour had just finished barrelling through the foundations of a building like a wrecking ball and was now striding down the road toward his dwindling comrades. His helmet also had a necrolisk motif, with actual mandibles protruding out. It was so realistic that it resembled a miniature version of a metallic necrolisk head.

No, it couldn't be him, surely? I knew who it was just by his monstrous size. Kalek, a man I *thought* I had already thrown into space long ago. It seemed not even *that* could kill him.

No matter, I'd do it a second time, and a third, as many times as I needed until he and his cronies took the hint. Like the others, I concentrated briefly, and a portal opened behind him in the middle of the street. The change in air pressure ripped him off the ground and towards the hole. His arms floundered madly, attempting to grab onto something like the others.

Another figure appeared next to Kalek in the blink of an eye. He plucked Kalek out of the air with his fingertips, stopping him in his tracks with ease. This new man floated in front of the portal, unaffected by the air current.

He was middle-aged and smaller than Kalek, but still large and muscular. Unlike Kalek, he didn't have a helmet. He had a chiselled look; short, black hair; furrowed, great brows; and a strong, wide jaw.

Although many obstacles separated us, he cast his gaze in our direction. I felt uneasy, as if this man knew exactly where we were in the dust. It wasn't over yet; I could still engulf them both in the portal by pulling it over them and closing it.

I tensed my hand and pulled the portal closer. The man saw what I was doing, whipped Kalek aside through some nearby open windows like a ragdoll and disappeared from the spot.

The debris between our groups obliterated in an instant as he appeared in front of our shield with lightning speed. The wall of dust whooshed and parted like revealing curtains. He briefly wound up a punch and smacked it into Tetsu's shield with such force that it broke through and blew all of us off our feet.

We all flew far into the air in different directions, but while I was still in mid-air, I felt a hand clutch around my neck and stop me. He wrenched it up and brought my face to his. Our eyes locked, his were dark, empty, and soulless. We floated upwards, and he studied me, up and down, as I hung there, choking.

'Aren't you going to defend yourself?' he asked in a deep, masculine voice.

I thrashed my hands and clawed at his tight grip. 'Who... *ack*... who are... you?'

'Does that really matter when I'm choking the life out of you?'

He was right, but the only thing I could think of was to suck us both into space. But like Kalek, I doubt that would faze him. I was out of ideas. I struggled to draw in air. Blurry vision. I needed to do something, *anything*!

My perception sensed my friends getting to their feet farther down the street. Tau saw us and pointed over. Noor fired in our direction. The stream of energy hissed past, missing us at first. It grazed into the man's shoulder but did nothing. My skin seared from the heat, and my clothing caught fire. His clothes, meanwhile, seemed impervious to damage like he was.

The man glanced over his shoulder and smirked, as if they were only a minor nuisance, before looking back at me.

'I don't know what they see in you, you're not ready,' he said in a relaxed monotone.

He tightened his grip further and I could feel pressure on my eyeballs. Overwhelming pain. Nowhere for my flesh and air to go. He broke my neck with a loud snap. His hand released and I fell back into fading darkness. He soared up into the sky and out of sight.

Three: Find Him

Tau

I sprinted towards where I thought Sacet was going to land, leaving the others behind.

'Tau, stop!' Amiki called, now in pursuit.

I hopped over the chunks of debris as fast as I could, but I wasn't going to reach her in time. Her body splatted onto the fractured pavement in front of me. I knelt next to her with my aura already activated.

One of Sacet's eyes had dislodged from its socket, and her neck was misshapen and purple.

Please, don't let this be one of those times my powers quit on me. The failure rate of my resurrection power had been getting worse as of late. Sacet was someone I couldn't afford to lose. This had to work!

I brought my hand to hers and got to work. As my aura intensified, so did the familiar tingling sensation throughout my body. Sacet's wounds began to heal, and I immediately felt the same excruciating pain she had experienced upon death.

First, her eye withdrew back into its socket, and my own eye felt like it was about to burst with immense pressure. Then the purple bruises around her neck disappeared, and my air supply was halted. I choked and desperately gasped for air. I heard a crack as Sacet's neck bones realigned, and my neck snapped to the side.

I collapsed next to her from the pain. Although I could resurrect more quickly than I used to, the pain that went along with it was getting worse each time.

All the bloodstains completely receded, and Sacet's eyes shot open. She leant forward with a loud gasp for air, thrashing her hands about for support. I exhaled in relief and grabbed one of her hands. The others arrived as she and I were sitting up.

'Tau?' Sacet said. 'What happened?'

'You're okay,' I replied, reeling from the pain.

Amiki offered a hand and pulled us both up. '*Now* can we leave, my Queen?'

Sacet's eyes fluttered, still adjusting to the shock. 'W-where is he? Where did he go?'

Noor held up his hands to calm her down. 'He's gone. He flew into the sky.'

Distant explosions continued; we were still in the danger zone.

'Tetsu?' I said.

He nodded back. 'Right.' Although panting, he brought up a new shield around us.

Sacet stared at the boys. 'Who... was he?'

Noor shrugged at Tetsu. 'Sorry, we've got no idea.'

Tetsu pointed to the battle still raging down the street. 'What if this is just a diversion?'

Sacet shook her head. 'No, he got exactly what he wanted.'

The rubble around us shook. The smoke behind us was clearing as a large battalion of our soldiers marched towards us, all clad in their new desert-camo armour and flanked by battle-damaged, rattling hover tanks.

Sacet's hands shook as she scanned the sky for her killer.

Amiki gave me an expectant glare. 'My Queen... let our reinforcements take over from here.'

I nodded, then nudged Sacet. 'Let's head back. The city needs its leaders, right?'

Sacet seethed, but closed her eyes to ready herself. Her portals appeared beneath our feet, her hands rose, and as they did, the portals lifted too, transporting all of us to the throne room.

Even with all the renovations in the throne room, the damage Sacet did to this place during the coup was still on display in certain areas. Even after almost a cycle, the vast chamber still had many chipped silver tiles. The gold columns needed fresh paint, and the upper level had broken guardrails. The gigantic doors at the end of the hall were still slightly warped, too, letting in a tiny shaft of afternoon sun.

All I could do was sit on my throne and wait for the news. Being unable to help was maddening, but Amiki had insisted I stay put on my silky teal cushion. When were we going to hear reports? I needed to know what was happening out there!

Amiki leant in, her long black hair draping over me. She gently gripped my hand, which had been anxiously tapping on the armrest.

'They'll be here soon, relax,' she whispered. She then pointed to the thirty or so Royal Guards that were lined up on both sides of the chamber, standing to attention in silence. 'And this is the safest place you can be right now.'

'It's not my *own* safety I'm worried about, you know that.'

Sunlight gleamed off the Royal Guards' armour and spears. Ever since I replaced the surviving guards with soldiers I knew, I had felt a *lot* safer. Of course, in times of crisis, I preferred to have my closest friends around, too.

Malu was standing on the other side of my throne, tapping her foot and clenching her fists. Noor and Tetsu were leaning on a nearby column. Every now and then I'd glance over at Tetsu and we'd lock eyes before he looked away.

A portal opened at the base of the steps to my throne. I straightened up, Noor and Tetsu came over, and both Amiki and Malu resumed their previous stances. I could see the Military Quad through the floating oval, and a line of people piled through shortly after.

The three nomad representatives entered first, followed by Pilgrim. He was struggling to carry an enormous gun, too large even for him. He barely fit through the portal with it.

He also had desert-camo body armour on now, although it was a mixture of different sized pieces that didn't fit properly, seeming as they were originally designed for women. They weren't locked into place, either, but rather just haphazardly strapped on. And draped over the top of it all was his desert cloak.

Malu pointed to his weapon. 'Impressive… rifle?'

'I believe it's technically a cannon,' he corrected, examining it with both pride and difficulty.

Next through were Tarsus and Coleo. As the Commander of City Defence, Tarsus had black-tipped, red streaks in her fringe. Coleo was the Commander of the Air Force, so her streaks were yellow with black tips.

Both gave a quick nod toward me and formed a line. Normally they were quite confident, always looking after me as their little sister and telling me why I was wrong about things. But now they avoided eye contact with me, ashamed.

Sacet could be seen through the portal, still giving orders to soldiers running about someplace in the barracks.

'Report,' Amiki commanded.

Tarsus closed her eyes and knelt on one knee. 'My Queen, the male strike force has fled, but not before… not before destroying several residential buildings all over the city. The casualties so far—'

'This was terrorism, my Queen,' Coleo interrupted. 'Pure and simple. None of our infrastructure was targeted, only our people.'

My heart sank like it was burying itself deep out of shame. How could I face the innocents I promised to protect after this?

'This is all *my* fault,' Tarsus continued. 'Our outer perimeter was down because of the upgrades and—'

I raised a hand to stop her and gestured for her to rise. 'I've known you my whole life, Tarsus. I *know* you weren't responsible for this.' I sighed. 'How did they get in, exactly?'

Tarsus' eyes widened and she gave a tense shrug. 'I… I… still have no idea how they got in and out. B-but I have my p-people investigating as we speak.'

Coleo squinted in thought. 'Maybe they were hiding in that last wave of refugees?'

Sacet came through next. 'Tau, I think we should revisit your choice of commanders…'

'Oh? What's the problem?'

Sacet joined the line and folded her arms. 'If it were up to me, our Science Commander would be in cold storage with Verre.'

'Well, I'm *sorry* to hear that, Acolyte Commander,' a voice coming from the portals said. Stepping through next was Siph. She had black-tipped, white streaks in her short, grey hair. The short, thin, frail woman was slightly older than Marid and wore a lab coat instead of a uniform.

She scowled as she walked over to join the others. 'You know, sound travels just fine through your portals.'

'Maybe I *wanted* you to hear me,' Sacet replied through gritted teeth.

At that moment Terel, the Special Ops Commander, walked through the portal. 'My Queen, are you alright?' She also respectfully knelt.

Terel wasn't usually this pleasant. She had a hefty build, although not unfit, just much bulkier than most. She had black-tipped, green streaks. During the coup, she was one of the few higher-ups to deliberately not interfere, hence why I kept her around.

Marid, the last of my New Elysian commanders, appeared through the portal next. She nodded at Sacet, who closed it behind her. Marid had black-tipped, blue streaks, being the Troop Commander. I didn't have any regrets giving her that position, given her experience. She also joined the line, lightly relying on her sword cane for support.

'Ah, Terel, Marid,' Siph said. 'Sacet here was just telling the queen how *untrustworthy* we all are.'

Sacet raised an eyebrow at her. 'No, just you. Those perimeter upgrades were *your* idea, weren't they? Funny how the MD knew exactly when to attack. And when that happened, *you* were nowhere to be found. I wonder why that was?'

Siph furrowed her brow, wrinkling further an already wrinkled visage. 'I had important business to attend to. As for the enemy knowing when to attack, maybe we have an information leak? That's Terel's department, not mine.'

Sacet and others now glared at Terel instead. Pilgrim, whose arms were now shaking from the weight of his giant weapon, broke the tension by placing it on the steps.

Terel didn't react, instead focusing on me. 'My Queen, I admit I deserve some of the blame here. I have caught and killed numerous spies, but our plans are still somehow getting out to the enemy. I have failed you.'

Siph gestured to the former nomads and the boys. 'Maybe one of these *outsiders* blabbed about our plans, did you consider that?'

Tamil, our feistiest nomad chieftains, whipped out her dagger and strode towards Siph. 'I will split your lying tongue down the middle, hag!' The other two chieftains had to restrain Tamil, and she eventually relented, but didn't break her murderous stare.

Marid chuckled. 'Why would nomads help the MD against our Concord?'

Having also been accused, Noor turned to face her. His eyebrows lowered, his posture strengthened, and his fingers twitched, at the ready.

The colour drained from Siph's face. She then pointed at Malu. 'Well… well what about her? This acolyte colonel shouldn't be eavesdropping on a commander meeting.'

Malu, one of Sacet's colonels, sported yellow-tipped purple streaks. When accused of being a traitor, she didn't react. Instead, she simply glanced at the door and then at me. 'I can leave if you want?'

I shook my head. 'No, stay.' I glanced at the other delegations as well. 'I need people I can trust here.'

Sacet scoffed at Siph. 'Speaking of, what were you *actually* up to, Siph?'

She sneered back. 'I was rerouting the power from downed city sectors before they overloaded. But I wouldn't expect an uneducated child like *you* to understand. Knowing you, you'd blow it all up instead.' She paused and noticed almost everyone staring at her. 'Why am *I* the only one on trial here?' She pointed at Tarsus. 'I thought *you* oversaw City Defence? Where was it?'

Sacet nodded in agreement. 'The MD was right on top of us. There was no warning.'

Tarsus sighed gruffly. 'You all knew I was installing Siph's upgrades today.'

Siph then looked expectantly at Coleo. 'And nothing on the scanners there, Air Force Commander?'

Coleo had a similar reaction. 'Nothing.' She looked back at me. 'I swear we didn't see this coming.'

I cleared my throat so I could get a word in. 'I trust them, Siph. They're my sisters, like Amiki here.' I pointed at my personal guardian, who gave me a small bow.

'Their inexperience will be the death of us,' Siph muttered.

Amiki slammed the haft of her spear onto the gold tiles. 'Show respect to your queen!'

The other Royal Guards lining the hall pointed their spears in Siph's direction.

'I ought to kill you right here...' Sacet added.

I pointed at each of them. 'Enough! Stop bickering. We're on the same side.'

After a tense standoff, Siph half-heartedly waved her hands in resignation. 'I apologise, my Queen. I am quite... flustered. Today has been one for the archives. In the hundreds of cycles that this city has stood, it has *never* been directly attacked.'

Sacet moaned. 'That's because the war was fake up until the coup. We *knew* this was coming eventually.' She shifted out of line and faced Noor and Tetsu. 'That man today... are you *sure* you don't know who he is?'

'I've never seen him before in my life,' Tetsu added with a shrug, before looking at Noor. 'Guess we weren't his only favourites.'

Noor crossed his arms and shook his head. 'The king never told us about him. But then... Havoc Division's always been pretty secretive about its members.'

Sacet stared at the steps. 'He was so strong... and fast. He could've done so much more damage. He practically beat us and then just... left. He was testing me... us, I meant us.'

I narrowed my gaze. 'Sacet? What did he say to you?'

'He... told me I wasn't ready—'

'Ready for what?' Marid interrupted. 'What do you mean?'

Sacet shook her head. 'I have no idea.' Her eyes unfocused and she brushed her neck. 'When he choked me, I froze; I didn't know what to do. And he just held me there like… he was toying with me.'

Marid left the line and tapped over to her. 'You were scared.' Sacet's posture stiffened. 'There's no shame in it. I would have been, too. We should be thankful that this assault was only a test, as you said. Next time we need to be ready.' She patted Sacet's shoulder reassuringly.

Tarsus had a finger near her ear, no doubt receiving a message from one of her underlings. 'I've got an update. We found out how the MD got through undetected.'

She strode to the group's side and placed a holo-throw on the ground, a tiny cube-shaped device that could project a three-dimensional image above it. It activated with a button press and displayed a fuzzy, reddish image of our soldiers in a dark building interior inspecting a cave-like hole leading straight down.

'A tunnel?' I asked.

Marid clenched her sword cane tighter. 'Then that slimy Colony is probably involved.'

I raised an eyebrow at her. 'That's not necessarily true. Tarsus? Is this tunnel connected to the ones made by the necrolisks?'

She bowed. 'I'm not sure yet, my Queen, but I'll find out.'

Sacet locked eyes with me. 'It wouldn't surprise me if he had betrayed us. Every day they get hungrier.'

Marid grunted. 'We can *barely* feed ourselves. My Queen, we must *deal* with the nest, before things get worse.'

'At least make them work for their food,' Noor suggested. 'You have no miners extracting resources anymore. Necrolisks are perfect for digging and tunnelling. Why not cut a new deal?'

The commanders turned to face Noor. Sacet locked eyes with him, smiled, and nodded.

'Who are you, again?' Siph asked.

'Me? I'm Noor.'

Siph pointed at him. 'Right. Well, I'm with Norn on this one. Pitch him that instead.'

'It's *err…* it's Noor?'

Tetsu elbowed Noor. 'And if Colony doesn't like it, we exterminate them. Right, Norn?'

Pilgrim pointed at him and laughed.

Elder Hati, who had been quiet up until now, stepped forward. 'Forgive me, Queen of Light, but things have been steadily getting worse for us. It sounds like your people don't know who to trust, and if we just sit here, stagnating, we'll eventually tear each other apart. Maybe we need to make some *new* friends.'

Terel waved a hand at him dismissively. 'Our cities are already bursting with your nomads. And, no offence, but we don't need more mouths to feed.'

'Not even an entire clan of sand acolytes?' Hati asked, followed by silence.

Terel shook her head. 'You're talking about The Shroud, aren't you? They're a myth.'

Hati smirked. 'A shockingly ignorant stance from our spymaster. I assure you, they are very real. It is said they can even teach their powers to others. Imagine doubling or even *tripling* your acolyte army...'

'Acolyte powers cannot be taught,' Marid said with a scoff. 'And why would you wait until now to tell us?'

Hati's smirk faded. 'Because I promised I would never reveal them, but... we are clearly desperate.'

Pilgrim glanced between Sacet and I. 'I've worked with members of The Shroud before. Remember Sabikah and Tern?'

It felt like so long ago now, but back when I was Sacet and Eno's prisoner, I did remember a beautiful woman named Sabikah who Pilgrim was enamoured with. She could wave her hands at the sand to cover our tracks.

Sacet nodded at me. 'Oh, those two sand acolytes that were with us?'

'Yep, well, they wouldn't tell me *how* they got their powers,' Pilgrim continued, 'but I did work out where they came from.'

Terel raised an eyebrow. 'Which is... where?'

Pilgrim looked intensely proud of himself. 'In the wastes, along the coast, far east of my old village in Metus. Too far to walk, but with an aircraft, I think I could find it again.'

There was another pause. Was everyone waiting on me to make a decision? I conceded with a shrug. 'Well, they sound like... they could be useful.'

Sacet's eyes widened, as though having a sudden realisation. 'I'll go with him.'

'What?' I shook my head. 'No, we need you *here*.'

'That man was after *me*,' Sacet replied, raising her voice and pacing around. 'I know it doesn't make sense, but… if I'm not *here*, they won't attack.'

Siph laughed. 'How arrogant to think that everything revolves around you.'

Marid rapped Siph with her cane. 'No. She might be onto something.'

Sacet approached the throne. 'I know it sounds… ridiculous and selfish, but these people have had it in for me ever since I was first captured. Maybe I can at least lead their attention away from the city.' She came up the steps and knelt in respect. 'With your permission, I would like to take an aircraft on a diplomacy mission. With my scouting ability, and Pilgrim's knowledge, we will find this Shroud.'

'If what you say is true,' I said in a caring tone, 'and the spies find out, it'll be a suicide mission.'

Sacet looked up into my eyes. 'At the first sight of trouble, either there or here, I'll portal back.'

I smirked and gave her an approving nod. 'You know, after all this time searching, maybe Eno is with these other nomads?'

Sacet smiled back. 'That *did* cross my mind.'

'Very well,' I replied and Sacet stood. 'But you two aren't going alone.'

'I'll go,' Noor said, joining Sacet's side. 'If that guy shows up, I wouldn't mind a second shot at him.' The two exchanged a quick nod. 'Maybe we can try the old magnify trick?' He looked back at me. 'I mean… only if we have to.'

Malu stretched on the spot. 'Count me in, too. I need a change of scenery.'

'And… *obviously* me,' Pilgrim said, stretching his arms and cracking his fingers.

I looked at Coleo. 'I have a job for you.'

She had been standing silently in bewilderment. 'Yes, my Queen?'

'I want you to prepare an aircraft, and your best pilot for them. And Terel? Choose some trustworthy soldiers to accompany them, along with any intel of the area you have.'

Terel bowed. 'At once, my Queen.'

'Can I go along, too?' Tetsu asked.

'Now, just hold on a minute,' Marid said, causing Tetsu to frown. 'Don't you think we're sending far too many of our acolytes, particularly the ones that we can trust? What if something was to happen and we lost them all at once? And I don't doubt the Royal Guard's abilities, but surely we need some more power with the queen at all times? Tetsu's shield would be perfect.'

'You're right,' I said. 'Tetsu? Could you stay with me?'

Noor chuckled. 'Yeah, bud, you should. You'll make a great Royal Guard.'

'But… um.' Tetsu and I locked eyes for a moment, and he bowed. 'I mean… I would be honoured.'

Sacet turned and opened another portal, this time to what looked like the armoury. 'We'd best be getting ready then.'

'I'll get that craft prepared,' Coleo said before darting through the portal. Terel bowed before following her.

'Wish us luck,' Malu said as she and Noor stepped through, too.

Siph rolled her eyes. 'Good luck.'

After a brief whisper with Hati, Pilgrim picked up his cannon and hauled it to the portal. He winked at Sacet. 'Don't worry, we'll find him this time. Got a good feeling.' He then staggered through as well.

Sacet took one step in before turning back to look at me. She smiled, nodded, and mouthed the words "thank you".

I nodded back as her portal closed. 'Find him this time.'

Four: Echo Chamber

Eno

Almost a cycle ago

The sun was setting on the forest treetops, staining them a deep red. The wind whispered through the leaves with an unsettling intensity, as though the souls of the dead were trying to shriek my location to the world. The four women I had killed to escape deserved what they got, I had no regrets about that. No matter how deep we went into this forest, I knew the soldiers wouldn't be far behind, wanting their vengeance.

I submerged myself in the murmuring river, the same waters Sacet, Tau and I had once swum in before all this horror had upended our lives. That was the last time I remembered being happy. What a different kid I was then, so naive and dependent on others. As soon as I dipped my head under the surface, the voices stopped, and I felt alone.

I wondered if I'd ever see my friends again. Pilgrim and Turen had been executed. Toroi? Probably still in those mines, poor guy. Tau? Who knew with her. She was a friend, but also still my enemy. And

Sacet? I didn't know how she did it, but she saved me. I hoped she was okay. If I knew my sister, she'd still be fighting them, even now two days later.

No, I didn't need any of them now. Their presence would be nice, but I needed to be strong, remember? I could do this alone. I could survive without my sister's help, without anyone's. That is how I was going to pay her back, to be strong, like her, like she and Grandpa were trying to teach me.

Something brushed my leg underwater, causing me to jerk, which in turn broke open the still-healing whip wounds on my back. I screamed, creating a surge of bubbles, then surfaced to regain my composure. Looking down, I noticed the likely culprit was a mantakrill peacefully swimming by. If I wasn't so tired from the lack of sleep, I'd attempt to catch the spiny fish for a much-needed meal, but instead, my gaze drifted to the shore.

The other former prisoners were still setting up camp. There were about twenty of us left all up. The original group had whittled down in size for various reasons: some because they didn't think I knew where I was going, and others had died of their various injuries and diseases along the way. One slow, but brave old man, knowing everyone was worried about pursuers, told us to go on without him.

I had led those who were left to the same shack where my sister and I were originally captured. Probably not the smartest idea I've ever had, but I didn't know where else to go, as Sacet had always been in charge of the map. There wasn't much left of the shack, for half the roof and walls had been converted to water by that acolyte, who I later found out was Toroi's sister.

Still, the men were doing their best to make do, gathering firewood and berries, and making fish traps out of reeds. A small campfire already crackled in the forest's tight embrace, illuminating the long and weary faces of broken men.

The red sky darkened, and I laid back, holding an underwater tree root to keep me in place while I rested my eyes. A small part of me had the urge to let go of the root, to be washed downstream to a new life rather than having to make one myself. The stars above peaked through the inky black, like a thousand eyes waiting to judge what I was going to do next.

That was enough rest for now. I'd rejoin the others by the campfire to dry off, hopefully eat something, and then discuss what to do next. The obvious answer would be to head deeper into the Promised Land.

I rose from the water and trudged out in nothing but my dripping underwear. I picked up my tattered prisoner uniform from the branch I had hung it on and moved towards the warming glow of the fire.

As I got closer, something felt off. Where had everyone gone to? Were they all inside the shack for some reason? I reached the fire and looked through the shack's gaping front hole but couldn't see anyone in the darkness. Had they all gone hunting at the same time? What was going on here?

'Hello?' I called. 'Guys? Where'd everyone go?'

Did they abandon me? Well, good riddance! I'd survive on my own if I had to.

The shadows beyond the fire's light briefly swirled: movement.

'Is someone there?'

A face appeared, floating low in the dark. A white skull with glowing red eyes.

My legs shook, but my hands were steady. I pointed my palms towards the creature and strained, sending a pushing wave of force into the dark. The face disappeared, but so did the fire, unintentionally snuffed out.

The nearby shack behind me shook, for my unfocused power had spilled over to it. Some of the logs came loose and rolled away with loud thunks and womps, and what remained of the shack loudly collapsed into a pile of debris.

In the pitch black, all I could see was the outline of the treetops on the starry night sky.

'If you don't answer me, I... I promise I'll keep doing that until you're dead.'

A snap, like a twig being stepped on. I sent another blast outwards and heard the wave splinter the nearby trees into pieces.

Another noise, a puff, followed by a sting in my chest.

'De... did some... someone stab meh... me?'

Everything went swirly. Was I going to fall over?

'The acolyte is secure,' a gruff voice said.

Several more skulls appeared, surrounding me from every angle.

Why were they higher than me? Looking down on me. Black sky. Red eyes.

I awoke with my throbbing head resting on a hard wall. I was in a cold, square room with no doors or windows.

A blond-haired boy was sitting across from me. No, it was my reflection. There were mirrors on every wall, creating a false infinity everywhere I looked. Even the ceiling had a mirror, which reflected the tiled, steel floor. Along the tiles were the only lights illuminating the room.

I propped myself up using the wall. My head was spinning, so I paused to rest. I waited until my vision had adjusted before standing up again properly.

What was this place, and where? The last thing I remembered was swimming. Then I… what was it?

I ran my fingers along the mirrored wall and did a circuit of the room, hoping to find an exit.

What happened after… oh. The skulls. The terrifying skulls with red eyes. Then, I remember being hit by something. And that was all.

My powers! Yes, I could easily smash these walls apart, it would be no problem. I had practised with it heaps when we were travelling. I held out my hands, closed my eyes and strained. A few uneventful grunts later, I peeked and saw that nothing had changed.

'That's not… going to work,' a resounding, raspy voice said from all around.

I retreated to the closest wall and frantically looked around. As soon as I had put my weight against the surface, it gave way. My stomach lurched. I almost lost my balance, but a strong hand caught my shoulder, holding me upright.

I spun on the spot and fell anyway at the sight of the enormous, grotesque man. He had a hunched back, yet still towered taller than most grown men. His entire body was misshapen; his skin had patches of veiny growths, like a burn victim covered in scar tissue; and his face was so bulbous, I half-expected it to explode like a balloon. He had a tuft of black hair sprouting from his skullcap, straightened and parted to the side.

As I scrambled away to the other side of the room, this mutant of a man stepped in through the secret opening. As soon as he was clear, the doorway closed and the view of the steel corridor outside was gone, now just a mirror again, showing my reflection staring back in horror.

The man was sheathed in black armour – it was much more menacing than other MD armour I had seen in the past. Perhaps it was because of his odd proportions? His upper body was somehow simultaneously both burly and contorted.

He lumbered forward, each step causing him to groan in discomfort. Was he going to kill me? I pressed up against the wall, pulled my knees close and wrapped my arms around them. My jaw quivered and my body shook.

'Hello, Eno. Don't worry, I'm not… going to hurt you,' he said in his deep, guttural voice. 'My name… is Mycol.'

There was something strange about the way he spoke, pausing every so often as if he was out of breath.

Two of the floor tiles in the centre of the room parted and a steel stool emerged from the hole. Mycol gently sat, as though the chair might break under his weight.

He chortled. 'I'm sure you're wondering… how does he know my name? The others you were with told me all about you.'

I lowered my face into my arms and peeked over to study him.

'So, I'd like to welcome you… to your new home, MDC,' he said with his hands out wide. He observed my silence with confusion. 'That's the Male Dominion Capital, boy, in case you didn't know.'

He cocked his head to the side. 'You must be *very* afraid of me, being so silent. It's my appearance, is it not?'

He was right, his looks made me feel queasy. Even his teeth varied in size.

He leant much closer. His breath smelled like a rotting corpse. 'That's alright, I'm used to that. You *can* speak? Surely you have questions?' He raised one of his thick eyebrows.

I slowly stood, still leaning against the mirror. 'Why did you bring me here?'

'To rescue you, of course!' he said with an uneven smile, one of the corners of his mouth travelling much higher than the other.

'Rescue? What a joke, you captured me!' I shouted as I bashed the wall with my fists. He was just another big bully in my life drawing lines for me to follow.

He rolled his eyes back and continued his malformed grin. 'Well, *some* people don't appreciate… when we try to rescue them. But soon you will call this place home… and be happy here.'

'What do you mean? So I'm not a prisoner, then?'

'For now, let's just say that you'll live with me and my friends in the Military Wing… and you won't be allowed to leave.'

I pointed down. 'I don't *want* to live here.'

Mycol stroked his bulbous chin. 'Is that so? Would you rather go back to a Female Dominion prison?'

I folded my arms. 'The others tell you that, too? Did you interrogate them?'

He gestured at my wrist. 'No, your prisoner uniforms and tattoos told me. And I didn't need to *interrogate* anyone. We're all brothers here, Eno. I often like to say… our brothers' strength is always within.'

I looked down at my tattoo, a permanent reminder of their mistreatment of us males.

'You know,' Mycol continued, 'my spies told me about what your sister did.'

My eyes widened and I pushed off the mirror. 'Where is she? What happened to her?'

'Brave girl. A shame she wasn't male… we'd be calling her a hero… for rebelling like that.'

I clenched my fists and strode up to him. Even when he was sitting, he was still taller than me. 'Where is Sacet? Tell me!'

He stood, too, towering over me again. 'Calm down, boy. You're not acting very… brotherly. And what do you think we do… with those that are unbrotherly?'

There was nothing I could do. I had no powers here for some reason. Or maybe I had lost my powers completely? I would have to do what he said. I relaxed my body and looked down at his legs.

He loomed over me, bringing his face close to mine. 'Good, no more outbursts like that again. It's not *me* you should be angry with.' He glanced back at his chair, felt for it with his closest hand, and sat.

He attempted what I assumed was a sympathetic frown. 'Because… as for Sacet, I'm sorry to say… she didn't survive… much longer after rescuing you.'

I shook my head and tried to remain calm. 'You're lying. And like you would care, anyway.' My fists continued to shake, and my breathing quickened.

'You don't *have* to believe me. Fact is, she died. She even tried to kill the queen herself!'

That part sounded like her, but she wasn't dead. She was too stubborn to be dead.

Mycol latched onto my shoulder, pulled me closer and lowered his brow. 'Don't let her sacrifice be in vain.' He grabbed my tattooed wrist. 'You know who *truly* deserves your wrath. And I can help you with that. Help you with your vengeance!'

A tear rolled down my cheek. 'You can?'

He slowly nodded. 'I can.'

I regained my now shaky breath. 'I *do* hate them.'

Mycol shook me slightly. 'I do, too. Not a day goes by that I don't picture burning their cities to the ground.' He let go of me and sat up as straight as he could. 'Here in MDC, my rank is… the Terror Patriarch, second only to the king himself. And lucky for you… I have a soft spot for those that have been… *torn down* by their evil.'

He stood again with a groan and staggered towards the hidden exit. 'I see much of you in myself. And I have a *collection* of boys just like you… under my guidance.' He turned back to me with a serious expression. 'You'll meet them soon. I promise that together… our vengeance will come.'

Five: New Friends

Sacet

The present

Entering the armoury

The weapon racks stretched out of sight, as did the number of soldiers rushing about every which way. Although the attack was over, Marid and I had placed everyone on high alert. So now, the armoury was filled with women suiting up and picking out their weapons, readying for possible deployment or extended guard duties.

With Noor and Malu by my side, and Pilgrim straggling behind, we marched through the room with confidence.

Some of our soldiers glanced over with curiosity, and almost every one of them saluted with an arm across her chest. Others gawped at Noor and Pilgrim with mixed reactions, still not used to them here.

As we passed, I glared at any disrespectful soldiers, who then broke their focus on the boys and stood to attention. One older soldier couldn't look away from Noor, clearly reviling his presence.

I got up in her face. 'A hundred push-ups, now!' I opened a portal under her feet before she could react, and she plummeted back down from the low ceiling.

I turned to a nearby corporal and heard a loud thud. 'Make sure she finishes.'

The corporal nodded, and as we kept moving, there were rapid, panicking push-ups behind us.

We arrived at an empty prep station and the young, low-ranking initiates rushed over with a trolley of desert-camo armour plates. I stood with my arms to the sides as they went to work removing my clothing.

A sudden thought occurred: this was the first time I had brought Noor and Pilgrim into the armoury with me, and they were about to see me naked. As one of the initiates was about to lift my shirt, I grabbed onto her hand to stop her. 'Wait,' I said and turned to the men. 'Do you mind?'

Noor raised an eyebrow. 'Hmm?'

Already suited up, Pilgrim awkwardly made for the door around the corner. 'I'll wait over here.'

Malu strode over to Noor and shoved him in the side. 'Turn around!'

'Okay! Hey, easy!'

Noor, having grown up in the MD and completely alien to the concept of modesty between the genders, seemed genuinely confused. But he complied, turning away and approaching the other racks.

The initiates continued their work, quickly undressing and then re-dressing Malu and I before getting to work attaching our armour. I recognised one of the little girls adjusting the straps around my legs. She was the one who suited me up the very first time I prepared for a mission.

I prodded her with my toe. 'Hey, remember me?'

She avoided eye contact, instead continuing to tighten my armour. 'Y-y-yes... Ma'am.'

'What's the matter?'

'Nothing.'

I stood up straight again to make it easier for the little sisters. 'I'm not going to hurt you, you know that, right?'

She shook her head. 'Of course not, Ma'am.'

'Although, last time I seem to recall you giving me *quite* a bit of attitude—'

'No! I mean… yes. I mean, I'm sorry… Ma'am!' She stood, rushed off to one of the racks, pulled out a long metal sheath and handed it to me before bowing. 'Please, maybe this will make up for it?'

I grabbed the sheath with one hand and pulled on the sword's handle with the other. I held the pristine, metal blade in front of me. It was so shiny that I could see my reflection in it. The blade crackled and zapped with blue bolts of electricity.

Now that I could teleport people into space, having a weapon was kind of obsolete for me to carry, but I still appreciated the gesture.

She knelt and continued with my armour. 'I remember you liked swords, right?'

I sheathed the blade and held it near my hip. I smiled down at her. 'I do. We're even now.'

She awkwardly smiled back. My mind wandered as I stood waiting for the kids to finish.

Something had been troubling me ever since the attack. Our enemy struck the heart of our city, undetected. But stranger still, we had only been a couple of blocks away. Coincidence? No. I bet they knew where we were. Maybe they were still tracking me somehow?

I had removed the tracking device implanted in my neck during the coup. But maybe I wasn't the one they were tracking? Tau had given the order for all tracking devices to be removed long ago, but it wasn't like I had personally checked inside everyone's bodies. What if one of my closest friends still had one and I didn't know it?

My second perception drifted. As it turned and faced Noor, I stopped. He didn't have a shirt on. His bare chest was exposed. Snap out of it. I flew closer and went into the back of his neck. I searched through his flesh, but I couldn't see anything. Maybe it wasn't in…

'Sacet?' he said.

Breaking out of my trance, I realised that I had been staring at him.

I shook my head. 'Uh, I…'

Malu looked between us, folded her arms and laughed so loud that nearby soldiers stopped what they were doing to also gaze over.

'I'm sorry, Noor. I was looking inside of you for devices,' I said, feeling like an idiot.

'Devices?' Noor said as the initiates finished placing a larger undersuit on him and began work on his armour plates.

I frantically shook my head. 'I mean tracking devices.'

'It's okay, Sacet, really.'

My face was red hot, so I turned away, hoping he wouldn't notice. I rolled my eyes, frustrated with my awkwardness. What was *that*, Sacet? Although embarrassing, it was good to hear Malu laugh again.

When the initiates were done with my armour, I glanced back at Noor. Our eyes briefly locked, and I pointed to where I had seen Pilgrim go. 'I'll be over there with Pilgrim.'

The others finished gearing up and joined us. Like Pilgrim, Noor's armour was oddly proportioned and didn't fit him quite right.

I led them out of the armoury, taking deep breaths as we walked, trying to calm myself down. As I walked as normally as possible through the hangar, Malu occasionally whispered and laughed with Pilgrim from behind, which I assumed was at my expense. Well, at least our mission was starting in high spirits.

There were aircraft everywhere. Lines of troops were in formation, ready to be deployed if the order was given. A lone aircraft idled nearby. Terel was already waiting beside it. We reached the back ramp and she waved the others up, but put out a hand to stop me.

She gestured into the cabin. 'Look in there and tell me what you see.'

Inside the craft, strapped into the seats along the walls were five soldiers. Their camouflaged armour matched my own, although theirs was a bit more colourful for some reason. A couple looked to be in their twenties, while the other three were in their 30s or possibly older.

'I see five dedicated women willing to perform their duties,' I said.

She narrowed her eyes. 'Good answer, but they're more than that to me. When I was asked to choose a team to accompany you, I chose the best I had.'

'And I appreciate that,' I replied.

'No, I don't think you do. Not yet. You see, they're more than *just* soldiers to me, they're my family. They can and *will* hold their own out there, but that's not enough when there isn't someone experienced looking out for them and their mission.'

'You're referring to me?'

Had Siph gotten to her? The two of them knew nothing about me or what I was capable of.

She prodded me sharply in my breastplate. 'You know how to look out for yourself, sure. But if you don't bring those girls back, if they die and you leave their bodies out there, then I promise I'll *kill* you, powers or not. And it will be your sun-bleached corpse rotting out there in the sand with no one to find it.'

I stood in silence for a moment, processing her excessive threat. 'Is this all because you think I don't trust you?'

'I couldn't care *less* what you think of me. You need to be more worried about *me* trusting *you*. Something you must earn by bringing them back. Got it?'

'I got it.'

Terel relaxed her expression and stood to attention, before saluting, bringing her right hand across her chest. 'Good luck, Commander.'

I straightened up and returned the salute, before turning and walking up the ramp. As I entered the compartment, I passed the seated soldiers, as well as my companions, and saw an empty seat closer to the front of the cabin.

At the far front of the cargo area was an open doorway leading to the cockpit, where our pilot was adjusting controls and bringing various flashing lights to life. She had yellow streaks in her elegant, long, sandy-blonde hair, which curled with green tips. Her skin was pale, and her eyes were green, matching her tips.

I sat and strapped myself in. The ramp hummed and began to rise. Terel was still in the same position outside, her gaze fixed on me. The ramp sealed with a loud whoosh of air and the compartment went dark.

There was a whir from the ceiling. A large, bright hologram appeared in the centre of the cabin. Our pilot's face appeared in the upper left corner. The rest of the hologram showed what the nose of the aircraft could see in front. In the top right corner, there was a map showing our position on the planet, which was currently locked on our city, New Elysia.

'Commander Sacet?' the pilot said over an intercom, still focusing on the controls in front of her. 'I'm Officer Nako. Is your team ready for take-off?'

I glanced back at Pilgrim, Noor and Malu. Each gave a nod back. 'Whenever you're ready,' I called out. 'Go straight up.'

Nako moved more of the gadgets on the control panel. 'Control, all final checks have been made. We're ready for take-off.'

'Opening launch shoot,' said another voice over the speakers.

The engines outside droned and I sensed that an opening had been made in the hangar's ceiling directly above. But we wouldn't be needing that.

I thought back to when I was first discovering my powers and when I first met Tau and Pilgrim. Pilgrim's old village was where I teleported Eno to. That is where we would begin our search. I remembered the day we arrived at that place, a serene, cloudless, blue sky hung over us. I closed my eyes and clenched my fingers.

My stomach shifted, for we were already hovering above the hangar floor. I separated my fingers, and a large portal opened above our aircraft. The desert sky was now above us.

'Are you sure about this?' Nako called back, looking up through her cockpit window at the portal.

'Sure about what?' Pilgrim asked, clutching his seat.

'Do it,' I shouted over the humming engines, 'full power straight up!'

The engines roared and our craft lifted into the sky on the other side of the portal. There was another lurch in my stomach as the air pressure outside abruptly changed. As I closed the portal, we entered free-fall.

'Now!' I yelled.

The engines wailed, as did everyone in the compartment.

'Full power, Nako. Do it!'

The turbines strained. Were they at maximum power? The sound was beginning to cut out.

'I can't, it's stalled!' she yelled back.

We were plummeting towards the desert surface, and the screen showed this, too. The others in the compartment were yelling and screaming. I had never seen Pilgrim so afraid, whereas Noor hooted like he was having the time of his life.

Even if the engines miraculously reactivated, they wouldn't save us from the impact in time. I focused on the ground below and opened a portal to receive us, with the exit placed nearby, pointing up.

We plunged through the portal and out the other, pointing back up again, and as it did, the gravity in the cabin shifted sickeningly. The engines whirred back to life, and the craft steadied. The turbulence levelled out and smoothed again.

Noor laughed ecstatically. 'We almost died!'

Nako glanced back from her cockpit seat. 'A little warning next time?'

I laughed, too. 'I'm sorry, that's not how I pictured it happening. But I knew our best pilot could handle it.'

'Well, you're right about that, if it was anyone else, though...' Nako trailed off.

The mini-map on the screen had updated, showing different cartography.

'Good job, Commander,' one of the soldiers said. 'We're in a completely different part of the world.'

'And good job, Sacet,' Pilgrim added. 'I'm going to need a completely new pair of pants.'

'I don't get it,' another soldier said. 'If you can teleport all of this way, why do you need an aircraft?'

'Because I can only teleport to places I can see or I've been to,' I said. 'We need an aircraft because once I get there, I'm not going to just *walk* through the desert to discover new locations, am I?'

'Where to now, though?' Nako interrupted.

We all looked at Pilgrim expectantly. He was holding onto his chest, breathing heavily.

'Ea-east...' he managed.

We had been searching most of the morning. The remnants of my childhood village were much farther east of here. I remembered it being well hidden, but unfortunately, the village disbanded after the tragedy involving my parents. I wondered if they'd approve of the woman I had become?

I was scanning the ground below with my second sense, a task made more difficult at this speed. Meanwhile, Pilgrim was consulting his maps on a nearby console. He was getting more and more lost with each passing moment.

'Heh, it's… been a while since I've used this,' he explained. He paused to give me a grin. 'By the way, I appreciate you bringing me along, like we used to.'

I nodded back. 'That's okay.' I went back to concentrating in silence.

He cleared his throat. 'Because… uh… I know things have been hard.'

I sighed and turned my attention to him. 'Look, I stopped searching because…'

All eyes in the silent cabin were looking at me, but I didn't care.

'I was tearing myself apart thinking about him being alone and afraid. All those times you and I went out here to look for him but found nothing. I kept asking myself what if he was just over the next horizon, and we quit on him early? And you were always so positive, I just couldn't…'

I sensed the tension I had brought, but Pilgrim had taken it in stride, simply nodding in agreement.

I chuckled. 'And you remind me of my dad too much. The same beard and the same upbeat attitude. And he's gone. And now Eno's gone. I failed them both.'

Pilgrim reached out and put his hand on my knee. 'I'll never give up on him and neither will you.'

It was a beautiful sentiment, but I couldn't say it was true. I could have devoted so much more time and effort into finding him, but Tau, the Concordites, New Elysia, it all needed my attention, too.

'Alright, I'll be the one to say it,' Pilgrim addressed the cabin. 'What makes you special forces so *special*?' He must have sensed the tension, too, and decided to change the subject.

The soldiers exchanged looks, their silence replaced with smirks and snickers.

'You mean besides the seventy-six male goons I've popped?' the sniper said, before side-eyeing Noor. 'No offence.'

'None taken,' Noor replied. 'I'm not one of them anymore.'

'Oh no, of course not,' the squad leader said, before pointing to a tiny illustration on her shoulder of a headless MD soldier. 'But had things panned out differently, it probably would have been us sent in to kill you and your hard-shelled friend.' This elicited laughter from most of her squad.

Pilgrim looked over to me. 'Ah ha, trash talk, I've missed this.'

The squad leader had yellow tips in her green streaks, making her a colonel, the same as Malu. She and her team had at least a hundred cute little cartoons drawn on their armour, each depicting themselves killing MD soldiers in varying, over-the-top ways. The male enemies were drawn ugly and exploding in gore. The sniper had the most pictures, probably one for each of the seventy-six she had killed, and it looked more like graffiti than camouflage now.

One of the more reserved soldiers, who had been glaring at Noor ever since we came aboard, leant across the gap and smirked at him. 'Not one of them anymore? That's hard to believe. We know all about you, King's Wrath. More like King's Pet. Daddy's Pet.'

Noor turned away, staring at the flooring instead. The compartment quietened. Many glanced at me to see if I was going to shut her down, but I closed my eyes and continued to concentrate on the desert.

The hardened soldier's eyes narrowed. 'You melted through three of my sisters' faces with that power of yours, and probably a thousand other women. Got anything to say about that, huh?'

Noor returned her intense stare with his own. 'They should have ducked.'

The woman's lips curled, showing teeth. 'That's it.' She fumbled and ripped at her straps.

'Alright, that's enough,' the Colonel commanded.

The soldiers to the woman's sides placed an arm across her to keep her in place.

She continued to struggle. 'You think I'm scared of you, you murderer? They were innocent you piece of...'

'Enough!' the Colonel repeated, which finally silenced the soldier, who eased back down.

I opened my eyes and looked at them all. 'I'm trying to concentrate here. And you should be, too, Pilgrim.'

'Sorry, Commander,' the Colonel said. 'We'll try and keep it down.'

Pilgrim went back to his map, but his usual cheery smile was gone. 'Sorry, Sacet. You're right.'

Noor continued to stare daggers at the soldier, but when he noticed me looking at him, he exhaled and nodded.

At that moment I sensed something moving below, maybe an animal? It was a person, no, there was more than one. Eight men were hiding in the distant foothills beneath a cliff.

'Wait!' I called out. 'Stop! I see someone below.'

There was a cave next to them, their hideout perhaps? They were ducking down and observing us from afar using some kind of telescope. Concealed under their desert robes were old, scavenged rifles; it looked like they were ready to fight.

'Okay, tell me where to go,' Nako said.

'Head right,' I said, and the ship veered to the side. 'More... a bit more. There, now head straight. Do you see that cliff?'

'I see it, should I land next to it?'

'Yes, but not too close, they're armed.'

Nako brought the ship closer and cut the throttle. She tilted the nose down and lowered us safely. We touched down on a dune's peak, the engines spraying sand everywhere.

'Noor, come with me,' I said as I loosened my seat straps and stood. 'The rest of you stay here, but be ready to enter a portal if I make one. Nako, lower the ramp.'

Noor loosened his straps and joined me. Malu and Pilgrim exchanged a look, confused that they weren't invited. The ramp mechanism hummed and lowered, letting a stream of desert heat and sand in through the opening. I strode down the ramp with Noor following close behind.

'I'm coming, too,' Pilgrim said, unbuckling and shooting up. He pulled his oversized rifle down from the overhead trays.

'No, Pilgrim,' I commanded, stopping in the middle of the ramp. 'If they see you with that cannon of yours, they'll probably open fire,' I replied.

'If we hear gunfire, we're coming out, Commander,' the Colonel said.

I nodded back at her and continued down the ramp with Noor. As our feet stepped and sunk into the loose sand, I raised my arms into the air, as if to surrender. 'Do as I do.'

Noor copied me before quickening his pace up the dune with me. 'Is there something I should be aware of? Like how I'm the only one out here with you?'

My concentration lapsed and I almost tripped in the sand. He was right, it was just the two of us out here.

I cleared my throat. 'These nomads might not know about the rebellion, so it will help to see someone from both sexes approaching. And if there are only two of us, we don't seem as hostile as a larger group.'

'Fair enough, but why not bring Pilgrim, too, him being an actual nomad?'

I avoided looking back at him. 'Ah, well… I didn't think of that. I guess I feel safer knowing another acolyte has got my back.'

Out of the corner of my eye, I saw Noor smile. 'Thanks. I'm glad you feel safe with me.'

I ignored his comment, hoping to end the embarrassment I had brought.

We were getting closer to the rise where the nomads were hiding behind. I could see them clearly with my power. They were crouching silently in a trench, possibly waiting for us to give up and leave, or maybe waiting until we got closer to ambush us.

I cupped my hands around my mouth. 'Hey, we're not here to fight, we're friendly!' I shouted over the desert wind, hoping they would hear.

The group remained silently crouched and were now signalling each other. They split into three smaller groups. Two men stayed put, while the others edged along the trench in both directions. They were trying to flank us; if they had heard me, they certainly didn't believe me.

'You can see them?' Noor asked.

'Yes. Just stay calm.'

They could attack us at any moment. I had to make this quick.

I focused on all their weapons and opened tiny portals in front of all their gun barrels. In a single quick, jerking motion, I forced the portals over the gun barrels, over the weapon, and out of their hands. The guns all dropped at my feet, leaving the eight unarmed nomads to gawp at each other.

'I'll say again, we are *not* your enemy. We just want to talk.'

The oldest nomad popped his head up over the rise. 'Don't shoot, we're unarmed!'

I rolled my eyes. 'I know. I have your weapons here. You can have them back if you promise not to shoot at us.'

The other nomads stood up in place, revealing their positions to a shocked Noor, who had no idea how surrounded we really were. The first nomad jumped out of the trench and traipsed down the sandy rise, and then the others nervously did the same. The old man stopped in front of us and looked down at the pile of guns at our feet.

'Sorry, but I didn't feel like being shot at,' I said.

'Hmph, well we know when we've been beaten,' he said in a croaky voice. 'I was hoping it'd be the *Male* Dominion that finally caught us, at least then we wouldn't have to be slaves, or dead.'

'Hey, do I *look* female to you?' Noor said in protest.

The man shrugged and gestured at me. 'Kind of... you're wearing *their* armour. You could be a traitor, or some other complicated trick to lure us out.'

'Look, you don't understand,' I said. 'We defeated the Female Dominion some time ago. I'm a nomad, like you, or I was. There was an uprising, and we have a new queen. We accept people from both sexes now.'

The man grunted. 'Interesting trick. After hearing that, do your prisoners usually follow you back to your fortress without a fight?' The other nomads folded their arms and sneered.

I smirked back. 'You're quite the stubborn old man, aren't you?'

Noor nudged me. 'Sacet, maybe we should fetch Pilgrim. He can vouch for us.'

I nodded and turned away from the men.

'Wait, your name's... Sacet?' he asked from behind.

Ignoring him for now, I held out my arm, focused, and then opened a portal in front of me, leading to our craft's compartment.

Not realising I could see him, one of the nomads quietly pulled a knife out of his robes and hid it behind his back. He glanced at the old man, who shook his head in disapproval.

'It's about time,' a voice yelled from inside the cabin, before Pilgrim burst out of the portal, gun first.

Upon locking eyes, Pilgrim and the old man froze. Each nomad in the circle had a similar gawping expression.

Pilgrim dropped his cannon into the sand with a heavy thud. 'Dad?'

Six: Welcome to the Feeble Fortress

Eno

The last light of day gleamed off the city's spikey steel towers. The reflected light wavered, highlighting the imperfections in the structures' designs, like corroded metal plating, rust-covered pipes, punctured sheet metal and grimy, almost opaque windows. Each city block in MDC was dizzyingly high, made all the more scary by the buildings' shabbiness, as though they could collapse at any moment. They were all brown and drab, reminding me of my time in the FDC mines.

We flew over it all on an equally rusty, rattling vehicle that was nothing more than a floating platform with railings to stop us from falling. The hovercarriage shook as its engines sputtered. Mycol took no notice, as though it were normal. There were plenty of other vehicles hovering about, too, mostly packed with soldiers, or other times used to transport raw materials.

We weren't alone. Several creepy guards— the Terror Guard, as Mycol had called them—accompanied us in silence. These well-armoured men wore red-eyed skull masks like Mycol's, although not as elaborate. Each had long, button-covered batons, which could probably do more than just whack people.

I leant over the guardrail and looked down into the streets, which were like thin, concrete gorges. There were walkways filled with shuffling, sickly citizens. We passed one particularly wide divide filled with green water, an aqueduct. Occasionally I'd catch a glimpse of men inside the darkened rooms, huddled together and conversing around a single light source.

Even the air had a brown tinge here, limiting visibility. It smelled dirty and thick, as though an exhaust was blowing into my face. Trash was in abundance; it blew about in the high winds.

Mycol pointed in front of us. 'Look, dead ahead. The Military Wing.'

The colossal facility he was referring to was like a mountain of metal, with its own network of streets and buildings winding up its sides. The tip of the mountain was a grand palace. The entire thing was sleek and clean, unlike the rest of the city.

Our hovercarriage passed over a huge barrier wall at the base of the mountain before descending into one of the massive, mostly concrete courtyards. The canyon-sized courtyard had several facilities opening onto it. Several lowered areas were spaced along the yard, blood-stained sparring arenas. The men here, some armoured and some bare-chested, were bashing each other and their equipment. Each seemed stronger and more menacing than the last.

We touched down in front of one of the many grey facilities, which all looked the same to me. The guardrails lifted and allowed us both to disembark, as well as the Terror Guard. Once clear, the hovercarriage took off again.

Mycol gestured to the facility. 'This will be your living quarters.'

'The whole building?' I asked in disbelief.

'No, you'll be sharing it. But *I* have my own building… on the other side of the courtyard.'

Each facility here was a few storeys high, with evenly spaced windows. Hanging above the main doors was a symbol – one that I had seen many times before. It was shaped like an "M", but it looked like necrolisk claws, the symbol of the Male Dominion.

My mind briefly wandered to thoughts of Sacet. I still didn't believe Mycol's story of her death. No, she escaped shortly after I did, I was sure. Right about now she'd be arriving at the forest shack, looking for me.

As Mycol staggered forward, his limping was becoming more noticeable. He groaned louder with each step he took. Was he recently in a battle? The Terror Guard were following us, but none came to aid him.

Mycol stopped, noticing my unease. 'I'll be fine. I have... a condition.'

'What do you mean?'

'It's all part of my... acolyte ability. Our abilities aren't always... a blessing, sometimes they are a curse.'

I looked down. 'I can't even control my power. I don't know how to use it. It just pushes everything away. Seems like a curse to me.'

'Nonsense,' he said as we continued closer. 'You just need practice. And besides, there are *far* worse abilities. You'll find out, soon enough.'

We reached the large double doors at the entrance, which opened automatically on our approach.

What would this collection of others be like? Prisoners or loyal soldiers? What if they wanted to hurt me? If I fought back with my powers and accidentally destroyed this whole place, would Mycol kill me?

'You'll like it here,' he said as we entered. Our footsteps echoed down the shiny hallway, which had numerous doors and stairwells off it. 'You won't be put with the other... stronger acolytes, not yet.'

I glanced back and noticed the Terror Guard had remained outside. We reached the end of the hallway, stopping in front of a transparent glass doorway. We peered through into another training area. There were other young boys in there, all wearing military fatigues. Some were sparring, others were sitting at tables scattered around the edges, and a few were eating meals.

'This is a pet project of mine,' Mycol said. 'Not all acolytes are created equal. The boys here all have powers that are... a weakness. By sheer misfortune, some of them have been... given blindness, or a cripplingly delayed reaction time, or an uncontrollable shapeshifting power. So here the aim is to rehabilitate.'

'Blindness is an acolyte ability?'

'Normal blindness or some other disability... are not powers. But our scientists have confirmed that in these cases... they are the boys' acolyte abilities.' Mycol lumbered inside. 'Come!'

As I followed, the boys around the room noticed Mycol, shot up, ran over and lined up in front of us. Most of them were around my age, maybe a little older, perhaps twelve to eighteen cycles old.

A pair of boys came over to line up hand-in-hand, one guiding the other. Both had tanned skin and black hair. They looked similar. Maybe they were siblings? The boy being guided had white eyes; the blind one. The other older boy, a calm-looking late teen, had neck-length hair and a few facial scars.

Another boy was still over at the tables, staring at his food. All the others but him had lined up in silence. The boys all stared at him, but Mycol seemed particularly patient, not saying a word.

Moments passed and then the boy shot a look towards the door we had come through, stood up and lined up with the others, bumping into them as though they weren't there. The one with the bad reaction time, I guessed.

'King's glory, boys,' Mycol said in an upbeat tone.

'And King's glory to you, Patriarch,' they said in unison. All but the boy with the delayed reaction time, who stood silently.

'What must I remember if I am ever without my brothers?' he quizzed.

'Our brothers' strength is always within!' they said back.

'And King's glory to you, Patriarch,' the boy with the delayed reaction time said. The others took no notice.

Mycol nodded. 'Yes, well, I have some good news. You have a new brother to join you.'

'Our brothers' strength is always within!' the slower boy said.

'He is new to the Dominion, too,' Mycol continued, ignoring him, 'and so I'll need one of you to show him around.' He paced the line. 'Now, unfortunately, I cannot stay today. I have a mission to prepare for. Keenu?'

One boy from the fourteen stepped forward. He had short, black hair and kind eyes. He gave a quick bow to Mycol. 'Here, Patriarch.'

'Young Eno here... will be staying in your dorm,' Mycol continued. 'Get him acclimatised. Look after him.'

'Yes, Patriarch!' Keenu said with another bow.

Mycol turned back to me. 'And Eno? Everything you need... has been provided for you here. Just stay in this building... and relax until I return, understood?'

I nodded. 'I uhh... yes... Patriarch.'

He turned and staggered back to the exit. 'If you try to leave, I'll know.'

All the other boys stood silently until Mycol left through the corridor and was out of sight. Then they went back and resumed their training, leisure and meals. All except the slower boy, who left a few moments later.

Keenu walked over to me and smiled. 'Hey. So, ah, as you heard, I'm Keenu.'

'I'm Eno, as you heard, too. Can you tell me what's going on? I don't trust that guy.'

Keenu gave a grim smile. 'You might want to keep that to yourself.' He gazed over to the boys who were sparring. 'I take it he promised you some vengeance?'

'Yeah, he... how did you know?'

He gestured around the room. 'Because we've all heard that promise before. Welcome to the Feeble Fortress. A place where those who would simply get in the way on the battlefield are brought.'

'Why do you say that? What's your power?'

'I'll show you.'

Keenu calmly walked closer. As he was about to reach me, he didn't stop. I backed away, but I wasn't fast enough. Our faces met and I expected a collision, but instead felt nothing as his body passed through mine entirely. He was gone, so I looked around, searching for him.

'Behind you,' he said.

I spun and sure enough, he was behind me, with a large grin on his face. '*Wow*, you can walk through anything?'

'No, only people, and any objects associated with their person, like their clothing,' Keenu said, pointing at mine and frowning. 'I can still get shot, crushed, burned and so on.'

'But your power is still pretty useful, right?' I argued.

Keenu shook his head. 'Maybe if everyone else wasn't using

firearms? With all the deadly weapons and powers, there's no need for someone like *me* out there.' He crossed his arms and gruffly sighed. 'The psych and I worked out I got this power because of my abusive father. I just didn't want to be hit anymore, and then one day, no one was able to ever touch me again.'

I furrowed my brow. 'What do you mean?'

'Because of the trauma?'

Trauma? I stared at him, trying to make sense of what he was saying. He slowly moved away and gestured for me to follow, and we paced the room.

'Aren't our powers something we get when we're born?' I asked.

'No. Acolyte powers come from trauma. No one ever told you that? That's why Mycol is so intent on helping us get revenge. He gets all of us to talk it through, wants us to meet the trauma head-on. If we... understand why, maybe we can fix our problems and become strong.'

We passed the group of boys that were sparring. One of the wrestlers suddenly convulsed, and his skin rippled, as though he was transforming.

'Wait, wait!' he said to the others, and they all stopped. We watched as the boy's skin morphed into random shapes and colours, before he eventually got it back under control, turning normal again. 'Okay, keep going.'

Keenu and I continued pacing.

I gestured back at the boy. 'So, you're saying we all got our powers because... something bad happened to us?'

'Yep. Look over here,' he said, pointing to a nearby wall.

There were a hundred or so steel picture frames showing teen boys, hanging in a big grid. Under each picture was a plaque that listed their name and acolyte power, and above them all was a larger sign that read "Feeble Fortress Graduates".

Keenu smiled as he inspected numerous plaques. 'These are our heroes. They all overcame their weaknesses and became powerful.'

I shrugged. 'What happens to those that don't?'

Keenu's smile faded. 'Le-let me point out our bunkmates.' He cleared his throat and pointed over at the boy with the slow reaction time. 'That's Sozha. The reason he's so slow is because his sister died in his arms, and he just wanted more time with her. From his perspective, something that was present for us wouldn't have happened yet for him.'

Sozha was tall with brown hair, and similar in age to my sister. He was now sitting back down with his meal, ignoring everyone around him.

'See the older guy over there?' Keenu then pointed at the long-haired teenager from earlier, who had sat back down with the blind boy at a table in the corner of the room. 'That's Nadan. He can kill someone just by looking at them, but he needs to be in intense pain to do it. That happened because bandits tortured him. Those bandits are dead now.'

Nadan glared at us; he probably knew we were talking about him. The scars on his face now made more sense.

'The boy next to him is his little brother, Mui, and he's blind. The bandits forced him to watch when they tortured Nadan. Obviously, he didn't want to. Are you starting to understand now?'

I nodded, but a part of me wished I wasn't hearing all of this.

'Come on, I'll introduce you,' Keenu said before walking over to Mui and Nadan in the corner of the room.

I hesitantly followed, brushing past tables and chairs. I watched Sozha as I walked. He looked up from his food and glanced at where Keenu and I were earlier, perhaps listening in on our past conversation.

'Here we go again,' I heard Mui say as Keenu and I approached.

'What?' Keenu replied as we arrived in front of them.

Mui shook his head. 'Oh, Keenu, sorry. I wasn't talking about you… I didn't know you were there.'

There was something off about Mui, he was slightly hunched over, looking down, and had his arms crossed tight, as though to hold himself comfortingly.

'I just thought I'd introduce you guys to Eno here,' Keenu said, taking a seat next to them and gesturing for me to do the same.

Nadan had his feet up on one of the free seats. He hadn't stopped glaring at me since I walked over, and it was making me feel uneasy. He looked me up and down, scrutinising me.

'I'll stand,' I said quietly.

'So, what's your power?' Mui asked, in a low tone, his milky white eyes staring vaguely in my direction.

'I can push things,' I replied, hoping I wouldn't have to elaborate further for fear of them interrogating me on my past.

'Can you be more specific?' Mui asked.

'I think he means he can telekinetically push things away. Right?' Keenu said.

I nodded in agreement, that sounded right. Not sure what that big word meant though.

'So, you probably had some bad people after you,' Nadan said. His voice was much deeper than the rest of us.

I took a step back. 'I… I'd… rather not… go into it.'

His eyes narrowed. 'I could hear Keenu telling you our stories from here.' Nadan pulled his feet back down off the chair and pointed at the other boys. 'It's not like there's much else to do around here while we wait for our inevitable death.'

'Death?' I asked, my voice a little higher pitched than I intended.

'Nadan is just paranoid,' Keenu interrupted. 'He thinks this is a prison for us.'

Mui sighed and turned away. 'It's something *much* worse than that.'

'What's your story, kid?' Nadan repeated, not letting up. 'Was it because the Dominion was chasing you?'

'Necrolisks?' Mui added.

Keenu noticed my unease. 'Maybe he's not ready to talk about it yet?'

'Don't tell me it was bandits,' Nadan continued. 'Or maybe it was…'

'It was a cave-in, okay?' I snapped back.

The three went silent for a moment.

Keenu shrugged. 'A cave-in is quite terrifying. Nothing embarrassing about being traumatised by that.'

Nadan leant back with his hands behind his head. 'Are you claustrophobic? Afraid of small spaces?'

Mui nodded without looking. 'Makes sense. That's why you push everything away, to give yourself more room.'

They were right. I had hated small spaces all my life. But I didn't know about my powers until recently. If I hadn't pushed those collapsing rocks away in the mines, I would have been crushed.

'You don't have to worry about cave-ins here,' Nadan said, before narrowing his eyes. 'Instead, maybe you should worry about impressing Mycol, because underperforming kids don't last long here. If you're not careful, you'll disappear like the others.'

Seven: It's My Fault

The Royal Gardens

I got up from the stone bench and wandered to one of the vibrantly coloured bushes. I smelt its flower petals, long and deeply, trying to enjoy the brief moment to myself. Amiki, Tetsu and a group of Royal Guards were watching over me, spread about to not crowd.

Before today's events, I had been locked in day after day of non-stop appointments with administrative assistants and provincial delegates. None had any good news for me. And now the MD had struck at the heart of our society, mere blocks away from one of the few places I found comfort in anymore.

Tetsu was pacing back and forth along the garden path. Ever since the others left, he hadn't been as confident and jovial.

'You'll be fine, Tetsu,' I said, trying to reassure him. 'This isn't your first time separated from Noor, is it?'

'No, of course not. I'm just… uhh, not into plants.'

I picked one of the brighter, blue flowers, wandered over and handed it to him. 'A shame. They're much easier to protect.'

He gave a quick laugh. 'Thanks.'

'Are you worried about him?'

He inspected the flower in the palm of his hand. 'A little, but I know he can take care of himself. Sacet, too.'

I nodded and stared into the gardens. 'Yeah, they'll be okay. They'll be okay.'

Amiki clutched her earpiece, before approaching and bowing. 'My Queen, the bodies have been delivered. It's time.'

I smiled at Tetsu. 'I'm glad you're here with me. I need all the moral support I can get for what comes next.'

Amiki came closer and stamped her spear's butt in the dirt. 'My Queen, may I have a word with you in private?'

Tetsu gave an awkward bow to me before heading back along the path towards an archway in the hedge.

Once he was out of earshot, Amiki bent closer. 'Ma'am, I must advise caution when dealing with him.'

'Who, Tetsu?' I whispered back.

'We don't know him all that well, my Queen.'

I shook my head and began to follow the path. 'He and Noor have been loyal since the coup. Where's this coming from, suddenly?'

Amiki strode alongside me. 'It's just that… the two of them have killed hundreds of women. For your own safety, I'm not comfortable with him being this close to you.'

I stopped and turned to her. 'Drop the formalities. Are you saying they've been pretending to be nice all this time? That they're spies?'

She locked eyes. 'I'm saying that the regret that you and I feel every day, I don't see it in them. They're all jokes and smiles. We shouldn't trust them, not fully.'

Although the boys' powers had been invaluable to us, it was true we didn't know much about them personally. Whenever the topic of their past had come up, they almost always deflected with unrelated stories.

'Maybe they're just better at hiding their regret?' I said softly. 'That doesn't mean it's not there.'

Amiki dipped her head. 'I will put more trust in him if my Queen commands it of me.'

'See that you do,' I immediately answered, focusing on the path again.

We passed under the arch and followed the winding path around the Citadel's perimeter to the front. The late-afternoon sun lit up the tower's golden walls, as well as the lush open gardens. Outside the gardens was the Residential Rim, a surrounding layer of apartment buildings that housed all the citizens.

Beyond that, the city's four corners were each designated a specific purpose. Behind the Citadel, up a large hill, was the old Prison Quad. The prison itself was empty now, but below it were the mines, a vast network of caves and tunnels that stretched underneath the city. They were the current home of Colony's necrolisks.

To my right was the Military Quad. The large, grey facilities consisted of numerous training centres, a barracks, a hangar, warehouses for our munitions and everything else our soldiers needed. To my left was the Science Quad where smokestacks spewed into the sky. There seemed to be less of that smoke lately, a sign of those industries producing less and less.

In front of me was the Commercial Quad, where the skyscrapers towered over all but the Royal Citadel itself. Now, in the aftermath of the attack, the fires were under control, and our clean-up crews were still digging through the rubble to recover our people's bodies.

Tetsu rejoined us with a macabre expression. I looked out at the rows of dead citizens lying in the gardens. There were hundreds.

My heart twisted. 'If only they understood how much pain they were causing.'

I had been offering my resurrection services daily ever since I took power. Since discovering it, my power hadn't always been successful, particularly on older bodies, so I always had Siph and her staff bring me the new dead at the end of each day. But seeing this many all at once made me feel like there was never going to be an end. To bring them back, I'd have to experience all that pain, one after another. The three of us stood there in silence, looking out at the sea of corpses.

I wondered what our lives would be like if Sacet never came along and rebelled. Would all these people still be alive?

Groups of white-streaked administrators unloaded corpse-filled hovering vehicles while the Royal Guards watched in silence. Many of the bodies were scorched, while others were in pieces.

I turned to an administrator standing nearby. 'Is this all of them?'

She turned with a grimace. 'I'm sorry, my Queen, but I don't know,' she said with a bow. 'These are only the ones we have recovered and processed so far.'

'Bringing back any memories?' Amiki said to a contemplative Tetsu.

His face screwed up. 'What?'

Amiki shrugged. 'I just mean, these are Havoc Division's usual tactics, right?'

Tetsu gazed at her for the longest time. 'Yeah… usual tactics.'

There was a loud commotion coming from the edge of the gardens. The entrance gates were closed, but through the bars we could see a large crowd had gathered in the streets.

'What's going on over there?' I asked.

'Another protest,' Amiki answered. 'I didn't want to trouble you with it. Troopers are on the way to disperse them.'

I shook my head. 'I don't understand. Do they think the attack is *my* fault?'

'My Queen, I know what you're thinking. But if you respond it will only make things worse.'

I marched toward the gates. 'No, I'm tired of being blamed for everything.'

'My Queen, please!' Amiki called.

'They just need to hear the truth,' I called back, now with Amiki and Tetsu in pursuit.

When I reached the outer wall, I climbed a set of stairs. Other Royal Guards had noticed what I was trying to do and converged on my position. They weren't going to stop me, either. I needed to put these people's minds at ease.

I ran along the wall until I had a clear view of the crowd from an open notch in the fortifications. I clambered into the crenel and up onto the wall. There were even more guards up here with me, pointing their weapons at the crowd, and when they noticed me they lowered them.

Amiki and Tetsu caught up. She gave me a pleading look, and he watched without objection.

I could see an army of soldiers approaching farther down the street. They were heavily armoured, with riot shields and shock weapons, which I hoped were set to non-lethal. I had to get this crowd under control before they arrived.

'It's the queen,' one woman yelled, followed by a barrage of boos.

'Everyone, please listen,' I yelled over them. 'Listen to me!' They eventually hushed. 'The attack was from the Male Dominion. I'm just about to start resurrecting the victims. I want to listen to everything you have to say, and I want to help with any problems you may have. There is no need for further violence.'

'This is all your fault!' a woman screamed, and there was a surge of approving yells throughout the crowd. 'This never would have happened with the old queen.'

I raised my hands for calm. 'Yes, we would have never been attacked, but we also never would have attacked them.'

A robed, nomadic man raised his cane. 'Some of us came from far distances to join your *Concordites*, but we were safer out in the desert!'

'I promise you, we will get this under control.'

'What about our food?' a younger woman shouted, followed by more jeers. 'How am I supposed to feed my children?'

'Why are there necrolisks living under the city?' yelled another. This brought the loudest of the taunts.

'We need a peace treaty,' shrieked another, 'and new leaders!' The crowd around her cheered and applauded.

A thrown piece of litter whizzed past my shoulder, and more was on the way. Tetsu climbed the wall to assist.

Something hot and sharp ripped into my chest as a high-pitched whine rang. I looked down at the gaping hole in my ribs. All noise now muffled. My breathing stopped. My body shook involuntarily, and then my aura exploded, coating me in light-blue flame. The hole sealed and I stopped shaking.

'Sniper!' Tetsu yelled as my hearing returned. He brought up a shield around us whilst also pulling me down from the wall. More laserfire collided and dispersed along his protective energy. Now kneeling behind the fortifications, he dismissed his shield again.

The mob shouted even louder; it was chaos out there.

'Are you okay?' Tetsu asked, inspecting me.

I nodded. 'Physically, yes.' I buried my face into my hands as Amiki now joined us.

'Citizens, return to your homes immediately,' an amplified voice from beyond the wall instructed.

I peeked over the wall to see. The soldiers banged their electrified weapons against their shields, over and over, sending a thundering, crackling sound throughout the streets. The crowd screamed, some in panic, others in riotous fervour. Weapons clattered and fizzed. Tetsu and Amiki pulled me back down yet again.

'My Queen, stay down,' Amiki begged.

'Please, just go!' I shouted, hoping that even one person could hear me. 'Go back to your homes!'

But it was no use. The bedlam continued: banging of shields, scattering laserfire, and a cacophony of cries.

Several golden guards surrounded me now, gesturing for me to descend the steps. I shoved off the wall and went back into the gardens, and my entourage followed close behind.

I stomped over to the nearest corpse, a small child. Her body was covered with searing laser burns.

I knelt and placed my hands on her singed wrists. 'This *isn't* my fault.'

My aura reactivated. The tingling sensation returned. It travelled through my arms and into her now-healing wrists. And then it hit me, the same pain she had experienced, multiple blasts hitting my own body. I moaned through the agony. My skin broiled, like I was sizzling away in a cooking pot.

Her burns receded and her cavity-like wounds filled with new bone, fluids, and flesh. Finally, the skin mended, leaving only burned holes in her clothing.

Any moment now she would come to; her eyes would flutter open, and she'd be alive, like us. I bent over and placed my hand in front of her nose to check for breathing. Nothing. I gripped her wrist to check her pulse. None. No.

Tetsu stepped closer. 'What's wrong?'

'It's happening again,' I said with a trembling voice. 'My power didn't work. This… this isn't right, I'm doing it the same as always. Let me try another one.'

I stood back up and knelt beside the next woman. She had suffered the same fate as the little girl. I grabbed onto her wrist like before and began. The woman's wounds healed and again I was wracked to the core. My sorrowful scream joined many others on the air. I turned her wrist over and felt for a pulse.

Amiki averted her eyes. She hated seeing me in pain like this. 'Anything?'

I shook my head. 'I don't understand. These bodies are new… I don't…'

I stood again and chose another body at random, kneeling over a dead nomadic man. He had suffered a different fate, his body had been crushed by falling debris. This time I placed my hands on his chest instead. I focused as much as I could, ready to willingly accept the pain.

The man's flesh healed, making a sickening churning noise as his innards rearranged themselves. I tried to scream, but was unable. My stomach ripped to the side. Wave after wave of crippling pain rolled over me. I cried instead, feeling so sorry for this poor soul. His final moments must have been horrific.

My guards stared as I checked again. The man didn't spring to life, and he didn't have a pulse. I looked up at those around me.

'What's wrong with me? I can't bring anyone back!'

Eight: Coming Back

Sacet

The cave walls were moist, indicating a water table nearby. There was a lived-in smell to the place, as though this was where they kept old meat. These nomads had found a great spot to hunker down.

Pilgrim was still hugging and reconnecting with all seven of his brothers. In the centre of the cave, his father had taken a seat on one of the many rocks forming a circle of natural chairs.

'We were about to fire on you,' he began. 'You know that, right? And my other son over there was going to stick you with his blade.'

I took a seat on what I hoped would be a comfortable stone, but quickly discovered it was anything but. 'I was aware, more so than you think.'

He stroked his long white beard. Now that I had more time to look at him, the resemblance to Pilgrim was strong. Unlike Pilgrim, though, he was bald and didn't share his son's usual toothy smile.

Noor, Malu, Pilgrim and the other nomads took whatever seats they could find. Per my request, our soldiers waited at the cave's small entrance, resting their backs on the rock walls. Our pilot, Nako, was back in the aircraft, ready to take off at a moment's notice.

'Now go through it again,' the old man continued. 'Why have you come for us?'

'Well, we didn't specifically come looking for *you*,' I replied.

The old man gestured at Pilgrim. 'Then why is *he* here?'

'Coincidence,' I said. 'We're looking for The Shroud.'

He shook his head, straight-faced. 'Never heard of them.'

His sons all exchanged looks.

I smirked and leaned in. 'I never said it was a "them". It could have been an object or a place.'

He copied my body language. 'In any case, they're not here.'

'Indeed,' I said, resting my elbows on my knees. 'Well, we're always looking for new allies. You're all welcome to come back with us.'

The man glanced at his many sons, who had stern looks and crossed arms. 'No. There's a reason we've been able to survive so long, and it's because we don't take stupid risks.'

'But this war affects all of us,' Noor interrupted, picking up a pebble and piffing it to the other side of the chamber. 'Don't you want it to be over?'

The father flicked his fingers at Noor as if to shoo him away. 'That may have roused me when I was young and foolish, but my answer is the same. We don't want any part in your fight.'

'Then nothing's changed,' Pilgrim said, staring at the cave wall with an oddly dejected expression, especially for him. 'You were too afraid to help Mum, too.'

His father shot a spiteful look at him. 'How dare you bring her up again.' He paused, looking Pilgrim up and down. 'How dare you *still* blame me. *You're* the one who brought them.'

Was he referring to us? I shrugged. 'I was the one that brought us here. Don't blame Pilgrim for this.'

The old man sneered. 'Pilgrim? Is that what you've got everyone calling you now? Too ashamed of the name I gave you?' He turned to me. 'His mother died decades ago, and it was his fault. He and Kirai went off looking for a fight, for blood. And they found it: an MD patrol.'

'You could have saved her,' Pilgrim interrupted again. 'She was out in the open and you could have at least *tried* to rescue us, but you hid up on that cliff instead.'

Their shouts echoed off the cave walls.

The old man stood and kicked sand towards Pilgrim. 'She knew the rule! And so did you: we… will… endure.'

The other sons put a hand on their chests and repeated the phrase. "We will endure."

Pilgrim mouthed out their creed, too, while rolling his eyes. 'Whelp, you're still alive so… well done.'

The father paced around the circle of stone seats. 'You were a stupid kid, you never listened to me.'

Pilgrim's eyes occasionally darted to his cannon lying in the sand. 'Oh, I listened alright. But Mum and I were tired of hiding in the dark.'

'Don't drag her into your shame. She only went to look out for your worthless arse. If you had stayed put, she'd still be alive.'

Pilgrim shot up and copied his father's body language, gesturing aggressively. 'No, she was a fighter! And then you… you acted as if nothing happened.'

'Oh, I've so *missed* this argument. You think I'm some kind of monster for not showing how affected I was? Is that it?' the father said before pausing. 'You're all still alive because of *me*. I was, and still am, trying my hardest to keep this family alive, and you're worried I wasn't crying enough? What is wrong with you?'

Pilgrim closed his eyes, defeated. 'I guess I just cared more about her than you did.'

The father pointed to the exit. 'Get out!' He picked up a fist-sized rock and lobbed it at Pilgrim, narrowly missing him. 'You continue to sully her name? Leave, and take your new masters with you.'

Pilgrim picked up the same rock and hurled it right back at his father, hitting him in the chest. He then picked up his cannon and stormed off to the entrance to leave.

Malu stood and smirked at me. 'This *Shroud* is probably just as cowardly as these guys.' She turned and followed Pilgrim out.

The cave fell silent other than a constant dripping. The nomads eyed the rest of us warily.

'I… I'm also looking for my brother,' I said, trying to cut the tension. 'He got lost to the west of here, almost a cycle ago. He's maybe… eleven. Light-brown hair, pale.'

I looked around at the other boys, too, hoping for some kind of recollection, but no one said a word.

The old man turned his back on us. 'Get. Out.'

I sighed, stood, and motioned for Noor and the soldiers to follow me out.

As the Colonel and her squad picked up their weapons, I glanced back. 'I understand having a code of survival. But know that you don't have to fear death anymore. Thanks to our queen's power, we can bring people back to life.'

The man's eyes widened, as did his sons. The soldiers made their way outside. The sons all looked to their father.

'We'll wait for a short while, in case you change your mind,' I said, turning and walking out with Noor.

The desert wind resumed its loud howling, battering us with stinging sand. A sandstorm was rolling in. Pilgrim was sitting on another rock at the entrance with Malu, and the others had gathered around them.

In this past cycle I had known Pilgrim, I had never seen him so angry. He had told us tall tales of his mischievous brothers and their dangerous childhoods, but never once mentioned his parents.

I approached, shaking my head. 'I'm sorry everyone. This wasn't what I was hoping for.'

Another sound carried on the roaring wind. It sounded like engines, but our aircraft was still grounded over the next rise. Another craft poked through the thick weather, approaching the landing zone.

'Everyone, take cover!' the Colonel shouted. 'Ready your weapons!'

As we ran to the same trench the nomads used earlier, the aircraft turned. Large doors on the sides rolled up to reveal the MD soldiers standing inside, holding handles on the roof for support.

One peculiar man was burly and hunched, and while the other soldiers had helmets with skull designs painted on them, his helmet was in the shape of a large, deformed skull with its jaws open.

The man let go of the handle and brought his glowing hands together. A sickly, pale green ball of energy formed between them. He took a strong stance for balance before lobbing it towards us.

The fizzing globe sailed through the air and hit the side of the nearby sandy trench, exploding on impact. The force rocked the ground, obliterating our cover and launching us backwards. The sand rippled outwards like a tidal wave.

As I landed, the wave overwhelmed and buried us all. When the barrage of sand stopped, I squirmed and struggled to pull myself out. There were muffled groans from my buried friends as they eventually surfaced and stood, too.

Two more aircraft landed next to our own. Enemy troops departed from the rear and sides, wearing standard helmets and gas masks.

Noor sprinted for the newly formed crater and dove in. He popped up and fired at the advancing ground soldiers with his devastating energy beam. He tore several to pieces in mere moments.

Our soldiers opened fire from the trench with their lasers, picking off some enemies at the base of the hill. Turrets fixed to the enemy aircraft swivelled to our position and returned fire. Our sniper perched herself on a nearby rock and shot back at one of the crafts. The precise laser zipped through the cockpit's window and into the enemy pilot's head.

Pilgrim rested his oversized cannon onto the trench's edge and aimed. He fired a thunderous blast on one hapless soldier, leaving nothing but spinning limbs. The rest of their body sprayed across the sands in smouldering charred clumps.

Malu placed her palms over the side of the trench and liquified the ground. The trickling creek streamed down the hill and underneath some of the soldiers' feet, causing them to fall into the newly created quicksand. They clawed at the air as their heads sunk below the surface.

I surveyed the battlefield with both of my perceptions, searching for the flying man, but I couldn't see him. I instead bolted for the rocks near the cave's entrance and took cover.

Focusing on the second landing craft, I opened a portal beneath it, ejecting it and a stream of sand into the black abyss of space. I closed the portal again before our craft suffered the same fate.

I felt a hand on my shoulder; it was Pilgrim's father. He nodded at me sternly before he and his seven sons rushed out of the cave and joined our soldiers in the trenches. They, too, fired upon the enemy soldiers.

The first craft containing the hunched acolyte was back, moving too fast for our soldiers to get a bead on. The enemy acolyte had grabbed one of his own men in the craft by the neck. The green energy returned, this time coming from the grabbed soldier. The acolyte was pulling the energy from his own soldier's body, and then into his mouth. The acolyte's hands reignited. The soldier, now limp, was tossed from the aircraft.

A far more immense, swirling ball of green energy was in the acolyte's hands now. He heaved the orb at us with an overhead throw. Having little time to react I made the widest portal I could in front of our group to meet the projectile, with the portal's exit up high, pointed back into the sky.

The orb flew through my portal and exploded in the sky far above us. The explosion was unlike anything I had ever witnessed; massive, perfectly spherical and continually expanding. It was so large, had it hit us, it would have destroyed us all, and demolished the cave, too.

The shockwave rolled through the air at tremendous speed, taking everyone off their feet and producing an ear-piercing hiss. The enemy craft got hit, too, and almost lost control in the turbulence before flying straight again. Flashing lights could be seen inside the compartment.

There was a whoosh as a stray rocket slammed into the cave entrance's mouth. Sharp stone stalactites whizzed down into the ground, penetrating the soft sand by my feet. Even larger chunks of rock were beginning to break loose, too.

I opened a portal below my feet and fell through, back into the trench. The stones were still falling, so I closed the portal just before any could pursue me through. The cave entrance now collapsed, replaced with a huge plume of dust.

More enemy troops were coming over the sand dunes; the two craft that we had already taken care of mustn't have been the only ones. I sensed several more craft landed just beyond our obscured view, beyond the veil of the sandstorm.

The nomads and the special forces to my sides continued to fire. One of the nomads was dead, shot in the forehead. And one of our soldiers had taken a hit, too. She was bleeding out onto the sand, barely conscious and close to death.

'Everyone, get down!' I shouted over the wind and laserfire.

As my allies ducked behind the trench, I adopted a strong stance, closed my eyes and clenched my fingers. Behind the grounded enemy aircraft, a vast portal to space widened. At first, it was only the blowing battlefield sand that was sucked through, clearing our vision. But soon each enemy soldier was picked up by the vacuum, along with their craft.

Many of them dropped to the disappearing ground, desperately trying to latch onto something. It was no use; they were soon sucked through.

The sand around my allies and I shook. The wind whipped around me, far stronger than before. Our own aircraft was starting to tilt, so I closed the portal. Everything dropped back down, and the sandstorm rushed back in from all sides.

My portal had sucked in so much that large linear streaks were drawn in the sand. I tried sensing for more enemies but there were none. The acolyte's craft had retreated beyond my range. Nako had been taking cover in her cockpit, anxiously aiming her pistol at the windows.

'Clear?' Noor called.

'We're clear,' I called back, exhausted.

Malu climbed out of the trench. '*Why* did I think coming out here was a good idea?'

The Colonel approached me. 'We can't stay here, Ma'am. That might only be the first wave.'

I nodded in agreement. 'Secure the craft. The rest of us will be down in a minute.'

'And what about Tannis?' she replied.

'Tannis?'

The Colonel looked at the girl who had been bleeding out, now dead, and back at me. 'I think my commander would appreciate it if she didn't become a... sun-bleached corpse?'

I stared at the body, remembering Terel's threats. 'Of course.' I pictured the gardens outside the citadel back home and opened a portal under the body. She fell through and I closed it. 'I'm sure the queen will resurrect her soon.'

The Colonel gestured for the soldiers to follow. They all hopped out of the trench, slung their weapons over their shoulders and ran down the dune.

Noor came over and gestured around. 'It's like they knew where we were again,' he said in a hushed tone, before eyeing our soldiers with mistrust. 'It's gotta be one of them.'

I joined in his scepticism, also watching our soldiers. 'It could just as easily be someone in administration, keeping track of us remotely.' I sighed.

Pilgrim's father approached, clearing his throat to interrupt us. He gestured to his dead son in the trench. 'You said you can bring back the dead?' His face was welling up, but he tried his best to conceal it.

'Not me, our queen,' I replied.

Pilgrim and the other nomads had gathered around the body to stoically mourn, but a couple broke down into tears.

'And how about my Kirai?' the man added. 'Their mother?'

I shrugged and partially nodded. 'So long as you have her remains, it should work.'

Noor looked over his shoulder at the sealed cave entrance. 'Something tells me you wouldn't have *endured* in there.'

The old man smirked. 'Yes, very humourous, but now we have no choice but to leave.' He gazed at each of his seven remaining sons. 'Can you get my boys somewhere safe?'

I nodded as Malu came closer. She raised a hand to stop my kindness. 'Wait, does this mean you're going to help us now?'

The man narrowed his eyes at her. 'Not cowardly enough for you?'

I closed my eyes and pictured the throne room in my mind. A portal opened next to them, and through it, we could see the throne, devoid of Tau. There were still Royal Guards though, who noticed the portal and advanced on it.

The old man got his remaining sons' attention. 'Go through and wait for me. Take Atu with you and bring him back to life. Don't let them tell you no.'

Each of the sons, still distraught over their loss, dipped their heads in both understanding and acceptance.

'What about you?' one of the older sons asked.

For the first time since I had met him, the father smiled. 'I'm going to get your mother.'

The sons managed to smile back, exchanging looks of surprise and excitement. Except for Pilgrim, they each farewelled their father in their own way, picked up their fallen brother and dragged him through the portal.

'Good luck, Dad,' the last son said before also stepping through. 'We will endure.'

The father repeated their creed back to him.

I caught the eyes of one of the Royal Guards on the other side, who lowered her weapon when she noticed me and offered to carry the dead man's feet.

I closed the portal. 'Your sons will be safe there.'

He climbed out of the trench and made for our aircraft. 'Good. Come on, it will be nightfall soon.'

Pilgrim, Noor, Malu and I all followed him back.

I caught up with him. 'I didn't catch your name by the way?'

'Doron,' he replied as he walked up the ramp, 'and my son there, Saladire, is my firstborn.'

Pilgrim seethed back at his father, before going back to ignoring him.

Noor smirked at Pilgrim. 'Saladire?'

Malu burst out laughing. 'Salad boy over here. No *wonder* you changed it. Is that why you never eat your vegetables?'

Pilgrim sighed and rolled his eyes. 'Yes, yes. Get your laughs out now.'

We reached the back ramp and quickly marched up. Malu and the soldiers took their seats, as did Nako in the cockpit. The ramp rose. Doron initially had trouble with the seat's straps, but our sniper leaned over and assisted him. He inspected her closely with disgust. I sat next to Doron, and Noor eagerly took the other seat next to me.

I turned to Doron as I strapped myself in. 'I'm happy to help retrieve Pilgrim's mother for resurrection. But what else can you help us with?'

The pilot glanced back from her seat. 'What's our heading, Commander?'

'We are going east to the resting place of my beloved,' Doron answered for me, 'which just so happens to be the village of my old clan. I believe you've heard of them.'

I grinned. 'The Shroud.'

Nine: Cold Snap

Tau

The rough, unkempt man stomped on the throne room floor. 'What do you mean you can't bring him back? We were told you could!'

Pilgrim's brothers all had different measures of shock and anger. One was pacing back and forth. Another was sobbing over the dead brother's body on the ground. Blood was spreading along the tiled floor.

I was sitting on my throne with my head in my hands.

With a hesitant, fleeting smile, Amiki knelt beside me and put a hand on my knee. 'My Queen, if you'd like I can get them to come back later?'

I looked up at the desperate men. 'I'm *so* sorry. I've been gradually losing my power. And today of all days, I can't seem to bring *anyone* back. I don't know what's happened…'

Tetsu was leaning against a pillar nearby. He was shaking his head now and then, perhaps sharing in my despair.

'Well… can't you at least try?' the brother at the front asked. He appeared to be the oldest and had the longest beard.

Amiki's smile faded. She stood and approached the top of the throne's stairs. 'The queen has told you it cannot be done. If you'd like, we can preserve his body in the city's morgue.'

The aggravated man pointed threateningly back. 'This is *not* what was promised to us!' Now that his voice was raised, the guards lining the chamber closed in and pointed their laser spears at the anxious group. But the man didn't seem to care, he bent down and grabbed his dead brother's legs. 'We're not trusting you with him.'

Amiki scoffed loudly. 'And yet you trust the queen enough to grant a free resurrection?'

One of the younger brothers, his previously hopeful demeanour now extinguished, brushed the corpse's hair and sobbed. 'No, Atu... this was not how we were supposed to go.'

Yet another brother elbowed the young man. 'We will endure.'

The sobbing man composed himself and sternly nodded, still with wet eyes. 'We will endure... without him.' He assisted in picking up the dead man from the other end.

'And without them,' the elder brother said, gesturing at me. 'Come on.'

I shot up. 'Wait. Please stay. Guards? Organise accommodation for them.'

'My Queen?' Amiki said in protest with a raised eyebrow. 'If they want to leave, we should let them.'

I shook my head. 'I'm starting to realise... that I'm already responsible for so much anger... and hunger and sickness and death. I can't have this on my conscience, too. Sacet sent you here for a reason, so stay.'

Amiki fully turned to me. 'My Queen, you must understand...'

'No, Amiki, *you* are the one that must understand,' I interrupted. 'If I hadn't taken power, none of this would have happened. Those people outside would still be alive.'

'But it would all be a lie?' Amiki replied. 'You and I fought together; we watched our friends die. It was all for nothing. What would be the point in living a life like that?'

I slumped back into my throne. 'My life *did* have a point, for a while, when I was just a healer. When I *knew* I was doing the right thing.'

The eldest brother let go of his sibling's legs. 'You're afraid of the responsibility, aren't you? Afraid to get your hands dirty?'

Amiki turned with a scowl. 'Watch what you say, nomad, or soon there will be *two* dead men on the ground.'

He glanced back at the throne room's doors. Their confiscated weapons were there on a table for when they left, thankfully both out of reach and unloaded. He locked eyes with me and approached the steps. 'If you can't make the hard decisions, then maybe you shouldn't be sitting there? A true leader doesn't give into weakness.'

'Enough!' Amiki leapt down the steps and kicked him in the stomach, launching him back. He landed at his brothers' feet, who all helped him up.

The eldest coughed as he regained his composure before looking back at me. 'Even in failure, they are *never* defeated, not while they still draw breath.'

He turned, and he and his younger brother picked up the dead man again. They hobbled towards the exit with the others trailing behind. Amiki gestured for the guards to escort them out. The men were ushered at spearpoint. They reached the end of the hall, took their rifles, and left.

We waited in silence as the doors were slowly closed by the guards. The last streams of daylight, which had been warming me and my throne, disappeared as the doors locked in an echoing sound of deep, resonant finality.

'He's right, you know,' Tetsu said from the side of the chamber before arching his back up from the pillar to stand.

Amiki shot him a surprised look. 'And what would *you* know about it? Your queen is giving it her all.'

Tetsu strode over. 'He's right about what a leader is. But he doesn't know you, Tau, not like we do. It's not too late to turn everything around, and to be a strong and decisive leader. It's time to go on the attack.'

I looked down at my feet and exhaled. 'And what, send people off to die when I know I can't bring them back? That'll just make things worse.'

Tetsu sighed and shook his head. 'About that, I think all the pressure is getting to you, gunking up your powers. It's all in your head. You need to retake control.'

Amiki leered at Tetsu and shook her head at me. 'I disagree. Maybe resurrection just doesn't work on everyone? Or maybe all this pain you're taking on is poisoning what limited power you have left?'

'Don't even suggest something so awful,' I said.

She gave an apologetic look. 'I'm sorry, my Queen, but we need to explore *all* the possibilities. We could visit the morgue and try interrogating the former queen again?'

'But Verre is dead,' I said.

Tetsu smiled. 'But you've resurrected her before, so it should work.'

'We didn't get anything out of her last time,' I argued.

Amiki nodded. 'Well, maybe we just weren't asking the right questions? At the very least, we'll learn a bit more about your resurrection problem.'

The Science Quadrant

The hallways were abuzz with scientists, pushing dead bodies on flat, metallic, hovering stretchers and arguing over where to put them. Because I was unable to resurrect the dead, they were rushing to preserve those who had been killed in the attack. They were so busy that they didn't even notice Tetsu, Amiki, me and my entourage of Royal Guards entering the facility.

Amiki snatched one of the nearby staff from her workstation. 'Initiate, where is Commander Siph?'

The wide-eyed, baby-faced initiate had completely white streaks. She frantically looked about to ask her superiors for help, but they were all busy in nearby corridors and chambers. '*Ah,* I'm sorry, I don't know where the Commander is. I...' Her face went pale as she finally realised who I was. 'You're the queen!' She fell and bowed at my feet.

Other white-tipped administrators and scientists had finally noticed us, too. Each abandoned whatever task they were doing to also approach and bow.

I always felt embarrassed by this. 'That's not necessary. Please get up.'

'Stand up, all of you,' Amiki commanded with more strength, and they did. She furrowed her brow. 'Your Queen demands to know where Commander Siph is.'

Their eyes darted nervously, perhaps unsure how to answer.

I raised a hand. 'That's okay, Amiki, I'm sure the staff here are more than capable of retrieving the body we're after.' I turned to the highest-ranking woman among them, one with green-tipped white streaks. 'Where is Verre being stored?'

The slender, middle-aged woman was the calmest in the group. She gave a small bow. 'Ah, yes. Right this way, my Queen.'

We were led down a sleek hallway to one of the many morgues, leaving the other staff behind. As the frosty, steel door creaked open, it released the misty, refrigerated vapours from within.

Amiki gestured for both the guards and our escort to remain outside. 'When Commander Siph arrives, lead her here to us.'

Our escort nodded. 'Yes, Ma'am.'

Amiki, Tetsu and I entered the large, dark, bluish morgue. No other staff were present, only operating tables and medical equipment.

On the walls surrounding the lab space were hundreds of small, transparent hatches, each stacked on top of each other. Some were at head height, while others were by the wayside. Each hatch had a handle, locking apparatus and label. Through each door, we could see the feet of the corpses, surrounded by icy mist. Most here were whole bodies, but some were only a few remaining body parts, like in Iya's case.

What a tragic case she was; so young, yet swept up in this fake war all the same. I remembered when Malu, Iya, and I had been charged with escorting Sacet around. I wanted so badly for the four of us to be friends. If only things had panned out differently.

On the far side of the room was a separate holding cell: an operating room, with thick, glass windows for others to peer in. There were even more medical tools inside, each sharper and more jagged than the last.

I remembered coming here once after the rebellion. We had resurrected and interrogated Verre, but she refused to answer our questions. The others were frustrated with me at the time for being almost apologetic to our captive. For the city's safety, Marid killed her again, which I wasn't comfortable with. That all felt like a distant memory.

'Now, where did we put her?' I asked.

Amiki pointed to an information screen by the door. 'Look here.' On the dossier was the room's floor plan. It showed each of the containers with a name. Amiki brushed a finger down the list. 'Okay, let's see... Latana, Wrai, Iya... Verre: S103.'

As the others checked the container codes, I made my way to a nearby surgical table and took deep breaths.

Tetsu wiped some built-up frost off a nearby hatch to make out the label. 'So, what are you going to politely ask her this time?'

I smirked. 'Assuming I *can* bring her back, I'm going to make her tell us everything.'

Tetsu nodded in approval. 'Good. No mercy.'

Amiki beckoned us over. 'I found her.'

She unlocked and opened the hatch, releasing a whoosh of cold air. She pulled out the tray Verre's frozen body was lying on. Although she was long deceased, there was no odour. Her skin, which was partially covered in a thin layer of ice, almost matched the pale blue of her hospital gown. She still had a huge stab wound in her stomach from when Marid had executed her a second time.

Amiki pulled over a nearby humming hover stretcher, side-by-side with the tray. 'Ready? Help me lift her.' She grabbed Verre's shoulders, Tetsu pushed from the side, and I held the feet.

We strained and heard a crack like broken glass. I had accidentally snapped Verre's right foot off. I winced and placed it back down on the tray. 'Sorry.'

Amiki sighed. 'Come on, push again.'

We struggled and heaved, and eventually, the sculpture-like body snapped off from the tray. We shifted it over to the hovering stretcher. Amiki and Tetsu pushed, and I led them into the operating room.

I didn't understand how, even in the face of repeated death, Verre hadn't given up any useful information. This time, if I wanted to loosen her tongue, maybe the only way was to do terrible things to her. Was I ready for that?

After bringing in the stretcher and transferring the body to the steel operating table, I pointed to the door. 'Thank you. Now, step outside.'

Tetsu glanced back. 'Both of us?'

'My Queen, when she's awake, I think you'd better let me take over…' Amiki began.

'No,' I answered in monotone, 'I need to do my own dirty work for a change.' I firmly pointed outside again and the two begrudgingly left with the stretcher, leaving me inside with the body.

Tetsu slid the door closed and locked it.

Amiki approached a control panel outside the window. 'My Queen, with respect… I don't think you have it in you to do this.'

I pointed at the panel. 'If anything goes wrong, turn on the sleeping gas.' I wrenched open a nearby steel cabinet and retrieved an inhibitor collar, which I then secured around the corpse's neck.

Amiki pressed a few buttons, and the collar activated with a subtle flashing light.

I took another deep breath and stared into their eyes. 'No matter what happens, do not open that door unless I tell you to. Understood?'

Tetsu gave another nod, seemingly impressed by what I was about to do to this woman. Amiki continued to frown.

I gripped the icy corpse's wrists and began. My skin glowed and my hair changed. The effect was immediate; Verre's blue skin started to return to a healthier, pinker shade; the ice started to melt, and her blood seeped back into her body; her stab wound closed.

Then I felt the inevitable pain, like a drill spinning and burning into my stomach. The pain stunned me, and I collapsed over the body. I felt my insides ripping and churning, as though my intestines were peeling.

My companions, who were used to this by now, weren't shocked, but they did wince as they watched.

Eventually, the pain subsided. I pushed myself up and saw that Verre's body had completely healed. I checked for breathing with a hand above her mouth. Nothing. I held onto her wrist longer, waiting, but she didn't wake.

'Anything?' Tetsu called out.

My hair changed back to brown, and my skin stopped glowing. 'Nothing.'

They both exchanged wide-eyed glances. My lip trembled, and soon after my wrists started to shake, too.

'It's okay,' Amiki slowly stated after a silence. 'We'll find another way. Do you want to come out?'

'There is no other way,' I muttered under my breath. 'This should have worked.'

'What?' Tetsu asked, unable to hear me.

I closed my eyes. When I first started resurrecting, it was rare for it to not work, but now it had just stopped completely. What could I have done wrong? Was my power finite, or was Verre's side responsible somehow? Was this a punishment for betraying them?

I had spent my whole life deceived by an illusion of this woman's making, devoted to it, shaped by it. She and her ilk had me fooled into thinking my unwillingness to take a life was a weakness, and I hated what I was, always trying to hide it from others.

My fists were now shaking. To my side was a tray of scalpels, so I picked up the largest of them and brought it down into Verre's chest. Blood spurted up and onto my clothes.

Amiki placed her hands on the glass. 'My Queen? What are you doing?'

Tetsu grimaced, also taken aback. 'That won't solve anything.'

'All I've ever wanted to do was to help people!' I shouted. I pulled the scalpel out and brought it down a second time, fresh blood splattering onto my hands. 'I've always been nice to everyone… but no matter what I do, they pull me deeper into this stupid war.'

Amiki shared a pained look with Tetsu. 'Please come out and we can talk about this.'

I shook my head and twisted the scalpel back out. 'If they're not expecting me to be a soulless killing machine, it's a cold tactician, or… or a cruel dictator.' I stared into Verre's closed eyes. 'Like you. Well, I don't *want* to be like you. I don't *want* to be the queen.'

'I'm getting her out of there,' Tetsu said as he started for the door.

'I said keep it locked!' I shouted back at him, and he stayed his hand. 'I gave you an order.'

Tetsu gestured to my blood-covered robes. 'You just looked like you needed help.'

'What I need is to stop feeling like this. I can't be myself. I'm sick of it!'

Tetsu placed his hand on the glass. He locked eyes with me and frowned, as though pitying me. 'Whether we like it or not, we all have to become something we're not to live in this world. We all want to be kind, like you, but we can't.'

In the heavy silence that followed, the painful truth that I had known all along grated on me. I looked at the blood on my hands and knew it wasn't just Verre's. If I couldn't make peace with that, then I may as well have surrendered long ago. To win, I needed to become something else.

My skin was red hot and sweat-drenched. I seethed at the dead woman and activated my withering aura to heal her again. 'I'm not leaving here until Verre tells me what I want to know.'

Ten: No More Safety Net

Sacet

The overhead screen showed a cooling, early-evening sky outside. Aside from an occasional glimpse at the southern coast, we could only see an endless stretch of desert as we flew deep into the Unclaimed Wastes. Doron still seemed to know where we were going based only on the gentle rising and falling contours of the dunes, and that was good enough for me. He was evidently a much better navigator than his son.

Our pilot and special forces were wide awake, but I could tell the rest of our tired passengers weren't used to long aircraft rides like this, strapped in the dark, climate-controlled compartment. I myself was completely drained because of the excessive use of my perception.

Unlike the first leg of our journey, Pilgrim had gone completely quiet. The rest of us knew better than to continue bringing up his history with his father, so we had mostly restricted our chatter to the mission at hand.

Malu had started this journey on a high note, which was so refreshing to see. But now she was back to her gloomy, down-in-the-dumps self again, staring at the floor and shaking her head every so often.

We briefly locked eyes, and I gave her a sympathetic smile. 'Do you need a break?'

She shook her head and avoided my stare. 'No. I want us to hurry up and get there already.'

Noor looked between us and gave me a knowing look. We had both seen Malu acting like this in the past, sometimes just before combat. In this state, she became unreliable and distracted. I'm not sure what dredged up her guilt this time — whether it was Pilgrim's familial tension or perhaps the extended periods alone with our thoughts. Regardless, it was best if we had a rest.

'GL-206, do you read?' a distorted voice called out. 'Officer Nako, come in.' It was from the electronic speakers built into the cockpit.

'Nako here. Go ahead,' our pilot replied.

'We're getting some interference. What's your present location?'

'We're still over the Unclaimed Wastes.' She briefly consulted a map on her console. 'Coordinates... O8A2.'

'We're showing that you're below ten percent power,' the voice said. 'You should have returned for a recharge by now.'

'Is Sacet with you?' a different, familiar voice said. It was Marid.

'*Uh*, yeah, hold on.' Nako looked back into the cabin and rested her eyes on me. 'Commander, just talk out loud, they can hear you.'

'I'm here, Commander, what's the problem?' I said from my seat.

'Seeing as you're coming back anyway,' Marid said, 'could you meet me in the briefing room?'

I got Doron's attention. 'How far off are they?'

The old man's eyebrows twitched. 'Slightly less than the last time you asked me.'

'Fine,' I called aloud, 'Nako, land here.'

As the aircraft tilted and the engines slowed, my perception flew outside and took note of the surrounding land formations so that we could return to this exact spot later. I pictured the centre of the hangar in my mind. The craft straightened and hovered as it got close to the ground. I opened a portal below our craft to the steel runway on the other side, lifted it over us, and closed it again. We gently touched down, and there were multiple relieved gasps around me.

'Alright everyone, listen,' I said as I unstrapped and stood. 'It's getting late, so we'll spend the night here at home. Leave your gear. Recharge and meet back here tomorrow at dawn. Understood?'

'Understood, Ma'am,' the Colonel answered, followed by a number of the soldiers repeating her.

Doron gave a gruff sigh. 'I suppose I'll just have to wait one more night to see her again.'

As the ramp wound down, the others unbuckled and stood, too. Everyone except Nako came down the ramp while she powered down the craft.

The hangar had at least a hundred women running about as usual: soldiers loading into aircraft to go on manoeuvres and engineers fixing technology I had no clue about.

The Colonel and her squad lined up to attention, waiting to be dismissed.

Doron's mouth was agape as he tried to take in the massive hangar. 'I... never imagined a building could be so... immense.'

I pointed at him. 'Can someone get our guest a place to stay? Help him find where we've put up his sons?'

I turned to Pilgrim, thinking it'd be the perfect chance for them to work out their issues, but he had already walked away.

Doron seethed and folded his arms. 'Thanks, son. Nice of you to show your old man around, at least.'

'You can sleep on the hangar floor for all I care,' Pilgrim called back without looking.

A silence followed. The Colonel had her mouth slightly ajar, perhaps about to offer her assistance, but Malu cleared her throat first. 'I'll show him. I'm heading to the Rim anyway.'

'Alright, thanks, Malu.'

'Until tomorrow, then, Commander,' the Colonel said. She turned to her squad. 'Dismissed.'

As the Colonel and her squad headed to the armoury, Doron awkwardly followed Malu with his neck craned up at the enormity of his surroundings. Which left Noor and I alone at the ramp.

We looked at each other briefly and smiled.

'I... uh, need to go see Commander Marid,' I explained.

He glanced around. 'Oh, um. I guess I'll... I'll—'

'You can come, too?' I added, a little more excitedly than I intended. 'We can go check on Tau and Tetsu afterwards.'

Noor chuckled and nodded. 'I'd like that.'

I hadn't much experience with boys in general, something that Eno would tease me about if he were still with us. Even so, something had drawn me to Noor as of late. He was close to my age, which was part of it, but that wasn't all.

We all knew Noor had a shady past, having killed many, many women. He even tried to kill me the first couple of times we had met, but he was clearly trying to make amends for that over the past cycle. Now that I thought about it, the fact that he was so potentially dangerous was what I liked about him. Like me, he was an incredibly effective weapon that others had callously used. Now that we were free, I was bitterly angry at those who used me, and he probably felt the same.

I concentrated on my memories of the briefing room where Marid wanted to meet.

After the portal opened, I gestured through. 'After you.'

He smiled and entered, and I followed close behind.

The briefing room was massive, circular, and had rows of seats on the ascending outer rings. All the lights were off, save for a spotlight near the central podium and the last strain of sunlight trickling in through a skylight overhead. The room was currently empty, except for Marid close by at the base of the podium.

I closed the portal and approached with Noor in tow. 'Marid, what's this all about?'

She pointed a finger at Noor. 'What's *he* doing here?'

Noor narrowed his brow. 'You didn't say I *couldn't* be.'

I shrugged. 'Does he need to go?'

'Only if you have doubts about his loyalty,' she said, now lowering her voice.

Noor folded his arms. 'You think I'm a spy?'

'I trust him,' I said resolutely before an argument could begin.

Noor relaxed and flashed a smile at me.

Marid's hands briefly tremored before she put them both behind her back. 'Alright. Then this is a secret the three of us must keep.' She gestured around us. 'I'm in the process of installing my own security patch into this room. Once activated, alarms will trigger whenever you make a portal in here, alerting the entire barracks to suit up and investigate this location.'

I thought about it for a moment. 'So I can call in reinforcements.'

She nodded. 'Exactly, you're going to need them. If we can't oust the spies infesting this place, then that ambush you fought off earlier today was just the beginning.'

I smiled. 'Well, this... this is *really* helpful. Thank you.'

Noor gave a weak salute. 'We won't tell anyone, Commander.'

'There's another thing. I've thought it over and... I think this scouting mission is a mistake.'

'What? But I think we're onto something big out there.' I clenched my fists. 'I thought you *supported* my idea?'

She raised a hand to calm me. 'I did, but I've also reviewed the city attack footage. That man that killed you... he's *too* powerful. You *need* more training. You and I should use this time to formulate a better strategy against him.'

I shook my head. 'No, we're going back out there tomorrow and completing our mission. Having these sand acolytes with us could change everything.'

Marid sighed and turned away. 'Alright, I was hoping I wouldn't have to tell you this myself but... if you die out there, there's a good chance we won't be able to bring you back.'

Noor and I shared a horrified glance.

She wrapped her hands behind her. 'Tau can't resurrect the victims of the attack. And same goes for that dead nomad you sent through earlier. Sacet, you were the last person she's been able to bring back.'

'Why didn't you tell us this sooner?' I asked. 'I thought you would have opened with that?'

Marid turned back to us. 'I assumed you would have listened to my sage advice, and Tau could have explained it herself. Now you understand why you need to stay close to home, we can't afford to lose you.' She dipped her head at Noor. '*Either* of you. There's no more safety net.'

The thought that death was permanent again was scary, I hadn't felt this way since the rebellion. But if my brother was still alive, death would have continued to be a very real threat for him. What if he had made it all the way to The Shroud?

I put my hands on my hips. 'Even still, I can't give up now.'

'What?' they both said in unison.

'I'm flying back out there tomorrow and finishing what we started. Where's Tau now?'

Eleven: Something I'm Not

Tau

11 cycles ago

The Unclaimed Wastes

'You're safe now,' a distant, echoing voice said. It seemed feminine but warbled in pitch. 'Be good, always. Now awake. Wake up and bring them back. Bring them back to me.'

My eyes fluttered open to the sight of a blurry orange sun sinking behind a rocky ridge. With its lower half obscured, the sun resembled a juicy fruit wedge. I was strapped in a seat, one of many in a row, and leaning at an uncomfortable angle. The seats were part of a crashed aircraft, which had a giant, gaping hole torn through the other side. The desert wind was blowing hot sand into the cabin.

Why was I here? And who had been speaking? Was I dreaming?

I squirmed, attempting to stand. I fumbled at my straps and found the release, ejecting me onto the sandy floor with a soft thud. I shook my groggy head and then sat up to take in my surroundings.

Children were sprawled around what was left of the troop

transport interior and in the sand outside, the sun glinting off their silver armour. Most of my squad-sister's bodies were still strapped into their seats. A lot of time must have passed, for sand mounds had caked around those lying outside. They were all motionless, aside from their hair flicking in the intense gale. Some had their eyes locked open.

Could they still be alive? Could our scientists fix them? Our acolytes even? It took me a moment to process what I was seeing. The answer was most certainly no. I had never seen death before, but this was definitely it. None of them would ever move or speak again. None would smile or laugh. My friends were all gone. Saylee, Cinyth, Kierlin… they were all dead, unfixable.

After noticing blood on my armour and seat, I checked myself for wounds but found none. The others hadn't been so lucky: drenched in blood and contorted at impossible angles. Their deaths had transformed them in grotesque ways, making them hard to identify. Some were also bullet-ridden, as though someone had been here to finish the job.

My fingers shook. The sensation travelled up my limbs until my whole body was convulsing. I screamed while frantically scrambling backwards, out of the cabin and into the desert. My hair whipped, and I spun around to search for the danger, but realised it had just been the howling wind. I was alone with the dead, in the centre of a rocky crater. I couldn't look away from the bodies. My stomach twisted as I squealed and cried, for I was only a little girl in a huge world of monsters.

It was coming back to me now. Our squad had been heading to Atrasia, our first posting. But the craft got hit by something. We plummeted down, and I saw the other little sisters ripped from their seats and blown into the sky. And then… blank. Nothing.

Remembering only made the shaking worse. I couldn't move, nor breathe. My wails descended into choking sobs. Outside, it felt like walls were closing in on me, like someone had their hands around my neck and hard on my ribcage. Blood was creeping, slowly covering every surface in red.

A new sound drowned out the still-howling wind – another aircraft. The engines blasted the nearby dunes, blanketing the grisly carnage in a fog-like haze, as though hiding the evidence, like my sisters never existed. My metallic saviour encircled the crash site and landed nearby.

The open eyes stared at me. As much as I wanted to, I couldn't help them.

The city of Aero

The darkened sky couldn't steal away the beauty of this place, for as the sleek, chrome surfaces hid, the grand, neon billboards and windows lit the high-rises like a bright collage. It reminded me of my city, FDC. It was scary to think that the war was just outside the city limits, on our doorstep.

My squad-sisters and I were originally going to make a new life together here, but now it was just me, alone. We were so excited to kill people we had never met. Why?

Looking down from the safety of a hospital window, I had never felt so much fear and uncertainty in my life. What were they going to do with me? Where would I live? Would I still have to fight?

I had also never felt this cold, so I cocooned myself in my bedsheets as I shuffled around the patient room, waiting to be discharged. When I was first brought here, the scientists seemed amazed by my perfect health. It was a "miracle" I was alive, apparently. A miracle...

'Tau?' a woman said from the door.

I spun, still gripping my blanket close. It was my den mother, Corporal Tallu. She wore her military fatigues and a sombre frown, sharing the same grief as I. I threw the blanket off and rushed over to her.

'Come here,' she said benevolently with open arms.

I crashed into her, my face hitting her stomach. She embraced me, something she had never done for any of us little sisters before. I latched onto her waist tight and wept into the smooth fabric of her clothing. My body stiffened, in case anyone tried to pry us apart.

Since this afternoon's horribleness, I had only been surrounded by strangers, no one to truly comfort me. But seeing her face caused me to burst into tears again.

'I know, I know…' she soothed, and after some time without speaking, she knelt to my level. 'I came as soon as I could. I'm so glad you're okay.'

I looked down, watching my teardrops fall and paint the tiles with my sadness. 'I'm sorry,' I said, clearing my eyes. 'I shouldn't be crying.'

Our superiors usually punished our squad with drills for being weak, for acting like kids or for crying.

'Hey,' she said softly. 'Look at me.' She caressed away my tears, before carefully pulling my chin up. 'It's okay this time.'

My breathing quickened and I shook my head. 'I couldn't save them. I didn't… I didn't know how. They were already… I wanted to, but I wasn't… wasn't awake. I… I…'

She shooshed me. 'Stop, it's okay.'

I tried pulling away. 'I'm… I'm the only one left. I'm sorry. You must hate me.'

'What? No. Why would I?' She hugged me tighter than before, nuzzled her chin on my shoulder and sighed. 'This is far too much for a little sister to go through. *None* of it was your fault, it was the nomads, understood?'

I nodded and tried to get my rapid breaths under control.

Tallu stood and placed a hand on my back. 'We'll get them back for this, I promise.' She then guided me back to my bed. 'Take a seat.'

I obeyed, even though it felt better to keep moving. I dared not question the Corporal. We both sat on the bed, facing the window.

She placed a hand on my knee. 'I know we were sending you here to fight… but after what's happened, I think you need more time with me.'

I wiped my eyes once more. 'But… I thought you weren't my den mother anymore?'

Her frown turned to a slight smile. 'My superiors agreed we could put you in my *new* little sister squad.'

My eyebrows furrowed. 'The newborns?'

She nodded and her smile grew. 'Yeah, you'll have a whole cycle head start on them, and they could learn from you. You'd like that, wouldn't you?'

I nodded back and tried to smile, too. If I stayed as a little sister longer, I wouldn't have to fight, I'd repeat my training instead.

'And I'll be honest with you,' she continued, 'you would have hated it here. The life expectancy of a soldier on this island… is very short.'

'So… I'm *not* staying?'

'No, I'm taking you home tomorrow.'

My breaths quickened again. 'I'm not flying!' I shouted as I shot up. My bedsheets ripped off with me and fell to the floor. 'Please, don't make me go back.'

Tallu stood and raised her hands for calm. 'Alright, relax, Tau. Relax. We can go back by boat instead. I'll be right there with you. It's all going to be okay.'

As I eased back onto the bed, she looked out the window. 'One day, this will be a distant memory. You'll look back and realise how many of your friends you've lost. But… you'll fight on, anyway. That's just what happens in war, you become stronger.'

My eyes narrowed. 'Did… you lose all your sisters, too?'

She briefly looked away before giving me a comforting smile. 'Yep. I'm the last one left.'

'So, you're all alone, like me?' I asked.

Her smile faded, and she straightened up and grabbed my shoulder. 'You're *never* alone. Even if *everyone* you know has died, there's always another sister behind you. Someone who has your back. Never forget that.'

We embraced again and she softly cradled me from side to side. I stared out the window and thought about the life, or death, that might've been.

Several days later

FDC

I jumped onto my old bunk and hugged my pillow with glee. The

Military Quad and its dorms – my home – hadn't changed since last I was here. It felt good to be in familiar surroundings, the war once again seeming far, far away.

The beds next to me now belonged to new little sisters. They were all mingling around the aisle, excitedly swapping their future battle plans. None had warmed up to me yet, I think they were still confused as to why I was here. I remembered what it was like to be them: equal parts afraid and unsure, but also buzzing with the FD ideals transferred to us pre-birth.

'I can't wait to shoot some MD scum,' one chirped from the next bed, a brazen little sister named Tarsus. 'I'm going to run up to him and slide on the ground, and then... and then shoot up between his legs!' She leapt from her bed and slid on the floor, mimicking her plan.

The others oohed and aahed, marvelling at her pretend bravery.

'Yeah? Well, I'm going to blow up a whole nomad village with *one* bomb,' another called Coleo boasted.

'Wouldn't that kill the girls, too, though?' one asked.

'Oh, yeah.'

As the gaggle of children continued to brag and gasp on repeat, unaware of what it was really like out there, the door at the end of the aisle opened and two figures entered. It was Corporal Tallu and another little sister I didn't recognise.

This girl had long, glossy black hair and bronzed skin. She was tall for a little sister, like me. She had stitches on her cheek, with red swelling around it. Her shoulders were slumped, and she avoided the gaze of others. She didn't have a trunk of basic belongings to keep at the end of her bed like the rest of us did.

Tallu led the girl to the closest free bunk, by the door, where she plonked down an extra set of fatigues.

The little sisters finally took notice of our Corporal's entrance, and we all ran to our beds and stood to attention by our trunks.

The Corporal smiled and gestured to the new girl. 'We have a new little sister joining us today. Like with Tau earlier, I'm sure you'll make her feel welcome.' She turned to the girl. 'Don't worry, you'll like it here soon.'

The girl stared at the floor and rubbed her arm nervously.

The Corporal faced the room again. 'I see some of you out of uniform, hurry up and get changed. I'll come back soon to collect you for your first drill.' And with that Tallu left the now silent dorm.

The sisters stared at the new girl and murmured to one another, and eventually went back to their original conversations. The girl sat on her bed and tucked her knees into her arms tight, continuing to look at the floor or the door, anywhere but at us.

I knew her downtrodden look well; I had been wearing it myself for days now. I got up from my bed and slowly meandered over, leaving the chatter behind. When I reached the end of the girl's bed, I leant sideways into her cone of vision, hoping to get her attention.

'Hello,' I said, before waiting for a response.

She turned even farther away, focusing on her pillow instead. 'Please, just don't talk to me.'

She had a deeper voice, but I was sure I was younger than her.

'Are you okay?' I quickly replied, copying what some of the others had said when *I* first arrived. 'Would you like to talk about it?'

She smirked. 'No, I wouldn't. Someone like *you* wouldn't understand.'

I shook my head. 'But I would, I do. I've lost my entire squad, all my sisters. I'm assuming you have, too?'

She slowly looked back with a mournful expression. 'Well, I lost everyone I knew, my whole family.'

It was an interesting way to put it, a "family". I liked it. I had never thought of my squad-sisters as a family before. It was fitting.

I sat on the end of her bed. 'I know it doesn't mean much, and that it won't bring them back, but I'm sorry.'

'You're right, that won't bring them back,' she began, getting off her bed and throwing her arms around in frustration. 'Why am I even here? I'm not a soldier, I don't want to fight.'

I glanced over my shoulder and to the door to see if anyone was listening in. 'I don't want to fight either.'

She stopped pacing, instead locking eyes with me. 'You don't?'

'I want the killing to stop,' I replied. 'Everyone around me wants me to be... something I'm not. It's not *me* that has to change, is it?'

She took a seat right next to me, now looking into my eyes. 'No, it's everyone else that should change.'

I smiled back. 'My name's Tau, by the way.'

'I'm Amiki,' she replied, before glancing back at the other girls. 'Do the others think like us?'

I shook my head. 'Not really. They can't wait to fight.'

'Well, I don't want to be alone here. Can maybe… you and I… we look out for each other?'

I nodded and gave the biggest smile I could. A friend! 'Definitely! But also, just so you know, you're never alone.' I stood up and pointed behind us. 'Come on, I'll introduce you to the others.'

Twelve: I Became a Monster

The present

The constant, humming freezers were the only sounds in the morgue. I was still in the operating room, sitting on the steel table, next to Verre's feet. Although her body was healed, complete with warm blood, there was no heart or brain activity.

I had been experimenting with my power, trying to find some version of my aura, some technique that still worked. I was still so angry, but also exhausted.

I was sure of it now, my power to resurrect had left me, there was no other explanation. Knowing that, I was afraid to return to the throne, to the responsibilities waiting for me there. I'd have to deliver even more bad news to everyone that relied on me.

Amiki and Tetsu were still outside the operating room, per my order, patiently waiting. They had pulled over a couple of chairs to sit, joining me in introspection.

I stared at the floor. 'These people... and this place have turned me into a monster.'

Amiki's eyes narrowed and looked down, too.

'Monster?' Tetsu said, his voice slightly muffled by the glass.

'I've known plenty of monsters. Trust me, you're not one of them.'

'You remember when we first met?' Amiki asked me, and I looked up. 'That huge dorm? And you had just lost your whole little sister squad.'

I flashed a smile as memories of my youth swirled. 'Yeah, we were both new there. And we both… needed a friend.'

She smirked. 'Took you a whole cycle to work out I used to be a nomad.'

Tetsu's face relaxed and grinned at Amiki. 'Oh? You were one, too?'

Amiki leant back again. 'Sure was, before they chucked me in with the little sisters.'

I gave an involuntary laugh. 'I didn't talk to you for days after that. I was actually scared of you.'

She slowly nodded. 'Yeah, but we were best friends, so that didn't last long.' She drew a deep breath and leant forward in her chair. 'For so long after, I hated the Dominion for killing my family, but you made me realise that all sides were suffering. And… I don't know if it was the mental conditioning they put me through or whatever, but… when I saw you couldn't defend yourself, I became a monster, for you.'

My eyes widened and I shot up. 'Oh, Amiki, when I said *mon*— I didn't mean it like that.'

Amiki continued to nod. 'I know you didn't.'

I approached the operating room door and Tetsu happily slid it open for me. Both he and Amiki stood and came closer. I immediately went over and hugged her. 'I'm so sorry.'

She hugged me back; her golden plate armour was cold on my skin. 'It's okay, my Queen.'

When we separated, I stared at the tiled floor. 'Do you think… Tallu would be disappointed in me?'

Amiki slapped my shoulder and grinned. 'Are you kidding? She'd be proud of you. Of how you've kept things together.'

I shook my head. 'But she always used to say that… I wasn't made for this war.'

She sighed and still nodded. 'Yep, she said that to me, too. She meant it as a compliment. That you're meant for better things than… this.'

There was a whoosh of air in the centre of the morgue. Sacet, Noor and Marid suddenly appeared, no doubt from using Marid's teleportation. Amiki and I released, and I wiped my tears away.

'*Urgh*, I prefer Sacet's way,' Noor said while holding both his mouth and stomach.

Marid smirked and nudged him with her cane. 'Harden up, *Norn*.'

Sacet darted over to us. 'Tau, what's going on?'

Noor approached Tetsu, and after a sturdy embrace, gestured to the operating room. 'Is that Verre?'

We all stared through the glass together at her.

I sighed. 'Yeah, I was thinking of interrogating her, but...'

'Your resurrection powers have stopped working?' Noor finished for me.

'Yes,' I replied, squinting at him. 'How do you know that already?'

Amiki joined my scepticism. 'Nothing was certain until now.' She then glared at Tetsu.

His brows lowered. 'Why are you looking at me? I didn't tell anyone! I've been with you two the whole time.'

'Then how does he know?' Amiki questioned, pointing at Noor.

'My brother doesn't lie,' Noor said resolutely, clenching his fists.

Marid banged her cane loudly on a nearby metallic cabinet, the sound echoing off the morgue walls. 'All of you, stop. *I* told them.' She glanced at Amiki and I. 'I'm sorry, my Queen, but gossip always finds a way of getting around.'

I closed my eyes. 'Then... it won't be long before everyone in the city knows.'

'How did this happen?' Noor continued. 'You can't just *lose* your powers.'

I sighed. 'It's been happening for a long time, ever since I discovered them. Misfires were rare at first but became more and more frequent. And after you left—'

'With respect, my Queen, you can't keep doing this to yourself,' Amiki interrupted. 'You've been taking on all this pain, all this darkness from others. We should head back; you need to rest.'

Sacet had been ignoring our conversation, squinting at the ground instead. 'What is Siph doing...'

Amiki raised an eyebrow. 'Commander Siph? She should have been here by now. Where is she?'

Sacet shook her head. 'Below us… what is she doing to that body?'

I stepped forward. 'Sacet.'

'She's in a small room. It's like the basement of the basement. She's in there and she's talking with someone on a float screen.' Sacet narrowed her eyes. 'I recognise him. The same face. That's King Tuloch!'

'Sacet!' I yelled, breaking her focus. 'Take me there.'

'Alright,' she said before glancing around at each of us. 'When we go through, stay quiet and we might be able to hear what they're saying, okay?'

Everyone nodded. Sacet closed her eyes again to concentrate and a portal opened next to us. She snuck through first, looked back and beckoned us through with her hand. I followed her through into the dimly lit corridor and could immediately hear voices from around the next corner.

'She's still up there, trying and failing,' Tuloch's voice remarked. 'Just keep her busy.'

Sacet put her back against the corridor wall and signalled for the rest of us to do the same. She edged along it, closer to the corner. Our entire group formed a line and copied Sacet. The portal closed, and the only light left in the dark corridor was coming from around the corner, probably from the screen.

'Of course,' I heard Siph say. 'This is the last body for the batch.' There were electronic noises, button presses perhaps. 'So, what of Sacet?'

'She's not your concern right now,' Tuloch replied. 'Leave her to us.'

'She is *very* much my concern!' Siph replied. 'Were you watching the way she spoke to me earlier? That girl wants me dead.'

'Sir, look at this,' a different male voice said. It sounded as if it was someone in the same place as the king.

'You've been compromised,' Tuloch said. 'Get out of there!'

'What?' Siph shrieked.

Sacet straightened up and rounded the corner. I followed and saw Siph standing in front of the float screen. To her side were numerous hover stretchers with dead bodies lying on them. Laser burns, probably victims of the attack. Our group confronted Siph as one.

Siph turned and noticed us. Her eyes and mouth opened in shock, and she backed up against the nearest table, causing some of the medical instruments to clatter and fall. King Tuloch's face was on the screen, but before I could study anymore details, it blanked out to an opaque green.

'What *is* this?' Sacet shouted as she stormed over to Siph and grabbed her by the scruff of the neck.

Before Siph could answer, Sacet tossed her to the side of the dark chamber. The old woman slammed against the steel wall with a resounding thud. She stayed down, doubling over in pain.

The rest of us spread through the ambient green room, searching for any clue that would tell us what this place really was.

Sacet bolted over to Siph a second time. 'What are you doing here?' She punched the old woman's wrinkly face. 'What is their plan? Answer me!'

Siph smirked, before spitting blood into her face.

There was no redness, only a dark green splotch dripping down Sacet's cheeks. Her face twisted in anger; every line pronounced like the edge of her blade.

'That's it,' Siph said slowly to Sacet, 'that's the killer look. I see it in your eyes. You like to pretend to be the hero, but deep down you want to be a hunter in this world of predators, don't you?'

Noor came to Sacet's side, while Tetsu and Amiki stayed at my own. Marid watched from the corner, shaking her head in disgust.

Sacet gripped Siph's throat and rammed her into the wall again, before unsheathing her glowing, blue sword and bringing its crackling edge to Siph's neck.

Siph simply laughed through pained squirms. Her eyes darted about and rested on me. 'Sorry to disappoint you, my *Queen*.'

Sacet tensed her muscles. 'Last chance. Talk!'

'I'm not telling you anything,' Siph replied. 'Hurry up and get it over with, you stupid girl.'

I pointed at one of the cadavers. 'What were you *doing* to these bodies?'

My question had stayed Sacet's blade. She shook out of her transfixion, instead waiting for my command.

I thought back to all the times my resurrection had failed. Siph and her team were the ones in charge of bringing them to me. 'Is this why I can't resurrect them?' I covered my eyes and shook my head. Who else was working for them? Was Terel a spy, too? My hand unconsciously clenched onto something in my pocket, the scalpel from earlier. I pulled it out and kept it low. 'I should have *never* trusted you.'

Sacet loosened her grip on Siph and backed away.

'*Oh, boo hoo*,' Siph teased. 'Go on, tell your goons to kill me already.'

I glanced at the others. 'Hold her.'

Siph's smile grew wider. '*Ah*, here we go. So much for the Queen of Light, a?'

Noor and Tetsu approached, and each pinned one of her arms against the wall. I meandered closer, brandishing the scalpel in front of me.

Siph gave a nervous giggle. 'Death by stabbing? Well, not particularly quick. But do it.'

'My Queen…' Amiki said with a hand raised.

Tetsu nodded at me. 'You can do this.'

I took a deep breath and drove the scalpel into Siph's stomach. She let out a pained grunt. Tears had already formed in her eyes, and her blood was trickling down my wrist and onto the ground.

Closing my eyes, I activated my aura, and the tingling sensation poured through me like an effervescent wave. It briefly lit the room with cyan flames, mixing with the green to make teal. I touched Siph's stomach and healed the wound, experiencing the same pain I had just inflicted. My knees gave, and I crumpled forward. I leaned on her body to stop me from collapsing.

Her brow lowered. 'What are you doing?'

I smirked back. 'One way or the other, you're going to tell me everything.' I grimaced, before driving the scalpel into her again, this time in the chest.

She screamed in agony as I rotated the knife. As she fell limp in the boys' grip, I healed the wound again, causing the same scream-inducing pain to cut through me like a bolt of lightning to the heart.

The healing was slower this time, and the pain was far more excruciating than anything before. My aura's light wasn't as intense as it usually was, it faltered, overpowered by the surrounding green. I fell to my knees, and Tetsu immediately reached out with his other hand to help me up.

'Stop it, just kill me!' she pleaded.

I shook my head slowly. 'No, we're going to do this over and over again until you talk. Let's see who will endure the longest?'

Siph gave a jaw-dropped, desperate look to everyone else in the room, like I was crazy, perhaps hoping someone would come to her rescue. Although the others did look horrified, shaking their heads or averting their eyes, none intervened. Both Noor and Tetsu were resolute, pinning Siph's arms even harder than before.

The scalpel was dipped dark green, almost black in this light. I stabbed a third time, this time into her neck.

Amiki stepped forward. 'My Queen... Tau, please. This is a bit much.'

Marid shifted uncomfortably. 'A bit much?' She focused on me pleadingly. 'If you keep this up then you're no better than they are.'

I turned away from Siph, prolonging her death throes. 'But she won't answer me? This... is all I can do now.'

Amiki approached and put her hand on my shoulder. 'Come on, this isn't you. Let me deal with her.'

Noor and Tetsu released Siph for the moment, who fell to the ground and bawled. She reached a hand up to me. 'No more!'

'So talk!' I shouted down in her face.

She continued shaking her head from side to side, crying, and crawling back towards the screen. 'Please, I'll talk, just stop. Stop it.'

'What have you been doing to these bodies? Why can't I resurrect anymore?'

She raised a hand to shield herself. 'Because... because these bodies *can't* be resurrected.'

'Why not?' I paced. 'How? I demand you tell me!'

Siph sniffled and rested her back against the base of a control panel. 'So little you understand about your own power.'

Sacet pointed at a nearby cadaver. 'Are you saying that... the bodies we have are fakes?'

Siph glanced up at the control panel. 'No, these are the originals. Although they may as well be fakes now.'

The rest of us exchanged bewildered looks.

Siph locked her gaze with mine. She had stopped crying and was calm again. 'I've said enough.'

I raised my scalpel. 'No, actually you're going to answer more questions.'

A weak smile returned to her face. 'No, *actually* I'm not.'

Siph reached a hand up to the panel and hurriedly pressed some keys. The screen came back up, and in large green letters were the words 'self-destruct'. I looked back at the others with shock.

'Tetsu, shield!' I yelled.

Tetsu brought his hands to his sides and a white orb stretched and enlarged from his centre. It immersed Noor, Sacet, Marid, Amiki and I as the control panel detonated. The shield was completely engulfed with fire; I could see nothing but shades of red and orange.

Tetsu's arms wavered under the power of the deafening explosion. There was a loud creak above. The ceiling's support beams snapped and fell.

'Sacet!' I yelled.

She closed her eyes, and a portal appeared beneath us. The beams clanged and tumbled into the weakening shield. Sacet raised her portals above our heads. I looked straight up and saw the shield dissipate, followed by the inferno taking its place just as the portals closed.

Thirteen: Fuel Your Hatred

Eno

Red was everywhere I looked above the Military Wing courtyard: in the polluted crimson sky, staining all the surrounding concrete surfaces, and dripping down the boys' faces in the sparring pit. An audience of burly soldiers from other units had come to watch, lingering on the rectangular pit's edge, baying at our ineffective techniques.

Per Patriarch Mycol's orders, all of us from the Feeble Fortress were here to train in hand-to-hand combat and also to "eradicate our weaknesses", as he had put it. Although a few were enjoying the sparring, leering with malicious satisfaction as they wailed on the weaker boys, most of us were too afraid to properly defend ourselves, shaking in place as we took hit after hit.

We had been forbidden from using our powers for this exercise, although that wasn't an option for some of us. Keenu, for example, being unable to touch his opponents, had remained sitting on the pit's edge with his feet dangling over.

The tiny and blind Mui, on the other hand, had been unfairly partnered with a much larger teenage boy, Ido, who revelled in the beating he was giving the practically defenceless child. All Mui could do in response was protect his face and back away, occasionally crashing into other fighters.

Sozha's sparring was even sadder, so one-sided that he looked like a punching bag. He was paired with the tallest boy in the dorm, Ateity. Sozha threw an occasional strike at thin air, but because of his abysmal reaction time, all Ateity had to do was sidestep to get the better of him.

Alongside the howling soldiers that comprised our audience were numerous skull-faced Terror Guard, silent as always. I had come to learn that they were Mycol's eyes and ears, carrying out his will, whatever it happened to be. They were aptly named, because whenever I caught one's gaze, a shiver ran down my spine.

My sparring partner was Nadan, another far taller and older, mismatched opponent. However, he was clearly going easy on me. At first, I thought it was because all that training with Grandpa and Sacet growing up had paid off. But then I noticed that his eyes kept darting to the side every time his little brother was struck. I had barely hit Nadan so far, and yet his expression strained more with each passing moment. What if he broke away to go help Mui?

I threw a weak punch to get his attention. 'We have to stay one-on-one, remember?'

Nadan's distracted eyes steeled and he leapt forward. He was on top of me before I knew how to react, putting me in a headlock and ripping me to the ground with his superior strength. I struggled for air and squirmed against his newfound intensity. The audience bellowed louder in approval.

'I need a favour,' he whispered hoarsely into my ear, before whipping me over and pinning me facedown. He leant closer again. 'I'm going to let you go, and then I want you to tackle me hard into Ido.' He released me, albeit roughly, before shooting up and backing away. 'Attack me for real. Come on, wimp!'

I was right, he was planning on interfering with Mui's fight. I stood, and my knees trembled with unease. What if Mycol found out I had helped with this? No, I couldn't risk that. I didn't want to disappear like the others. I shook my head.

Mui took another blow to the ribs.

Nadan's eyes widened. 'Come on weakling, attack! Do it!'

I didn't like being pressured like this, and he didn't look like he was giving up on the idea. I'd have to leave no doubt that I was attacking him for real. I breathed deeply, before gritting my teeth and charging with all the energy I had.

Nadan glanced over his shoulder, lining himself up with Ido. My mass made contact, plunging into Nadan's stomach and driving him back. It was easy, too easy; he let me take him off balance, and he tumbled into Ido as if by accident.

A bruised and bloody Mui lowered his arms and stared in our rough direction. 'What just happened?'

As I got to my feet, Nadan and Ido did, too. The rabble above booed and jeered.

'Sorry, brother,' Nadan said to him with palms raised. 'Didn't see you there.'

'You did that on purpose!' Ido shouted as his face began to droop unnaturally. His ears and cheeks lengthened to three times their normal size. His power was to reshape his body in minor ways, and it was often involuntary, according to him.

Nadan chuckled in response to the boy's goofy new look. 'I didn't, I swear.'

'Yes, you did,' Ido continued, now resuming his aggressive stance. He looked just as much at the mob as Nadan. 'You just wanted to save your blind brother.' Various parts of his face engorged and shrunk, seemingly at random. 'We're supposed to stand on our own, not have family swoop in every time things go bad.'

Nadan pulled out a previously hidden blade from his pants. 'So, you're calling me a liar? Funny, coming from you.'

'Put it away, filthy nomad scum,' one voice from the crowd yelled.

Nadan, clearly realising the jig was up, directed his glare to the others, too. 'Or what, puppet? You'll go snitch on me?'

The boos continued. The other sparring pairs stopped to watch the spectacle.

Mui clawed at the air around him until he eventually found and latched onto his brother. 'Stop, Nadan. Just let me fight.'

Nadan ignored him and stood his ground.

One soldier directly above me, a bearded giant of a man, pointed at Nadan. 'Young brother, no weapons! Face your partner and fight!'

Nadan laughed. 'Or what? You'll hurt me?' He pulled up his sleeve, revealing more scars on his wrist and arm, before hovering his blade over it. 'Go on, do it. Find out what happens.'

Ido and several other boys backed away. Meanwhile, a few of the larger men jumped into the pit and strode closer without hesitation. Nadan held his ground. The men crowded around, staring him down for the longest time. The Terror Guard did nothing.

One soldier looked down at Nadan's steady blade, then back into his eyes. He smiled back at the bearded man. 'Fearless as a feral necrolisk, this one.'

The other man grunted. 'As dumb as one, maybe.'

A deep, distorted droning sounded through the courtyard and beyond, bouncing off the tall buildings and warbling in our ears. Everyone stilled, aside from exchanging wide-eyed stares.

'What's that?' I asked.

'Everyone out of the pit!' the bearded man shouted. 'Now!'

The crowd above sprinted away as one, towards the far end of the courtyard.

'Stay together,' the man continued to yell. 'Faster!'

The Terror Guard had remained, staring down at us menacingly. They raised their batons and activated them, producing a puff of greenish-yellow mist out the ends. Sharp, crackling electricity then ignited the gas with bright flashes.

All previous tensions in the pit were dropped in lieu of the circumstances. Me and the other boys all made our way to the nearest recessed ladders built into the concrete wall. Nadan shepherded his blind brother, even guiding his hands to the recesses. Once Mui was up, Nadan followed, and then me.

When I reached the top, Nadan held out a hand for me, but I ignored it and pulled myself up on my own.

'We've got to move,' Keenu said, running ahead of us to catch up to the others. 'We can't be the last ones, come on!'

The soldiers in the other pits had also emerged, and hundreds more soldiers from the surrounding barracks streamed out, many already in full black Male Dominion armour. It seemed everyone was heading to the far end of the enormously long courtyard. The alarm continued to drone.

Bloodied and bruised, the boys from the Feeble Fortress ran together, led by Keenu and some of the other senior boys, with Nadan and Mui trailing behind.

'What's going on?' I shouted over the sound as we ran. 'What's that alarm?'

'It's the king,' Keenu called back between breaths. 'He's going to address the entire Dominion.'

We sprinted past several more sparring pits and training areas before merging with the hundreds already gathered under an immense, floating screen. The screen displayed a crimson-red room, with steel walls and banners draped on them donning the Male Dominion symbol. A solitary red leather chair faced the camera, curiously empty.

A wide raised platform was below the screen, and several red-robed Patriarchs had already ascended it, including Mycol. He had his terrifying skull mask on, but thanks to his misshapen body we could all tell it was him. Since coming here, I had learned that the scarier and more detailed your mask was, the higher your rank.

The other Patriarchs wore similarly intimidating masks. One had necrolisk-like jaws and fang-filled teeth: the Havoc Patriarch. The man was enormous. His hulking body was familiar to me, but he couldn't have been the same guy. What was his name again? Kalen? He'd still be in that FD prison, right?

Another Patriarch's mask featured a more robotic design, with dark, fiery pits for eyes and various hoses and nozzles covering his mouth: the Destruction Patriarch, leader of the rank-and-file troops. Yet another appeared as a monster, his mask hideously twisted like a mutated freak: the Corruption Patriarch.

Throughout the mob, many higher-ranking soldiers growled deep, guttural commands at their troops to whip them into formation. The crowd, including those of us from the Feeble Fortress, eventually lined up into our units and stood to attention.

The majority of those around us were fully armoured, muscle-bound behemoths, which obscured a lot of my view. However, I could still see the screen above, as well as Mycol stomping along the stage, inspecting us from on high. He looked in my direction and paused. Was he looking at me specifically? It was hard to tell because of his hideous skull visage.

Nadan, who was still arm-in-arm with Mui, placed his free hand on my shoulder. 'Another opportunity to brainwash the masses,' he whispered.

Mui elbowed him. 'Shut up! Someone might hear you.'

Hundreds more soldiers gathered behind us as we waited. The shouts of our superiors shifted away, directing their ire towards any latecomers and dawdlers.

A huge silhouette entered the screen's frame: a man with an illustrious red robe and the biggest, scariest mask of them all. The army roared with explosive vigour, as though they had just won a victory of epic proportions.

The man's mask was pure black, like necrotic bone. Eyes like impossibly dark caves; teeth as big as fingers and sharp as daggers; and horns so wide that they probably affected his balance. It had a long snout with locked open jaws, as though in mid-cackle, or about to swallow his prey whole.

As the crowd roared and stomped, so loudly that I felt the ground rumbling, the man hung his robe on the back of his chair, revealing a more official dress uniform underneath, covered in pins of rank and commendations.

The crowd, more an army by this point, began to chant: 'Tul-och… Tul-OCH… TUL-OCH!' They beat their chests with each syllable, adding to the already thunderous reception.

The king removed his helmet and placed it on his desk to reveal his older, distinguished face. He had black hair with some grey mixed in, and a big, grey moustache. The visual on the screen was so convincing that it was like an enormous version of King Tuloch was in front of us. I could see every line and wrinkle in perfect detail.

The king sat in the red chair and faced the camera. He brought his hands in front, each finger pressing against its counterpart. His dark, hazel eyes were piercing, as though he were staring at and judging me. The crowd quietened, waiting with bated breath.

He scowled. 'My brave sons, it saddens me to hear the lies that have run rampant through my Dominion. First, rumours of a successful rebellion in our enemy's ranks. And now, an absolute falsehood grows that the Female Dominion accepts both men and women.'

'What's he talking about?' I could hear one of the boys say.

'Silence!' a nearby soldier said.

'This is weaponised propaganda,' the king continued, 'designed to shake your resolve. And anyone caught spreading them will be punished. In reality, the rebels were quashed long ago.'

The screen changed its image to that of a young woman on her knees, her hair concealing her face, with another woman holding a gun to her head. At the top of the screen were the words 'Intercepted footage – Prisoner execution 316SC'.

The woman looked up towards us and I couldn't believe what my eyes were seeing. It was Sacet! The laser fired and her head snapped to the side, before her body collapsed off-screen.

'No!' I shouted.

A hand quickly stifled me from behind. 'Quiet!' Ido whispered. 'You want us to get punished?'

Almost every nearby soldier had glanced back at me, lips curled, and eyes widened in disgust.

I shook free from Ido's grip. 'It's not true,' I said to the boys, although quieter than before. 'She's not dead. *He's* the one lying.' I didn't have any evidence to prove my case, I simply knew it couldn't be true.

Nadan and Keenu shared a concerned look but didn't respond. Maybe they wanted to believe me, but couldn't? Sozha was staring at me, too. It was disconcerting, he was looking right at me.

One of the huge men in front of me who was previously partly blocking my view turned, grabbed me like a ragdoll, clasped a single hand over my entire lower face, and forced me to look forward. 'Just watch in silence, or I'll snap you in two.' I couldn't move, and I believed his threat. The only thing I could release was a tear.

The screen had changed back to the ugly king again. 'Do not forget, our enemy is cunning. By deploying this misdirection, they were attempting to coax the weakest of us into the open.' The king's voice was getting louder as his speech continued. 'But we are not so *easily* fooled. Clearly, they fear our strength, our *power!*'

'That's right!' one of the men shouted, and the mob joined in with cheers and chest-beatings shortly after.

Tuloch was now yelling. His chest heaved, and his posture

straightened in his chair. 'Too long have we fought in this war with no end. No more, I say. We will bring it to an end in less than a single cycle.'

Each sentence now elicited a wave of roaring approval. 'And when I stand in their Capital, in a field of their bones, surrounded by dust and burning ash, only then will we show a hint of mercy. But until that day, you will continue to demonstrate your loyalty, your resolve, your fury!'

The entire courtyard was now shouting with deafening ferocity.

The king smashed his fist onto the table in front of him with each sentence. 'They will fall. We will rise! And together, we will transform this world, permanently!'

Feet stomped. More chests were unendingly beaten. It was the most excitement I had ever seen. All I wanted to do was fall to my knees and curl up into a ball, but I couldn't even do that.

The usual gloominess of the Feeble Fortress had disappeared. Most of the boys had smiles plastered on their bruised faces now, inspired by the king's speech. Most except for me, of course.

I played with my food with no intention of eating, making a little shack out of the saucy necrolisk giblets. I'd probably be willing to live in a shack made from dripping meat if it meant leaving this place. Although I had finally gotten used to the strange aftertaste of the food here, I just wasn't hungry. Seeing the last of your loved ones die does that.

I sighed and glanced around the mess hall. The others were sitting at the tables, too, excitedly discussing the future of the Dominion and the battles they hoped to soon be a part of.

'Eno?'

I looked up with indifference.

A frowning Keenu was standing there, holding his meal tray. 'Can I sit with you?'

I shrugged and looked back down at my giblet shack. 'I suppose.'

'Are you okay? Do you want to talk about it?' he asked, placing his tray down and sitting opposite me.

'Not really.'

'Well, I think you need to. I'm guessing that you knew her?'

'We've all lost people close to us,' another voice behind me said. It was Mui, and with his brother's help, they both sat at the same table and plonked down their food, too.

'We're not going to make fun of you or anything,' Nadan added. 'That girl, she was apparently the rebel leader. So, how'd you know her?'

I sighed and wiped my eyes before they had a chance to tear up. 'She was my big sister. She helped me escape.'

'Sacet, right?' Nadan whispered with a raised eyebrow.

I shot him a look. 'Yes. How do you know her name?'

Nadan glanced around to make sure no one was listening. 'Those rumours the king brought up? Let's just say it's not the first time I've heard them.'

Keenu leant closer. 'I heard she took on the whole FD by herself. Is that true?'

I remembered Tau healing the men who were about to be executed in the tournament, but I doubt she would betray her kind to help Sacet.

I sighed. 'Maybe. I don't really know.' Sacet rarely trusted others, so it was doubtful she had made allies. 'No, she *was* alone. She was strong, she didn't need help from anyone else.'

Mui cocked his head. 'Well, in the end, maybe she *did*?'

Nadan gave a dour expression. 'Either way, she sounded like a pretty awesome person. Very brave.'

I nodded and managed a smile. 'She was.'

'Mycol's coming,' Mui interrupted.

The far door opened and Mycol trudged in. All the other boys screeched their chairs along the floor at once as they stood, ran to the centre of the room and lined up, leaving their meals behind. Nadan again assisted with Mui. It was just Sozha and I still at the tables.

With my head down, I slowly stood and joined them. We all looked over at Sozha, who had only just noticed the commotion, and he shot up and ran over as well.

'King's glory, boys,' Mycol said. He was gritting his teeth, perhaps involuntarily. Was he in pain?

'And King's glory to you, Patriarch!' the others said.

I remained silent, instead eyeing Mycol's feet as he paced up and down the line.

He clenched one of his massive, bulbous hands. 'Today, you saw the great King Tuloch… and I hope his words… inspired you. That they will fuel your hatred… for your enemies.'

'And King's glory to you, Patriarch!' Sozha interrupted.

Mycol stared at me and took a deep breath. 'Starting tomorrow… your training will be far more challenging. So, you all need your rest… it's time to head to your dorms. Dismissed!'

The others dispersed and made for the nearby stairs, and so I followed. Mycol raised a hand in front of me. 'Not you.'

He placed his hand gently on my shoulder and waited for Sozha to catch up with the others. My knees shook. Was he going to punish me for helping Nadan earlier? Sozha finally left the room.

Mycol forced a quivering smile. 'Did you enjoy the address, Eno? Did it inspire you?'

'Ye—yes, Patriarch.'

His grip tightened and his smile disappeared. 'You're a bad liar. You and I both know… that was Sacet being executed. Now… *don't* lie to me again.'

I stared at the floor to avoid his intense stare.

'You see now I was telling you… the truth all along. I was only trying… to help. You trust in me now, yes?'

My breathing quickened. I closed my eyes and nodded. 'Yes, Patriarch.'

He let go of my shoulder. 'I have something to show you… come.' He turned and strode to the far corridor, one loud clomp at a time.

I was too terrified to move at first. He paused and looked back at me expectantly, and I eventually summoned the courage to follow.

We left the mess, and I trailed behind him in silence. This corridor had even more portraits of former Feeble members.

I remembered back to what Nadan told me when I first came here: that kids that didn't impress Mycol disappeared. Was this it? Was he already doing away with me?

Every step I took wobbled before it touched down. We wound our way along the corridor and stopped in front of a locked training room, one I hadn't yet entered.

Mycol pressed a button on the door's keypad. A mechanism above shot out rays of red light, scanning us, before beeping. The door whooshed open, revealing the dark, cold interior.

He entered and beckoned for me to continue following. I took my shakiest steps yet, beyond the door and into the cavernous room. Every tiny sound echoed back at us.

The door crashed closed, and the lights flickered on at the same time, causing me to jump and yelp. The large training area was mostly bare, aside from three steel rectangular blocks on the far side of the room, standing upright. They had a slender profile, meaning they could easily be knocked over.

'I've had this room outfitted for your needs,' Mycol began, before taking a few painful steps over to the blocks. 'The door will only recognise you or I.'

The wave of relief that washed over me was intense. My heart, which thought it was pounding its last beats, finally slowed. 'This is for me?'

Mycol nodded. 'I realised that you needed a space… away from others. The walls here are reinforced, more than enough to resist your power.'

I also walked over to the blocks and inspected them. 'And what exactly will I be doing in here?'

'Starting tomorrow, you will spend all your… assigned personal training time here.' He gave the middle block a minor shove and it toppled over with a loud metallic clatter. 'You will work on using your power to push this block over, but not the other two.'

That made a lot of sense. If I could choose what I pushed, I'd be far more effective.

I tested the balance of the left block with my hand and found it flimsy. Even a slight breeze could tip this over. 'I don't know if my power can do that. What if I can't?'

Mycol bent down and locked eyes with me. 'Right now, both you and your power are… unfocused. But if we give you something to focus on—'

His eyes widened, and his misshapen muscles tensed. Mycol's body glowed green, and he pivoted towards the right block with a mighty punch. The now flaming block careened into the far wall with an eardrum-shaking dong. Its original form now lost, the warped block gave a few last pitiful bounces before coming to a smouldering rest in the centre of the room.

'Aren't you angry, Eno?' Mycol roared. 'Over what they did to your sister? Don't you want to rip them apart, one limb at a time? Burn their cities down? Deny them from existence? Don't you want to show them *true* power?'

I took a couple of steps back, in awe of his strength, but also partly fearing that his violence would spill over to me.

His aura eventually faded, and he returned to his original pained stance. 'Before you sleep tonight, I want you to focus… on what they did to her, on how that makes you feel. Because only when your mind is focused on what must be done… will your power also be.'

Fourteen: A Fearsome Aura

Sacet

The present

The throne room

Tau arched back into her throne and stared at the ceiling. Everyone around her had solemn frowns, unsure of how to comfort her. Noor and Tetsu were leaning against nearby pillars; Marid and I were both standing to attention; and Amiki was by Tau's side, staring at her own feet.

'So stupid,' Tau said to herself, breaking the uncomfortable silence. 'I can't believe how stupid I've been.'

The massive doors at the end of the hall opened and Terel marched in. 'My apologies, my Queen. I've only just heard,' she called out when she got halfway.

Tau slowly levelled her gaze and glared at Terel as she fell into line. 'How did you let this happen, Commander?'

Terel glanced at both Marid and I with a furrowed brow. 'I'm sorry?'

Tau leant forward and brought her fingertips together. 'You're *supposed* to be a master of information. Siph was working for the enemy all this time right under our noses. How did this happen? Was she at least being investigated?'

Terel looked down in shame. 'I accept that this was my failure. My best interrogators are with her senior staff as we speak. I promise something like this won't happen again.'

Tau curled her lips. 'I thought I could trust Siph, but if I was wrong about her, maybe I could be wrong about you, too.'

Terel shrivelled her face and went red. 'I would never! With all due respect, just because I failed you, that doesn't mean I'm a traitor. I am loyal to you, my Queen.' She knelt and bowed.

Tau shook her head, unconvinced. She glanced at Amiki and the guards by the pillars. 'Arrest her.'

Terel's jaw dropped. 'My Queen, you can't be serious?'

Everyone in the room did a double-take. Nevertheless, Amiki nodded, and the Royal Guard complied, surrounding Terel and grabbing her by the arms.

I broke formation, ascended the steps and stopped halfway up. 'Tau, please, I don't think this is right.'

Marid nodded but stayed put. 'I agree. I've known Terel for many cycles, I can vouch for her.'

Tau raised a hand at the guards to stop them and looked at me. Her glazed eyes twitched, as though she was about to break down and cry. Behind her firm expression I could see she was still the same Tau, but putting on a tough exterior.

'How can we be sure?' she said quietly. 'What if she *is* one of them?'

I pointed back at Terel. 'Every one of our true enemies has been uncaring for the lives of others. But Terel showed genuine concern for her soldiers. I trust her.' I looked back at Tau. 'And *you* shouldn't be the sort of leader that persecutes the innocent on a whim.'

It was as if everyone's eyes grew two sizes. I was surprised Amiki wasn't telling me off, she must have been in shock, too.

But Tau didn't get upset. She looked down and closed her eyes. 'You're right, Sacet. Thank you for reminding me.' She waved a hand dismissively at the guards. 'Release her.'

Amiki rejoined Tau by the throne and the guards returned to their pillars.

Terel resumed her kneeling position. 'Thank you for your mercy, my Queen. I understand your anger. I, too, have my doubts about those I once trusted.'

Marid relaxed her stance. 'Some good news for you at least, my Queen. If what Siph said is true, your resurrection power is not lost at all, just that she was interfering with the bodies somehow.'

The floor trembled. Everyone raised their arms for balance. Tau grabbed her throne's armrests. Small cracks appeared on the nearby pillars.

At the far end of the hall near the doors, the tiles rippled, then launched outwards, as did clumps of dirt and concrete. Necrolisk claws emerged and thrashed around the hole's edge. Several of the beasts pulled themselves up and out, before scrambling throughout the chamber.

Climbing out after his pack was Colony. 'Where… is… our FOOD?' Colony bellowed at the top of his lungs, his voice echoing off the chamber's walls. The necrolisks roared to amplify their puppeteer's rage.

The Royal Guards aimed their lances and advanced. I could hear turrets overhead humming to life and spinning up their cannons.

Colony had gritted teeth and clenched fists. He strode forward with his monsters to meet the guards.

'Stop! Do not attack him,' Tau called, and the guards froze in place.

The necrolisks also thankfully stopped just short of their prey. Their jaws chattered with anticipation; globs of disgusting saliva dripped on the now rubble and mud-ridden tiles.

Amiki bent down by her side. 'Please, give me the word to rid you of this parasite,' she whispered.

'Let him approach,' Tau ordered.

Colony glanced at the guards with a contemptuous snarl. Even from here, I could see the guard's confused expressions. They raised their lances and stood to attention once more. Colony marched towards us with a trio of necrolisks. When he reached the steps, he stopped and glared at each of us one by one.

Tau gestured at the creatures. 'Let us settle this with words, not claws.'

Colony smirked. 'With words, *huh*? I tried that. You've betrayed me and my family, *Queen of Light*. If it wasn't for *our* efforts, you wouldn't even be *sitting* there.'

'You need to be patient,' I said.

He turned back to me. 'Shut up, peon! I'm speaking to your leader.'

Noor had pushed off from the pillar to join Marid and I. 'Oh, look who's talking? Mycol's favourite feeble little pet.'

Tetsu followed with his arms folded.

Colony rolled his eyes. 'I've had to endure your insults for a long time, Noor. I found solace knowing at least *I* have a family that *wants* me.'

Noor's eyebrows lowered and he pointed both hands at him. 'What did you say to me you pathetic little underling?'

Tetsu jumped in front of Noor and thrust his arms back down. 'It's not worth it, brother.'

Noor tried pushing past Tetsu. 'Get out of my way, I'm going to kill him.'

One of the hissing necrolisks clomped over and stood between Colony and Noor.

Noor settled for peeking around the creature and throwing out a rude hand gesture. 'They're not your family, you freak!'

'Colony, you're right,' Tau interrupted, breaking his attention away from Noor. She sat up straight and composed herself. 'You *did* help us. But the fact of the matter is, no one is getting special treatment here. There is simply not enough food to go around.'

Colony shrugged and gestured back at his necrolisks. 'My family is dying. There are too many for you to resurrect. And even though I'm in control *now*, they have a breaking point. What do you think they'll do when that happens? When there's a viable food source right above them?'

Marid scowled at him. 'Your thinly veiled threats are not welcome here, Colony.'

At least fifty more guards, some with golden armour and others without rushed through the main doors and surrounded the necrolisks from behind. They trained their weapons on the skittering brown mass. Terel pulled a pistol from her holster and faced Colony. Marid and I got closer to the queen and each placed one hand on our sword handles. Tau gripped her armrests tight.

Amiki raised a hand so that the guards would be at the ready. 'And if you make a threat like that again, I guarantee you will need all of those claws you brought with you.'

The entire room paused in a stalemate.

Colony seethed, perhaps mulling over his options, before pointing at Tau. 'I'm not leaving here without food.'

Tau stood. 'Enough! I'm sick of this. So, listen, Colony, and listen well. When food becomes available, we'll feed you. But we're fighting a war here if you hadn't noticed? And your constant whining is a complete waste of my time.'

Tau's aura had activated, and she stomped down the stairs. 'You're ungrateful for what I *do* give you, you selfishly only care about these creatures and none of *my* people, and look at what you've done to my throne room!'

There was something off about her flames, they lacked their usual light-blue tinge. If anything, they looked a bit teal, even green. Her eyes darkened, too, and her hair became more grey than white.

Tau passed the necrolisks, as though ignoring them. She got right up close to Colony's face and prodded a finger into his chest. 'If you can't handle living here with the food we do manage to give, maybe you should look farther afield? *Maybe* you should leave?'

Colony's tough façade broke, and he went even paler than usual. Gone was any form of smugness. The necrolisks shared their master's fear, receding from her and hissing.

Tau had a fearsome aura about her. Although this is probably how I would want to handle the situation, something was very off about her.

She grabbed his collar and wrenched him closer. 'Because if you ever come here again complaining like this, I'm going to give the order for your family to be exterminated!' She threw him back onto the cracked tiles. 'Now leave, or I will *make* you leave.'

Colony scrambled to his feet and backed away. His eyes were still locked with Tau's. He stared for the longest time and eventually turned. 'I thought this place would be different.' He calmly walked back through the hall with his now-silent army in tow. 'But you're the same as them.' When they reached the hole, his necrolisks entered first and he jumped in to follow.

Fifteen: Just A Chance

It was a new day, and I had a good feeling about this one. Today we'd find The Shroud, Tau would fix her resurrection problem, and our farms would finally report a surplus harvest. I had to stay positive, for all our sakes.

The initiates finished up with my armour and handed me my sword. I fetched Noor from the neighbouring changing racks, and together we strode back through the armoury and into the hangar.

With my perception, it would have been easy for me to spy on him from afar as he had suited up, but I resisted the urge this time. It felt wrong. Not only that, but we didn't have time for that kind of selfish frivolity; so *many* people were counting on us.

Our aircraft was still where we had left it. As planned, everyone was waiting, also fully armoured and ready to head out again. The Colonel and her troops were lined up by the ramp. Pilgrim and Malu were already inside the cabin, sitting across from one another and talking. Nako was powering up the engines. And Doron was at the bottom of the ramp with two large metal boxes, wheelable supply crates of some kind.

'It's probably better we don't tell them about last night,' I said as we marched across the steel-plated floor. 'About Siph… and Tau.'

Noor gestured ahead with a nod. 'Yeah, it probably wouldn't help Malu's mood or Pilgrim's either.'

Whatever Malu and Pilgrim were talking about was causing her to tear up. The last thing she needed was more bad news, and it was a surprise to see Pilgrim here again after all that drama with his father. And yet, here they were again, still helping. Was it because of a sense of duty, or because they *needed* to do this, like I did?

'Right,' I added, 'we need them focused. But I was more referring to Doron. If he suspects that the resurrection might not work, even a little…'

'Got it,' Noor said with another nod. 'And, uh, thanks again for yesterday.'

I kept my eyes forward to avoid blushing. 'For what?'

'For trusting me,' he answered. 'With all that's going on right now, it means a lot.'

I couldn't help but smile, and my cheeks warmed. 'Oh, that's okay.' I briefly glanced at him but then looked forward again. 'I mean, I assume you trust me, too?'

Noor stopped in place and gawked. 'You're kidding, right? You showed me the truth of this war.' He waited until I stopped, too. 'You saved me… from who I was, and from who I was becoming: someone motivated only by hate. You gave me a chance when all I deserved was the same fiery death I had given others.' He gave the warmest smile I had ever seen from him. 'So yes, I trust you.'

As Noor strode ahead, I paused. I never realised he felt so strongly about me. My smile persisted and eventually, I jogged to catch up with him.

The Colonel noticed us approaching. 'Attention!'

Our soldiers straightened up and saluted with an arm across their chests. Malu saw us and cleared her eyes to compose herself.

'Morning, Colonel,' I said, before pointing at the crates. 'What's all this?'

Doron slapped the nearest box with a metallic thud. 'Insurance.' He opened one of the lids for us to see inside: it was filled with fruit and cured meats. 'In case The Shroud doesn't like what you have to say.'

Although I agreed it was a good idea to bring a gift, I couldn't believe anyone in the city would willingly part with two whole crates during a food crisis. 'Where did you get all of this?'

'The slimy murkfish stole it,' one of our soldiers said from the line with a scowl. It was the same woman that had grilled Noor yesterday.

The Colonel and I shot her a look for talking out of turn, and she snapped to attention again.

'Scavenged,' Doron corrected before either of us could open our mouths. He pointed back at her. 'Now help me load them onto this shrieking sky deathtrap of yours.'

The soldiers sneered at their colonel, who in turn raised an eyebrow at me.

I folded my arms and turned to him. 'Doron, you have no rank here. You can't order my people around.'

He grinned with an exaggerated bow. 'Oh, oh my, of course not. How silly of me. Please, Commander Sacet, your guidance to The Shroud would be an honour beyond measure. Lead on, dear Commander.'

Everyone looked at me expectantly, probably surprised over how I was letting this elderly, dishevelled nomad disrespect me without reprisal.

I had little choice but to let him. I sighed and glanced at the Colonel. 'Load them up.'

As the Colonel ordered her team around the crates, Doron wandered closer and draped an arm over my shoulders. 'Stunning, this place. This… *city* of yours. Truly staggering to behold up close.'

Noor, who was also assisting with the crates, stopped and glared at Doron.

I began peeling the old man's arm off me. 'Hmm, yes, well, I'm glad you enjoyed it.'

Just as I was about to free myself, he wrenched me in closer. 'Enjoy is the last word I'd use. I spent all night looking for my sons, but no one knew their whereabouts, including that useless Malu girl. Now, you tell me where they are right now, or this deal is off. '

My eyes widened. I had completely forgotten about his sons, and I honestly had no idea where they were now. 'They… um… they—'

'They're in the Commercial Quad,' Noor chimed in. 'Saw 'em last night, they've got a cushy apartment while they wait for this mission to be over.'

As unbelievable as I knew it was, Noor's face showed no hint of a lie.

Doron's face, meanwhile, lit up. 'So, Atu's alive again? He's okay?'

Noor shrugged. 'I didn't know that was his name, but yes. They were out celebrating. And they probably don't want me to say this, but they were very concerned for you.'

Noor even had me believing him. We had been with Tau at the Royal Citadel most of last night as security, so if it were somehow true, when would he possibly have had the chance to see them?

I successfully squirmed out of Doron's grip and gestured to Noor. 'Satisfied?'

The old man closed his eyes and nodded. 'Yes, you don't know how much of a relief that is to hear.' As though invigorated by the news, he darted over to the crates. 'Come on, we have a clan of sand lickers to find.'

I breathed a quiet sigh of relief and mouthed the words 'thank you' to Noor.

He answered with another smile, waited for me to reach him, and joined me up the ramp.

The craft's main compartment shook as we hit another patch of turbulence. Our global map showed us close to the southernmost coast of the Unclaimed Wastes, a place I remembered trekking through as a child. Occasionally we'd pass a familiar mountain range or a white, streaking L line in the sky.

'You're veering too far left, head right a little,' Doron instructed the pilot, who turned us in response. 'We're almost there.'

'So, what made you choose to leave these… sand lickers of yours?' Malu asked. 'Was it on good terms, or are we expecting a fight?'

'They wanted to fight both Dominions from the shadows,' Pilgrim said with folded arms. 'Dad just wanted to stay in the shadows.'

Doron glared at him. 'So, we left, as a family. And that's all.'

'*Uh*... okay,' I said, trying to distract from their now intense stare-off. 'Is there anything else we should know about them?'

Doron glared at me instead. 'They excel at ambushing Dominion patrols, so this time we're going to approach them on foot, not fly over and land right next to them like a bunch of rockheads.'

I returned his look with an awkward nod. 'Uh, whatever you think is best.'

'How soon should I land, then?' Nako called back.

'Soon,' Doron replied. 'I don't even know if they're still there, it's been many cycles since we last saw or heard from them. When we land, I'll go first and—'

Doron was interrupted by the aircraft making a sudden jolt. We all rose in our seats and fell back down. The rumbling continued, and the craft sickeningly swayed and rolled after multiple more strikes.

'More turbulence?' Noor yelled next to me.

Doron pointed at the screen. 'No, it's them.'

Whirlwinds of sand had appeared all around the aircraft, surrounding us. One of the tornadoes spun into us, and we spiralled with it briefly, throwing all of us to one side in our seats. Although the crates were locked to the floor, their metal seals rattled and whined.

Pilgrim sneered at his father. 'What now, rockhead?'

'What is Urias doing this far out?' Doron shouted to no one in particular, before turning to the cockpit. 'Land this thing!'

Another twister whipped at our rear, destabilising our tail. Everyone was thrown around in their straps. Outside, my perception saw nothing but a sandstorm consuming us.

The engines waned. The sand was choking their sputtering turbines. Our nose dipped forward. I knew there was no flying out of this, we were going down.

I sensed stony canyon walls to our sides. The tempest was in the shape of a gargantuan hand, which was plucking us from the sky and plunging us towards the rocks below.

Nako was pulling her control stick back with all her might. 'I can't... pull up!'

While being thrown side to side, the special forces reached up from their seats and pulled their weapons down.

Noor reached for my wrist with his free hand. 'Sacet!'

We were moments away from smashing into a cliff. My perception searched for a patch of ground below. There wasn't time for individual portals. I clenched my fingers and opened a large portal on the floor of the cabin. We all saw the sand below, still and safe, and only a short drop down.

'Jump!' I shouted as everyone else unbuckled and dove through at once. I opened one more portal in the cockpit for the pilot. 'Nako, bail out!'

Noor and I were all that was left now. He noticed I was focusing on the portals, so he ripped off my straps, yanked me out of my seat and fell back into the portal with me.

As I was in freefall, I heard the eruption. Our craft had slammed into stone, and the fiery explosion chased us through the portal. I hit the ground harder than expected, but quickly closed the portal above, cutting off the fire.

We had finally stopped. My head spun. I pushed myself up and noticed that it was Noor who had broken my fall.

I rolled off him and stood. 'Ohh! I'm sorry, Noor, are you okay?'

Clutching his ribs, Noor gave a quiet thumbs-up through gritted teeth. He eventually composed himself and stood.

The aircraft had splintered into fiery pieces upon impact, each falling near us at the base of the cliff. Pieces of fruit rained down surreally, too. The smoke drifted up briefly before coiling with the wind and joining the maelstrom of sand above. We couldn't see the sky anymore.

The others were scattered about near Noor and I. Most had gotten up and were training their weapons in every direction. Both Pilgrim and Doron were still sprawled out on the sand.

Pilgrim sat up and looked at the wreckage. 'No, my cannon! Does someone have a spare weapon?'

'Here,' Malu called out, chucking Pilgrim her sidearm.

Pilgrim caught the much smaller pistol and examined it with disdain. 'Hmm, thanks.'

Doron struggled to his feet and trudged away from us towards the sandstorm. 'Stop! We're not the enemy!'

'Doron, come back!' I called, but he ignored me.

'Urias, do you hear me, brother?' he hollered over the still howling wind. 'Do not attack us!'

Noor positioned himself in front of me like a shield. I waded forward and stood beside him instead.

The sand rippled around us, like waves in an ocean. The waves converged on us, congregating at our feet. The sand quickly piled up, already submerging our knees.

I brought my hands up and clenched my fingers ready to make another portal, but as I did, a massive surge of sand sideswiped and bowled me over.

'Commander, do we fire back?' the Colonel yelled.

'Fire at what, Ma'am?' one of the soldiers added. 'I can't see any targets.'

The sand was overcoming their legs as well. We all tried digging ourselves out, but the sand rose quicker than we could climb. Soon it was waist height, then at our chests.

'Do *not* fire!' I shouted back, before realising that we were running out of options.

As the sand piled up, I swam my arms to try and reach the top.

My perception showed Doron still waving his arms around. Malu tried turning the sand into a pool, but it only made her sink deeper.

Noor fired his powers wildly upwards, also trying to escape, but whatever sand he destroyed was immediately replaced by more.

I could sense the sand acolytes, too. Men and women dressed in robes, masks and goggles, were buried in the distance. Only their heads peaked above the ground, which had wide-brimmed camouflaged hats covering them.

Would I really need to hurt these people to get them to stop? I'd been patient enough. I opened a portal beneath my feet and ripped it up. It spat me and a mound of sand outside the pile, next to Doron.

Then, while looking up at the sandstorm, I opened a portal into the vacuum of space. The wind whipped most of the airborne sand straight up, and our visibility began to clear. Doron and I could see the acolytes' heads with our own eyes.

He continued to wave and shout, and eventually, the sand stopped moving of its own accord. I closed the portal, and the air returned to normal.

The mountain of sand that was drowning my friends shifted and dispersed to the sides, releasing them. They all slowly got to their feet, some coughing and heaving, trying to clear their throats of what they had swallowed.

'Doron?' one of the male masked acolytes ahead of us said.

He made some hand gestures to the others around him. Their heads burrowed back into the sand, and the ground trembled. The man and two other brown-robed acolytes burst out of the ground beside Doron and I.

The quakes intensified and my perception sensed them burrowing at great speed underneath us. Each launched back up near my people with eruptions of blinding sand.

'Stop!' I shouted again, before quickly finding a long blade beneath my neck.

It belonged to the first man. 'A Matriarch? What a prize! Tell your people to drop their weapons.'

His mask was now down around his neck. He was old with tanned skin, and had grey hair like Doron, but had stubble instead of a beard. A long scar arced over a closed eye.

'On your knees!' one of the nomads commanded with a hostile stance.

'No, you get on yours!' the Colonel shouted back with her weapon pointed at him.

'Urias, this isn't necessary,' Doron began. 'We're all on the same side.'

The man called Urias raised an eyebrow but still didn't look away from me. 'They managed to brainwash someone as stubborn as you, *old friend*?'

Doron screwed up his face. 'Will you just listen to me, you unbelievable dolt? The Female Dominion was overthrown a cycle ago. These... *Concordites,* as they're so-called, are looking for new allies. They accept both men and women.'

Urias' eyes briefly looked down at my sword. 'They look like plain old Female Dominion to me.'

'Commander?' the Colonel called out.

I glanced back. 'Do not... shoot. Everything is under control.'

The nomads and soldiers were still in hostile stances towards each other. Without any weapons, Nako was left cowering behind a dripping-wet Malu and a slightly singed Noor.

Urias bent in closer. 'That's right. Now, tell them to drop their weapons.'

My perception didn't sense any more acolytes hiding beneath the sand. There were twelve altogether, all visible to me and standing still. Easy.

'In a moment,' I said with a smile. 'First, I want to show you something.'

I pictured one of my favourite footway intersections in the Commercial Quad back in New Elysia. Then, without moving, I placed an individual portal under all twelve and simultaneously whipped them up, sending the nomads to our home. They were all gone in a flash and all the agitated sand came to rest.

I turned to the group with a well-deserved, smug smile.

'Did you just—' Malu began, before pointing up at the sky.

'No, not that,' I said, shaking my head. 'Just showing them what home looks like.'

At this time of day, they'd now no doubt be surrounded by both female and male citizens rustling and bustling. They wouldn't be able to cause any trouble without their sand. Although, some did have blades. Maybe that was long enough.

'Alright everyone, lower your weapons. I'm bringing them back.'

As my team relaxed their stances, I opened another wide portal to our sides, and through it we could see the awestruck nomads standing on the street corner. Their jaws sufficiently dropped, I gestured to the sand on our side of the portal.

'Seen enough?' I called through.

Captivated by the city's sights, sounds and smells, the nomads eventually noticed the new portal beside them and came back through a couple at a time. With wide eyes and rapid breaths, they were understandably shocked, but when they saw that we had lowered our weapons, they didn't continue their hostility.

The city's residents, both female and male as planned, stared over with curiosity, but none ventured closer. After the recent attack, I didn't blame them for their hesitation.

Urias lowered his blade. 'You weren't lying…'

Once they were all back through, I dismissed the portal and folded my arms. 'Let's talk, yes?'

He raised a shaky eyebrow. 'Er, yes, yes.' His eyes came to rest on Pilgrim. 'Is... is that you, Sali? The lil' sand-slapper himself?'

Pilgrim nodded and presented a giant, toothy grin. 'Sure is, Uncle Urias.' He gleefully dropped his pistol and strode towards him. 'It's good to see you again.'

Urias returned his smile and hugged Pilgrim so strongly that he lifted him off the ground. 'You too, my boy. Oh, ow!' He released him and feigned pain in his back. 'You're a giant. What are you doing with all these degenerates?'

Pilgrim laughed. 'These degenerates are my friends,' he said as they let go of one another. He then pointed at me. 'Uncle, think back. That's Sacet — you visited her when she was a child. She's the one who could make portals, remember?'

'Her?' Urias said in disbelief. 'That sweet little kid turned into that?'

I lowered my eyebrows. 'Sweet?'

'*Ha*, take it easy.' He lowered a hand down by his hip. 'I remember when you were *this* high.'

I quickly nodded, wanting to cut to the chase. 'We've come with a proposition for you.'

'Hold on, wait,' another masked nomad interrupted. 'Let me see if I understand all of this. The Female Dominion has been defeated and now accepts men and nomads... and you chose Doron as your spokesperson?'

The nomads laughed, including Pilgrim. My soldiers were not amused.

Doron gruffly sighed. 'I'm just here because they promised they'd bring Kirai back to life.'

Urias bent back and chortled. 'And you believed that?'

'I've been brought back from the dead twice,' I said as I walked over and joined my friends.

Pilgrim raised his hand. 'Me, too. But just the one time.'

Urias raised an eyebrow at Pilgrim. 'Really? Was... there an afterlife?'

Pilgrim stroked his beard for a moment. 'Uhh. Well, I don't recall anything... except that death is *very* painful, as expected.'

'Do you believe us or not?' a still-wet Malu asked, twitching her fingers in anticipation.

Whatever smiles the nomads had faded.

Urias pointed back at Malu. 'Easy there, sweaty.' He came and studied the rest of us before grabbing both of Pilgrim's shoulders. 'I trust *you*, Sali, but not the others. Is what they're saying true?'

He nodded with a far more solemn expression. 'The war is almost over… one side down, one to go. This is what you've wanted all this time, right?'

Urias' brow furrowed and he closed his eyes.

'So, what do you say, Urias?' Doron continued. 'Care to see your sister again?'

'Let's go see her together,' Urias responded with a grin, before signing more symbols to his people.

As the others encircled us, Urias pointed at some nearby smouldering wreckage. 'Sorry about your craft, but we travel differently out here.'

'We brought you food, too,' Noor mentioned, before looking down at some of the fruit scraps still in the sand.

Urias shrugged. 'Our food's better. You'll see.'

Each sand acolyte faced away and lifted their arms. The sand beneath us rumbled, solidifying into a large circular platform. With another motion of their arms, we levitated up and glided over the dunes, away from the crash site.

We careened across the desert's surface almost as fast as our aircraft could. It wasn't until we rose above the surrounding cliffs that we saw a beautiful, blue line on the horizon. Noor's hand gripped mine. We looked at each other for a moment before gazing back at the sparkling ocean.

Sixteen: Only Just Begun

Tau

I looked out at my domain of peril from the highest room of the Citadel. The city shone like a beacon under the darkening sky as if to say: here we are, come kill us. The stars twinkled through the thin clouds like thousands of little eyes. How many spies were watching me right now? How many enemies were ready to pull their trigger? It was only a matter of time before they struck again.

I was sitting in my personal chambers with Amiki and Tetsu, facing the enormous window. Unlike the rest of the Citadel and its ongoing building works, this room was unchanged, without a single renovation. It had the same extravagant furniture as before the coup, the same ornate wooden desk by the window, and the same cushioned seats behind me for my guests.

Today had been another barrage of bad news, like one long endurance test. The worst of it was receiving an official declaration of war from three Concordite territories: Utos, Suralia, and Elysia, which had decided to secede. Each was crucial to our cause in their own way, but mainly the loss of their food production was the most damaging. Within days, our food crisis was going to become a food catastrophe.

Their commanders, now Matriarchs again, had decided their peoples would return under the Female Dominion banner. I thought about all those men who had joined their societies in the last cycle, only to now be rounded up and enslaved.

At least yesterday provided one good revelation: my power wasn't broken. And with the switch to Tarsus and her City Defence now collecting the dead, starting tomorrow, maybe I could focus on resurrecting people full time?

Although my leather chair was the pinnacle of comfort, I couldn't stop tensing. I didn't belong in it.

'I… I can't do this anymore,' I began, still facing the window. 'I'm quitting.'

Amiki was silent. She had been quiet all day, as though this duty had been eating away at her, too.

Tetsu, on the other hand, stood and approached. 'Don't. Just hang in there, you're doing fine.'

I spun my chair to face him. 'I said I can't do it, aren't you listening to me?' I pointed at him just as he was about to open his mouth. 'And no advice about being a strong leader is going to help me. This is just… not something I'm capable of anymore. I can feel my very soul being eaten away. I've got nothing left to give.'

Amiki and I stared at the golden-edged, white floor tiles. Her knee bounced unendingly. Tetsu groaned in frustration as he paced.

I slumped onto my desk, head in my arms. 'I just want to *heal* people. That's all I ever wanted. When Sacet comes back I want her to take over. Or maybe Marid.'

Silence returned, other than the ventilation's soft hum and the distant city noises.

Tetsu stopped, folded his arms and leaned on my desk. 'When I was young, it was just me and my dad. We were nomads, too, and everything was bad. Necrolisks, Dominion patrols, bandit ambushes… the works.

'Then the Male Dominion captured us, and you know, I actually thought things would be easier, but the thugs in the city were just as bad. Dad never fought back. I still remember, he'd hide me under this pile of dirty grease rags. And… I would hear the beatings…

'One night when they came, I burst out to defend him and that's when I got my powers.' He stared outside and shook his head. 'But it didn't matter. He was ill and I lost him anyway. My shield couldn't protect him.'

I tried reaching out for his hand. 'I'm sorry.'

He backed away. 'I was forced to fight, of course, now an acolyte. I met Noor, some abandoned kid with no family either. Over there, everyone is your "brother", but he and I really *were* like brothers, you know? Noor's powerful, but dumb sometimes. Without someone to watch his back…'

His eyes squinted. 'I realised that no matter how hard you try to protect others, sometimes you still lose them. But if you let that eat at you, you'll let the times when you could have done something pass by.'

Tetsu came over, grabbed my hand and smiled. 'Tau, you're the most kind-hearted person I know. You remind me a lot of my mother.' He then gestured around us. 'But this city… this *world* needs you to be *more* right now. I think *you* are the one that's supposed to lead us, so after we win, you can teach us to be kind again.'

He pulled something out of his pocket. It was the bright blue flower I had given him in the garden, now slightly wilted from being in his pocket. He placed it on the table. 'But it's not time for kindness yet.' He turned and made for the elevator.

As if anticipating his need, the circular elevator platform rose to our level and opened its see-through doors. Two Royal Guards were already standing inside. Amiki gave them a nod, and one nodded back at her.

Tetsu hopped on the panel and faced Amiki and I. 'Ground floor.'

My lips trembled as I gave Tetsu a solemn frown. The panel disappeared below the floor, and he was gone.

I rested my head on the desk. 'And what do you think, Amiki? Should I keep doing this until I get everyone killed?'

Amiki's eyes darted, as though she were trying to find the words. 'I… think… you should quit. Both of us should.'

'Oh?'

Her indecision turned to groaning frustration. 'I have to show you something.'

She stood and pulled out a little cube-shaped device, a holo-throw, and placed it on my desk. She pressed a button, and a blueish beam fired up, forming a portable float screen. It showed a man and a woman in a plain room, sitting at a table and facing the camera.

'Amiki,' the woman began with a huge smile. 'It's... it's us. It's Mum and Dad. We're okay.'

Like Amiki, they had glossy, black hair and bronzed skin. Both wore generic civilian clothing and sombre expressions, with occasional smiles of joy breaking through.

I glanced at Amiki. 'Didn't you say you saw them—'

'Die? Yes.'

The man chuckled. 'I wish I could see your face right now, little hapoyo.'

The woman frowned. 'Yes, I *so* want to be there to give you a great, big hug. We've missed you so much.' Tears trickled from her eyes. 'Missed... watching you grow into a young woman.'

'We've heard all about what's happening there,' the man continued. 'And... every time we hear what they're doing to you and your friends, it makes us sad. You probably already know, but... you can't beat them, hapoyo.'

The woman wiped her tears, but they were quickly replaced with more. 'That's why you need to come home to us. The whole family is here, waiting for you. And your friends can come, too! Just come home.'

The man's eyebrows lowered. 'There's just one thing you've got to do.'

Amiki leant forward and pressed the same button as before, stopping the playback.

What home were they referring to? I shook my head, flabbergasted. 'Wow. The level of... the lengths they'll go to—'

'Hapoyo... that's what Dad used to call me.' Like the woman, Amiki began to tear up. ''Cause I'm sweet like the fruit.'

I stood and pointed at the holo-throw. My body tensed beyond belief. 'Amiki, you don't... you don't think this is real, do you? Those aren't your parents; they've faked it somehow. Your parents are—'

'They're real,' she interrupted again, moving to the window and staring out. 'Before you discovered resurrection, I wouldn't have believed it. But now? And even if it is a fake, maybe they'll show you and me mercy if we give up? My dad's right. We can't win this.'

I slowly reached for the emergency button under my desk. 'If your mind is already made up, then why did you show me this?' I hit the button.

'So you understand,' she answered. 'So you can forgive me.' She glanced over and noticed where my hand was. 'I already deactivated it. It's just you and me.'

I launched up from my chair and backed away. The chair fell to the side.

Amiki hit a nearby panel on the wall, opening a secret cabinet. Inside she retrieved what appeared to be a shock dart gun and an inhibitor collar, the same type we use on our acolyte prisoners. How long had those been stashed there?

I rounded my desk, keeping my distance from her. When I reached the elevator, I pressed the call button, but it didn't respond.

'That's been deactivated, too,' she explained as she turned to me fully.

My breathing quickened, and I naturally activated a weak aura to defend myself. I leant up against the elevator tube. Maybe I could pry the doors open? No, they were sealed tight.

There was nowhere else to go, except for my bedroom or the side office, and both of those were dead ends. My power would not affect her, and she completely outclassed me in hand-to-hand combat. I was trapped.

'How long?' I asked, buying more time to think.

She meandered over to the centre of the room, between me and the desk. 'How long what?'

'How long have you been spying for them?'

Amiki winced. 'You think I'm a spy? I only received this message a few days ago.'

The window behind her. I could leap through the window and survive the fall. It was my only shot, now or never.

She put her hand over her heart. 'I'm not one of them, Tau. I still—'

I darted to one side before she could finish and sprinted alongside the wall towards the window. She turned and vaulted over the table to intercept. I'd need to leap through to break the glass, so I bent my knees at the last moment and dove forward.

Her foot, a flying kick collected me in the side midair and smashed me into the wall. Several shelves and the knickknacks they displayed crashed down with me to the floor. Although my aura was active, I still felt discomfort, the smallest amount of pain.

I flipped over, attempting to stand, but was pinned by Amiki's knee on my shoulder. My face rammed into the white tiles. A loud, metallic click rang in my ears as the inhibitor collar was attached around my neck. What was left of my aura dissipated, replaced by a piercing pain in my back.

'I still care about you,' she said, voice now trembling. 'I'm doing this for *us*.'

I writhed under her superior strength and position. 'Amiki, stop this, please! If you really do care, then you'll stop.'

There was a loud pop above me. A sharp prick in my arm followed. My vision went fuzzy, and my body convulsed. My view of the tiles spun. Dark blotches filled my eyes.

'Rise and shine.'

My blurry eyes could only make out vague, swirling shapes. 'What? Where is… where's Tetsu? Amiki… where are we?'

I was lying on a bed in a small cell. There was a seatless, chrome toilet to my side and a steel wall behind me. The other three walls were translucent, like a greenish glass. They had a feint hum, as though electrically charged, the whole place did. The far wall had an open door. My cell was one of many, side-by-side in an aisle, with a corridor beyond the doors to access them. A prison.

A still-hazy figure was standing in front of me, and her familiar features were coming into focus. This middle-aged, blonde woman wore a simple and sleek uniform I didn't recognise.

'Verre?' I uttered in disbelief.

She grinned with overwhelming smugness. 'Correct, usurper.'

'But you're… you're dead?' I said, sitting up and shuffling back to the wall. 'I couldn't resurrect you.'

Verre shook her head and tsk-tsked. 'You can't resurrect someone already alive, stupid girl.'

We weren't alone. Standing out in the corridor with a shameful frown was Amiki, and next to her was the much shorter Iya, folding her arms and scowling like she always used to. Amiki couldn't even look at me. Both Verre and Iya had black wristbands on, not for decoration, but to house small glowing screens.

Unconscious in the cell next to mine was Tetsu. 'Tetsu!' I shouted, hoping to wake him. I looked down and saw that I had no restraints. I threw my feet over the side. 'Who are you people? What do you—'

As I stood, I saw a huge, dark figure enter my cell's door behind Verre. It was the same man who led the attack on New Elysia and killed Sacet. I backed up against the wall again and slid down it into the corner.

'You,' I said.

His piercing eyes locked on me, unmoving. His face was devoid of all emotion.

'You know, I saw what you did to my body,' Verre continued. 'That wasn't very nice.' She then gestured around my tiny cell. 'Get comfortable, Tau. You're not going anywhere until we are finished *ruining* Sacet's life in every way we can think of.' She joined the man by the doorway. 'Her Harrowing has only just begun.'

Verre and the man stepped back out of the cell. Verre waved her wristband over a panel by my door to close it, before they both strolled along the corridor and out of sight.

Iya shoved Amiki in the side and indicated for her to follow. Amiki complied and averted her eyes as she passed my cell, possibly out of shame.

Iya brought up the rear and flashed me a fake smile. 'Enjoy your stay.'

Seventeen: A Quick Death

Eno

Another night in the most comfortable bed I had ever laid on, yet I couldn't help but stare at the dorm ceiling. The distant but ever-present hum of the surrounding facilities and factories filled the curfew-imposed silence. My mind repeatedly filled the darkness with what I had seen earlier: Sacet's head rocking to the side and hitting the ground.

Our little dorm had six beds, a couple of windows that overlooked the courtyard, and a single door leading to the stairwell. Snoozing nearby was Nadan, Mui, Keenu and Sozha. The sixth bed lay in wait for a new recruit. I wondered who originally slept there, before being taken away by Mycol.

Although some of the boys here were nice, particularly those in this room, I doubted they'd defend me if my life were in danger. If it were me next, they'd look the other way, like they did for all the others. I was alone now. The only person I could rely on to protect me was me.

I rolled over and saw Sozha with his bruised face buried in his pillow. Poor guy, I should make more of an effort to get to know him. Everyone else overlooked him, even shunned him at times. How much longer would he last?

Someone was tossing and turning in his bed, while on my other side, Mui was sitting up and crying softly. I closed my eyes, scrunched up my face and ignored him as best I could, hoping he'd stop and that I'd finally fall asleep. But another memory surfaced, of Sacet comforting me when I was little. There were so *many* times, actually. Each sob gnawed on me from within until I couldn't take it anymore.

I slinked out of my sheets and tip-toed over to him. 'Mui?' I whispered, pulling on his sleeve.

He jumped in surprise and turned to where he thought I was. 'Who's that?' he whispered back.

'It's Eno, sorry.'

'No, I'm sorry. Did I wake you?'

I knelt beside his bed. 'I was already awake. Why are you crying? Can I get you a cold towel for your bruises?'

He frowned. 'No, it's not that, it's… it's better you don't know.'

'What? You can't say that. Just tell me,' I said, my voice getting a little louder.

'*Shh!*'

There was a rustle from one of the other bunks, but it didn't sound like we woke anyone.

'Alright,' he continued. 'But you have to promise never to tell anyone.'

I nodded, but stupidly realised he couldn't see me. I gripped his hand. 'I promise.'

'You have to understand, I've only told Nadan. If they know I know, they might kill me.'

'Who?'

'Mycol. When one of us disappears, Mycol just says they were transferred… or promoted or something. But I know *exactly* what he does with them.'

I peered through the dark at the empty bed.

He leant closer. 'I'm blind to everything that you can see. But I can *see* things you can't. I see the pain people feel, even through walls. It sort of looks like… little green flames where their veins should be.'

He pulled me closer and pointed to an empty corner of the room. 'There…'

I paused, trying to picture what he might see. 'You can see someone right now?'

'Mycol's building, it's filled with people in pain.' Mui then pointed slightly down. 'He's in his basement right now.'

I tried following Mui's gaze but could only see the floor. Although that direction *did* go across the courtyard towards Mycol's quarters.

'I can see a girl… I think it's a girl. I can't see faces, only the pain they experience.'

'What's he doing to her?'

'I don't want to say.'

There was a silence between us before he continued.

'It's almost over anyway. There… she's gone.'

'What do you mean?' I asked.

'Mycol just ripped her flames out of her body and kind of… ate them.'

'She's dead?'

'No, I can still see her in pain, but now she's inside his body, floating around, trapped. I always know where Mycol is, because I can always see him in pain, but it's not him experiencing the pain, it's the people inside him.'

'That's his power?'

'Yeah. Sometimes he invites one of us to go on our debut mission with him, and then they never return. But I can see the kid floating around inside him.'

'That's terrible.'

Mui wiped away his tears. 'I know.'

'Well… so, what do we do?'

'There's nothing we *can* do but wait for our turn.'

It was so quiet in the training room that I could hear my heartbeat. I had been kneeling beside the three toppled blocks for so long that I had lost track of time. Mycol would probably be back soon to check on my 'progress'.

Knocking over just the centre block while leaving the other two up seemed more and more impossible with each attempt. If I couldn't perform this simple trick for him, how many more days did I have left alive?

The infuriating part is that when I used my power at Pilgrim's old village and created that crater, everything around me was pushed back *except* for the other prisoners. How did I do that? I still had no clue.

As if sensing my dread, the only door opened behind me with a squealing shudder and Mycol stomped erratically in. He looked down at my blocks and sneered, leaving me unsure if it was due to his pain or his irritation with me.

I spun and backed up close to the wall. 'Oh, uh, King's glory to you, Patriarch, sir.' He didn't respond so I gestured down. 'I was close a few times,' I lied. 'But... but the... they're too thin. Even the slightest push—'

'Follow me,' he interrupted, before turning and leaving the room without another word.

I knew better than to disobey, so I pursued him out into the corridor and back to the mess hall, which was currently empty. The others were probably still in their own training areas, each with different challenges aimed at bettering themselves.

Mycol was quieter than usual, keeping his eyes forward as we exited the Feeble Fortress and into the massive courtyard. Several Terror Guards were waiting outside and accompanied us. We passed at least a hundred soldiers training in and by the pits, and whenever one looked over and saw Mycol and his cronies, he'd avert his eyes and go back to training, more intensely than before.

Mycol's dark grey building lay ahead, a facility-sized spire with spikes on its awkwardly angled surfaces. The windows on the higher floors were blacked out, although I did notice a faint sky-blue light through one of them. The reinforced entrance doors whined open as we approached.

I spotted Keenu and Nadan doing push-ups and gave them a pleading stare. Noticing where I was heading, they gawped back.

Nadan took a step forward, but Keenu shook his head at him, so he stopped.

I dawdled behind Mycol; each step was harder and harder to take. This was it, wasn't it? I was being led to my death. I wondered how much it would hurt. Would he at least make it quick? I froze in the open doorway, too terrified to continue.

'It's alright, Eno,' he said, glancing back with his widened, bulbous eye. 'You can enter.'

Once inside, there was probably no going back. I'd be alone with him in there. Fine. If he tried anything, I'd kill him first. I'd show him my unfocused power, unrestrained. And if I were to die, I'd at least go down swinging, as Grandpa used to say.

I stilled my shaky legs and stepped into the entry hall, avoiding Mycol's unsettling stare.

His home was covered in rugs and furs that looked more like they belonged in a nomad's cave, as well as poorly stitched leather furniture.

I gestured to the decorations. 'You like to… hunt?'

He smirked as we strode down the next hallway. 'Certain things, yes.'

As we moved, the Terror Guard took up positions one by one to block the path behind us.

'My… my grandpa and I used to hunt sunshy eels with our spears,' I said, trying to get on his good side.

'Mmm hmm…'

To our sides were many closed doors, behind which I could hear an occasional muffled whimper. Lining the walls between each door was even more creepy decor: hanging bits of necrolisk chitin and mandibles, dead animals posed like statues and dressers with screaming skulls carved into them.

On top of the dressers were stacks upon stacks of journals, as well as many colourful, sealed jars, containing floating bits of preserved flesh. People's names were written on the journals' spines. It smelled worse in here than the Teersau sewers.

Probably the most unsettling piece was a huge, framed painting of Mycol himself with his skull mask on, and a column of green flames twice his height extending outwards. Beneath his feet was a field of bones that stretched into the picture's horizon. Was this supposed to be him when he was younger?

There was another door at the end of the hallway, rusty and stained with dark splotches. Unlike almost every other door in this city, it had a handle to manually open it. Long scratch marks on the door, from its centre to the handle side, hinted at a past struggle.

Mycol lurched ahead and clutched his monster-like fist around the handle. 'I've taken you away from your training... for a very *special* reason.' He noticed my renewed hesitation and paused. 'Come, boy. I promise... you *need* this.'

'Patriarch,' I began, 'I'm sorry if... if I've disappointed you. I just know that... if... you give me more time, I'm sure I'll be up to your standards.'

Mycol's larger eye twitched, and he turned fully to me. 'Of course you will.'

'What's... in there?' I asked, my voice wavering.

He pondered for a moment. 'In here you will find... the *end* of your childhood.' He opened the door and revealed a dark staircase leading down. He then stood aside and gestured for me to go first.

I peered into the dark. There was another room down there with a light, but I couldn't make out any details from here. 'Do I have to?'

Mycol nodded solemnly. 'You must.'

I begrudgingly went down one step at a time, with Mycol following close behind. The old door shut behind us with a metallic groan, making it even darker. Definitely no escape now. When we reached the bottom, my eyes adjusted to the dimly lit room.

There was a blood-stained steel table with built-in restraints. Saws and knives of varying shapes and sharpness were hanging on a wall nearby. Several padlocked metal boxes were off to the side, each large enough to fit a person, but not tall enough for them to stand. The number one fear of all nomads was to end up in a Dominion torture chamber like this.

Movement in the far corner of the room: a woman was slumped down in a small transparent prison cell. Glass, or maybe plastic? I wasn't sure. She was restrained with chains from the floor and blindfolded for good measure.

Mycol led me over to her to take a closer look. She seemed familiar, but with her head down it was hard to tell. Aged somewhere in her thirties, she was thin and malnourished, and purple bruise marks could be seen through the rips in her tattered prison clothes.

'My present… to you, Eno,' Mycol said with a gesture to her.

'Eno?' the girl said weakly, her voice slightly muffled behind the wall. She looked roughly in our direction. 'I *know* that name…'

'Who is she?' I asked.

Mycol fiddled with a latch on the transparent door and opened it. 'You don't recognise her?'

He then reached into his pocket, pulled out a small device and clicked a button on it. A small hologram shot up: it was a still image of Sacet being executed. He pressed another button, and the image zoomed in on the executioner.

'It has been over 100 days since you arrived here,' Mycol began, 'and since then I've… been *hunting* this person, all so that you… could take your vengeance.'

There was no doubt, she looked exactly like the one that had shot Sacet. For so long now I've had restless nights, not only worried about my own safety but also fantasizing about what sort of violent acts I would do to this woman if I ever met her.

I turned back to Mycol. 'You brought her here just for me?'

'Of course,' he continued, 'I made a vow that day… to help you.' With that Mycol took a step back and pointed to the torture instruments on the wall. 'You may do to her as you wish.'

The girl winced and breathed quicker. 'Please, please no…'

I focused on her with a seething gaze. 'Why? Why did you do it?'

She clawed at the empty air and bawled. 'Please let me go.' She crawled forward pitifully but was immediately stopped by her chains. 'Eno, right? I remember that name now. You're her little brother?'

'Yes,' I answered, stepping through the door. 'Why did you kill my sister?'

She shook her head. 'No, that wasn't me, I promise.'

Mycol chortled. 'We know you're lying.'

She went stone-faced. 'Please, I… I… I just want to go home. Or… women who cooperate can be incubators, right? I'll do that, please… just don't hurt me.'

Incubators? Whatever, it didn't matter. I grabbed her by the shoulders and shook as hard as I could. 'Why did you take her from me? She didn't do *anything* to you people. We just wanted to hide in the desert in peace, but you kept *chasing* us. Why couldn't you just leave us alone? *Why?!*'

She sobbed and continued shaking her head, so I pushed her over. I couldn't hold back my tears any longer either. I turned away from them both and cried into my hands.

Mycol grabbed a machete from the wall with a cold, metallic ring. He hobbled back over and stood in the door frame, offering the blade handle to me. I knew what he expected, but I didn't know if I could. I reached out to it with a trembling hand.

'I gave her a quick death,' she said calmly and bowed, exposing her neck to me. 'I ask for the same.'

I coiled my fingers around the machete's grip. Mycol let go and stared at me expectantly. I turned to the woman and raised my weapon. The room went silent, apart from my rapid breathing.

'Do it, Eno,' Mycol interrupted, 'feel that thirst for vengeance. She'll be one of many.'

I took several breaths, thinking how hard I'd need to swing to slice through clean. I had killed in self-defence before, but this felt different. Although I had been training for most of my life with Grandpa, readying for the horrors of war, I never thought I'd have to execute someone.

I could see my reflection in one of the shiny metal boxes on the edge of my periphery. With the blade held up, I looked like a violent psychopath, the same as those who had oppressed my people for generations. This version of Eno wasn't me.

I dropped the blade and watched it clatter on the tiled floor. 'I can't do it.' I closed my eyes. 'I'm sorry, but I don't want to be like her.'

Mycol was silent.

'Are you... upset with me?' I asked, before finally looking back at him.

The cell door slammed closed with a solid thud and click. Mycol had already moved to a nearby control panel. 'I had a feeling you'd say that.' He pressed a button, and the transparent walls glowed green with an electrified hum.

'Patriarch?'

Mycol peeled open a toothy grin. 'If you won't kill her, then maybe you'll save her instead?'

He pressed another button, and the ceiling panels whined open. Sprinkles of something fell into my eyes, and I backed up to clear them. A deluge of continuous sand began filling the cell.

'*Ack*!' the woman wailed as she squirmed against her now-buried chains. 'What is this? Please, please, I don't want to die…'

'Patriarch, Sir, please stop!' I yelled as the sand rose to my waist.

The deluge hadn't ceased. Although the woman struggled, she couldn't break free of her restraints, and so was buried completely. Her screams were now a sickening muffled choke.

'You can stop this, Eno,' Mycol said, stepping away from the controls. 'Go ahead and use your power. Push it all away.'

My fear was palpable: my sweat dripped, my jaw quivered, and my arms shook. I wasn't going to die here.

I pointed my palms up and screamed. Waves of force rippled through the air, sending the falling sand back up. The sand already beside me vibrated madly against the cell walls. The walls didn't move. Were they immune to my power?

Snap!

A huge crack appeared in the cell wall, and it quickly grew. All the lights in the chamber flickered as I continued to scream. Mycol's former calm grin was replaced with a concerned gawp. He stepped back as the cracking worsened into more forking paths. The electrified green flickered, too.

Mycol summoned his aura, sheathing himself in his sickly green corruption. 'Yes boy, show me!'

I gritted my teeth and tensed my arms. I would survive this, no matter what. My fear evolved into some kind of savagery. It felt good. My scream was now a roar.

The humming of the cell walls distorted and spiked, ear-piercingly so, before failing. The wall shattered out in a mighty burst of sandy glass hail. Mycol was thrown off his feet, all the furniture and weapons flung away. The unprotected walls warped. And finally, I stopped.

I glanced back to the corner and saw a horrifying sight: the woman was twisted in knots of unnatural contortion. Her eyes were open, blank. Her body was motionless, dead, because of my lack of control. I must have gotten lost in the moment because I didn't mean to hurt her.

Mycol, who was lying in the rubble, cackled madly. He had a huge shard of glass impaling his abdomen. He gripped it with both hands and ripped it out, before sitting up. 'See? It wasn't that hard. Vengeance!' He awkwardly rose to his feet and lumbered closer. 'Now imagine if only… you could focus all of that raw power… you'd be unstoppable.'

Eighteen: Trust Us

Sacet

The present

Our flying sand platform hurtled over the unending beach. We had been following the ocean's edge for some time now, propelled by the rhythmic sway of the nomads' sand powers. The sun was setting far out to sea over the horizon, its rays scattered vibrantly throughout the atmosphere in a blend of red, pink, and orange.

The salty marine tang breezed past, clearing my sinuses and somehow reinvigorating me. The peaceful churn of the waves stirred many great childhood memories, some of the only fun Eno and I ever had. Everyone but the nomads stared out at the sun-brightened waters, in awe of its natural majesty.

Unlike the others, I could sense what was beneath the powerful surface. My perception had dived in to spy on the underwater inhabitants several times now. Such strange and wonderfully colourful varieties of fish and predatory creatures swam just beyond our concerns – creatures that I never knew existed.

Urias elbowed Pilgrim in the side. 'Hey Sali, remember that time when you were a teenager, and I snuck you some liquor without your stuck-up pa knowing?'

Doron, who had been focused on maintaining his balance, furrowed his brows in annoyance.

Pilgrim gave an incredibly goofy, almost child-like smile. '*Ah*, yeah, and I vomited all over your legs?'

Urias nodded. 'Yes! But then what happened after?'

Pilgrim's cheeks reddened. '*Oh*… was that the night I set Dad's beard on fire while he was sleeping?'

Urias and Pilgrim laughed until they were hoarse, as did a couple of others.

Doron pointed at his son. 'That was *you*? I should have known.'

Urias pointed at his own chest. 'You mean you thought that was *me* all this time? No wonder you wanted to leave!'

Others from both sides joined in the laughing, even the Colonel.

All the wrinkles on Doron's face creased like bad leather. 'It's not funny, I could have been seriously burned.'

Pilgrim shrugged and pointed at Urias. '*He* put me up to it.'

Doron's eyes widened. 'I blamed *you*, Urias because you gave me lum nut oil for my beard the night before!'

Practically everyone joined in with the laughter now. Noor and I guffawed, and even Malu giggled. The laughs eventually died down.

There was a rocky mountain ahead, its higher surfaces lit like a beacon in the last light of day. It was right next to the beach, and beyond it were cliffs that continued over the horizon.

'We're here,' Urias said, before signalling to the others.

The nomads slowed and lowered the platform. When we reached the mountain's base, they merged our makeshift vehicle back into the sand from which it was made, and we stepped off as though it never existed.

I sensed a well-hidden cave entrance into the mountain nearby. It was cleverly submerged underwater, but once you passed through, the tunnels then weaved upwards into larger cavernous areas.

'You still haven't moved, after all of these cycles?' Doron asked.

Urias shook his head. 'Never needed to abandon the perfect home.'

'Uh, where is it?' Malu asked. 'The mountain?'

The nomads waved their arms at the submerged entrance. In

doing so, the sand from the seabed floated up through the water in cloggy chunks to the surface. It solidified, forming a wet dam and blocking the tide from bringing more water in. The water behind the dam drained away, leaving an empty, but still moist, tunnel to enter through.

'Very clever,' the Colonel said. 'No wonder we never found you.'

'Wait,' I asked, before turning to Nako. 'While we're still above ground, try and contact home. See if everything's alright.'

Nako nodded and procured a small device from her belt. Some of the nomads exchanged glares.

Urias approached. 'As I said, I trust *Sali*. But I don't know what sort of person you've grown up to be. So, until we have you figured out, no contacting potential reinforcements.'

One of the nomads snatched the device out of Nako's hand, and the soldiers shifted uncomfortably.

I raised my hand at them. 'Relax.'

Urias looked around at each of us again. 'While you're here, it's radio silence.' He held up the device to me. 'Unless you'd prefer to go home now?'

I shook my head. 'Keep it until we leave.'

He put the device in his pocket. 'Gracious of you.' He pointed his palms at the trench and tensed. More sand rose from the seabed and formed a solidified staircase. 'In we go.'

One by one the other nomads and soldiers climbed down and landed with loud squelches. They followed the tunnel and climbed out after the dip on the other side.

Urias prodded me in the back. 'A former nomad like you wouldn't be afraid of a little mess on her fancy armour, would she?'

Malu skipped the staircase and leapt into the muck. 'Sacet and I are more nomad than anyone here, old man.' Her legs sunk into the slush up to her knees.

As Malu plodded under the dip, Urias looked back at me. 'Indeed. And now your turn.'

I could have easily teleported all of us from one side to the other, but Urias was eagerly watching what we'd each do. I descended the staircase like the others. Several slippery steps in, I reached the dip and ducked under. After that, hands were waiting to pull me up.

My eyes adjusted after a few moments and realised there was more light here than I initially thought. On the rock walls, thousands, maybe tens of thousands, of tiny worm-like creatures dotted every surface. They were bioluminescent, each lighting the cave with a pinkish hue and twinkling as they crawled.

As the last stragglers climbed through, I examined the creatures on the nearest wall more closely.

'*Whoa*,' Noor said as he was pulled up. 'What are those?' His voice echoed off the walls.

They were eyeless and had tiny, soft spikes growing from their spines. They reminded me of necrolisks a little bit, except these were actually kind of cute. I reached out my fingers to one of them.

'Don't touch that!' Urias yelled back. 'Their venom will kill you instantly!'

Noor and I jumped back and looked back at them in shock. Pilgrim and a few of the nomads laughed. Urias gave a big toothy grin. 'Just kidding, you can eat one if you'd like.'

One of the burlier nomads groaned. 'Every time we bring someone here, you make that joke. *Every* time.'

Doron folded his arms. 'It was already old when he told it to me twenty cycles ago.'

It was amazing how alike Urias and Pilgrim were. The family resemblance was strong. Meanwhile, Pilgrim was nothing like his father.

Malu wandered over to one of the worms and gently rubbed it. 'What are they?'

'Necrolisk larvae,' Urias said, picking one up from the cave floor and placing it in his mouth. He chewed as he spoke. 'We breed 'em and eat 'em.' He finished chewing and swallowed.

'You... breed them?' I asked.

'Should we be worried about their mother?' the Colonel asked, voicing my thoughts exactly.

'Not at all,' Urias said. 'We cleared out this nest *many* cycles ago now, the queen and all her soldiers. When we were done, there was nothing left but the eggs, which can be fed, and so long as you *keep* feeding them, they produce more larvae. The eggs and larvae both eat mould, and they only grow into their larger forms once a queen fertilises them with her mist.'

Malu's face contorted in disgust. 'I don't like them.'

I watched one of the crawling creatures hanging from the roof. 'I wish my village had done this, too. It's ingenious.'

Urias smiled, then tread towards a nearby narrow gap. 'This way.'

We all followed in a single line through the tunnel. Noor pushed past a soldier to be right behind me.

I glanced back at him. 'Hey, thanks for stepping in front of me earlier. But I *can* take care of myself, you know?'

'Of course, yeah, I know you can,' he said.

I raised an eyebrow at him.

'It's… uh,' he said, before looking around and scratching the back of his neck. 'Just something I do, I guess. Never mind.'

'So, you've built a home inside the nest,' the Colonel called ahead. 'That's pretty smart. Our scouts rarely venture near nests if we can help it, let alone go inside.'

'Kind of confined in here, though?' Malu added.

'You just wait and see what's up ahead,' Urias said as he squeezed through another narrow gap.

I already sensed what he was talking about. Many surrounding tunnels twisted into the mountain's core like the roots of a tree. And at that core was a vast cavernous chamber, with a hidden settlement nestled in the centre.

It wasn't just any settlement though. Rather than a collection of shanty shacks and shabby tents, like Pilgrim's old village, this place was one huge building: a monolithic, terraced sandstone pyramid. Each terrace was filled with solidly constructed, aesthetically pleasing sandstone homes.

Instead of torchlight, the entire cavern was lit by hundreds of thousands, maybe *millions* of its larval residents, bathing every surface in a warm pink glow.

There were sandstone sculptures of people, geometric shapes, and creatures, each carved with care and whimsy. And most importantly, the village was home to hundreds of nomads, more than any other settlement I had ever seen. I paused in the tunnel, analysing the enormity.

Malu noticed me stopping and allowed Pilgrim ahead of her. 'You first.'

'Thanks, Mal'sy,' he said, heading through.

She lowered her brow. '*Don't* start with that, salad eater.' She then waited for me to catch up to her. 'So, what do you think? Are they gonna' help us?'

'They will,' I answered as I squeezed through the last gap and took in the sight for real.

Malu also came through and joined the rest of us on a small precipice overlooking the cavern. All my people were awestruck by the grandiose city under twinkling pink starlight.

'Like us, they've got something worth fighting for.'

Nineteen: Satisfaction

Colony

Under New Elysia

The dark tunnels were cold as usual. But that didn't matter when I was in the warm, coiling embrace of my necrolisk queen. I patted and rubbed her soft abdomen underbelly. Her stomach growled and churned, eating itself further out of starvation. She had no larvae left to cannibalise.

Even when weakened, I admired her beauty. She was at least five times larger than any of her children, and far more elongated.

She opened her jaws and bellowed, shaking the cave. I sensed and shared her anger. Our patience was running thin. The swarm snarled, snapping their claws and legs in a macabre dance, one they soon wouldn't have the energy to perform.

'I know, I know,' I said gently, letting my thoughts drift into theirs. 'But if we attack, many more of us will die.'

On the far side of the city, one of my family was in the perfect position to strike, burrowed under a street. It sensed a person step over it. *Oh*, how easy it would be to let that one loose and go on a spree. To spring out and taste that warm bag of blood, before letting it drip down the hole to the others.

'Just one,' it begged. 'Just one bag. Rip. Tear. Taste and feast. The warm filling dripping on our tongues.'

I couldn't take this anymore. It was so hard to keep my family in line when a banquet of easy prey roamed just above them.

I thought back to my encounter with Tau earlier in the day. I didn't think she had it in her to terrify me like that. I went in there intending to have every one of my demands met, only to leave with my tail between my legs.

If I didn't know any better, I'd say she had the same power as my old Patriarch, Mycol. Her aura reminded me of his, one of bitter spite, selfishness, and death. When she grabbed me, my very life was draining away, just like with him. The entire brood shivered, feeling my fears.

Maybe they were right. Maybe it was time for us to leave this place. To be free of these despicable acolytes and their politics.

One of my scouts by the mine's entrance excitedly shared its thoughts. Soon all the guards were buzzing. 'Intruder! Intruder! May we feast?'

It was a solitary man, large and muscular. Hooded robes concealed his face. He approached the entrance, ignoring the obvious necrolisk presence.

Tau's people knew our agreement, to never come here. What was this juicy morsel doing?

He grabbed hold of his robes with one hand and tore them clean off, revealing a dark blue undersuit. He had a strong jaw and big eyebrows. His hair was short and black. I had no idea who this man *thought* he was, but if suicide was what he wanted, then we would appreciate the free meal.

'Kill him,' I whispered.

All twenty-three of my entrance guards shrieked in joy, clanging their claws together in anticipation. They charged out of the cave towards him.

The man's face showed no emotion at all. I had to admit, quite brave.

The first of my family reached him, slashing at his torso, but each pincer bounced off as though he were made of solid steel. The necrolisks reeled back in surprise, but went in for a second attack, this time to bite. As one placed its jaws around him, the teeth clamped down and shattered in places.

The man continued to take no notice of them, instead levitating off the ground and flying overhead. As he floated into the cave, his clothing lit up and illuminated his surroundings.

My family tracked him with their eyes. 'What is that? Is it edible? Why is it here? Do we follow?'

'Defend me!' I yelled, jumping up from the queen's warm belly.

The entire nest reacted, retreating to me through the thousands of winding tunnels.

The man was taking every correct path towards me, as though he knew *exactly* where I was. He was almost upon my innermost sanctuary.

The queen reared up, preparing to defend me with its life. Hundreds of others poured into the chamber with a cacophony of roars and skitters.

And then he entered, hovering above all. He was upright with his arms folded. He floated calmly towards the queen and I, completely unafraid. His bright light was blinding, so I raised my hand to block it.

The swarm now shared my hesitance, unsure how to act. 'Let him approach,' I mentally instructed. 'If he is hostile, kill him.' A small patch of necrolisks in front parted.

The man floated down and landed in the space they made, several paces away from the queen. 'We meet the same way again, boy.'

Now that my eyes had adjusted, I poked my head out from behind the queen. 'Do I know you?'

He looked around at my family, and then back to me. 'I suppose you were *only* a toddler then. Naked, with a blood-covered mouth, and snarling like one of these beasts.'

It was something I would never forget: being abducted from my birth nest when I was little. The Male Dominion then 'civilised' me, teaching me their language and forcing me to obey. But I had always thought it was Mycol who brought me to MDC.

'That was you?'

He nodded.

'You turned me into the MD's slave.' I shook my head and gritted my teeth. 'You took my life away from me!' My family roared with me.

He reached over his shoulder for something on his back. He produced a case, unlocked it, and threw it to the ground between us. It landed and flew open.

It was my old uniform: a black suit of protective gear, with tubes and a vat filled with corrosive acid I could wear on my back. A gas mask rested on top of it all, shiny and brand new.

'And now, I'm here to give it back.'

I stared into his cold, dark eyes and waited.

He tilted his head slightly. 'Have you ever wondered what happened to your parents?'

I laughed. 'I couldn't care *less* about them. What you see before you is my *real* family.'

He brought a hand to his chin for a moment. 'I see.'

I pointed at him. 'I know *exactly* why you're here. And you're crazy if you think I'm going to attack the city. The citizens would be easy pickings, but their soldiers and acolytes would massacre us.'

He smirked. '*Hmph*, what if I *guaranteed* you wouldn't fail? You wouldn't be attacking them alone.'

'Guaranteed, *huh*?'

He nodded again. 'What is it you want, Colony? What would give you satisfaction?'

I paced and chuckled. 'What is it *I* want, he asks me. That's the first time the MD has ever cared.'

'Name it and it's yours.'

I paused and stared at him. 'I want Sacet dead. I want Tau… dead. I want all their lackeys dead. Especially Noor…' I looked back at the queen and placed my hand on her shell. 'And I am no longer a slave to the MD. Your guarantee includes that we will be left alone after this is all over. You do this for me, and I promise you we will leave nothing alive above.'

He smiled. 'We have a deal.'

Twenty: The Source

Sacet

Although the pink dots were mostly scattered throughout the cavern, there was a bright patch at the peak of the central pyramid. My perception surveyed a high concentration of larvae on the roof, gathered around several fleshy, open necrolisk eggs – or at least, that's what I assumed they were. The amassed light shone like a prismatic crystal, bouncing off the rocky ceiling and stalactites, which in turn washed over the terraced town with a peaceful ambience.

It was then I realised that all the structures weren't made from sandstone at all, but sand, hardened and moulded into shape by the artistry of the acolytes. Even now some were shaving away rough edges in the distance with their powers. Almost everything they owned was made the same way here, even their beds and bowls. Sand was their way of life.

The only thing that wasn't sand-ified were doors. They simply didn't bother with them, all of them were open archways instead.

I sensed at least fifty nomads already staring at us from the various levels of the terrace, none of whom seemed happy about our arrival. They watched from arched windows, flat roofs, and long balconies.

As our group approached the pyramid's base, many townsfolk took defensive postures.

Urias raised his hand of authority. 'At ease, family, we have some new guests.' He then sighed and turned to each of his accompanying warriors. 'Just to be sure, go spread the word. We don't want anyone getting hurt.'

We began to climb the stairs towards the peak, and Urias' people dispersed throughout the town to disseminate the news. The rest of us kept following Urias, one step at a time.

Like with the cave walls, the necrolisk larvae also crawled on the settlement's walls, floors, and steps. It seemed the villagers lived side-by-side with the creatures without stepping on them.

I noticed tiny, smiling faces roughly cut into the steps. Unlike the larger sand sculptures, these didn't have as much detail or skill on display.

Urias glanced back at me as we ascended. 'Admiring the artwork?'

I smiled back. '*Oh*, yes. Very… cheery.'

Our group spotted a small boy carving more little faces into a nearby wall using his sand powers. A man, perhaps the boy's father, came out the doorway. He noticed me and gave me a dirty look, before pulling his son inside.

How did all these people have the same power? They couldn't have *all* gone through the exact same traumatic experience, could they?

Urias gestured up at a cluster of youngsters scurrying along the rooftops and upper layers. 'The children here love to decorate.'

There was a tiny necrolisk larva on the next step, so I paused, sparing it from being crushed. It squirmed away to a nearby crack in the step.

The kids pointed at our group and whispered to one another. I caught the eye of one little girl. She was tanned, with short, brown hair, brown eyes and a button nose. We exchanged a smile.

Doron was panting. '*Argh*, my knee.'

Urias chuckled and jogged on the spot. 'What's the matter, old man? Can't handle the steps anymore?'

Doron muttered something incomprehensible. 'Why am I even climbing this thing? I came to see Kirai!'

Urias' elated expression sunk into a grave frown. '*Ah* yes. We haven't moved her from the crypt, I assume you remember where?'

Doron didn't delay; instead of continuing up the stairs, he turned and hobbled along the terrace's edge.

The rest of us eventually reached the topmost platform and entered another large structure. Many more nomads were inside, preparing food on long moulded tables. The warriors who had ambushed us were explaining what had happened, and the townspeople's initially fearful glares gradually changed to smiles.

There were even more children playing up here, chasing one another from room to room. When they saw us, they screamed and ran back outside.

Pilgrim shrugged. 'We're not scary, right?'

'I am,' Malu said while maintaining a deadpan expression.

Noor and I smiled at what we hoped was a joke.

The chamber was perfectly square; its edges were somehow impeccably straight. Larvae lit the room like every other, but rather than crawling freely, they had been clumped together in glass lamps suspended from the ceiling.

Urias gestured all around. 'We normally use this space for important gatherings and great feasts.' He raised his arm at all of us. 'And now that the Female Dominion is no more, we will feast in here again!'

The nomads around the room cheered and my soldiers, who were still in a bit of shock, murmured less excitedly. I sensed the building was surrounded by the village's children, who were eavesdropping and spying on what was going on through the windows.

Most of the nomads took off their masks, waved their hands at the floor and fashioned chairs for us to sit on. Others made beds on the far side of the chamber, and then covered them up with walls, each with their own doorways. Another started morphing a third long table and joined the three together. They even made hangers on the wall for our weapons and equipment. Even more nomads piled in through the entrance with platters of food and small wooden barrels.

Now that things had calmed, our two groups began to chat about the day's events and even bantered like friends. Everyone either took a seat along the massive table or gathered around it. The kids outside climbed through the windows and sat in their frames to be closer, too.

Pilgrim plonked himself on one of the chairs and let out an

exasperated sigh of relief. '*Awww* yeah, that's better. When will this day end?'

Malu found a place next to him to sit. 'We've spent half the day sitting.'

'And we've spent the other half *fighting* for our lives, so what's your point?' Pilgrim replied. 'Besides, I can't help it if those aircraft seats were originally designed for smaller frames. My back is killing me.'

One of the masked nomads approached them. 'It was always like you to *complain* after a hard day,' she said.

'*Ha*, yeah I…' Pilgrim began. 'Wait, do I know you?'

She put her hands on her hips. 'You don't recognise my voice?'

'*Hmm…* I'm sorry, but I think you might be confusing me with another dashing ruffian.'

'Pilgrim, you idiot,' she said, taking off her mask and revealing a familiar face. 'It's me, Sabikah.'

I remembered her. She was one of the nomads from Pilgrim's old village. She had long, black hair, brown eyes and tanned skin.

'Sabikah? I *thought* you were dead,' Pilgrim said, shooting up and embracing her.

'And I thought *you* were dead,' she said before looking at me. 'I remember you, too, Sacet.' Her eyes narrowed. 'You're the one who brought a Dominion soldier into our camp. And then the Dominion attacked.'

'Ah, yeah, I'm so sorry about that,' I said. 'She's the new queen now, so… *hooray*?'

'I don't understand, how did you survive?' Pilgrim asked.

She focused back on him. 'Tern and I got separated from the others. We didn't know if anyone survived, so we came back to the source of our powers.'

'What?' I asked. 'The… source?'

Her eyes fluttered and she frowned. '*Oh*, no, I just meant that I… draw my strength from my people.'

Urias shifted to the head of the table and raised his hands for quiet. 'Please, everyone? Before we enjoy each other's company I just wanted to say something.' He picked up a hardened sand cup and poured the contents of one of the barrels into it. 'Firstly, I hope Kirai is returned to us.' He put down the barrel and took a sip from his cup. 'And if that works, perhaps all those in our crypt can be brought back as well.'

The nomads all murmured and nodded in agreement.

He pointed to me. 'Secondly, Sacet, I understand why you've come. And you can *indeed* call us an ally. And we will all celebrate our new friendship tonight.'

All in the room cheered.

I waited for the noise to die down a bit. 'That's fantastic news.'

Urias raised a hand at me. 'However, we will *not* be leaving our territory, our *home*.'

There were confused mutters all around.

Sabikah stood. 'But we *want* to fight, Urias. Like we have been *doing* all this time.'

He shook his head. 'We *know* these lands, so this… is where we'll *continue* to fight.' He noticed the downtrodden looks on his people's faces. 'We are not equipped for a war in city streets, places with no sand. And we are happy here, are we not? We have everything we need.'

I shrugged at him. 'You will be provided for in our city?'

Sabikah gestured around at the nomads. 'We are warriors, no matter what terrain. And since when have *you* ever shied away from a fight?'

He looked at Sabikah. 'I wouldn't give up what we have here for anything. *If* we go there, our culture will *cease* to be. We'll just be… nameless people in their crowds, like the ones I saw today.'

I put my palms out on the sandy table. 'That's not true. Urias… look at me at least.' I waited until he looked back at me. 'Shouldn't you let your people decide for themselves?'

'My mind is made up. We will continue fighting the Male Dominion from here, and we will never attack your people again. Maybe we can open up trade as well?'

The room was so silent that I could hear the lamps squirming.

I took a deep breath. 'When all this started, *my* clan sent me on a mission to unite all the nomadic peoples together. And I learned that no matter the distance between us, we have all suffered… and we are all family.'

Urias grinned. 'A cute sentiment. But The Shroud is *too* precious for me to just… merge them with everybody else. It wouldn't be *my* family anymore.'

I shook my head again. 'Yes they would?' I glanced at Malu and Noor. 'And you'd find new family along the way. Your family doesn't disappear just because they move. They disappear when… when you fail to protect them.' Eno entered my mind, and my gaze drifted. 'If I thought like you did, then I'd have no family left.'

Pilgrim reached out to my arm. 'Sacet…'

I locked my welling eyes on him. 'Eno's dead, Pilgrim.'

Everyone at the table stared at me in complete silence.

Urias brought his palms together in thought. 'Everyone here has lost someone in this war.' He gestured at a couple of my nodding soldiers. 'Even the Dominion. Death is everywhere, and it is always tragic. That is why I'm doing this, to protect my people. I'm sorry, Sacet.'

Malu clenched her fists. 'This was a waste of our time.'

I pulled away from Pilgrim and stood, then made my way around the table. I reached Urias and looked deep into his eyes. 'You don't want to fight? Fine, but maybe you can help us another way?'

Urias shrugged. 'And what way is that?'

I narrowed my eyes. 'We will resurrect your dead… if you share the source of your power with us.'

His darting eyes widened two sizes, and he laughed. '*Wha…* what are you talking about?'

I could see right through his act. 'Don't play dumb.' I pointed at the other nomads. 'You're going to stand there and tell me *every single one* of your people has the same power by coincidence? Even the ones not related by blood?'

He shrugged again. 'There is no *source*. It's our culture, our way of life!'

I folded my arms. 'Hmph, another *shroud* to hide behind. You say you want to fight, but when the *real* war comes to your doorstep, you're the same as Doron, hiding in a cave.'

I turned and stormed towards the chamber's exit. All eyes were still on me. I paused in the doorway, remembering the necrolisk larva on the steps earlier, and how I chose to spare its life.

'You're both like… a necrolisk larva. When a foot comes, you hide between the cracks.'

I didn't look back, but I didn't need to; my perception could see all their shocked faces. I left without another word, stomped down the first flight of stairs and stopped at one of the upper-layer edges. The edge was like a balcony that overlooked the lower terraces.

Yet another larva was on the parapet wall beside me, motionless. I hopped up on top of the wall, sat next to the larva and dangled my legs over the edge. The larva's head reared, almost as if it were looking at me.

'He's just like you,' I said, frowning at the larva, but immediately feeling stupid.

'What's your name?' a voice to my side said, and I jumped.

It was the little girl from before; she had snuck up behind me. I had been so distracted that my perception didn't sense her coming.

'*Oh*, hello,' I said. 'I'm Sacet.'

'Who're you talking to?'

'*Um*, I was talking to… your food. I'm not sure why.'

'Hey, I do that, too!' the girl said with a giant grin. 'Hang on, that's my one.'

The girl noticed the larva to my side, ran over to it and picked it up. 'Come here, Nevin.' She patted it gently with her little finger, opened her robes and placed it in her glowing pink pockets.

'I'm Meevi,' she said, also jumping onto the parapet and sitting beside me. She gave me a closer look down her pocket where at least 50 of the creatures were wriggling around. 'I love keeping them all together, like a family. I give them names, too, but there's so many to remember that sometimes I forget.'

I nodded. 'I know how you feel.'

Her smile turned to a frown. 'You're not going to tell my dad, are you?'

'*Uh*, no? I'm guessing he doesn't like you playing with your food?'

Meevi shook her head. '*These* ones are not food. But maybe they can help you fight if my dad doesn't want to? They're *great* warriors, like this one here, Arty. He's my favourite.'

I smiled. 'Eavesdropping on us, were you?'

'Meevi,' Urias called out from behind us. 'Go back home.'

Meevi hid the larva with the others, then jumped back onto the terrace floor. She smiled at me. 'I like your hair.'

As she ran away, I glared at Urias. 'Relax, I'm not trying to recruit your children.'

He sighed. 'Come with me, I've got something you should see.'

I narrowed my eyes at him, but he turned and began descending the stairs before I had the chance to question him. My curiosity piqued, and I hopped off the parapet wall and pursued him. In the time I took to catch up, we went down three layers of the pyramid.

'Where are we going?' I asked.

He raised a finger to his mouth for quiet. 'Not yet.'

I nodded and patiently waited for him to lead me to the base of the pyramid. From there we followed the settlement's outer perimeter until an outcropping of cave rock obscured much of the settlement's view and light. There was another hardened sand wall back here, rougher than those in the pyramid, as though made to naturally look part of the cave wall.

Urias looked around to make sure no one was watching, then placed his palms on it. The sand loosened and parted to the sides, revealing a hidden passageway. It was never hidden to me, of course, I could see it when we first arrived in the mountain. There didn't seem to be anything special along it, just more squirming larvae to light it and eventually a dead end.

'Stay close,' he instructed. 'Watch your step.'

'Can you tell me now?' I asked again as I followed, careful to avoid standing on anything pink.

'To where we originally found the eggs.'

We trudged forward and weaved through another twisting tunnel. At one point, jutting out from the wall was an ancient stone column. To the untrained eye, it looked like any other construction in the pyramid, but this was far older and carved with actual tools.

'Petroglyphs!' I said, pointing at the collection of symbols carved in the column.

Urias raised an eyebrow. 'Ah, you recognise the dead language of our ancestors?'

I nodded. 'My grandfather taught me. Don't tell me *this* is the source?'

He smirked and gestured farther down the tunnel. 'No, no. The source is far stranger. You know… it's been a long time since someone looked better than me in an argument. And from a *teenager*, no less. How old are you now, anyway?'

'Seventeen,' I said as we continued to walk. 'I think. I've honestly lost track.'

'*Ha*, seventeen?' he replied as he hopped over a boulder partially blocking our path. 'When I was seventeen, all I thought about was survival… and girls. But look at you, trying to conquer the world. I'm sure Aberym would be proud. Azua and Enni, too.'

I jumped down from the boulder but then stopped. 'How well did you know them?'

'Very well,' Urias said. 'Although, we *both* know they weren't your *real* parents.'

I looked down at my feet as we walked. The density of the larvae was growing with every step. I accidentally stood on one with a squelch. '*Whoops*.'

'They begged me to be allowed to adopt you,' he continued. 'Most of us thought you needed to die though.' He smiled. 'But Enni, she truly did love you, and you were a cute kid. So, uh… we just… banished your family from The Shroud instead.'

'What? We were in The Shroud?'

We reached a dead end; another wall was made of sand. But again, I sensed a hidden chamber beyond it.

Urias snorted. 'Only for a little while.'

In the centre of the hidden chamber stood a stone pedestal, and atop it was a glowing piece of metal. It was only a rusted piece of shrapnel and yet it had a strange white aura about it that lit the whole chamber. I could faintly hear sand shifting nearby. A draught? Here?

Urias gave me a serious look. 'My answer still hasn't changed; I don't want my people dying in some faraway city.' He placed a hand on my shoulder and smiled. 'But… maybe *this* will help.' He threw his hands at the wall, which shifted like before, opening the chamber.

We entered and approached the pedestal. The strange piece of shrapnel was emitting a low hum. He picked it up and closed his eyes. Its glow intensified like a blinding flare. After a few moments, I peered through the adjusting light and saw him offer it to me.

'*This* is the source of my village's power. Providing it *remains* here, it is a power I'm willing to share with your armies.'

I looked at it hesitantly and then at Urias, who nodded with approval. I reached out and cupped it. As soon as I made contact, there was a flash of light, and the blinding energy swirled around my arms. It seeped into my skin, brightening it. It even lit my veins.

It felt as though my muscles were on fire and every part of my body convulsed. My rib cage was tugged upwards, and the room blurred completely. I tried to let go but it was as if my hands were fused onto it.

The artefact dimmed and the white lines faded away, as did the burning pain. I regained control, staggered forward and carefully placed the still-glowing shrapnel back onto the pedestal.

While still shaking, I examined my hands and my body to see if I had been burned.

Urias chuckled. 'You're fine, trust me. You're *better*.' He gestured at the cave's sand floor.

I turned and brought my hands up, and as I did so, the sand on the floor floated. It was the strangest feeling; it felt like I was tugging on an invisible, weightless sheet. The sand followed my hand movements, and as I twisted my wrists in a circle, so did the sand. I released my fingers to let it all drop to the ground.

He folded his arms. 'The power you have now isn't permanent. The longest it has ever lasted is half a cycle. Sometimes it's only a few days with extended use. Eventually, it runs out and you have to touch this again to recharge.'

'Incredible...'

His smile faded. 'Yes. But you must understand how important this object is to us. If it is ever taken from here...'

I nodded. 'I understand. I can portal my soldiers here under the strictest supervision.' I leaned down and inspected it closer. 'What *is* it, exactly?'

He leant over it, too. '*Oh*, I have *no* idea. I was hoping *you* would know. It was scavenged from... *your* aircraft.'

'What?'

Urias circled the pedestal. 'About eleven cycles ago, Doron and I were on a patrol. He wasn't afraid of fighting back then. He even brought his eldest son along.'

'You mean Pilgrim?'

Urias smiled. 'My nephew, Saladire, yes.' He stopped smiling and circled back. 'There were others, a whole scouting party. We shot down an aircraft and then checked the wreckage. It was filled with children. Do you remember?'

I clenched my fists and breathed quicker. 'That... was you?'

He saw how tense I had become. 'I'm sorry.'

I lashed out, punching him in the chin. He fell back into the sand.

'We were little kids! Little kids and you killed them!' I raised my hands, and a blanket of sand wrapped around him.

He used his powers back to keep the sand at bay. 'Your people had killed hundreds of mine before then, *including* children. It was war! Sacet, please, enough!'

I lowered my hands and turned my back on him. 'You monsters...'

We both breathed deeply. My memories were letting me relive that day all over again.

'I'm sorry to tell you... but... your parents were there that day, too.'

My mouth contorted and I turned back around. 'Don't you *dare* lie to me!'

He raised his hands in defence. 'It's true. They didn't take part in the killings. They stayed back. Enni was too afraid to even watch. Then we all saw *you*.'

'Up on the rocks.'

He nodded. 'That's right. It was Azua, Sali then Enni that chased after you. Enni was adamant, she didn't want us to shoot.'

He paced around the pedestal. 'After they left, that's when we saw the light.' He gestured his hands out like an explosion. 'It was a flash in the sky... and... sunrays beamed down in random directions. One of them hit this piece of the aircraft debris.' He looked at the shrapnel. 'And it started to glow white. Looking back on it now, I was pretty stupid to pick it up. But something drew me to it, I couldn't help it.'

'And the *source* of the light?' I asked.

'We don't know,' he replied. 'A gift from a higher power, perhaps?'

I shook my head. 'This doesn't make *any* sense. Your people *shot* me that day. As I was running, I felt a pain in my back, and I fell. Are you going to try and tell me that was my parents?'

He frowned. 'I'm being completely honest with you, Sacet. *No one* shot you.'

Twenty-One: When I'm With You

'Have a drink, Sacet, you should be celebrating,' Doron said, breaking my concentration. He shoved a drink into my hand from the other side of the long table. It was the first time I had seen him sincerely smile.

Everyone was either sitting at the long table or lounging on the new sandy furniture throughout the chamber at the pyramid's peak, conversing and generally just having a good time. There were even more nomads than before, the chamber was almost full.

More barrels had been brought up since I was gone, each filled with the same alcohol Aberym used to drink. I knew well enough what it did to *his* behaviour, so it was probably best I didn't have any.

Our soldiers and the nomads were watching Malu with anticipation as she reached for a larva on the table and picked it up.

'Come on, Mal'sy,' Pilgrim slurred, before hiccupping, already affected by the liquor.

She winced, quickly popped it in her mouth, closed her eyes and chewed. Many cheered and some laughed.

Eventually, she swallowed and opened her eyes again. 'It's actually not as bad as I thought.'

'Told you,' one of the young men said, passing her a drink.

'What is this stuff anyway?' she asked, staring down into the black, murky liquid.

'What?' the man replied. 'Are you telling me you don't know what bomb juice is? I thought you said you used to be a nomad?'

Malu shrugged. 'Well, maybe my people up in Revus had better taste.' She took another look at it before taking a sip, but then immediately spat it out.

The table burst into laughter again.

Malu coughed and retched, before glaring at them. 'Are you playing a joke on me? What is this, really?'

They all looked at each other and smiled. 'Bomb juice!' they shouted, almost in unison.

Sabikah gave a firm pat on Malu's back. 'It's a mix of water, yeast, a few herbs and chemicals to give it a kick. Fermented to perfection.'

The others kept chatting and knocking their mugs together; the banter echoed off the chamber walls. The nomads were much louder than our soldiers.

Nako was leaning against the entrance. She seemed to be avoiding the nomads, like they disgusted her. Hopefully, she'd get over that.

Sabikah had a seat with a now-drunk Pilgrim. He pulled her in close and tried to discretely tell her something. However, he was pointing at me, and every so often he'd let a word slip at excessive volume. I locked eyes with Sabikah and rolled my eyes. She smiled.

Doron was eyeing me and gesturing at my drink. I finally took a swig. Awful, it burned all the way down. The old man gave me an approving nod.

I pictured the desert outside the mountain and created a tiny portal inside the bottom of my cup. The liquid splashed onto the desert ground. I closed the portal again, raised my cup at Doron and nodded back. 'It's good.' I pretended to take another giant swig and swallowed.

Noor was passed a mug as well but looked at it with confusion. He took a quick sip, shrugged, and then took another.

The Colonel and her troops surrounded a barrel, eagerly testing it for themselves. It was like everyone's egos were tied up in the drink itself, and they were all pretending it tasted great to one-up each other. I didn't get it.

Malu raised an eyebrow. 'It can't be *good* for you, surely?'

Doron smiled. 'Definitely not. But we don't have to worry about that now that we have this healing queen of yours.' Doron's dead wife, Kirai, was outside the building, her remains wrapped in a large burlap sack.

I thought back to Tau. 'About that, maybe it's time we headed back.'

Those who heard me booed and jeered, even one of my own soldiers.

The Colonel approached me from behind and placed a hand on my shoulder. 'Commander, are you sure?' She knelt beside me with a drink in her hand.

'Colonel,' I began, 'I…'

'My name's Kinru, by the way,' she interrupted, taking a swig.

'*Oh*, right. Sorry, I… should have made the effort to…'

She grinned. 'That's alright. It's easy to forget to ask when you've got so much on your plate, right? May I speak freely?'

'Of course. What's wrong?'

'Nothing is wrong. Look around you.'

I did as she suggested, and saw laughter, smiles and camaraderie.

She pointed at her squadmates. 'Tactically speaking, staying the night will be good for morale as well as building trust.' She gestured to Malu as well, who was locked in a conversation with the young man who gave her a drink.

'I guess you're right about that,' I said. 'I suppose I've just felt a bit…'

'Rushed?' another voice behind me suggested. It was Sabikah. 'So don't you think you've earned a small, one-night break?' She looked at Kinru. 'Can I steal her for a moment?'

Kinru happily nodded and stood. I stood, too, and Sabikah guided me away from the others.

'Sabikah, again, I'm so sorry about what my brother and I… what *I* caused back then.'

She raised her hands. 'Sacet, enough. You weren't the one who burned down the village and killed those people. And you've tried to make it right since then.'

My eyes darted when I realised that Noor had been involved in that attack. We reached the side of the chamber and leaned against the wall.

'I still *feel* awful about it,' I continued.

She punched me in the shoulder. 'Would you just cheer up? Is it always doom and gloom with you? Everyone else is having fun, you should, too.'

I shrugged and nodded. 'Sure, I'll *try*.'

'You know that Noor boy likes you, right?'

My eyes widened. '*Errrr*?' I felt my cheeks go warm. 'What?'

I looked over and saw Pilgrim sitting next to him. Noor looked just as awkward as I did.

Sabikah smirked. 'Pilgrim tells me he's a nice guy. And from what I hear, he's *crazy* about you. What do you think about him?'

I shrugged and looked at the floor. '*Uhhh*, he's… nice.'

'Have you considered… you know?'

I pushed off the wall. 'We're at war, we don't have time…'

'Why not? What about your parents? They had time. And what about the rest of us? If Pilgrim stopped drinking and making a fool of himself, tonight I might even…'

'Please, stop…' I sighed. 'Back when I was a nomad, maybe. I thought about boys then. But now I just feel *angry* all the time.' I folded my arms. 'Look, I have noticed him sometimes acting… *strangely* towards me.'

Sabikah giggled and folded her arms. 'I bet you have, too. And the poor guy *has* lived in the MD his whole life. He's probably very confused.'

I raised my eyebrows at her. 'We only *just* got everyone off the hormone suppressants. Could that have something to do with it?'

As Pilgrim was coaching him, Noor briefly glanced over his shoulder at me.

'Probably.' She looked at him for a moment. 'Have you ever just *talked* to him? About something other than the war and acolyte powers?'

I shrugged. 'Sometimes. But he closes up whenever I ask anything personal.'

'Well then, maybe tonight's the night you pry it out of him?'

I nodded with confidence. 'Okay, I'll go over and do just that.'

She nodded back. 'That's right. You're just going to talk. Nothing scary about that.'

'Right.'

Sabikah took another gulp, emptying her mug this time. 'I'm going to get another drink, and you're going over *there* now,' she said, gesturing at Noor with her eyes.

She turned and walked back to the barrel for a refill. Pilgrim noticed her walking by, so he stood and left Noor by himself.

Noor looked back at me from his seat, and we locked eyes.

I shook my head and smiled, before approaching and sitting next to him. 'Did you just get the same speech I got?'

'Yeah, pretty much. Awkward, *huh*?'

One of the nomads reached over the table and handed me another cup of liquor. 'Here you go, have a refill.'

I forced a smile. 'Great, thanks.'

After he left, Noor looked back at me. 'What do you think of the drink?'

'I don't think it's for me.'

'*Ha*, yeah, I've never had anything like this in the MD or in New Elysia, that's for sure.' He paused and briefly scanned the room before looking back. 'So, you have this sand power now, right?'

'Yeah.'

We both looked silently forward at the table. Noor played with the necrolisk larvae in his bowl, stirring them around with his finger. It seemed like we were the only ones not talking much.

He cleared his throat. 'I… meant to go after you before when you walked out.'

I smiled. 'And why didn't you?'

Noor gestured to Urias on the other side of the room. 'He got up after you left and said he'd handle it, told everyone to stay.'

I felt my cheeks warm again. 'I probably would have liked it if you had come out to talk with me.'

'Then let's talk now. Is everything going okay with you?'

I shifted in my seat. 'Well, there is a war going on, and my brother is probably dead.'

'Eno isn't dead. He's probably missing you, very much. Don't give up hope.'

'I'll try.' I shifted closer to Noor and gave him a solemn look. 'Speaking of family, when are you going to tell me what happened to yours?'

Noor shifted awkwardly in his seat. 'I'd rather not. I don't even think about them… it's no big deal.'

I reached out and grabbed his wrist. We locked eyes. 'Please. I *want* to know.'

He paused again and slowly nodded. I let go of his wrist.

'When I was a… a baby, my family apparently had this big floor in a complex all to ourselves. We were powerful and well-liked. I had an older brother, two uncles, three cousins… and my dad.' He looked away. 'I never knew my mother. I was told she died in prison.'

He shrugged. 'I was too young to remember, but the story goes that one day they collectively sort of… snapped. They went from loyal soldiers to always looking over their shoulders, paranoid. One day, they bundled me up in rags and escaped MDC.

'With their connections, they got pretty far: across Avarut's Bay, past Falerra, and even reaching the Unclaimed Wastes. But in the end, they were hunted down and shot for being traitors. The soldiers took me home, and I was raised in the barracks.'

Noor put his face in his hands. 'When I grew up, I hated my family *so* much. I got my powers from that hate.' He leant back in his seat. 'The king visited me a few times. I should have killed him then and there, had I known what I know now. He made me feel ashamed of my family. Convinced me to be better by hating women even more.'

He closed his eyes and took a giant swig of his drink. 'I have over… three thousand confirmed kills in his name. Before you freed me, the last count was three thousand… two hundred… and sixty-seven.'

I rubbed his shoulder. 'It's not your fault.'

He shook his head. 'It is, I did it all *willingly*.'

'It was their brainwashing.'

He straightened up and narrowed his eyes. 'And when I learnt the truth about this war, I finally realised *why* they were executed. They must have found out the truth.'

'Do you miss them?'

He winced, as though I asked something embarrassing. 'I miss my dad. But if he was brought back… I wouldn't be able to… tell him how I felt. The truth destroyed the old me, but it also didn't. I have to live with what I've done for the rest of my life.'

I didn't know how to comfort him, so I kept rubbing his shoulder.

'Sacet, drink your damn drink!' Pilgrim yelled from his seat on the other side of the table. He and Sabikah had been casually watching us this entire time.

I gruffly sighed, picked up my cup and showed it to Pilgrim, before having the tiniest of swigs.

Noor stared into my eyes again. 'You're the reason I'm still here, Sacet. I love how *brave* you are, how you take charge. You and I, we have a lot of anger inside. But when I'm with you, it doesn't feel so bad.'

I nodded. 'Yeah, it's more like... justice. What's right. I'm tired of being their puppet.'

Noor had a determined look in his eyes. 'Me, too, of being their weapon. No more for either of us.' He shot up from his seat and raised his cup. 'Everyone, listen!'

The entire room turned after hearing his deep, commanding voice.

'Raise your drinks like me,' he instructed, and everyone did so, including me.

'What's this?' Malu interrupted.

'Tonight, we salute those that have fallen in the face of the Dominion. And tomorrow, we avenge them!'

With that, Noor downed the rest of his drink in one go. The room cheered again and joined in.

I sipped my drink, too, and did my best to keep it down. My face still felt warm, and I couldn't help but smile. This was the most passionate I had ever seen him.

He turned to me. 'I feel energised, like I could take on the whole MD right now. Feels good.'

I frantically nodded. 'Do you want to maybe go get some fresh air? Or... fresher air? We'd still be in a cave.'

'Okay,' Noor said as I stood.

Pilgrim was now elbowing those around him and signalling in our direction. He had a huge grin. I noticed a few others watch as the two of us exited. We headed to the nearest balcony.

Noor leaned over the parapet. 'That felt really good. I think I really needed to get that off my chest.'

I offered my hand for him to hold. 'I'm glad you told me.'

He turned, took it and offered his other free hand to mine. I couldn't help but smile again as I grabbed it.

He gently pulled me closer to him. 'I'm glad you asked.'

We both closed our eyes and tilted our heads. I felt his lips press against mine. They were soft and smooth. The larvae on the cavern walls twinkled as if everything was right with the world.

After a short while, I pulled away. 'Your breath tastes like that drink.'

He laughed. 'That wasn't part of the plan.'

'This was planned?'

We both shared a short giggle before I pulled on his arm for another kiss.

Twenty-Two: It's War

The sand beds were surprisingly comfy, and we had plenty of sheets over us made from some sort of animal skin. And the robes the nomads gave us to sleep in were warmer than our armour, but I still couldn't fall asleep.

Noor had gone out like a light pretty much immediately after we spooned. I was glad he didn't insist on taking the next step tonight. I glanced back at him as he peacefully slept. He was so cute like this. I smiled and rested my head back on the pillow.

Instead of moonlight, the countless pink larvae shone through the window right next to our bed. All the small noises of life throughout the cavern were gentle, yet constant. None of that bothered me either.

It was Urias' story that had me perplexed. It just didn't make sense. How did light beams come from the sky and grant an inanimate object acolyte power, which could then be shared by anyone who touched it?

As I closed my eyes again, I sensed someone still wandering about outside on the upper terrace balcony. It was Sabikah. What was she still doing up?

She was oddly silent, each step producing almost no noise. She approached our window and stopped to look in, so I pretended to be asleep.

Sabikah slowly climbed through and slunk closer, almost floating. I didn't move a muscle. Whatever she was doing, I'd catch her in the act. Her clothes and even her flesh shifted away like sand as she reached into her stomach and pulled out a dagger. I waited patiently, not even breathing.

She raised the dagger over us. As it came down over Noor, I opened my eyes and grabbed her arm. 'Noor, Noor! Wake up!'

Sabikah's free hand formed a fist and thwacked me in the head. I released my hands but kicked my leg out from the sheets into her body. She stumbled back.

Noor shook himself awake, jumping up from the bed and pointing both his palms at her. As I clutched my cheek in pain, he let loose a red beam of intense heat. On contact, her body exploded in a cloud of sand.

Noor turned and helped me up. 'Are you hurt?'

The sand was shaking and shifting on its own. It rose and spun like a whirlwind before breezing back out the window.

I pointed at the sand. 'I'm fine. After her!'

Noor pulled on my hand, and we gave chase, running and vaulting through the window. But she was already gone.

'Where did she go?' Noor asked. 'Was that Sabikah? What was she doing?'

'Wait a moment.' I closed my eyes and observed my surroundings in greater detail.

By our feet, I sensed splits in the hardened sand. The parted sand had left a trail down the pyramid steps, through the village and into the tunnels. The floating cloud of sand rapidly flew under the tidal lock and had reached the ocean already. It was almost out of my perception's range.

'Hold onto me.'

Noor grabbed my arm. I opened a portal under our feet, dropping us onto the beach directly in the would-be assassin's path. The two of us separated and held our hands up at the floating cloud, which stopped and hovered in place.

The moonlight illuminated the deserted shore with a soft glow. The deep, dark-blue tides crashed at our feet.

'That's far enough, Neva,' I called out.

Noor raised an eyebrow and glanced at me briefly. 'The one you sent to space?'

The sand reformed into a body we recognised. It was the pilot, Nako. She smirked. 'Where to, Commander?'

'Nako?' Noor and I exclaimed together.

She laughed and reformed again, this time into Neva's regular body. She had even longer, luscious blonde hair. Her clothing morphed into golden, sparkling robes with intricate patterns. 'No, you were right the first time.'

'What are you doing here?' I shouted.

She groaned and played with her hair. 'To kill your new boy toy. But we both know I'm not answering any more of your stupid questions. That was a freebie.' She started walking towards us, so we backed away. 'And you don't have the means to kill me. So, either send me to space again or get out of my way.'

I gritted my teeth and strained my wrists.

She froze in place and her smirk disappeared. 'Impossible. I'm not made of sand!'

I shrugged. 'Close enough to.' With that I smacked my hands downwards, pinning her to the ground. She tried to transform again but I clenched my fingers and kept her together.

Noor nodded, impressed. 'Nice work. We should get reinforcements.'

I nodded back. While still keeping Neva in place, I closed my eyes and concentrated back on the pyramid's peak. A portal back to the upper terrace balcony opened beside us.

Neva was clawing the ground, trying to escape my grasp. 'I was going to settle for just him, but now I'm going to kill them all!'

'Shut up,' I said, before using my power to slam her face into the ground.

Noor covered me as I forcibly dragged Neva's body along the sand and through the portal. After Noor came through, the portal closed.

Commotion had spread across the village in our absence.

Hundreds of nomads were running about the walkways below, no doubt searching for enemies.

'I'll get the others,' Noor said as he ran into the building.

'Hurry.' I clenched my fingers tighter again and Neva moaned in pain. 'Why were you trying to kill him?'

She gave a long, drawn-out laugh. 'You're so pathetic. You *still* haven't worked it out? If we were *actually* trying to kill you, you and your friends wouldn't have lasted a day.'

I didn't let up, I wanted answers. 'Why did your leader say I wasn't ready? Ready for what?'

Neva remained motionless but continued smiling, amused by my confusion. My hands were shaking.

'Answer me!' I screamed. She cackled in response.

There were footsteps inside the nearby chamber. Noor and a mass of others sprinted over to us. Malu, Kinru and her soldiers, Pilgrim and his father, the *real* Sabikah and a bunch of other nomads piled out of the room and surrounded Neva. The nomads saw what I was doing and joined in, taking over for me with their powers to keep Neva in place flat on the ground.

'Who is this?' Sabikah asked.

'I'm a Concordite spy,' Neva answered with another smirk, 'here to steal your *precious* shrapnel.'

'What?' one of the nomads said. Others joined in with similar shocked noises. Over half of them turned to our soldiers aggressively.

Sabikah narrowed her eyes at me. 'Sacet, if that's true, our alliance is off!'

I shook my head. 'She lies, she's an *enemy* spy.'

'And a shapeshifter,' Noor added. 'She was hiding among our ranks.'

Malu's fingers twitched. 'Her name is Neva. One of the former queen's lackeys.' She looked at me. 'I have the power to kill her.'

'No,' I said. 'We need answers first.'

'Where is it?' I heard a man shout from the bottom of the pyramid steps.

It was Urias. He had seen our congregation. His death stare was intense. He pointed his fists to the path and then thrashed them up. This exploded the ground at his feet, launching him up. He careened through the air all the way to the peak, then used his power again to cushion his fall.

At least 100 more nomads from the village below ran up the stairs, too. All got as close to the group as they could.

'Everyone back!' Urias bellowed, and the crowd gave him space to come through. He pointed at our prisoner. 'Does she have it?'

Neva was still smiling, enjoying all of this. 'Our plan was to steal the shrapnel *all* along. This has all been an elaborate hoax. My commander here is hiding it from you in our city.'

Everyone looked around in a panic.

I calmly raised my palms at them. 'All lies. Please trust us, we are *not* the enemy. *She* is.'

'The artifact is gone?' Doron asked.

Neva chortled again. '*Looooong* gone.'

I remembered Neva's dagger from earlier, and that she had concealed it inside her own body. 'It might be inside of her.'

Urias gritted his teeth. 'Rip her apart!'

At least ten nomads clenched their hands towards Neva and ripped them back. Neva screamed as her body was torn apart. Each piece converted to sand again. There was nothing else there.

Urias' face was now red. As the nomads let Neva piece her body back together, Urias stormed over to me and grabbed me by the collar. 'What did I tell you? This is *exactly* why I didn't want to trust you with it.'

Noor quickly intercepted him and pushed him away from me.

Urias turned his wrath instead to Neva, stomping over to her. 'Tell me where it is, or we will…'

'Urias, don't touch her!' I called out. 'Her power can melt you.'

Neva sighed. 'It's fine, Sacet. Why bother hurting him when Tau will just heal… oh… no, wait? Maybe she *can't* anymore?' She turned her head and looked up at me. 'While you've all been drinking and celebrating your mediocrity together, we *took* your queen.'

My jaw dropped. I stumbled back, almost falling over.

'No!' Doron shouted. 'No, no, no! You scumbering trollop, I'll… I'll…'

'You'll what, old man?' Neva interrupted. 'Invent more dumb-sounding words?'

Noor bent over her. 'Where is she?'

'Far. *Faaar… faaar… far, far, far…*' she sang while giggling. 'Hey? Hey, Sacet? I saw your brother, you know?'

My knees weakened to jelly. '*Wha*-what?'

Pilgrim put his hand on my shoulder. 'She's trying to mess with you. Don't listen.'

'No, truly,' she continued. 'I saw him. I made him think that I killed you. Isn't that funny?' She gave a fake cry. 'Oh, he's so sad now. And angry.'

Sabikah's lips curled. 'That's enough poison from you!'

She brought one of her fists down like a hammer in the air, and as she did, Neva's head was crushed into the sand and exploded into grains again. The nomads helped crush up every bit of Neva and formed her into a hovering sandball.

Urias glared as though he were about to kill me. 'If you… don't find it.'

I didn't respond, instead dropping to my knees and staring ahead. How could I even begin to sort Neva's truth from lies? Was my brother truly alive, after all this time?

Noticing my inability to speak, Noor stepped closer to Urias. 'Wherever it is, our queen will be there, too. We're in this together.'

Urias glanced at his tribe. There must have been a few hundred of them gathered around the peak. Warriors and their families. He looked back at me. 'I have your word they'll be provided for? Treated as equals?'

I nodded as I slowly stood.

'Everyone,' he yelled as he shifted to the top of the steps. 'It is no longer safe here. We must… retreat to our new ally's city. Bring only what you can carry.'

As a village full of murmurs echoed throughout the cavern, Urias turned back to me. 'If I find out that *you* orchestrated all of this…'

A portal to the Military Quad opened. I clenched my fists as I walked through it. 'If *I* was your enemy, Urias, you'd already be dead.'

Noor, Malu, Pilgrim, Doron, Urias, our squad of soldiers and at least twenty nomads followed me down the steel hallway. The rest of the villagers were being escorted to the mess hall until we had a place to put them. Neva floated alongside us as a ball against her will. Kirai's body bag was slung over Doron's shoulder.

The doors to the meeting room opened automatically as we approached. The room was filled with soldiers, all anxiously conversing. Sitting in the highest chair on the podium was Marid. The other commanders, Terel, Tarsus, and Coleo were in the other seats.

My nomad guests shot dirty looks at the soldiers in the audience. The uneasy chatter quieted. We descended the stairs, and I approached the podium alone.

Marid shot up. 'Where have you been? We thought you had crashed. We've been searching—'

'Never mind that,' I interrupted, 'what have they done with Tau?'

Malu approached, looked at Commander Coleo and gestured to the hovering ball of sand that was being pulled down the stairs. 'The star pilot the queen asked you to assign us was Neva in disguise.'

Coleo looked genuinely shocked. 'What? But she—'

I pointed at Coleo. 'Arrest her!'

Everyone was taken off guard. Including a shocked group of podium guards, who eventually sprang forward and grabbed Coleo.

'What is happening?' she said as she was dragged away. 'I didn't do any—'

'Until you are cleared of suspicion, you are *relieved* of your duties,' I said with a scowl. I turned back to Malu. 'Colonels Malu and Kinru. You, your soldiers and some nomads escort Neva to a cell in the inhibitor prison. Heavy guard detail. Interrogate her. No mercy.'

Kinru saluted. 'Yes, Commander!'

'With pleasure,' Malu said. 'I'll liquefy her grain by grain if I have to.' She looked at the nomads restraining the ball. 'This way.' They led them back up the stairs and out the door.

Marid frowned. 'Commander Sacet, I think we should speak privately about this. Terel, you can go over the defence plans.' As Terel got out of her chair and ascended the podium, Marid climbed down with her sword cane and approached me. 'One moment.' She pulled out a small device and pressed a button, then looked back at me. 'My chambers. Your friends can stay here.'

'*Uh*, no,' Urias said. 'There's going to be no secrets between us.'

Doron nodded angrily in agreement, as did their remaining comrades.

Marid gave a short, respectful bow to them. 'Very well.'

I pointed at Marid. 'What was that button about?'

She showed me the device. 'This? I was deactivating… the *thing* we talked about before you portalled. Or would you rather have *me* arrested, too?'

I huffed, closed my eyes and pictured Marid's chambers. The Troop Commander's office was a nearby private room. The portal opened and she entered first. The rest of us followed, leaving Terel to address the troops, and I closed the portal once we were all through.

Marid went behind her desk but didn't sit down. 'I see you've heard. The queen was taken last night from her personal chambers.'

Malu shook her head and whimpered. 'Poor Tau.'

I gritted my teeth and tensed my whole body. 'Who, Marid? Who did this?'

'The security footage was corrupted,' Marid explained, bending over her desk. 'But I recovered some of it with Terel's help. It was Amiki, and several other Royal Guards under her command.'

Doron gently sat Kirai's bag up against the wall, sat in one of the chairs and dropped his head. 'I knew this was all too good to be true.'

Marid frowned at Noor. 'I'm sorry to say Tetsu was taken as well.'

Noor burst forward and smashed the desk with his fists. 'Where was the rest of the Royal Guard? Where were you?'

Marid went red. 'No, where were *you*? We tried contacting you over and over!' She averted her eyes. 'Amiki manipulated the roster. We only discovered what happened when the next shift came through.' She shook her head. 'I told you all to stay. I practically *begged* you.'

Doron looked up. 'Where is this queen of yours now?'

Pilgrim's eyes widened. 'MDC?'

Marid shook her head. 'I doubt it'd be *that* obvious. She could be anywhere.'

I gestured over my shoulder. 'Then what was that meeting for if we don't know where she is?'

Marid sighed. 'When news of the queen's abduction leaked, riots broke out throughout the sectors. New puppet leaders are taking over. Bombs have gone off in every one of our cities. Every aircraft in our hangar here was detonated as well. Our defences here have been hacked and crippled. Spies... everywhere. This was all coordinated.'

She sat in her chair and put her head in her hands. 'Estimates of over twenty thousand people dead, and that's just the beginning. The puppet governments are blaming *us* for the attacks. Some of our stupider citizens believe them. Without the support of those cities, we won't have enough food and supplies coming in to survive. Long-term, we don't have much time left. That meeting was... to organise our last stand here.'

I waved my finger at her. 'And be their puppets yet again? Waiting for death? No, we counterattack.'

Marid gawked. 'Sacet, haven't you been listening to *anything* I've said?'

I paced back and forth. 'We give them an ultimatum. Obey or be destroyed.'

Noor gestured to me. 'She's right. We can't just sit here.'

'Sacet, really...'

I clenched my fist. 'We attack one of these puppet governments with so much force that it sets an example of fear to the others. We keep the target secret between us in this room until the very last moment. We execute the traitors.

'Once the other sectors are back under our control, we finally do it. The big push we've been talking about. We obliterate the MD. Bring justice to their king. And then we scour every corner of their cities until we get our queen back.' I looked back at Urias. 'And your property, too.'

Urias nodded, although he stared at me with reluctance.

Noor stood beside me. 'Let's do it.'

Marid continued shaking her head. 'Insanity... we'd be leaving the city defenceless.'

I leant on the desk. 'Then we attack fast, surgically, before the spies can report to their masters. Before they can make another plan to mess with us.' I pointed back at Urias. 'I've seen the sand acolytes' power. With all of them together they could blanket the target city in a thick sandstorm. No one will be able to see but us.'

Marid folded her arms. 'And what if that man shows up again?'

I glowered back. 'Then I'll fight him, and this time I *won't* be afraid. I'll find a way to kill him.'

She closed her eyes. 'In times of crisis, all commanders must defer to the acolyte commander's orders, so I have no choice but to do as you say. You're really going to go through with this, aren't you? I can't talk you out of it?'

'Where are my sons?' Doron interrupted, slowly looking up at us.

We all looked at him, confused. I looked at Marid, hoping she would know.

'Your Pilgrim's father?' Marid asked and Doron nodded. 'I'm sorry, but they left. As I understand it, the queen couldn't help them. They insulted her and left without saying where they were going.'

Doron shot up, picked up the chair and flung it at Noor.

'Ow, hey!' Noor responded, raising his palms at him.

I wrenched them down again. 'Not in here.'

Doron seethed at the two of us. 'You lied to me! I've been following you fools around for days when I should have been finding my boys.' He turned and jabbed Urias in the chest. 'This is why we left you. There is no winning this cursed war. It just drags you deeper and deeper until the people you love start dying, one by one.'

Urias held his tongue but looked equally as furious. Doron picked up Kirai's body bag and made for the door. He left without saying another word.

'Should I go after him?' Urias suggested.

Pilgrim shook his head. 'No, he made his choice a long time ago.'

I turned back to Marid. 'And we've made ours. Prepare for war.'

Twenty-Three: The Lone Fool

Eno

'Wake up,' I heard a voice say. 'Guys, come on. Get up, please!'

It was Keenu and he was pacing around the dorm between our beds. The other boys and I slowly came to, rubbing our eyes and yawning, before pushing our sheets aside and hopping out of bed.

Keenu's hands were shaking. 'Where is he? Someone must know.' I had never seen him so agitated before.

Mui felt his way closer to us. 'Who?'

'Sozha,' Keenu said, pointing over at Sozha's empty bed. 'Did anyone notice what time he woke up?'

'Relax, he probably just went downstairs early,' Nadan suggested. 'Maybe he's having a bog?'

'No, I've looked there already,' Keenu replied, his entire body now swaying anxiously. 'We looked everywhere. He's *not* in the building. Did he speak to any of you?'

This all felt too surreal. Mui's eyes widened, probably thinking the same as me: Mycol had taken Sozha away in the night and killed him.

I glanced out the window to the courtyard and saw over a hundred armoured soldiers in formation. Their superiors were barking orders and sending them in different directions. It looked more serious than the usual morning drills.

'What am I going to say to him?' Keenu said, pulling his hair and making for the door. 'Come on, Mycol is waiting.' He led us to the stairwell.

As we descended, Nadan, guiding his brother as always, looked back at him. 'I'm not going to let him get away with it this time. Enough is enough.'

Mui feverishly shook his head. 'No, say nothing! Promise me you won't say anything.'

But as we landed at the stairwell's bottom, it was too late to make that promise, for we could see the main living quarters from here. The other two dorms had already lined up in formation. A line of at least ten Terror Guards mirrored the boys with their batons ready. It was the first time I had seen them inside the building.

Mycol was pacing back and forth along the line. He seemed even bigger, more bulbous than yesterday. We assembled at the end of the line and stood to attention, waiting for his usual King's Glory greeting, but it never came.

'Dorm... leader... three,' he uttered with a hint of anger in his otherwise quiet voice.

Keenu stepped forward, still shaking. 'Y-y-yes, sir!'

Mycol leered in Keenu's direction. Everyone was silent. Keenu's knees shook.

'Does your... dorm... know anything?'

'No, sir, I asked them but—'

'Enough,' Mycol interrupted. He pointed back to the line and Keenu rejoined. Mycol's forehead vein looked as if it was about to explode. 'I know... you wouldn't lie to me, Keenu. The rest of dorm three... step forward!'

Nadan, Mui and I did so.

Mycol sauntered over in front of us, moving with less trouble than usual. 'Boys, Sozha is in danger. We don't know where he's gone. He could be hurt; you know what he's like.' Mycol mustered a half-smile, bent down and stared into my eyes. 'If you know something, you *must* tell me, for *his* sake.'

Mui stared blankly forward, and Nadan looked over to me.

'Sir, if I may?' one of the other boys from farther down the line said.

Mycol straightened up. 'Of course. What is it?'

'I apologise if I'm out of line, but aren't there ways for us to track him down? Don't we all have tracking devices inside of us?'

Mycol smirked and took a moment to construct his answer. 'Not… all of you have one.'

'Patriarch, sir,' Nadan said with a solemn expression, 'Sozha isn't the first to go missing. Maybe whatever has happened to the others, happened to Sozha as well? We're all a bit confused about it. Maybe you could shed some light on it, sir?'

A brief, minuscule grimace appeared on Mui's mouth.

Mycol tried to keep a straight face. His lips trembled and his eyebrows twitched. 'Those boys you speak of… all broke the rules,' Mycol lied. 'But they were *caught*… and sent *far* away as punishment.'

Nadan thought about it for a moment. 'Maybe he went to go join them, sir?'

'Don't… *TOY* with me, Nadan!' Mycol shouted, stomping in front of him. 'Don't you *ever* try to make a *fool* out of me!'

One of Mycol's hands burst into green flames. He roared before furiously hurling it towards the corner of the room. The projectile exploded the table that Nadan and Mui normally sat at, vaporising it and coating half the room in green light. All the boys in the line took a step back except for Nadan.

Mycol pointed one of his flame-covered fingers at him. 'If you have something to say, then let's hear it. I want only *constructive* things coming out of that mouth of yours.'

Nadan's face went pale. His eyes widened, he shivered uncontrollably, and his mouth drooped, as though he had seen something horrifying. A small, floating, green ball of light was slowly exiting his mouth, and streams of the light peeled from the ball, gravitating towards Mycol's finger.

Mui's mouth was open in horror, too. His blind, white eyes stared directly at Nadan, understanding his brother's pain.

Nadan leapt back, fell to the floor and coughed as the light, his very life force, receded into his body.

Before the fire spread any further, Mycol opened his palm. The green flames whipped back towards him and entered his mouth. He then grinned as he leant over Nadan. 'I bet you know exactly… where Sozha is hiding. It's time you and I… had a little… chat.'

He grabbed both of Nadan's ankles with only one of his warped, monstrous hands. Nadan coughed himself back awake, clutching his sides in pain. Mycol dragged him past us back to the Fortress' entrance, and the Terror Guard followed him out.

'Nadan…' Mui weakly said, too afraid to intervene.

Nadan closed his eyes and slipped back into unconsciousness.

'Pair up and scour this building!' Mycol yelled as he made for the exit. 'If Sozha isn't found by day's end, then I'll just have to question each and every one of you.'

Although it was getting dark outside, hundreds of soldiers were still patrolling in the courtyard, persisting with Mycol's manhunt. After the Feeble boys paired off, I was thankfully the odd one out. And while the others did offer for me to join them, I preferred to be alone.

I had initially pretended to search like the others, but now I had been hiding in the shower block for so long that I had lost track of time. Once I had inspected the deserted shower stalls, I decided to lock myself inside one and curl up into a ball, hugging my knees tightly to my chest and resting my head against the tiled wall. I wondered how long I could hide here before Mycol would come for me, too.

I kept imagining what he was doing with Nadan right now, or if he was even still alive. I doubted Nadan would help Sozha hide or escape. When Mycol realises that, would he let Nadan live? And what about me when he discovered I also knew nothing?

If Sozha *did* escape, then he certainly had the right idea. If *I* wanted to survive, I'd have to work out how he did it and do the same, quick.

The closed stall door rattled with a gentle rapping. I couldn't see feet or shadows beneath the door, nor had I heard anyone coming in. Was I imagining things? I stood as quietly as I could, then froze, waiting for a sound other than the marching boots outside.

The room brightened overwhelmingly, as though the downlights were short-circuiting. Blinding whips of golden energy spiralled inside my stall with a reverbing, otherworldly hum.

I shielded my face and backed up against the wall completely. When the light and humming finally ceased, I opened my adjusting eyes to see a figure standing in the stall with me. It was Sozha, staring at me with concern.

'Sozha?' I began, pushing off from the wall. 'What are you doing here? Everyone's looking for you.'

He stared at me in silence for what felt like an eternity before finally bringing a finger to his pursed lips. 'Sshhhh! They'll hear you.' He reached out to me. 'Quick, take my hand.'

My eyes darted about to see if we were still alone. I needed to turn him in, right? No, what was I thinking? I couldn't do that to him, but I also couldn't be seen helping him.

I shook my head. 'You... you need to leave. Mycol's going to—'

Sozha's eyebrows lowered, and he leapt forward to grab my wrist. The golden swirls returned. My vision spun with them and fizzled with glittering pops. As quickly as the disorienting effect came, it faded.

'What was that?' I whispered.

'It... it worked,' Sozha said at normal volume. His surprise transformed to a grin. 'It's okay, we can talk now.'

I tilted my head, confused. 'You understood me straight away?'

He tightened his grip, pulled me towards the stall door and unlocked it. 'Yeah, we need to go.'

'What? Hang on. Everyone's been looking for you!' I repeated.

'I know, I heard you the first time,' he replied as he continued pulling me to the shower exit. 'I'm slow, but I'm not an idiot.'

'So, you know that Mycol is furious? He's going to kill you.'

We left through the open door into the main corridor and made for the Fortress' entrance. 'Yeah, I saw the way he yelled at you guys.'

What did he mean he saw? How?

My head was on a swivel, expecting to see someone else at any moment. I'd have no choice but to give Sozha up at this rate. What would I say to the others? Maybe just: hey, I found him hiding in the shower?

We reached the main doors, which beeped and opened for us. 'He was going to kill me eventually, anyway. Kill *all* of us.'

Realising an entire army was possibly outside the door, I planted my feet and pulled back on him. 'Wait, wait, wait! They'll see us.'

'No, they won't.' Sozha slammed the button anyway and the door whooshed open. He forced me outside the barracks, refusing to let go. He was surprisingly strong, although I suppose most of us regularly underestimated him.

A starry night was sprayed above like grains of glistening sand in deep, dark water. Groups of Terror Guards patrolled up and down the courtyard walkways, but none had noticed us yet.

'Now just hang on!' I whispered as I directed us to a nearby pillar to hide behind. Sozha finally stopped. 'I'm not taking another step until you tell me what's going on.'

He frowned and looked at our joined hands. 'Okay, but I'm not letting go. I don't think my power will work on you if you let go.'

I nodded. 'Alright. Huh? Just... explain, please.'

He gestured back to the Feeble Fortress. 'I heard you and Mui talking about Mycol killing us off,' he began, not caring how loud he was being. 'It scared me. Made me realise I was next. All this time, I've been so focused on my sister's death, when I should have been worrying about my own. I've been living in the past, but now I'm focused on my future, literally.'

I shrugged. '*What?*'

'See, I was always a few moments behind, yeah? But I think now I'm a few moments in the future.'

'I... still don't understand.'

He looked at one of the guards patrolling on a nearby catwalk. 'Watch this. Hey! Hey you ugly idiot! We're over here!'

I wrenched him back behind the pillar. 'What are you doing? Stop, they'll hear!'

'No.' He looked back and shook his head. 'They won't. See? No one can see or hear us now, because we don't exist to them yet.'

We peeked out and sure enough, the guard hadn't taken any notice of Sozha's yelling, in fact no one in the courtyard had. I couldn't make sense of it.

Sozha slowly led me out from our hiding spot. 'Last night, I got up and knew I had to leave. It took all morning, but I reached the edge of the city. I found a way out, Eno. I walked right past them all.'

'So why didn't you leave?' I asked.

'I saw the desert and I *would* have kept going. But then I remembered you and your sister, and I felt bad.' He gestured to the barracks again with disdain. 'I hate all the jerks here. They think that because I'm slow, I can't hear what they're saying about me.' He smiled. 'But *you* weren't like that to me. And I didn't want to do this alone, so I came back to break you out.' He pointed to the main gates at the end of the courtyard. 'So, are we doing this?'

I cast my eyes across the courtyard to Mycol's building. Nadan was in there somewhere. And without him, Mui was probably a goner, too. Was I really considering abandoning them?

Stop, focus Eno. You need to look out for yourself, remember? Sacet didn't keep rescuing you over and over so you could die here.

'Just you and me?' I said with a sigh, before glancing back to take one last look at the Fortress. Then I nodded at Sozha. 'Okay, let's get out of this terrible place.'

Twenty-Four: Yes, Commander

Sacet

The armoury initiates had completed suiting me up. Rather than a full helmet, one of them passed me a headset. It had an earpiece, as well as a holographic display to cover one of my eyes. It was already lighting up with information about my vital signs, a local map, and the status of various communication channels.

Noor was beside me, my loyal personal guard. We gave each other a firm nod.

There were thousands of others gearing up for battle in the other bays. We all wore the same sandy camouflaged pattern of armour.

Terel's face appeared on the screen near my eye. 'Commander Sacet, do you read me?'

An initiate passed me a new sword and a sidearm. I attached them to my belt. The girls all saluted me as I walked away from them. 'Go ahead, Terel.'

'As you requested, my scouts have live video surveillance of the first target.'

The image of the outskirts of a former Concordite city was on my screen. Much of the city was still on fire from the rebellions.

The snipers holding the cameras must have been hiding in a nearby jungle because tropical leaves and branches obscured some of the shot.

'Which city is that?' I asked as I marched through the armoury. I inspected my troops as I went. Every single one of them saluted me.

'Eclise, from the Utos sector.'

'Tell them to get a closer view,' I instructed.

'What? You're kidding? They're already in an exposed position—'

'And what about the other two live streams I asked for, Commander?' I continued. I didn't have time for complaints.

'They're still moving into position.'

I helped adjust one soldier's helmet. 'Get it done.' I kept striding through the armoury towards the Mechanical Bay. 'Until this attack begins, no one will know the true target but me.' I tapped a button on the headset to end the communication.

I reached the other side of the armoury and entered into the munitions warehouse. There were bombs everywhere, at least a thousand laid out in a grid on the giant warehouse floor. Each bomb was as large as a person, some even larger. I did my best to memorize the layout of the room. Soldiers were running back and forth with trolleys, unloading even more.

One of Coleo's colonels approached me. 'Ma'am, we've shifted about three-quarters of our bomb munitions so far, as ordered.'

'Are they live?' I asked.

She nodded. 'If you drop them from a sufficient height, they *will* explode. But Ma'am, without our aircraft, how do we—'

I pointed at her. 'Just leave them here. And if I discover even *one* has moved without my permission, then I'll throw you in prison with your old commander, got it?'

She rapidly nodded. 'Y-y-yes, Commander!'

She saluted as Noor and I passed, and we continued towards the mechanical bay.

Another face appeared on my screen. This time it was Commander Tarsus.

'Commander Sacet,' she began, 'your MASU is ready for you in Bay One.'

'Understood, I'm on my way.'

Noor touched my arm as we marched. 'Are you sure you don't want me to accompany you?'

I shook my head as we walked. 'Not this time. We need your power on the front line.' We reached the entrance to the Mechanical Bay and paused. I reached out to him. 'I'll be okay.'

He grabbed my hand back and nodded. 'I know you will.' He looked down at our feet. 'But… just in case one of us doesn't come back… I need you to know…'

I smiled, reached for his neck to gently pull him down, and then kissed him softly. I took a moment to enjoy it, everything else could wait. I smiled, placed a hand on his chest and slowly pushed him away. 'I love you, too. Now get to work.'

He straightened up and saluted, before turning and marching towards the hangar. I faced the mechanical bay and entered.

There were war machines everywhere in here, some hanging from enormous metal chains, others powering up and already rolling out. There were various hover tanks and mechs of different kinds. Spare parts were strewn all over the floor. Red-streaked mechanics were rushing about getting everything operational. I made my way to the giant area labelled as 'Bay 1'.

Also hanging from two large hooks was the massive suit of armour I'd be piloting. It was at least five times my height and maybe 50 times my body's size. Like our soldiers, the mech had been repainted in camouflage instead of the usual silvery shades.

Tarsus was already in the bay with her hands behind her back. She turned to me as I approached. 'Say hello to your Mobile Armour Support Unit, Commander.'

'I know what a MASU is, Tarsus. I've had the training.'

She sneered back. 'The beginner's course.'

I lowered my eyebrows. 'Do you have a problem?'

She shrugged. 'No, no problem. I just hope we find Tau soon. You weren't the only one she called friend.'

'Yes, I heard the stories about how you, Amiki and Coleo would kill innocent people for her so she wouldn't have to.'

She folded her arms in front. 'You're wrong about Coleo, too. She's my best friend and… we were both loyal to Tau *long* before you came along.'

'I guess we'll see how far that loyalty goes. Do your duty and defend this city while we're gone.'

Her lips curled. 'Yes… Commander.'

As I approached the MASU, some nearby engineers activated a ladder from the ground. It lifted and lined up with a hole on the MASU's side. Exterior spotlights beamed forward. The front part of its torso buzzed and eased forward, revealing the hollow insides.

I ascended the ladder and climbed into the person-shaped interior. My arms and legs each had their own areas to control. The suit closed and sealed with a whoosh of air, initially putting me in darkness. Lights blinked to life all around me, on various panels and control sticks. Screens flickered on showing every direction around the machine. The inner workings hummed and vibrated.

'Release the restraints,' I ordered, my voice amplified by the machine's speakers outside.

There was a snap, and my stomach lurched as I was dropped. My great metal feet hit the ground with deep metal clangs, reverberating throughout the bay.

'Performing diagnostics,' I heard an engineer say through the communicator. 'Just stay still for a moment.'

'Understood,' I replied, before switching off all the communicators.

I was alone now. I breathed deeply and closed my eyes. Eno, where were you? How could they do this to you, to me, to this world? It was all too much for me. I was acting as tough as I could, as long as I could, but my heart felt broken.

Tears welled and ran down my cheeks. My lip trembled and I began to bawl. I let it all out.

I hopefully only needed to hold myself together a bit longer. In the face of so many people I had to kill, I wished I could be as strong as Noor. To get through this, I had to be like him. I would butcher all the traitors, no mercy.

'Sacet?' I heard a voice say. 'Sacet, come in?'

It was Marid. Her face was on my headset's screen.

I quickly wiped away my tears and tried to compose myself again. 'Ye-yes, Marid? What is it?'

She paused with a saddened frown. 'You don't have to go through with this if you don't want to. It's not too late to call it off.'

I sniffled. 'I *have* to do this. I must do *something*.'

She slowly nodded, but kind of looked sorry for me. 'I understand.'

I could see the engineers outside waving to me on the screens, so I turned the communicators back on.

'Diagnostics complete, try to move, Commander.'

I grabbed hold of the control sticks in the arm slots and shifted them forward. My machine lumbered forward, each step banging on the ground and shaking the entire suit. Like when I had my training, it felt like I was invincible in here.

'Sacet, if the man shows up again,' Marid continued, 'remember that he was testing you. That means he'll be holding back at first. You might only have *one* shot at taking him down. And I've… been thinking about it.'

I stomped forward, heading for the bay exit. More MASU and hover tanks activated and followed me.

I left the Mechanical Bay through giant double doors and entered the hangar. 'I'm open to suggestions.'

There were thousands of soldiers lined up in formation. The aircraft lining the sides were all now smouldering wrecks.

Marid was at the front of the army with the other commanders, colonels and officers.

She was looking right at me with a hand on her own headset. 'You and I have trained together for over a cycle now. Do you remember our session when you changed the size of your portals?'

There was a division of nomads in the army, too, our sand acolytes. I saw Urias and Pilgrim among them. They all had modern weapons now but still preferred their own goggles and clothing.

I moved my mech into position in front of the army alongside Marid. I bent the machine to look down at her. 'I remember.'

'Well, if you can change their size, maybe you can change their shape, too?'

'I don't follow.'

I looked down at Marid and saw that she had raised a finger to her mouth to silence me. I understood immediately, that spies might be listening in on us. I watched as she then cupped both her palms and brought them together in the shape of a ball.

What was she trying to explain? It looked like she was gesturing for me to create a pair of crushing portals.

'*Hmm*, I think I understand. Thank you, Commander.'

She nodded. 'I will coordinate our ground forces. Good luck out there.'

'And to you.' I turned to Terel, who seemed to be having a conversation on her own headset. 'Are we ready, Terel?' my voice amplified through the MASU.

She turned and looked up at me. She nodded and said a few more words into her communicator.

The screen in front of me showed three different cities at once. Each was labelled: there was Eclise in Utos again, which had jungle surrounding it; Vemos in a sector called Suralia, where a thin haze of sand was already enveloping the city; and finally, a city nestled in the mountains called Esprit from the Elysia sector. I had made my decision.

'It's time,' I said to those below me.

I fiddled with the control panel and adjusted the speaker volume to the maximum. I stood my mech tall and looked out over the troops. I could see a visual of me appear on every one of the soldiers' faceplates.

'All of you, listen up!'

The various officers and captains throughout the hangar commanded their squads to attention. The entire chamber saluted, almost simultaneously.

'I know some of you still don't trust me. We have not always been on the same side. But know that my only goal in this life is to crush the Male Dominion and the ones in charge of them. We are surrounded by enemies, including traitors amongst us. After this attack, if you suspect someone, *even* a superior officer, report them directly to your commanders.'

I paced the mech out front. 'Today, we strike a city that has betrayed us. Our targets are their leaders and any brainwashed soldiers that get in our way. Do *not* attack the civilians. And if possible, give the enemy soldiers a chance to surrender. The sand acolytes will create a sandstorm cover, so use your updated sensors to see. Before this day is over the other provinces will fall back in line. And if they don't, we'll crush them one by one until they do.'

I paused for a moment. 'Do I make myself clear?'

'Yes, Commander!' the entire hangar replied together.

I focused on the footage of the desert just outside of the city known as Vemos. I imagined in my mind that I was actually there. I turned away from the army and opened a portal to it. I stretched my arms wide, enlarging the portal so much it went from one side of the hangar to the other.

'Forward!'

Twenty-Five: The Darkest Corner

Tau

Location unknown

I hadn't been able to hear a single word from Tetsu. The greenish glass between our two cells was too thick. We stared at each other in silence. He'd give a reassuring smile or rest his palm on the glass every now and then, and I'd reach back to him, but that's all we could do.

We had both tried to use our powers when we thought no one was watching, but we must have been in inhibitor cells, just like the ones we had back home. And even if we did have our powers, what could Tetsu or I possibly do with them to escape? We lay on our beds, alone with our thoughts, waiting for all this to be over.

Amiki's betrayal still stung, and although I understood why she did it, I could never forgive her. She wouldn't have been pushed to do that if I was never forced to be the queen in the first place.

I had repeatedly told them all I ever wanted was to stay at the hospital and heal the sick, injured, and dead. Every day, I'd feel innocent people's pain, but it was all worth it to receive their gracious smiles. I even missed the fame… well, the positive fame. People loved me back then; everywhere I went, they would rush over to adore me. That's what I wanted for myself – a life filled with love. Not this desperate, endless war I kept getting dragged back into.

My growing frustration weighed on my heart more than any physical pain ever could. I lashed out, smacking each of the walls, screaming and throwing my sheets on the floor. 'Let me out of here! Let us out, you monsters! I just want to go home… I want to go home.'

Tetsu waved to get my attention and again put his palms on the glass to soothe me. He then gestured that I should breathe in and out slowly. I tried to calm down, sitting on the bed and mimicking him.

There was a noise to my side. The cell door smoothly slid open, and the diminutive Iya walked in. 'Hey there, Tau. How ya' feeling?' She had a piece of orange fruit in her hand, which she took a bite of before leaning in the door frame.

I was still breathing heavily. I glared at her. 'Like *you* care.'

'You're right, I don't.' She took another bite, chewing slowly, before groaning. 'There's nothing to do up here. It's *so* boring.' She then gestured around my cell. 'Especially for you, huh?'

I turned away to the wall.

She shrugged and threw her unfinished fruit into the corner of my cell. 'I get it. It's not like I've ever been *nice* to you.'

I sat silently, inspecting the detail of the chrome wall, hoping she'd just leave.

'Really, Tau? The silent treatment?' she said, wandering in and standing over my bed. 'I practically invented that. Come on, talk with me. You've probably got a million questions.'

I shot her a seething look. 'I know why you're here, so you can stop it. You just want to torment me. My reactions give you some kind of sick pleasure.'

She smirked. 'Oooo, where did *this* Tau come from? Feisty. I like it.'

'I don't care what you like,' I replied with a sneer. 'You kill innocent people without remorse.'

'Yeah, but they're not dead *now*.' She rolled her eyes. 'Basically, everyone you have *ever* known that has died has been brought back. They're fine, promise.'

I huffed. 'Lies.'

'There's no point in lying to you. After all, you're one of *us* now.'

'What?' I said, sitting up straight and looking at her. 'How *exactly* am I—'

'Because it's over for you now, you don't have to worry about the war anymore. Just relax.'

'Relax?' I kicked my legs off the side of the bed and shot up. 'RELAX? Are you kidding?'

She narrowed her eyes, stiffened up and pointed a finger in my face. 'Yes, relax and get over it! You... lost! And when all your dumb friends have been slaughtered, it will be over for them, too.'

Tetsu watched us from his cell. His wide eyes gestured to my cell's still open door. Did she forget to close it, or did she just think I was that little of a risk?

I exhaled and shook my head. 'I just want to go home.'

'What, so you can be surrounded by people that hate you again?'

I ignored her comment, instead planning how I would overpower her. Could I knock her out somehow, or would I have to kill her to get out?

Iya's stern frown softened. 'You'll get a new home soon enough.' She smiled and sat on the end of my bed, dangling her legs off the edge. 'You know, all things considered, you were an okay leader, if I'm being honest.'

'What?' I said, completely taken off guard by her lack of sarcasm or malice.

'We've been watching you this whole time from here. Sometimes we sent spies to sabotage you, other times we messed with you remotely. And... yeah, I really thought we would have broken you and your friends by now. But you all kept fighting. It's... pretty admirable.'

Iya avoided my gaze, embarrassed from her candid admissions. Now was my chance.

I burst forward and hooked my arm around her neck. She struggled and screamed in surprise. I tensed my arm to choke her. She squirmed and reached for the door, so I pulled back and quickly overpowered her. Physically she was no match.

'Wha… *urgh*… what are… you doing?' she wheezed. 'Tau… I… I…'

I couldn't let her use her power on me, so I kept her facing forward. I heaved her onto the bed and tightened my hold. 'Be quiet and stay dead this time!'

Although only a child, Iya was also a psychopath, so I didn't need to feel bad. She deserved this.

'I… thought… *ack*… we could be… friends?'

Iya tried clawing my face, but I tilted from side to side, dodging her. Her arms flailed and managed to slap me before she ran out of breath. She gave one last rasp before falling limp in my arms.

I continued straining a little bit longer to make sure, then let go and pushed her off the side of the bed. She crumpled onto the metal tiles with a fleshy thud.

I sprang up and darted through the cell door before immediately heading to Tetsu's. I pressed random buttons on the panel, nothing.

Tetsu gestured to Iya's body. She still had her wristband on. Of course. I went back into the cell, ripped it from her wrist, ran back out and waved it over the panel.

His door slid open and Tetsu lunged forward to hug me. 'You did it.'

After a brief celebration, I released myself. 'Come on.'

The corridor went in two directions, so we chose one at random and bolted. Now that I was out of my cell, I felt my power coursing through me again, repairing the bruises sustained from tussling with Iya.

'What was she saying?' Tetsu asked as we closed in on a door at the end of the line of cells.

'It doesn't matter,' I replied. 'Let's just get out of here.'

We reached the door and again I swiped Iya's wristband over the panel to open it. We both dashed through, but then immediately stopped in our tracks, for two guards were running at us along the next corridor.

They pointed their rifles at us. 'Stop right there!'

They wore grey armour with a minimal design that I had never seen before. Their helmets were smaller, and they had bright neon green faceplates.

'Hands up,' the female guard commanded, taking aim as her male counterpart continued to charge.

Tetsu threw his hands out with a worried expression, but thankfully produced his shield as normal.

I scowled at the guards and summoned my aura. There was no tingling sensation this time, only that same sense of weight on my chest. As before, my flame aura was closer to sickly green than light blue. Some of my fringe flicked in front of my eyes, and I noticed dark-grey strands. My vision narrowed like a tunnel.

Tetsu's shield flickered and disappeared. He fell back against the wall, clutching his chest.

'Get... out... of my way,' I said, so low it came out like a growl.

Both the guards' faces turned white. They dropped their weapons and backed away, but I changed my mind. These underlings needed to be punished. I felt compelled, and strode forward faster than they could retreat. My hands now raised, like how I would if I were to heal them, the life-saving energy that normally radiated out from me instead reversed course.

'I just wanted to heal people! Was that too much to ask?'

The guards choked and grabbed their necks. Their skin continued to lose its colour. Their eyes sunk. Green energy rose out of their mouths and then dissipated in the air. Their bodies collapsed, dead.

As my aura subsided, I gradually shook, more and more until I lost my balance. I collapsed against the wall to my side and took rapid, shallow breaths. '*Ahhh*! What is this? What's happening to me?' I knew that wasn't me, but I couldn't stop myself.

Tetsu was slumped against the other wall, also catching his breath. He got to his knees and crawled over to me with pained groans, looking as though he had just been in the fight of his life and only barely survived. It took me a moment to realise that *I* had done that to him.

'Tetsu!' I yelled, grabbing him with my shaky hands and inspecting him. I wanted to heal him but was too afraid to activate my aura again. 'Are you okay? I'm sorry. I'm so sorry I... I didn't mean to... to hurt you. What's wrong with me? I would have never... I...'

I sobbed into his shoulder, apologising over and over, and he hugged me back. With my ear on his chest, I could hear his irregular heartbeat struggling back to rhythm. As his chest rose and fell, I listened to his breathing. We waited, slumped against the wall together.

'It's okay… there's nothing… wrong with you,' he said between breaths. 'You're not a monster.'

I didn't know if he truly meant that, or if he was just trying to calm me down. Either way, I wasn't so scared anymore. We closed our eyes and hugged tighter. Slowly, but surely, both our breathing rates returned to normal.

'Are you sure about that?' a voice echoed down the corridor.

Tetsu and I sprung apart and up from the steel floor. The doors had disappeared; the corridor now stretched endlessly into the distance in both directions. The guard's bodies were gone, too, as were their weapons.

'Verre,' Tetsu called, glancing around for her. 'What did you do to her, you *evil*—'

'Nothing,' the voice interrupted, bouncing around us. 'If you're referring to Tau's new killer instinct, she did that *all* on her own.'

I cleared my eyes. 'No, I… I… I'm not like that. Like this…'

'You are now,' Verre's voice reverberated, blending with her other sentences in sickening layers. 'Our powers reflect our inner selves. What did you *think* was going to happen by bottling up all that anger and hate for so long?'

Tetsu stood, almost losing his balance. 'Drop these illusions, right now!'

I closed my eyes, placed my hand on the wall for support and slowly rose. 'Please, make it stop.'

Verre chuckled. 'Iya is only a child and you killed her. She was sent over to welcome you to your new life, to become one of us, and *that* is how you repay her kindness? You really are a monster.'

'Stop it!' Tetsu yelled, his voice curiously not echoing like hers was. 'Stop toying with us, you've had your fun.'

'I must remember to put a collar on you, Tau, before you kill again.'

Tetsu locked eyes with me. 'She's not sorry. I would've done the same.'

I shook my head and lowered my voice. 'I don't want to become that again. I *can't*.'

He sighed and looked up. 'Tell us what you want.'

We waited in silence for Verre's response, but none came. A visual distortion passed us like a shockwave, revealing the true nature of the corridor again. The doors, bodies and guns reappeared.

Verre was beside us with her hands behind her back. Three more guards accompanied her, each pointing their weapons at us.

I wasn't sure when it happened, but an inhibitor collar had appeared around my neck. I tried to pull it off but failed. One of the guards approached and snatched the stolen wristband out of my hand.

'We want you to behave,' Verre said. She gestured down the hallway. 'This way.'

Verre turned and made her way towards the far end of the corridor, and we hesitantly followed at gunpoint. She led us to a set of double doors, the largest we had seen in this facility so far. They opened on our approach, and we stepped through into the large space, a cross between a control room and a meeting room.

To our left and right were many rows of workstations: control panels and screens with workers operating them. In the centre of the room was a long, sleek silver table surrounded by chairs. Many were already sitting there, some of whom I recognised as both former allies and foes.

Most notable was Kalek, who I did not enjoy seeing again. He glanced over and I shuddered, remembering the time he had crushed my ribcage. He grinned creepily, as though happy to see me.

Also in attendance were Verre's old colonels, some of the most powerful acolytes of the FD. I spotted all except Neva. As we walked over to the table, they exchanged sniggering whispers and smirked with malicious delight.

At the far end of the table was an older man with a wide moustache, King Tuloch. He wore a fancier uniform than the others, formal and adorned with military pins and insignia.

The expansive room had wide, curved windows lining the far edges, and standing by one of them was the invincible man who had killed Sacet. He was staring out the window into what I thought was the night sky. But it wasn't just the stars taking up most of the view. There was an enormous object; it was a mixture of yellow and brown, with significant patches of blue and a tiny bit of green.

I rounded the table and stepped to his side to get a closer look. I placed both my hands on the window with my mouth agape. It was Seron, our planet, and we were orbiting it in space.

Twenty-Six: Letting Go

Eno

Sozha and I walked hand in hand down the dark, deserted city walkway.

Earlier, when the sun had yet to set, the city was teeming with males going about their business. Flying vehicles whizzed past overhead, transporting all manner of workers and materials. Hundreds of shop owners were hawking their wares, yelling their prices outside. Gangs of thieves not much older than myself raided those businesses, usually as one of them distracted the shop owner with inane questions and would then run out with arms full of much-needed food.

It was the first time I had seen the regular people of the Male Dominion up close, and they weren't what I expected. For my whole life I was under the impression that they were all muscly, giant, cold killing machines, but that was just their military.

The civilians, at least those in this part of the city, had barely any meat on them, rags for clothes, and no hope in their sullen eyes. In a way, they weren't much different to nomads, doing whatever they could to survive in this harsh environment, even if that meant preying on each other.

When darkness fell, the guards came in droves and ordered everyone inside. We watched the city basically shut down: businesses closed, and civilians fled to their homes in panic, sheltering as though the city were about to be bombed.

The only ones left outside in the relatively silent city were Sozha and I, and the occasional guard patrol. Our footsteps on the pavement echoed eerily. Without Sozha's incredible new power, there was no way we could have snuck past these guards.

Sozha was getting noticeably more tired with each step, as was I. Our pace had slowed as the night stretched on. How much longer could we keep this up?

'We must be close to the outskirts by now, right?' I asked, unafraid to be loud.

Sozha's sweaty fingers almost slipped off mine before clenching tight again. 'Maybe… I don't remember where we are.'

'What? I thought you said you escaped this morning?'

Sozha groaned as we reached a walkway intersection under a dull streetlamp. 'Look, the city isn't infinite. We'll get out eventually.' He peered around, looking for something familiar, before pointing left. 'This way, I think.'

We kept walking, occasionally cutting through dirty junkyards and dumping grounds. Every run-down building we encountered was more depressing than the last. Most were rust-covered and in disrepair, as though no effort had gone into maintaining them for many cycles. No lights were on inside. Occasionally we'd see faces through the windows staring out at the streetlamps.

They reminded me of the other boys, still locked away in their Feeble Fortress, judging me for escaping. I did feel bad about abandoning Nadan, but if I wanted to survive, I had to let go of any attachments I had to others.

'The Male Dominion sucks!' I shouted at the top of my lungs, enjoying the echo and the following silence. 'You're all idiots!'

Sozha gestured at a pair of guards on a street corner the next block over. 'Imagine if we could really do that, without being killed.'

We reached another intersection. Although the buildings were less built up here, there was still no sign of the city's outer wall. Every direction appeared the same.

Sozha pulled on my hand to stop and catch his breath. 'Hold on. I… need a rest. I've been walking… *all* day.'

I turned and noticed the same pair of guards from before, following the same path we had taken. My heart skipped a beat. 'Are those… guards following us?'

Sozha shook his head while panting. 'Can't be.' He winced and fell to his knees, clutching my hand even tighter. 'Just a… a coincidence.'

'Are you okay?'

'It's nothing,' he answered with a pained expression. 'I… *argh*!' He grabbed his chest with his free hand and doubled over.

I knelt beside him. 'What is it?'

He shook his head and tried to stand. 'It's okay. Come on. We need to keep… *aruurgh*!' Again, he doubled over, this time using his free hand to break his fall.

'What's wrong? Tell me what to do!' I glanced about for anything that could help. Somewhere to sit maybe.

'I… I don't know.' He struggled to even look at me, so instead closed his eyes and gritted his teeth. 'I've never felt… I… I think I need to let go of you.'

'What? No, not yet!' I tried pulling him to his feet again. 'We're close, right? We're almost out of here, just hold on a bit longer.'

He kept shaking his head. 'I can't… I… I can't. It hurts.' His voice was reduced to strained murmurs.

I could feel him releasing his fingers, but I grabbed tighter in response. 'No, hold onto me!'

'I'm sorry,' Sozha said as his hand finally managed to slip out from mine.

A vortex of gold blinded me, and I stumbled back, landing on the pavement. The flash soon passed, leaving nothing but my hand outstretched into the empty crossroad.

'Sozha, come back!' I called out. 'Sozha!'

'*Whoa*, where did *he* come from?' I heard a deep voice say behind me.

'Did he say Sozha?' another voice added. 'That's a Feeble Fortress uniform.'

I shot up and spun on the spot. It was the two guards, looking directly at me. Oh no, I was visible again. They had caught up, already on the other side of the intersection. Their rifles were still slung over their shoulders. Their red-eyed, black helmets hid their no-doubt astounded expressions.

'Who're you talking to, kid?' one guard asked with a shrug, slowly reaching for his rifle.

'You know you're not supposed to be out here,' the second one said, stepping closer. 'How about you tell us who you are, *hmm?*'

My heart pounded and my body shook. They were only a few paces away, but what should I do? Should I run and hide?

The closer man offered his hand to me. 'Now… take it easy. We're going to get you back to the barracks. Everything will be fine.'

He was lying, of course. If they took me back, Mycol would kill me.

'I… I know where Sozha is,' I said, stepping back, and both guards exchanged a look. 'I'm going to go see Patriarch Mycol right now.'

As I took another step, the closest guard dove at me. 'Come here you little—' He latched onto my wrist and wrenched me up into the air. 'Got him!'

'Let go of me,' I shouted as I struggled, hanging from his raised grip. 'Someone, help! Let me go!'

As I kicked and flailed, the guard lowered me again and wrapped his arm around my throat in a chokehold. 'How about you tell *us* where Sozha is first?'

The first guard aimed his rifle at me. 'Come on, kid, do us a favour? We'll get a promotion this way, and you can get off with a warning.'

'Where is he?' the other bellowed in my ear. He produced a pistol from somewhere and shoved the barrel against my temple. 'Tell us where he is, now!'

'Get away from me!' I screamed at the top of my lungs as I activated my power.

The two men were flung away. A shockwave rippled out along the intersection, fracturing the pavement and warping the steel streetlamps. The foundations of the corner buildings buckled. Concrete chips and chunks smashed through distant windows. Without the foundational floors below, the buildings' upper floors teetered and crumbled away from me.

One of the guards rammed into the nearest building corner and was buried in the shifting rubble. The other tumbled head over heels farther along the walkway with a torrent of debris, eventually rolling to a stop.

He stirred with a groan, eventually sat up, then began shuffling away from me. 'TDC team needed on my position, now! I have a loose acolyte here!'

'Sozha, please,' I said to the empty walkway again. He either wasn't there or was choosing not to help me. I was on my own.

I soon realised the guard wasn't crawling away from me out of fear, but rather he was crawling to his gun laying in the rubble nearby. Just as he was about to reach it, I sprinted to the intersection's least destroyed left path.

Boom, boom, boom!

Narrow misses: each hit the still collapsing walls behind me. The projectiles' sizzling heat singed the back of my neck. The thundering crackle echoed down the walkways, probably waking everyone in the city.

As soon as I was out of the guard's sight, I turned into the nearest alley and kept running. My legs were already tired before, and now it felt like they could give way any moment. I couldn't run forever.

The narrow alley was even darker than the walkways, having no streetlamps. High buildings flanked either side of the twisting, winding path.

I passed multiple back doors and more windows with faces staring out, but none intervened to help me. They all only cared about themselves, their own survival.

I reached the end of the alley and stopped at the corner, just short of another well-lit walkway. This street was even wider than the last. Many shabby apartment buildings overlooked it, some with attached fire escape stairways.

A high-pitched whine cut through the night air, distant at first, but then close in mere moments. Several bright orange jet streams arched above the street, before disappearing over the next row of buildings. What they belonged to were too fast to get a good look at.

I peered into the street to make sure it was clear, as well as back in the alley, but caught a fleeting glimmer on the upper edge of my periphery.

It was a soldier crouched on the roof, overlooking the alley. He wore a sleek, black armoured suit, lit in various places with orange. His helmet was huge, with bright-orange eyes each bigger than my head, I had never seen it before. I didn't know how long he had been staring at me.

He pointed at me, and an audible puff followed. My hands came up, and I instinctively pushed everything away in a quick burst, then fell into the street behind me. A few bricks fell near my feet with sharp clacks, and something tiny smashed in the alley, a combination of a metal ting and a glass clink.

What I assumed was a man above and not some sort of robot cocked his head to the side, as though surprised. Whatever it was that he fired lay in pieces nearby. He rolled back onto the roof and was gone from view.

The high-pitched, screaming rocket sounds were back. At least ten more men like the first landed on the rooves across the street, five storeys up. Their backpacks built into their suits were allowing them to fly. Six soldiers leapt and slid down the side of the building, either by slowing their descents with long, spark-producing claws, or by acrobatically flipping and tumbling down the fire escapes. The other four aimed their rifles down at me, remaining on the roof.

I chose a random direction and scrambled along the walkway, running as fast as my aching legs would allow. The curving path I took thankfully had plenty of street signs and closed vendor stalls to block their shots.

The six claw-wielding soldiers landed in the street and gave chase, each skittering down a different path. They ran along walls, vaulted over tall obstacles, and dove under barriers, almost in complete silence. Were they part of the Terror Guard?

Thuds and glass smashes as more projectiles barely missed me, hitting the surrounding concrete surfaces. More were being fired. While I ran, I strained my muscles and sent out a pulse of force. It collected some of the projectiles as planned, and briefly brought my street pursuers to a grinding halt.

Two landed in front of me, catching me off guard. They swung their fizzling, electrified claws at me, high and low. I sent out another pulse just in time and sent them flying. As they careened through the air, they activated their backpacks and stabilised themselves midair.

Those claws could have sliced me in half. Were they trying to kill me?

Impressed as I was with using my power on the move for the first time, I knew I couldn't keep doing this. Even if I miraculously dodged all their attacks, they were far faster and more coordinated. They'd never let me escape.

A crackle behind me. I rolled to the side just in time as claws went over my shoulder. I gritted my teeth and tensed, sending out the greatest shockwave yet. He launched back and crashed through a window.

I had to fight, just like Sacet would have. Another volley of shots and another pulse. I found a stall that blocked the snipers' line of sight and stopped. The six claw users caught up and slowly encircled me. I stared at their giant orange eyes as they closed in, which began to flicker and brighten. Be brave, Eno, be fearless.

The ground beneath me trembled, causing the loose rubble to vibrate. It quaked a second time, and a third, each time getting louder. Two large mechs stomped around the street corner and turned perfectly to my position.

A loud aircraft droned above, blinding me with its spotlight. A mass of soldiers ran towards my position from every connecting street and walkway. What felt like a thousand weapons were all pointed at me.

I tensed, trying to send out another pulse, but nothing happened. How was I being inhibited? It was the six bright-eyed soldiers; they were stationary and surrounding me perfectly. Their suits must have had inhibitor technology built in somehow.

I shook my head in disbelief. All this just to stop me from leaving? They were so coordinated, so effective at working as a team. I raised my hands in surrender, knowing it was hopeless.

As I got down on my knees, Mycol, wearing his horrifying skull mask, appeared from the crowd of soldiers and hobbled towards me. Hundreds of pale faces stared at me from the surrounding windows, and over a hundred more through cold, emotionless soldier masks. Mycol stood over me with clenched fists. I was as good as dead.

Twenty-Seven: I See You

Sacet

The portal my mech was levitating on in the sky briefly stumbled due to the high winds, so I stabilised it. I was so high that the hazy city of Vemos below was only just within my second perception's range. My supporting portal's other side led to the desert ground outside the city where the rest of my army was poised to strike.

My mech's exterior cameras weren't providing me enough detail of the city buildings from up here, even when fully zoomed in. I wasn't quite flying blind though – one of my mech's internal screens displayed a city map and my position over it, highlighting points of interest in red. Hopefully my forces would hijack the city's security grid soon, and I'd have all their cameras at my disposal.

Of course, I could also rely on my perception if I was a little closer. I lowered the portal, slowly but surely towards the city. I wasn't moving particularly fast, but this mode of travel was far less conspicuous than a screeching aircraft. Those below would only see the bottom of my portal, which from their point of view was just another patch of sky.

That's if they could see the sky at all. A strong gale had already been blowing before we arrived, and now with our sand acolytes kicking up even more of the surrounding dunes, it was a genuine sandstorm down there.

All according to my plan: my forces and I wouldn't need eyes. I had purposefully instructed for my force's helmets to be equipped with the most advanced sensors possible to see through the haze.

Over the past cycle, my second perception's range had increased significantly, allowing me to scout several city blocks at a time. Although the range was impressively far, I wasn't omniscient. I could only look at one thing at a time, so it was hard to pay close attention to every detail.

Now that I was almost directly over the city centre, I focused on the Council building, a tall tower that overlooked the rest of the city. Although not as immense as the Citadel in New Elysia, it was similar in that it had large gardens and walls separating it from the rest of the city.

My sense sped from one room to the next, searching for their leaders. Their soldiers were completely unaware of the impending attack; there were no alarms, and no one was running about. They must have thought the storm outside was natural.

There, in the Council building's peak were the rebel leaders. I could tell it was them, even if I hadn't seen pictures of their faces ahead of time. It was a room full of high-ranking dignitaries and military personnel, all with excessively decorated uniforms and smug faces. Several surrounding screens showed male faces, possibly MD, and it looked like they were conferencing with them. More traitors to eliminate.

'Alright, Marid, I've found them,' I said. 'Strike team ready?'

'Affirmative, everybody's in position,' she replied.

I opened portals under the leaders' feet to space, one after another. Each futilely clawed at the floor as she fell through. I did the same to as many people on the top floors as I could, ejecting them from both the building and life. Good riddance.

Once they were dealt with, I closed the portals and opened new ones, allowing my special forces to safely infiltrate those now-empty rooms. Terel led them personally. They got to work immediately securing doors and commandeering the various control panels that managed the city's defences.

'Patching us in now, Commander,' one of my soldiers said through the comms. It sounded like Kinru. 'Done, we've got access.'

My screens lit up with hundreds more options than before, and I could already see many were remotely being taken over by my forces. I now had thousands of cameras I could access, and some of the most important views were already on screen, such as the Council building interiors and the barracks.

Turrets all around the city were now under our control, too, swivelling to life and preparing to fire on key targets if needed.

I cleared my throat and pressed a button to access the city's array of loudspeakers. 'Citizens and soldiers of Vemos, this is Commander Sacet of New Elysia, representing your Queen of Light. We've already disposed of your traitorous leaders. Order will soon be restored, simply follow these instructions: drop your weapons, stay in your buildings with your hands up and you will be forgiven. Or, come to the Council building for a quick death. The choice is yours.'

I muted the channel, then waited and watched.

'Commander Sacet,' Terel said into my earpiece. 'We have pushback.'

The cameras showed gunfights breaking out in the Council building between Terel's troops and the many council guards I missed.

I opened various portals throughout the tower at different levels. My own acolytes poured through in groups of five. I spotted Noor, Malu and Marid. No sooner had they entered did they unleash on the scrambling guards with laser, water and sword.

Many quickly noticed the purple streaks of our troops, as well as their superpowered displays, and surrendered on the spot. One knelt in front of Noor upon noticing him dispatch of another guard. He showed mercy, instructing her to lay flat on the floor.

Marid teleported behind various guards and brought her sword to their necks. If they didn't immediately raise their hands, she slit their throats. Malu held up her hands at the incoming fire and liquefied each projectile with her fingertips. Those guards gave up, too.

I opened more portals outside, along the tower's walls and in the gardens. With my troops' superior vision, they were able to sneak up behind most of the still unaware guards and force them to surrender.

On one of my screens was a live feed of their barracks. I watched the screens intently, hoping that they would just all surrender. Each chamber there was buzzing with activity like a disturbed necrolisk nest. Hundreds of soldiers were leaping from their bunks, arming themselves and sprinting to the exits.

I sighed, before bringing up the volume again. 'Those of you in the barracks.' This gave most of them pause again, making them look up. 'I can see *every single one* of you.'

I chose one at random from a bigger crowd of soldiers. 'You with the all-green streaks and her hand on the red control panel.' About 30 of her comrades stared at her. 'Yes, you. Or you, the blonde girl picking up the sniper rifle.' She dropped the weapon in shock. All of the surrounding soldiers looked just as freaked out. 'Do you want to die? Then keep doing what you're doing.'

Large groups threw their weapons to the ground.

'That's right, now raise your hands above your head and kneel.'

Most complied, kneeling in large, terrified groups. My message didn't get through to all of them, though. The higher ranks commanded many of the fully armed drones back into formation and out of barracks' front entrance.

I cycled through cameras and found one with a better angle, then activated the heat vision. A pack of over a hundred rebels were sprinting towards the Council building.

'Some of you aren't good listeners,' I continued. 'And I'm out of warnings.' I muted the channel again, then pressed a button on my headset. 'Colonels, instruct your squads to give the front gardens a wide berth. We have incoming, as expected.'

Their charge was just coming into range of my second perception. I could easily send them to space like the others, but it was time to make a statement. Those inside the barracks needed to understand how much of a mistake it was to come out those doors.

I thought back to the warehouse, and all the bombs I had seen. I created a portal under several of them, with their destination being the sky above the enemies in the gardens. The bombs dropped through, and the nearby cameras picked up the high-pitched whistling as they descended. Some of the soldiers dove for cover, no doubt hearing their squealing doom on the wind, but it was too late.

The resulting explosions' yield was far larger than I had anticipated, obliterating the targets in a firestorm. Walls crumbled. The outer gardens disintegrated. Charred body parts flew. Distant windows cracked. Streets fractured. The inferno burgeoned into the sky, parting the sandstorm.

After hearing the bombs, hundreds of civilians evacuated their homes. Some had their hands up, but most scattered, searching for safer cover.

I cycled through more live feeds for different viewpoints of my advancing army. MASUs and hover-tanks were entering the city's limits, as were swarms of camouflaged soldiers. They went from street to street and apartment block to block, ensuring no resistance.

'Commander, enemy aircraft!' a voice transmitted.

In my haste to control the ground, I had neglected the skies. I switched the camera to their hangar and saw the last of their aircraft powering up and taking off.

I couldn't see or sense them now, they could be anywhere. 'I need eyes on them. Someone give me eyes.'

'Sending you my feed,' one voice said.

Her visual appeared on my screen, which had a remarkably clear view of several aircraft above the sandstorm. I opened portals in front of their paths leading directly to the desert floor. As though crashing into a wall in the sky, each predictably exploded in a fireball, raining shrapnel down on the city.

My army breached the barracks from all sides at once, encountering hundreds of kneeling soldiers. Each was restrained with electro-cord. The harder some resisted, the stronger the shock they received.

The enemy was completely outmatched and overwhelmed. It was over, without any casualties on our side that I knew of. A flawless victory.

I rested back in my seat and exhaled. 'One down.' I pressed a button on my headset. 'Tell the nomads to stop. Everything is under control.'

The sand across the cityscape slowly subsided. The laserfire in the Council building eventually ceased. My army had spread to every corner of the city, breaching doors and windows, and restraining any who put up a fight.

I opened portals in the desert to allow the auxiliary troops and artillery to head back to New Elysia. The excess troops and nomads marched through to return home.

I tuned the comms screen in front of me. 'Auxiliary guard, are you clear? Notify me once everyone is through.'

'Affirmative, we're clear,' one of the colonels eventually answered.

As I closed their portal, every other voice channel on my comms screen lit up with chatter. I tuned in to an officer's channel and heard several raised voices overlapping incomprehensibly. Another channel had more of the same, there was panic coming up the chain of command.

'What's happening?' I asked. 'Officers, get your squads under control.'

Many of the soldiers in the streets had craned their necks up to the sky.

'Sacet,' Marid said into my ear. 'Look up.'

Coming within range of my sensory power, far above both me and the clouds, were hundreds of red-hot, rocket-powered missiles plummeting at an alarming rate. They looked nothing like any bomb I had ever seen. Each left a fiery trail behind them.

'Commander?' Terel said. 'What are your orders?'

Like I did to the other aircraft, I opened ground portals in the sky along some of their projected paths, but they dodged each attempt with insanely good, perhaps automatic reflexes. After focusing on just one, it made contact and detonated, creating an explosion at least five times larger than what I had done to the rebels.

The other missiles were spread so far apart that the first explosion didn't take out any of the others. At the rate they were falling, I wouldn't be able to destroy them all in time.

'There's too many!' I yelled.

'Sacet, we need to get out of here, now!' Malu's voice yelled over the comms.

I flicked up the volume. 'Everyone, either retreat through the nearest portal or… or take cover. Incoming missile barrage!'

My message spread to every loudspeaker across the city. Every citizen I could see panicked at once, screaming and diving for cover. My army's previously stealthy and professional approach was abandoned as they scarpered back the way they came, seeking portals that hadn't appeared yet.

I was overwhelmed by the number of people I had to help. My eyes darted from one screen to another. No matter how fast I breathed, I couldn't get enough air.

'Sacet!' Malu shouted again. 'Portal us out!'

'Right, right,' I replied, shaking my head to snap out of it.

Starting with the Council building, I reopened as many portals as I could for the troops to escape. The safest place I could think of short notice was the Royal Gardens in New Elysia.

Terel took her special forces back through immediately. I made sure to open portals next to our acolytes first. Some soldiers dragged subdued guards through to safety. I focused on the largest clumps of my people rather than individuals, and prioritized soldiers over civilians.

A second wave of missiles was approaching from above the first. I breathed quicker and gripped the sweaty handles around me tighter. 'No! I have to... everyone, just run! Retreat!'

I opened portals inside the barracks and next to the larger swarms of soldiers in the streets. The first wave of missiles hurtled down through the clouds and past me. They were moments away from impacting all over the city.

People from both sides piled through the portals to safety. There were too many to count, and all so spread out. It was impossible to help them all.

I turned my attention to the missiles again. The lower the altitude, the closer they were together. I managed to block one with a portal, which detonated, causing a chain reaction and taking a few others with it. The explosion was so large that the portal I was balancing on tilted to the side. My stomach lurched. The MASU slid. The portal disappeared.

I plummeted just as the first wave of remaining missiles went off all across the city. My screens fizzled, my MASU shook. I heard only intense, deafening rumbling. Red and orange painted the sky. Buildings vaporised. Thousands of lives instantly rubbed out.

A giant, black smokestack billowed in my headfirst freefall path. The rumbling didn't stop, but did decrease. I sensed the flame-covered ground approaching fast.

Was there anywhere the bombs hadn't hit? There, the Council

building itself was shockingly untouched. I opened a portal in my own path, with its destination pointing up in the gardens. I careened through, and the gravity flip spun my innards, almost making me vomit. The momentum launched me back into the air of the smoke-filled gardens.

Now the right way up, I reached the apex of the launch and activated my jump jets to cushion the fall. Small boosters on the MASU's back and elbows fired down. I landed in the scorched garden grounds and got my bearings.

The entire city was aflame. Truly shocking that they'd rather destroy the city than allow us to take it back. And even more shocking was that they had this kind of firepower this whole time.

My senses sped about looking for survivors but found very few. My cockpit was drenched with sweat. I could feel the heat radiating from the burning buildings, even from inside the MASU.

I looked up again. The second wave of missiles was almost here, but thankfully much smaller in number. The missiles' shape was quite different from the first wave, more capsule-like. Jets fired down from underneath each to slow their decent and to make precise reorientations.

They were coming directly for the Council building. Each slowed even more and landed in relative safety. Their doors burst off, revealing soldiers in dark-grey battle suits.

High above them, another single projectile was blazing down. This one was much faster than all that had preceded it. It wasn't a missile, it was a man, and he was coming straight for me. He wore a minimal, dark grey battle suit. It was *him* again.

Twenty-Eight: Every Last One

There was only a fraction of my army left that I could sense, the others had either escaped or been wiped out in the bombing. It was possible some survived, buried under rubble or lost in the smoky miasma, but I had bigger problems to deal with right now.

At least thirty enemy drop pods dotted around the ashen city released their cargo: MD acolytes. Each got to his feet, scanned his surroundings for targets or buildings that hadn't been destroyed and unleashed his powers.

'Sacet!' I could hear someone yell outside. 'Get ready.'

Marid had teleported to my mech. Bloodied and blackened, she looked up at the man in the sky with her sword drawn.

'Marid, what are you still doing here?'

'Never mind that. I'll distract him. Remember what I told you.'

The man in the sky was still hurtling towards us. I opened a space portal along his path, but like the missiles, he dodged it with lightning reflexes. He realigned and descended even faster. More portals, as many as I could. I created a veritable minefield between us.

He gracefully weaved around them all before bursting through the remaining cloud cover, trailing its vapour in his wake. He reached the peak of the Council building in a flash, bringing with him a thunder crack. He stopped and floated upright with his arms folded.

Marid brought a finger to her headset. 'If anyone reads me, fire on the Council peak, now!'

Several projectiles were fired from scattered tanks and MASU around the city, each focusing on the man. He didn't bother dodging or even acknowledging that he was being fired upon. The lasers hit him, and he absorbed them like a gentle breeze.

I targeted the man with my rocket launchers and let loose a screaming salvo. Each zipped up at him and exploded, enveloping him in a fireball. The nearby peak shattered and showered steel beams and debris, which clanged against the tower on the way down.

We eventually ceased firing, and the flame cloud cleared, revealing the man unscathed. He hadn't moved at all. He was looking out at the destroyed cityscape and smiling.

Marid smacked the side of my mech with her sheath. 'Sacet, when I get close to him, fire salvo-5B on my position, got it?'

The man looked down at the smouldering gardens and surveyed it. He spotted Marid and I.

I turned the mech to her. 'What? I can't attack when you're—'

'Just do it!' A tear was in her eye.

I switched the settings, unsure of what she had planned at first, but when I found the correct salvo and the words 'inhibitor net launcher', I understood. I hadn't ever used these in my training, I didn't even know a MASU could be equipped with them.

Unperturbed by our counterattack, the man casually floated down into the gardens.

Marid stepped forward and glanced back. 'Promise me you'll escape before he puts a hand on you.'

'What? I'm not abandoning y—'

'Promise me!' she shouted and glared back at my mech. The tip of her sword had a slight waver.

My hand shook over the trigger. 'I promise.'

The man landed on the ground over a hundred paces away and stared us down. I targeted him. As the burning city's anguish carried on the wind, the three of us silently waited for the other to make a move.

Marid teleported behind him. I pulled every trigger I had and unleashed the second volley. Marid swung her blade at his neck. The rockets whistled through the air. He just stood there.

The salvo collided with the ground, making a circle around the two of them. And just as the blade was about to make contact, I blinked, and he was gone. Marid sliced nothing but air. The inhibitor spikes in the ground electrified and Marid fell to the ground, unable to teleport.

'You dare attempt…' a deep voice shouted as the front panel of my MASU was ripped clean off, 'using inhibitors against *me*?'

He was hovering within arm's reach. I threw up my hands to summon a portal, but his crushing grip instantly latched around my wrists, squeezing until I screamed. With his free hand he rapidly ripped my MASU to pieces, chucking each aside with effortless flicks. My wrist bones could snap at any moment.

Marid was crawling out of the field, dragging her sword behind and reaching out to us. 'I'm not finished with you!'

He continued ripping until the remains of my machine fell to the ground and he was holding me up by the wrists, like freshly slain prey. He inspected me with disgust, before flinging me away. I hit the ground hard and rolled several times before stopping. I held my wrists in pain and moaned.

A stray hover-tank crashed through a nearby wall and briefly surveyed the situation. It aimed its turret at the man and fired. The massive projectile ricocheted off his head and into the Council building, blowing a hole in its side.

Unamused, the man appeared in front of the tank. He picked it up with one hand, lifted it above his head as though it were a toy and turned to me.

'Catch!'

He flung it at me. I sat up and opened a portal just in time like a giant shield. The tank whooshed through and out into the sky behind me.

'Get out of here, Sacet!' Marid screamed.

She teleported to the man's side and stabbed at him. He didn't move this time. The blade fractured as it collided with his ribs. In another flash, he backhanded her and launched her across the gardens into a stone column.

'Marid!' I yelled.

I shot up and strained my fingers. A pair of ground portals appeared at his sides. I slammed them together, but he was gone again before they hit. My perception darted about, trying to relocate him.

There was an ear-shattering crash to my side as the tank landed. I jumped back. I didn't even notice how close it was to splattering me. My heart felt like it was about to explode.

'Girl.'

The man was behind Marid. He had one large hand gripping the crown of her head. Bloodied and barely conscious, Marid gave a pleading stare. My eyes widened. Teleport away, Marid, what are you doing?

He twisted his arm and snapped her neck with a sickening crunch. He had spun her head completely backwards, and then forwards again. She dropped her sword. He let go and we both watched as she crumpled into a heap.

'NO!' I screamed. My whole body trembled, and I futilely reached out to her.

'Weak,' he said back, now meandering over to me. '*She* is why you failed to put up a challenge.'

What could I do to fight against this man? He was too fast, too powerful. My jaw quivered.

He was getting closer. 'And now…'

I shuffled back and hit a wall. I felt around it and shook my head. 'Stop this. Please.'

He stopped and glared, then gestured around. 'You brought this city to its knees, but *still* you cower? What is it going to take?'

I was shaking uncontrollably. I couldn't move.

He burst forward with his fist raised. I winced. He punched the wall behind me instead, sending most of the bricks crumbling. He leant in so close that I could feel his breath on my skin.

'I will destroy *every* last city. Kill *every* last ally. Every friend. Every innocent mother and child on this *wretched* world. *Every… last… one*. And unless you stop me, I will leave *you* to last.'

He grimaced, then slowly backed away. I saw his knees bend briefly and he launched into the sky with such force that the ground quaked.

And just like that I was alone. He was already above the clouds again. The fires had grown, and the distant screams wouldn't stop.

I collapsed to my knees and screamed at the sky, again and again until I was hoarse. I punched the charred ground repeatedly, furious with him and my failure.

How dare he? How dare he put the whole world on my shoulders like that? Just kill me! You had me in your grasp again, just end this!

My shaking eventually stopped, and my breathing returned to normal. I had never felt as ashamed of myself as I did now. I crawled uneasily forward, dripping tears in the mud as I went, until I reached Marid's body.

I put my arms around her and squeezed while crying. 'I'm sorry… I failed you.'

I had to keep telling myself that they weren't dead, not really. As long as we rescued Tau, there was still a chance we could bring everyone back. Marid was counting on me for that, so many were, so I couldn't stop, not yet.

The city was lost. Thousands fled from the chaos, many covered in severe burns. The sky was so dark that it was practically night, light unable to pierce through the ever-growing shroud of black smoke.

The few soldiers that survived were struggling against the MD acolytes. Although the man had left me to wallow in my failure, these other targets were no match for me, even in my weakened state.

While still hugging Marid, I closed my eyes and opened space portals behind each remaining enemy until they were all dealt with.

I then spent some time trying to locate my remaining soldiers and sending them back to the armoury at home. I was sure there were more out there, but the search would have to wait, I needed to retake command of my forces.

I wiped away my tears. When I panicked earlier, I had teleported many of the troops to the Royal Gardens. I pictured the greenery in my mind again and opened a portal under Marid and I. As the portal raised over us, it wobbled oddly and dispelled before I was ready to close it.

Sure enough though, the Royal Citadel towered above, casting a long shadow. I gently released Marid onto the garden path. There were troops scattered about in broken formations all around, including a few wearing silver, those captured from Vemos. We were safe again, but something still felt off.

'It's the Commander!' a nearby soldier yelled.

Malu and Noor came running down the path and through the parting troops.

Malu stopped in her tracks upon noticing Marid's body. 'Is she…?'

Noor didn't stop. He rushed over, knelt and hugged me. 'Sacet, what happened?' He inspected all the bloody gashes, bruises and dirt stains on my face and armour. 'Are you okay?'

I stood up, looking through him. 'Something's wrong.'

I tried sensing into the distance, but for some strange reason I couldn't. I couldn't sense *anything* at all. My power wasn't working! I threw my hands at the air nearby, trying to make a portal, but nothing appeared. I looked at Noor with wide eyes.

He furrowed his brow, pointed both palms to the sky and tried firing, but there was no beam. Malu bent down and touched the grass with her fingertips, but nothing changed to water.

Terel pushed through the crowd with some of her own troops. 'Out of the way!' She stopped when she saw Marid, before scowling back at me. 'If this is all about *you*, then I'm tired of my people dying for it.'

I closed my eyes and nodded. 'I am, too.'

A siren sounded on the wind. It was a long, deep, distorted tone that swung up and down in pitch.

'Now what?' Malu said.

All of us cast our gazes over to the Residential Rim for an answer. We couldn't see anything, but we heard the screams of innocents again.

'All of you, spike formation!' Terel roared. 'Move it, go, go, go!'

The mass of troops all shuffled at once as Noor helped me to my feet.

I miraculously still had my sword and sidearm on my belt. Noor didn't have a weapon, so I passed him the pistol, then drew my sword.

The soldiers continued shifting, putting artillery and snipers in the centre, the five-remaining hover-tanks and MASUs around them, and then the remainder of our soldiers pointed out like spikes in multiple directions.

There were several loud clangs coming from the nearby garden gates, causing what was left of my unsettled army to nervously turn and murmur. I didn't blame them; I currently couldn't sense beyond my own two eyes.

'Arrow formation!' I heard Terel shout over the clanging metal. 'Gate side!' The troops moved again, this time all facing the gate in the shape of an arrow.

We could hear necrolisk screeches accompanying the civilians' cries. There must have been hundreds approaching, the sight of which terrified me to my core.

We had been played from the beginning, from birth, for who knows how many cycles. I had no powers and no control over the situation. No matter how brave I thought I was or needed to be, I couldn't shake the idea that our deaths were imminent.

I reached out to Noor's hand and squeezed it. 'I'm… scared.'

He squeezed back and gave a sombre smile. 'That's a first, coming from you.' He slowly nodded. 'I'm scared, too. Stay together, no matter what.'

The gates burst open and the voracious necrolisk horde charged in. Countless more scaled the walls and leapt over, coming from different directions. They were coming for us.

Twenty-Nine: No More Failures

'Open fire!'

The soldiers fanned out and fired on the stampeding beasts. The front rows ducked, allowing those behind a clearer shot. It was hard to tell without my powers, but it looked like we had a few hundred soldiers barely holding their formation together.

The first wave of necrolisks splattered to bits as the wall of heavy projectiles met them. More poured through the gate and over the fortifications faster than could be dispatched. The gun emplacements along the walls weren't firing. Were they powered down?

'Shift back!' Terel shouted, her voice becoming hoarse.

Everyone hurriedly dashed back while continuing to fire. Our three tanks fired their huge flame cannons, igniting entire lines of necrolisks at once. The two MASU launched salvo after salvo of rockets, devastating the next wave.

Noor was firing his pistol into the mass, but every second shot deflected off the creatures' armour. He let go of my hand so that he could focus on his aim. Malu had borrowed a rifle and was manically firing it over and over whilst roaring a desperate battle cry. I gripped my sword tighter.

'All posts, all posts,' Terel yelled into her headset as she climbed onto one of the hover-tanks. 'Reinforcements required at Royal Gardens. Repeat. All posts…'

The encroaching swarm reached our frontline, swiping and tearing through several soldiers. The girls screamed as they were torn to bits by the giant teeth and pincers.

Terel pointed back to the Citadel. 'Fall back! Fall back!'

Everyone retreated, including the vehicles. Most kept firing on the move, while some soldiers had completely abandoned the line and were sprinting back to the Citadel doors.

'Get those doors open!' Terel yelled to them.

Nearby patches of dirt and grass burst upwards as more necrolisks emerged from their burrows to join the chase. One mounted a MASU and slashed its chest open, before ripping out the hysterical pilot and feasting. The lumbering machine teetered and fell on its back with a ground-shuddering thump.

The first of our soldiers reached the enormous golden doors, currently closed. They banged on them repeatedly, shouting for help. The mechanism to open the doors was inside.

A lone soldier hadn't noticed how much we were withdrawing. The necrolisks flanked and slaughtered her. The necrolisk encirclement was almost complete. They drew closer, slicing and killing another group of our dawdling soldiers.

'I'm going to kill Colony!' Noor yelled as we picked up the pace with the others.

'You're *surprised* by his betrayal?' Malu shouted back.

We kept backing up until we had also reached the Citadel doors. Our dwindling army was pinned against the entrance.

'What do we do?' one younger girl shrieked.

Kinru appeared at my side. 'Keep shooting! Protect the commanders!'

Even more soldiers joined in banging on the doors. Another had crouched by the wall to cry. I pulled a sidearm off her and helped fire into the swarm. Like Noor, my shots rarely connected. I got lucky as one exploded my target's head, spraying everyone nearby in green pulp.

Some of the necrolisks climbed the side walls to drop on us from above. One landed right next to me. It raised its pincers in the air. I stabbed my sword into its head, spilling its mucousy brains onto the already blood-strewn path.

More necrolisks ambushed from above, one landing on Terel's hover-tank. It began peeling its outer plating with some difficulty, the sound of which was an ear-piercing whine.

I went back-to-back with Noor. My aim was improving with each shot. Our numbers dwindled with every scream, but so did theirs. Necrolisk corpses fell onto our own as they were shot off the wall.

Was this our end? Our fledgling empire dealing with one embarrassing loss after another until finally succumbing in a last-ditch battle, crying and clawing for survival?

Distant pops, and shortly after, another missile volley slammed into the monstrous clusters. The expanding, sizzling fire consumed the foul creatures and showered us in charred gore. A swath of rapid-firing lasers cut through their lines from the side, tearing even more to shreds. Reinforcements had arrived.

The necrolisks collectively squealed, as though linked in both pain and failure. They withdrew as one, even those in mid-swipe. The blood-smeared mass scurried back towards the gate, the fortifications and their burrows. We kept firing, taking out many more before they escaped.

Some around us cheered, but most breathed a sigh of relief. I sheathed my sword, turned around and hugged Noor. Body parts littered the gardens. Green and red blood smeared every patch of grass. The siren still droned. The other army, roughly four times the size as what we had left, marched through the hedges to join us.

'Tarsus, what is happening?' Terel shouted into her headset. 'Where is City Defence? Tarsus, come in.'

Malu approached me, arms shaking. 'What do we do now? Those *things* are attacking our people… our families.' She paced from side to side, eyeing the Residential Rim.

Terel glanced at me, and then to Kinru. 'Give the Commander your communicator.'

I hadn't even noticed, but mine had come off at some point. Kinru obliged, taking off her entire helmet and putting it on me.

As this was happening, the other army reached us, and their troops blended into our own. Several surviving officers emerged and broke everyone into smaller formations, before turning to Terel and I and awaiting further orders.

The crowd quietened, and most of the soldiers looked out at the city again. The sounds of chaos again carried to us, visibly shaking morale. The whining sirens twisted in pitch and in our minds. The soldiers closest to us watched Terel and I intently.

Terel nodded and stared at the ground. 'Okay, start again, Tarsus.'

'Commander Sacet?' I heard Tarsus say. 'Is she on the right channel?' I could see a small picture of her in a control room. She and a small team were frantically operating the panels.

'I read you,' I replied.

'Power is out to most of the city,' Tarsus said. 'I have a backup system here, but I'm not sure how much time I've got, so I'll be brief. You've noticed there's a citywide inhibitor field?'

'Citywide?' I shouted in surprise.

Terel scowled. 'Siph's defence upgrades…'

'Yes,' Tarsus agreed. 'I didn't think one this large was technically possible. There's no telling how large it *really* is.' Several screens were dividing her attention.

I approached Terel and shrugged. 'So, we just blow up the power, like I did last time?'

Tarsus fiddled with some buttons. 'Hold on. Okay, it should just be us three in the channel. Can you still hear me?'

'Yes,' Terel and I both said.

Tarsus shook her head. 'They'll be expecting that. But… there *is* another option.' She frantically typed at her workstation. 'I never trusted Siph, or *any* of you for that matter. Only Tau and Coleo. I always had a feeling *someone* would turn this city's defences on us at some point…'

Terel rolled her eyes. 'Get to the point. What's your plan?'

'Updating your maps… now.'

A map appeared on the little screen in my helmet, highlighting a building in the Science Quad. It was a block over from the place Malu used to take me for assimilation procedures.

'That's a city defence nexus station,' Tarsus continued. 'The one I'm in has been locked out of every subroutine, and we can't access that one over in the Science Quad, but from here it looks like it's still green.'

I shrugged at Terel, unsure of what any of that jargon meant.

'Meaning what, Commander?' Terel asked her.

Tarsus sighed. 'I need you to go there and reroute the subroutines to us. Uploading my access codes to your communicators now.'

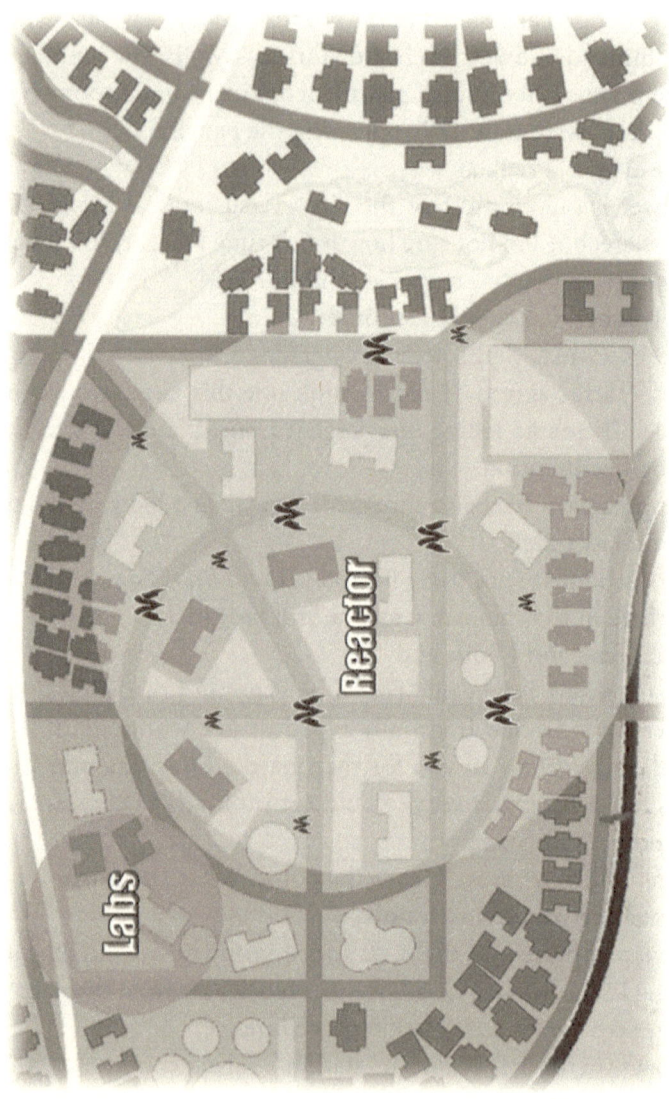

The map zoomed in on the building and highlighted one room, in particular.

'Just plug into the main workstation there. That'll bring control to us here.'

I clenched my sword. 'Is Colony dead? Is that why these things turned on us?'

'There's a high concentration of necrolisks around the reactor, so I doubt it. It's like they're defending it.'

She highlighted the other building where the reactor was. Hundreds of red dots appeared to represent the necrolisks, too. Our target was on the other side of the swarm.

I scrunched up my face. 'But Colony *can't* be there. The inhibitor field would…'

Terel waved a hand dismissively. 'Irrelevant. You'll deal with him when you get your powers back.' She inspected the new formations surrounding us. 'Tarsus, send every soldier you can spare towards the reactor. I'll lead the attack. At the same time, a smaller team will accompany Sacet to the second location.'

The surrounding soldiers, especially those close enough to overhear our planning, whispered amongst themselves nervously.

I looked back at Kinru. 'Colonel, get your team together and several more you trust.' She saluted and ran off. I turned to Malu and Noor. 'You two are with me.'

They both approached: Noor stern yet eager, and Malu willing but anxious, with darting eyes and glances.

Terel glared at me. 'Do not let our diversion go to waste, Commander.' She saluted strongly and I returned it. 'Everyone, listen up,' she roared to the murmuring soldiery, silencing them. She climbed the hover-tank again. 'We're assaulting the Science Quad via the main boulevard. Spear formation behind this tank. Move out!'

She opened the hatch and lowered herself in. Officers barked orders down the lines until all complied and mobilised. The tank floated towards the gate, leading the army out of the gardens.

Kinru returned with a full squad of fifteen green-streaked soldiers. 'Ready when you are, Commander.' She and her augmented squad saluted me in unison.

'You trust these soldiers, Colonel?'

She nodded. 'With my life.'

Satisfied, I turned away and took a closer look at the target's location on my map and noticed a line cutting across it. 'Tarsus?'

'Yes, Commander?'

'Is the hover-car system operational?'

There was a pause as she leant over a screen. 'You're not going to believe this. They are, but only in the Science Quadrant.'

'Why?'

'I'm guessing the spies are still using them, hoping no one notices. Head west and I'll guide you to the first functioning station.'

'Right.' I glanced back to the others. 'Let's go.'

We followed in the army's wake towards the gate. We passed Marid's body again and the feeling of shame returned.

'No more failures.'

At the station

Malu manually accelerated the hover vehicle out of the station and along the winding, elevated track. Our team barely fit inside, as the interior was normally designed for only ten occupants. Each row of seats was crammed with soldiers, and those left were forced to stand and hold the handles on the ceiling.

Our soldiers sat patiently without speaking. Some checked their weapons. Most looked outside at the bedlam in the streets below. One girl was drawing on her armour with a thick, black pen. I recognised her, she was the sniper we brought along to find The Shroud. She had found one final patch on her leg to begin outlining a cartoon necrolisk.

Outside, there were fleeing citizens and wandering necrolisks everywhere. Blood stains were common, but bodies were not; victims were either being dragged underground or eaten whole. Burrows punctured the battlefield ground like innumerable stab wounds.

Most of the surrounding apartment buildings' doors and windows were smashed in. In fact, the overall structural integrity looked very much weakened thanks to how the necrolisks had entered them, with holes in walls and floors where they had no doubt burst through. It was a wonder how some of the buildings were still standing.

The sirens had finally ceased. I wondered how many people evacuated in time. Would there still be a city left after we saved it?

Terel's army could be seen in the distance, marching parallel to us in the next street over. Like us, they fired on any stray necrolisks along the way. They'd engage with the bulk of the reactor swarm any moment now. The diversion was set.

Malu seemed particularly disturbed by the carnage below. 'The next station is where I used to get off to visit them.' She glanced back at me.

I nodded. 'I'm sure they're okay.'

She gripped the control stick tightly and narrowed her eyes. 'You mean like how Eno is *okay*?'

I shook my head and sighed. 'Hana is strong and cautious. She would have been the first to move at any sign of trouble.'

Malu gazed forward at the track. 'Sure. That would be the most *convenient* thing for your mission.' She glanced to the apartment buildings we were passing, and then pulled the stick back to slow us.

I raised an eyebrow at the Colonel and gestured to Malu. 'What are you doing, Malu?' I asked the question but already knew the answer: she wanted to stop at the upcoming station. Kinru and I approached Malu in the driver's seat.

Malu huffed. 'It's only a couple of blocks walk from here. I can make it on foot.'

'We have a mission, Colonel,' Kinru said. 'You think you're the only one with loved ones out there?'

I reached out for the stick. Malu turned in her seat and punched me in the jaw. I fell back against the cabin's side. Kinru and three others including Noor tussled with Malu.

'Stop!' Malu shouted as she was dragged out of her seat and to the back. 'Just let me off here; you can still complete your mission…' Tears welled as she continued to struggle against her restrainers. 'My family could be dying right now. Let me save them!'

Another soldier took the driver's seat, pushing the control stick forward again to accelerate. We passed through the station and along the next track.

I glared back at Malu for a moment, stunned by her cowardice. Noor and I traded a frustrated head shake, exhausted by her antics; this was the worst we had ever seen her.

I slowly rose, rubbing my sore jaw. 'The quickest way to save this city is by getting our powers back. We're doing this for everyone.'

Malu sneered. 'If you died right now, they'd probably stop attacking us. If anything, we're doing this for *you*.'

Kinru grabbed Malu's collar and forced her up against the wall. 'If you disrespect your superior one more time you'll spend the rest of this ride unconscious.'

I raised my hand for Kinru to take it easy and she let Malu down. 'Keep it together, Malu. Please. I'm asking you as a friend right now, not your superior. We *need* you.'

Malu shoved the other soldiers away, staring daggers at all of us. As the cabin awkwardly silenced and emotions calmed, she eventually slumped down and hid her head in her arms.

Our destination, the ugly, monolithic, grey laboratory, was within view. The driver gradually slowed our approach.

I squeezed through the soldiers in the cabin and approached Malu to begrudgingly hand her back her weapon. She snatched it with a sneer, stood, and lined up at the door with the others. The farther we had gotten away from the apartments, the more composure, and perhaps sanity, she seemed to regain.

'Everyone, ready up,' I instructed, glancing back at them all.

They all stood and checked their rifles.

I gestured to my headset. 'This communicator has the code that will bring down this inhibitor field. When I get my powers back, I'll need cover while I exterminate the necrolisks. If I die, one of you must take this to the central computer and connect it instead. Colonel?'

Kinru nodded and pointed at her squad. 'Check your corners.

Keep each other covered and stay together. We go in as quietly as possible.'

As she continued with the specific tactics, the vehicle reached the station. The doors opened, and we piled out to survey the area. Beyond the station, a column-lined path led to the lab's front entrance.

By the entrance was another group of soldiers, slightly smaller in number than our own. The women wore the same armour we did. What were they already doing here? They turned and noticed us.

I led my squad out of the station and along the path. Terel's forces were now fully engaged with the necrolisks over at the neighbouring block. The sounds of unending laserfire echoed off the tall lab buildings.

The other group strolled to meet us at the path's halfway point. They were mostly higher-ranked, older soldiers. Their streak colours were mixed. Leading their group was a dark-haired woman with green-tipped purple streaks. She seemed vaguely familiar, where did I know her from?

'Commander Sacet,' she called out before saluting. The others gave a delayed salute, too. 'It's good to see you alive. We've just finished securing this building.'

She had a strange electronic neck brace, like an inhibitor collar. Whatever it was, its tiny lights flashed, as though currently active.

I glanced at my squad, who appeared as sceptical as I was. 'Then you won't mind if we double-check it?'

Her eyes darted before resting back on me. She gave a wide smile. 'As I said, we have already checked it.' She gestured to the chaotic battle a block over. 'The necrolisks have surrounded the main reactor. We'll join you for the assault.'

I pointed at her. 'I remember you. You got a promotion from Verre for killing a hundred men. Aki, right?'

She dipped her head in an impressed bow. 'It was only eighty, but I'm honoured you remember me, Commander. You're a fan of my work?'

I shook my head. 'No, not really.'

I raised my pistol at her and fired, and my soldiers simultaneously did the same. The normally lightning-fast projectiles stopped in midair. Each crackled wickedly.

Aki, as though anticipating my actions, had raised her hands at the same time as me. She grinned, lowered her brow, then waved at the projectiles to manipulate them. The energy floated closer and flattened into a red haze, which surrounded her like a spherical shield.

Taken aback, my soldiers fanned out. Aki's group didn't counterattack, but rather appeared to be waiting for her command.

Although just as shocked as the others that she could use her powers, I kept my cool. I remembered what Malu said: that this would all stop if they killed me, but they would've already done that if they wanted. Their ultra-powerful leader made a point of saying he'd leave me to last. This was all a game to them, a blusterous show to us and their masters.

I shook my head at my own foolishness, lowered my weapon and stepped towards her.

'Sacet, what are you doing?' Noor called out, his pistol shaking.

Aki gestured at Noor. 'You should listen to your *pet*, Sacet.'

I continued shifting closer and pointed at my chest. 'Go ahead. Kill me.'

Thirty: They're Always Watching

Aki's lips trembled and her grin faded. She waved her hand about, causing the humming energy to swirl. 'You think I can't kill you?' Her voice distorted and crackled through her shield.

I smirked and took another step. 'You *could*. But you and I both know… *he*… wouldn't like that one bit. Do you *really* want to take my death away from him?' I stopped in front of Aki and glared at each of her soldiers. 'I wonder how he'd punish you all?'

Aki returned my smirk. '*Ha*, got it all worked out, do you? It's true, you're off-limits.' She looked over my shoulder. 'But *they* aren't.'

She burst forward and kicked me in the stomach, thrusting me back. Both groups opened fire and took cover behind pillars, benches and raised garden beds. My side's projectiles were instead being drawn into Aki's shield.

Aki pointed at my squad and the pulsating energy redirected to them like bolts of lightning from her fingertips. The focused energy obliterated three of our people into bloody particles.

I jumped to my feet, stowed my pistol and drew my sword instead. Knowing that I was untouchable, I charged the closest enemy soldier and stabbed her through the head.

'Cease fire!' I yelled back to the others. 'You're giving her more ammunition.'

My squad complied, taking cover instead.

Aki glowered. 'Fine, I'll make my own.' She pulled out her pistol and pointed it at the ground. She fired it repeatedly, and each projectile hung over the ground next to the others. She then waved her free hand at them, and they floated up.

As her shield reformed, I ran to the next closest soldier. The soldier aimed her gun at me but hesitated, unsure of what to do. I stabbed her chest, making the decision for her.

'Idiots!' Aki yelled. She flung a second arc of lightning at my friends but hit a pillar instead.

She turned to me and aimed her pistol at my legs. I leapt for a low wall as she fired. The projectile missed and I rolled into cover.

'For Empyrean's sake, don't just *let* her kill you,' Aki said back to her squad. 'Non-lethal shots on Sacet.'

I had to rethink my strategy instead of just charging in again. Aki was vulnerable whenever she discharged all her energy to attack. In that moment, providing no one fired their weapons, she'd be defenceless.

I clambered along the wall and went behind a pillar. Aki and her soldiers were ignoring me, firing on my squad instead. Aki fired her pistol again for another surge of energy. This was it.

As she raised her arm up at my squad, I jumped out from the pillar, raised my sword behind my back with both hands and hurled it at her. The electricity discharged from her finger. The sword spun through the air. She turned, too late.

The sword plunged into her chest. Her eyes widened in horror, as did mine in surprise for how lucky that throw was. She spat blood onto her chin and knelt.

The enemy soldiers noticed, exchanged anxious looks before turning to the facility and running.

I whipped out my pistol and aimed. 'Shoot! Shoot them now!'

My soldiers popped up from cover and fired on the retreating spies' backs. Together we fired and took the last of them down.

I looked back at my squad and noticed the others tending to Kinru. She had a large chest wound gushing with blood.

I scrunched up my face, ran over to Aki, grabbed my sword's handle and twisted.

She screamed in agony and grabbed the blade with both hands to stop it turning farther. 'Killing us… means nothing. We'll come back again… and again.'

'Then tell your masters I'm sick of playing games.'

She coughed up blood onto the ground. 'Tell them yourself, they're *always* watching you.'

'Then they're *also* watching you fail.'

I wrenched my sword out, then sliced it sideways to finish her. Her now lifeless body slumped to the side. I flicked the blood off the sword and rejoined the others.

Kinru was dead. My companions stood up over her and closed their eyes in grief. She wasn't the only one down, five others had lost their lives as well.

Malu stormed over to me. 'You wanna tell us what *that* was about?'

All but Noor eyed me with distrust.

I raised my hand up at them. 'For some reason they want me to suffer the most, so they're trying to kill me last.' I gestured at the fallen. 'I am truly sorry for their losses. Kinru was a good woman.' I looked at the other bodies. 'And the others fought bravely, too.'

The laserfire and explosions on the wind sounded closer than before.

'But we've run out of time.' I pointed back at the facility. 'We have a job to do. Come on.'

Inside the facility

This corridor was lined with large vats suspended from the ceiling. Unconscious little girls were floating in a white fluid inside them. Each had a series of tubes and wires plugged into their mouths and skin. There were catwalks above looking down on the vats, with ladders along the walls to reach them.

The nine of us ran cautiously towards the main room, clinging to any cover we could find and checking our corners. The lab was eerily quiet, aside from the humming equipment and occasional bubbling vat.

Noor lagged behind, horrified by what he was seeing. 'What *is* this? What are they doing to these children?'

I crouched by one of the control panels that regulated the vats for cover. 'These are the little sisters, Noor.'

One of the soldiers paused to tap the glass on a nearby vat. 'Born and raised like this until we're five.' The little sister kicked her legs, perhaps hearing the taps.

'Not me,' Malu said from a nearby railing. 'I'm all-natural.'

Noor shook his head and groaned, as though this was somehow an assault on his senses. He caught up to me and ducked. 'You were *in* one of these... prisons?'

'Yes, but I don't remember it,' I quickly replied before raising a finger. 'Now quiet! We're getting close.'

The last corner was in front of us. The map showed one more corridor and then our destination would be through a door. I double-checked the map to confirm it.

The building's layout was coming back to me. I remembered being in the next room numerous times for my assimilation procedures. They had this big machine called an Awakener, which I'd sit in to help amplify my powers.

Our group dashed around the corner but then stopped upon seeing a most ghastly sight. The final corridor was lined with vats like the last, but they were all smashed open. Glass shards were scattered everywhere, as was the white liquid. All the little sisters were missing, leaving only ripped cables and tubes.

I had already seen so much death today, but nothing as despicable as this. My jaw wasn't the only one dropped, the others looked equally as revolted. I closed my eyes, shook my head and continued forward.

'Why attack little sisters?' a soldier said from behind.

The others eventually trod over the broken glass with me. We passed broken vat after vat. Most had pooled blood at the bottom. There was a severed hand on one of the control panels. One soldier saw it and vomited onto the steel grated floor.

'This wasn't an attack,' I explained. 'It was a feeding.'

We traversed through the horror show, kicking shards out of our way, eventually reaching the closed double doors. I clenched both my pistol and sword handle tight. The others stacked up to the sides.

'What's that sound?' Malu whispered.

There was something making a loud inflating and deflating noise in the next room.

'I'll run to the control panel,' I instructed. 'Cover me.'

They all nodded. I stepped forward to trigger the doors. They slid open and I began to charge through but immediately stopped again.

The lab was filled with necrolisks. They collectively turned to me. Behind them in the centre of the room was an enormous, swollen, worm-like creature breathing in and out.

A scrawny, armoured man wearing a gasmask was sitting in the Awakener in the far corner of the room. Colony.

'New plan,' I said as the necrolisks roared. 'Run and shoot!'

I took aim at Colony and fired, before backing off and firing into the necrolisks. My first shot missed. Colony rolled out of the machine and took cover behind it. The necrolisks rushed towards the doors.

The others joined me, retreating along the corridor and firing. The bottlenecking doors forced the necrolisks to come through one at a time into our projectiles. We downed several already, forcing each successive creature to climb over the corpse of those that preceded it.

Malu was leading the way. 'Up the ladders!'

None of us needed much convincing, we all sprinted to whichever ladder was closest. Noor and I stayed below to cover the last soldier, firing at a charging beast together and downing it. We holstered our weapons and scrambled up, too.

Another necrolisk was coming straight for me. I was halfway up the ladder. It leapt into the air and snapped its pincer, but a crack shot from the catwalk above stopped its momentum dead, and it fell to the floor with a rattling thud. It was our sniper, who gave me a nod before recharging her weapon for another shot.

More necrolisks continued to surge out of the room. All my comrades aimed their weapons over the catwalk railings and fired down.

I continued climbing. Noor reached out and pulled me up the

last rung. I readied my pistol and joined the others to shoot over the railing, but nothing happened when I tried to fire. A red error symbol lit up on the pistol's side. I threw it over the side and unsheathed my sword instead.

Some of the necrolisks hopped on top of the vats, attempting to reach us. Others dug their claws into the walls and began to climb. One creature was getting close to reaching the catwalk. I ran over and sliced the puncturing claws, sending it tumbling down on the others under it.

Three more necrolisks clambered onto the narrow catwalk from the other end of the corridor. Our soldiers over there were distracted by other targets.

'Look out!' I yelled at them.

The first necrolisk impaled the closest girl. The other soldiers counterattacked, shooting it in the head. The dead necrolisk slipped off the catwalk, pulling the still-alive soldier down with it. She wailed as they both fell to the floor. Other necrolisks surrounded her and sliced at her body repeatedly until she was dead. The other soldiers focused fire on the necrolisks on the catwalk and downed them both.

A colossal roar shook the facility. Many of us reached out to the nearest railing to stop from losing our balance. The necrolisks below parted to the corridor's sides. There were several loud stomps coming from inside the Awakener chamber. The creature couldn't possibly fit through the double doors.

The walls around the doors crumpled with a mighty crash. The spindly, coiling monstrosity rammed through the new opening and into the corridor. Its terrible, thorn-filled maw had clicking incisors the size of forearms. Each of its six legs frenziedly stomped towards us. Its elongated body stretched up to the catwalk level. This was the necrolisk queen.

The soldiers fired on the behemoth, but every shot deflected off its thick, gleaming carapace.

'Run!' Noor shouted, and we all raced away along the two catwalks in different directions.

The queen bit onto the end of our catwalk and tore it backwards. The damage cascaded along until there was nothing to stand on. I began to fall.

'Sacet!' Noor yelled as he flailed his hands to mine, but our fingertips only grazed.

I hurtled down to the floor and smacked into it. My vision went fuzzy. I got back on my knees and looked up.

Noor vaulted over the railing and landed by my side. Brandishing only his pistol, he fired on the encroaching necrolisks, as did the girls still up on the catwalks.

Noor killed two more, but one scuttled unnoticed behind him, fixated and moving in for the kill. I sprung up and leapt. My sword penetrated the monster's mouth interior. Both it and I crashed at Noor's feet.

The necrolisk queen bellowed again. The thunderous boom was deafening, replacing the sounds of laserfire with endless ringing. The beast charged with even more of its brood. Each stomp quaked the floor grates loose.

I pulled Noor behind a vat and glanced back up at Malu. 'Distract it!'

Her eyes practically doubled in size, and she shook her head. 'I *hate* you, Sacet!'

'Please!'

I gestured for Noor to follow me down a different corridor.

Malu glanced at the other soldiers. 'Focus fire on that thing!'

Noor and I ran as fast as we could. According to the map, this new corridor was longer, but it would lead back around to the Awakener chamber eventually. The corridor opened into another large laboratory. There were jars all over the place with preserved foetuses inside, perhaps experiments that had gone wrong over the cycles.

Noor shook his head at me.

'Lecture me later,' I said.

The floor rumbled. More nearby stomps. Was it still chasing us? A door on the far side of the laboratory burst open and Colony ran past with two of his creatures, not noticing us. Was he trying to escape?

'Traitor!' I yelled to him, and giving the angriest death stare I was capable of.

He stopped by one of the lab tables and looked back at us. I darted forward and jumped up on the closest table. Noor aimed his pistol and fired at the necrolisks. They turned and skittered towards me.

I sprinted along the tabletop and leapt over the first necrolisk, which was then shot dead by Noor. I landed in front of the second necrolisk, which thrust its claws forward. I slid between its legs with my sword pointing up, splitting and spilling its innards onto the tiles.

Colony raised his hands as though in surrender, but I was ready for his deception. Green, corrosive fluid spluttered from the tubes on his wrists. I rolled under another table, avoiding it entirely, then flanked him from the side.

There was another loud crash from where Noor and I had entered as the queen forced its way in. Bits of the wall, the jars and entire tables launched in every direction. Noor quickly backed away from it, but it didn't have eyes for him. It instead reared its head up at me. Noor aimed at it, unsure of what he could do.

While I was distracted, Colony had redirected his hands to my face. I ducked just in time again and went behind him. I choked him with my blade and grabbed the top of his gasmask with my other hand. I ripped it off and flung it to the floor to better expose his neck, but discovered another electronic collar, just like Aki's.

'Call it off!' I shouted into his pasty ear.

The queen stomped closer, hissing at me.

'Do it! Or its master dies.'

The creature froze, going back to breathing in and out. The smell of its breath was of putrescent meat.

Refusing to take his eyes off it, Noor quietly edged his way around the lab to join us.

'Morons,' Colony said. 'We've been through this before. If you kill me there will be nothing to stop her from swallowing you both whole.'

Colony's chest heaved. If I took too long, he'd probably turn his acid on me again. The necrolisk queen crept closer, each step splintering the floor tiles. Its drool gathered and splashed onto the ground, forming large viscid puddles. Noor continued to edge closer to me.

These collars around both Colony and Aki's necks were so similar to normal inhibitor collars. But while the rest of the city couldn't use their powers, they still could somehow. Was the same technology being used to reverse the process?

I glanced at Noor and gestured to the door on the other side of the lab. He nodded. In one quick motion, I brought my blade to Colony's collar, sliced it off and shoved him forward at the queen.

I chucked the sliced, fizzling gadget to the side and cautiously edged around the room's perimeter towards the exit like Noor was.

Colony glanced up at the queen and smiled. 'You give me back to my family willingly?' He turned back and aimed his hands at us. 'Big mistake.'

The queen's head was hovering directly over him, looking down.

Noor shrugged and gestured up. 'You sure she's still family?'

Colony raised an eyebrow and looked back up at the queen. A glob of drool splattered down his shoulder. Soon his smug grin disappeared, replaced with a petrified gawp. 'Their voices… are gone.'

The queen's jaws spun and gaped open.

'No… no! STOP!'

The head dove and snapped shut over his cowering frame. We heard Colony's muffled screams as he was torn apart inside the maw. The queen then tilted its neck back to consume him in a single gulp.

Thirty-One: All I Do Is Destroy

'Run!' I yelled to Noor.

While the monster was busy, we both sprinted around the queen to the door and burst through. The Awakener chamber was just ahead; we could see the smashed doors from earlier. We kept running.

Up on the catwalks, Malu and the others were still locked in combat with the remaining necrolisks.

The floor behind us rattled; the queen had given chase. The stomps picked up speed. Its mouth was filled with Colony's acid. Although the creature's insides sizzled, it wasn't slowing down.

We sped through the door, slid over tables and benches, and finally reached the main computer. I pulled off my headset and frantically searched for a place to connect it.

'Here!' Noor shouted, snatching it from me and driving it into the correct slot.

The terminal screen went gold. A message reading 'Hack-choo' briefly flashed before showing a map of the city. Various symbols flickered from red to green.

The queen entered through the hole it had made earlier and roared, spitting blobs of acidy saliva.

A wave of psionic force rushed over me, returning my second perception. Like an out-of-control aircraft, it spun around the building in an instant, through the multiple floors and outside into the gardens.

I clenched the nearby desk and glanced at Noor. 'Hold onto something!'

He held onto the same desk, which was thankfully bolted to the floor. I threw my free hand at the beast and opened a portal to space behind it. The black void spiralled. My ears popped as the air ripped.

The creature slammed its claws into the floor, pegging itself in place. It squealed in anger and confusion.

My legs floated up, lifted by the violent current. I retightened my grip on the desk with both hands. The creature wasn't budging. If I made the portal any bigger or closer, Noor and I would probably be sucked through as well.

The queen crawled forward, one claw at a time. Its jaws snapped at my feet.

Noor noticed this. He hooked his legs around a nearby metal bar, let go of the desk, and pointed both palms at the queen to fire his energy beam. It hit the monster in the face and continued burning it in an endless barrage.

The queen squealed as its face fell apart, but its jaws still snapped at us. Noor instead aimed at its pinned front legs. His laser cut through the spindly joints in moments.

Now with only flailing stubs for front arms, the queen soared and tumbled back into the void.

I closed the portal. Noor and I fell to the floor and panted. I slowly sat up and he did the same.

There was a cacophony of roars as if every necrolisk in the building was crying out at once. They echoed down the corridors.

I could see them all now, there were thousands around the building. But every single one had stopped in place to quiver and writhe in pain. Some collapsed, unable to move. The rest dove back into their burrows and scurried deep underground towards the mines.

I glanced over at the Awakener and back to Noor. 'Time for some justice.'

He smiled, brushed my shoulder and continued panting for air. 'Yes… please.'

I forced myself up, groaning in pain, and made my way over to the Awakener. I had seen it operated plenty of times, so I didn't have any difficulty turning it back on. I sat in the seat and closed my eyes.

The range of my vision exploded out. I could see the whole city and then some.

Thousands of civilians aimlessly wandered the streets, and many more were hiding in their homes. One woman was kneeling in a crater and crying over another. So many were giving into despair, others stood in silence, in awe of the seemingly innumerable dead. The suffering was overwhelming.

Terel and what was left of her army were cheering in the neighbouring facility gardens, so loudly that Noor and I could hear them through the walls. They raised their weapons high in the air, some even firing in celebration. All the tanks and MASU were gone, their flaming wrecks littered the pockmarked battlefield.

I could see members of The Shroud had joined their cause, too. Pilgrim and Urias were among them, meanwhile Doron and his other sons were nowhere to be seen.

Malu and the four remaining soldiers in our squad were staggering down the corridor towards Noor and I. Malu was limping. She had a large gash on her leg. Someone had tied a tourniquet around it to stop the bleeding.

Without a leader to psychically manipulate them, the remaining necrolisks were retreating to the mines, going as deep as possible. After breaking their mental link to their queen, many had simply died on the spot.

Malu and the others entered the room and stopped in front of the machine.

'Sacet?' Malu began. Her eyes narrowed and her lips curled. 'Exterminate them all.'

I clenched the armrests. 'Gladly.'

My attention sunk to the mines. Even with all the necrolisk causalities, they were still thousands strong. But without their queen they were lost, stumbling all over the place and bumping into one another like feral, individual agents. I focused on the mine's main shaft. It was a massive, wide hole at the surface of the Prison Quadrant.

I thought back to the ocean besides Urias' village. I remembered the awesome power, the crushing pressure and immensity of it all. I felt the muscles in my wrists ache. My whole body convulsed as the largest portal I had ever created took shape. It opened over the shaft, with the exit deep in the ocean.

The deluge showered down like a gargantuan waterfall, wetting the edges of the cave. The mighty torrent reached the bottom of the shaft and onto the necrolisks' heads below, filling a rising pool under their many feet. They paid the water no attention, still in cerebral disarray.

Noor was fidgeting with the controls at the terminal, bringing up live footage of scenes around the city. He stopped the visual when he noticed my gigantic portal over the mines.

He stood back, folded his arms and nodded. 'That's it. Do it, Sacet.'

'Drown, you damn monsters,' one of the other girls uttered. 'Every last one of you.'

The ocean water trickled down into the many branches and paths, but even still, the flow's throughput would take far too long to fill them all. I pictured inside the mine's other vast open areas and created additional portals. One after another more waterfalls flooded the already filling chambers, rapidly eroding the cave's edges, and destroying whatever mining equipment remained.

As planned, most of the necrolisks were submerged against their will. Their pincers splashed upon the water's surface as though desperately trying to swim. Their heads bobbed and contorted as they choked. The water reached the cavern's ceiling in most of the chambers, cutting off any chance of escape.

The creatures smart enough to notice the water somehow paddled to the nearest walls before attempting to climb or dig their way out, but soon they were overcome, too.

Some of the ocean's creatures had been sucked through the portals as well, and unlike the floundering necrolisks, they adapted to the new conditions immediately, swimming around the deepest recesses of the sunken cave and nibbling on my drowned victims.

The water surged through the tunnels beneath us, underneath all the city streets and buildings. Geysers sprayed out of the burrows, washing the bloodstains away.

I exhaled and closed all the portals. Most of the necrolisks had stopped moving, only twitching in the cold dark.

When I first rescued Colony, I had hoped we could come to a mutual understanding. Even with him and all his 'family' dead, I felt guilt-ridden and worthless. What a fool I was for giving him a second chance.

I released my shaking hands but brought one of them to my nose. A stream of blood was pouring out, caused by the straining. My brain felt like it had been split in two. I climbed out of the seat, before immediately collapsing. I had no words.

Noor knelt and helped me to my feet.

Malu wasn't as empathetic. She still had the same angry look as before. She hobbled over, shoved Noor away, grabbed me with both hands and pulled me close. 'My... family... now!'

Noor forced himself between us. 'Malu, enough!'

I raised my hands to stop them both. 'It's fine.' I looked Malu in the eyes. 'I'll take you there.'

I nodded at the four final soldiers. 'Thank you... so much. I'm sorry about the others. I don't know what to say to make their deaths mean something. What I *can* say is... I'll try my best to find Tau and bring them back. All of them.'

None of Kinru's original squad were among them. Each remaining girl was young and close to breaking down like I was.

'Your final order,' I mumbled, barely able to concentrate, 'is to make sure your fallen sisters' bodies are collected. And... then find someone to help.'

'Yes, Ma'am.'

They gave a tired salute, turned and staggered away. Malu continued to glower.

My brain was still reeling from the Awakener, showing after images of things that weren't there. I leant on Noor for support and closed my eyes again. My second perception's range was still far-reaching, so I flitted through the Residential Rim. I stopped with a view over one of the many damaged apartment complexes, specifically the one Malu's family lived in.

There, under many demolished walls and caved-in floors, I sensed the family of three, hunkered down in a corner under what used to be their kitchen cupboards. Something wasn't right: Kowi, Malu's little sister, wasn't moving. Malu's mother, Hana, and brother, Toroi, were huddled around her, squeezing her gently.

Kowi's body was twisted. Had she been crushed by the room's collapse? Or had she fallen a great height? The tears on their cheeks had dried. Kowi's eyes were closed, and her heart had stopped.

'I found them,' I said in a low tone.

Malu's face drooped, her bitterness fading to fear. She gripped onto my shoulders with both hands. 'Please, let me see them. Send me there.'

I opened a portal leading to what was left of her family's living room.

She rushed through and began frantically searching for them. 'Mum?' she said, her voice travelling through the still-open portal. 'Mum, where are you? Kowi?'

Malu's family were obscured by the fallen debris, but they still heard her. Both Hana and Toroi carefully laid Kowi down. They stood and crept out of their cover, back into the living room.

Malu saw them and dashed forward, but Hana raised her hand in the air for Malu to stop. Both Hana and Toroi looked livid. The three of them stood in silence for a moment.

'Where's Kowi?' Malu asked.

'Go away, Malu,' Toroi said. 'We didn't ask for your help.'

'I told you we *never* wanted to see you again,' Hana added.

Malu's entire body languished. 'I came to see if you were okay. I was worried.'

Hana shook her head. 'Were you worried when I asked you to not join their military? Or when I asked you to take us back to the desert? Or when I *begged* you to get your father and brother out of the mines? Were you worried *then*, Malu?'

On our side of the portal, Noor and I stared at the ground in embarrassment.

Hana stomped on the barely stable apartment floor. 'Did you even *feel* anything when you killed your father?'

Toroi pointed at his mother and shrugged. 'Or when you dobbed on Mum and had her sent to re-education?'

Malu slowly nodded, averting her gaze. 'I… did all of those things. And I was… so wrong. And *sooooo*, so sorry.'

Hana shook her head and turned away. 'How many chances are we supposed to give you, Malu? It's too late. You've had endless chances to care about us.'

Malu stared back at them and her face went neutral. She had given up arguing. 'Where's… Kowi?' she asked again.

'She's dead!' Toroi shouted.

Hana glanced back. 'Are you going to kill us next?'

'Just leave, traitor,' Toroi added. 'I'm ashamed to be related to you.'

Malu stared at the floor for a moment, before striding forward. Toroi picked up a piece of debris from the floor, a long steel pipe and thrust it towards her.

'Let me see her!' Malu screeched as she stopped in front of him.

I looked back at Noor with concern, and he nodded back.

'Get away!' Hana screamed again. 'Stay away from us!'

Toroi held the pipe firmly, ready to strike.

Noor and I dashed through the portal. 'Malu,' I called, and she turned back to me. 'Just leave them be.'

Hana and Toroi both scowled in my direction, the same look they gave to Malu. I could feel their hate.

I slowly shook my head at Malu. 'This isn't something you can fix today.'

'It can never be fixed,' Toroi said, staring daggers at me.

'Please, come with us,' I said to Malu, trying to ignore the others.

Malu stared at the debris behind them with wet eyes, perhaps hoping to spot Kowi. She gave one last look at her family, turned and stormed out the apartment's front door.

Toroi pointed the pipe at me. 'Another family betrayer. You're all Eno ever talked about in prison, but you never came for him. You abandoned him.'

I closed the portal and shook my head. 'You don't know the whole story.' I turned and chased after Malu.

'Then where is he?' Toroi yelled as I left. 'Where's Eno now, Sacet?'

I followed Malu all the way to the elevator at the end of the ruined corridor. 'Wait. Malu, stop.'

She turned on the spot and raised her hands at me. 'If you come any closer, I *swear* I will liquefy you this time.'

I stopped and raised my hands in surrender. 'Just… *talk* to me. I'm your friend, remember?'

'It's always talk with you. You gaslight me with your words more than the Dominion ever did. All of you… shaming me for what I had to do to stay alive, to keep *them* alive.'

Noor had caught up and joined my side. 'Is all of that true? Did you really turn your mother in?'

As though reaching her breaking point, Noor's question finally shattered her. She lowered her hands, lips trembling and eyes continuing to well. 'Yes… yes, I'm a monster, alright?' She turned and rested her head against a wall. 'All I do is destroy.' The wall liquefied and splashed along the carpet by our feet.

Noor shook his head. 'I would have turned my father in, too. And… I imagine he'd still hate me if I had. But just because I was wrong in the past, that doesn't make me bad now. You're *not* a monster, Malu.'

She barely responded, not even a glance in our direction. Whenever she got in a mood like this, nothing I ever said would help. I'd always try to correct her behaviour, tell her why she was wrong.

'Malu,' I began. 'I'm not going to say anything else.'

She glanced to the side and raised an eyebrow at me.

I lowered my hands. 'I just want to listen.'

Noor relaxed his stance, too. 'Me, too.'

We looked at her in silence.

She wiped away her tears and sniffed. 'You're going to listen to me? That's a new one.' She shook her head in astonishment, then stared through a dark, nearby hole in the wall. 'You wanna know the last time I was truly happy?'

Noor and I glanced at each other, then waited.

She gave an exasperated snort. 'It was before I met Sacet. The Dominion back then gave me… purpose. They promised me power, respect… love. '

Noor slowly nodded, as if knowing the feeling well.

Malu looked at her feet. 'I know they were lying now, but I miss it. And I know betraying my family all those times was wrong. But I had a *new* family.' She locked eyes with me. 'Sacet, you took that away from me. I know you're right, but I still *hate* you. Ever since I met you, you have made my life miserable. And when this is over, if it is ever going to *be* over, I *never* want to see you again. You're a constant reminder... I cannot heal.'

She grunted and gestured back to the apartment. 'My family hates me. That's *my* fault and I can't fix it. So, I've only got *one* thing left.' She approached me. 'I hate the MD *far* more than I hate you. My only goal now... is to destroy them.'

Noor glanced down in thought. 'So why don't we?'

I scoffed. 'What do you think we've been trying to do all this time, Noor?'

He shook his head. 'No. No more relying on an army filled with spies. Just the three of us.'

Malu and I exchanged a raised eyebrow.

'We three want the same thing,' he continued, gesturing at us. 'So, we know we can *trust* each other. They've known our every move before we make it. They have eyes everywhere. But imagine only us, a small but powerful team.'

I slowly nodded. 'We go off grid...'

'Yes,' Noor replied. 'To places with no cameras.'

'We get rid of this armour,' Malu added. 'Probably filled with tracking devices.'

'I lead the way,' Noor gestured in an imaginary direction. 'I'll show you how to get there.'

I looked up at them both. 'We don't play their game anymore. We strike from the shadows like they do. Noor and I can devastate them from afar.'

Malu scowled at me again. 'And I'll kill your precious rival for you. If I can get a hand on him, I'll liquefy him into a puddle.'

We stared at each other, weighing up our plans. I placed my hand between the two of them. Noor copied me almost immediately, placing his hand over mine. Malu took longer to think about it but eventually put her hand on top of ours.

I nodded and threw my free hand to the side, opening a portal to Doron's desert cave, the most remote place I could think of. Malu strode through first, then Noor. I took one last look at my surroundings and gave a single laugh. Why didn't we do this from the beginning? I stepped through and closed the portal.

Thirty-Two: We Fight Together

Eno

Cold. Every part of my body touching a cold surface. Steel, maybe? I was laying down, and... wait. Where was I? My eyes sprung open and I shot up to sit. A tiny space I couldn't stand up in. A box. Vertical metal bars on the sides. A cage. I was in a cage.

A familiar room was outside the bars, one that chilled me to the bone. No windows, no daylight. Overhead spotlights dimly lit my surroundings. Nearby stairs, although I couldn't see from here, I knew they led up to the room's only exit.

A blood-stained table in the room's centre, with restraints waiting to latch onto their next victim. Behind that, various blunt and sharp instruments hung from a chrome rack. So much blood.

I was a prisoner in Mycol's dungeon, the realisation wrapped around me like a tight blanket of knives. Last time I was here, I was the one dolling out punishment to that woman; there were still mounds of sand and glass shards over in the corner.

Now it was my turn. Mycol was going to hurt me, then kill me, and shortly after my life force would be taken, consumed like a paltry snack.

There was an unsettling, grinding noise coming from somewhere, and at first, I thought it was my own teeth, but it was too high-pitched for that. I had to get out of here.

I strained my hands, trying to use my power on this cage. No effect, not even a rattle from the gate. Was this tiny space an inhibitor cell, like the one I was in when I first came to the city? The rusty, simple frame didn't seem very high-tech.

A metal brace was around my neck, but it wasn't chaining me to anything. I tried pulling on it, but all I did was choke myself. Perhaps it was this collar stopping me?

Why did you let go of me, Sozha? Maybe you had no choice, but you didn't even come back for me. You left me to die.

I tried kicking the cage's door, but nothing budged. It was no good, I was a goner.

'Eno?' a voice whispered, and the grinding stopped. Over on the other side of the room was another row of cages, and inside one was another hunched boy, obscured in shadow. 'You're finally awake.'

Although I couldn't see him clearly, I knew who it was. 'Nadan.'

He shuffled closer to his own bars and grabbed them with both hands. 'What happened? What did you do?' I could see that both his left pinkie and right middle fingers were missing. The wounds had black stitches and dried blood all over them. He, too, had a metal collar around his neck.

I grabbed my own bars. 'It was Sozha... he...'

Nadan rapidly waved his hands and shook his head, as though trying to get me to stop. Although his face was still in darkness, I could see the whites of his eyes widening in fear. He raised a single finger to his mouth, then pointed to the ceiling. I quietened as he cupped a hand on his ear. Maybe I needed to be careful what I said.

'Yeah?' he prompted. 'Sozha was...?'

I cast my eyes down and released the bars. 'I was worried about him. I went out looking for him but... I got caught.'

Nadan slowly nodded and relaxed back into his cage. His silhouette reached for a metal object behind him, the light briefly glinting off it. He had somehow smuggled in yet another knife, even to this place. Rather than going for the cage door, he brought the blade's tip to his collar and, with tiny grinding scrapes and jiggles, tried to break it off.

'Oh, is that all?' he continued. 'I thought that maybe you had come to break me out. Guess I was wrong.' He spoke louder with each sentence, maybe trying to cover the sound of his scratching. 'I mean, I'm always trying to look out for the rest of you, but does anyone look out for me? No.'

I stayed shamefully silent, unsure how to respond. It was true, after all, that Nadan and his brother, and to a lesser extent Keenu and Sozha, had always been supportive of me as the fresh meat here.

Although the thought of rescuing Nadan did cross my mind, shamefully, I chose to flee instead. Mycol's dungeon was just too terrifying to even consider breaking into. But if I was being honest, it wasn't just that. I had been so preoccupied over my own survival that his didn't even register to me.

He grunted as he angled his knife. 'Almost...' His knife slipped, causing a metallic shriek. 'Ahh, come on!' He ceased his picking, sighed, and leant back. 'Sometimes I feel like I'm the only one still fighting them.'

Is this what Sacet would have wanted for me? She fought against the Dominions until her end to protect me. But did she do that so I could spend the rest of my life hiding in a shack somewhere, to turn my back on others?

Knowing her, probably yes. But maybe she just wanted that until I could grow up and continue the fight? Grandpa wanted me to be a warrior, and if Sacet could see me now, I bet she'd want that for me, too. Simply surviving wasn't brave and it wasn't enough. We had to fight these people with everything we had.

My eyes welled as I realised my cowardice. 'I'm sorry.'

Nadan grabbed his bars again. Another sigh. 'No, I'm sorry, I... I didn't mean to make you cry. Expecting a rescue from here... it's a tall ask, of anyone. This place is just getting to me.'

We sat in silence for a while, me sniffling as I cleaned away my tears.

'You know, it wasn't bandits that tortured me and my brother,' Nadan began. 'It was Mycol.'

I shook my head. 'What? Why?'

'Male Dominion captured us, brought us here. And Mycol wanted to know where our acolyte dad was.' He pointed out his cage to the table. 'He hurt me really bad, in this same room. When I got my power, I killed his assistants, but I couldn't kill him.'

He groaned. 'When he got up, he… he didn't seem angry anymore. He was… *happy*. Happy he had another acolyte to add to his collection. He let us stay. Said we had to lie about what happened or we'd be right back in here again.'

Nadan clenched his bars. 'But no matter what he does to me, I'm never going to tell him what he wants to know.' He craned his neck up. 'You hear that, you soul-sucking creep? You will get *nothing* from me!'

A loud metal groan resounded, shattering the dungeon's stillness and causing me to jump. The door at the top of the stairs had opened, and now footsteps clomped down, each so heavy that they shook the nearby cages.

'Time to wake up, boys,' Mycol's gravelly voice crooned as he reached the bottom of the stairs with a thud.

His burning eyes locked with mine. I receded in my cage, my back to the wall. He drew closer, slowly, purposefully. His horrid face lit under the spotlight; an unnatural smile twisted up like a sickly, open wound; and his bulbous, swollen cheeks quivered in anticipation.

He stopped short of my cage, leant in and brought his shaking head level with my own. 'I'm so… disappointed in you, Eno. You had so much potential. I could have helped you… to become something far greater.' His carcass-smelling breath wafted in.

I lowered myself, attempting to bow in the restrictive space. 'Please, Patriarch Mycol, sir, I wasn't running away. I-I-I was tr-trying to find Sozha, like you asked.'

Mycol turned and made for the rack. '*Oh* Eno, I thought I already told you? You're a bad liar.' He reached out and twiddled his fingers over the various torture instruments, unsure of which to choose. 'Our security system showed that you simply… disappeared, just like he did.'

'Eno's telling the truth,' Nadan said from behind him. 'He doesn't know anything.'

Mycol ripped a cleaver from the rack and pointed it at him. '*You* be silent, boy! Or I'll have your whole hand next.'

He then pointed the weapon at me, but as I cowered, he inspected the cleaver and shook his head at it. He placed it on the table and regained his composure. He stared at me and slowly approached again with another sick grin. 'Eno, I've decided that… torturing you would be a waste of time. You can keep your secrets. Let's skip… right to the meal.'

He raised his hands, which ignited and engulfed in green flame. I panted rapidly. My heart thumped. I needed an escape, right now! Was the door upstairs still open? Maybe someone, *anyone* was up there.

'Someone, help! Help us!' I called.

His breathing intensified, chest now heaving. 'A shame about your size. If only you had *grown*… a little bit more.' His asymmetrical eyes glinted with sadism.

'Heeeelp! Help, please!'

No one was answering my pleas, and Mycol didn't seem concerned anyone would hear them either.

'Alright, stop it, you psycho!' Nadan yelled, his voice bordering on a roar echoed in the chamber. 'I know where Sozha is, so just… just leave Eno alone.'

This gave Mycol pause, but he didn't extinguish his flames. He glanced back. 'Oh? What happened to "you will get *nothing* from me", Nadan? Enough stalling.' Mycol leapt forward, grabbed my cage with both hands and lifted it above his head.

I screamed in fear and pushed against the bars with all my strength to stop from falling towards him, but his flames were already making me feel woozy. Everything was fading. I needed to vomit.

'It's Sozha's new power,' Nadan added.

'What?' Mycol shouted back, before hurling my cage aside.

My miniature prison clanged and slid along the dungeon floor, eventually coming to a stop. Mycol had completely abandoned his focus on me, approaching Nadan's cage instead.

Nadan pushed his face up to his bars, revealing even more fresh scars all over his face and body. 'I've seen it. He showed me just before he escaped. What you've been saying all this time about becoming stronger through suffering, I… I think it finally got through to him.'

Mycol, enraptured by the news, actually twirled on the spot and laughed with delight. 'Yes! I knew it!' His flames subsided and he darted over to Nadan's cage. 'What could he do? What did it look like, exactly? Tell me everything!'

Nadan sighed and sat down flat again. 'You'll just kill me if I tell you.'

Mycol's misshapen eye twitched. 'Or I'll kill if you *don't* tell me?' He clenched one of his flame-filled fists, whilst retrieving a metal key from his pocket and unlocking Nadan's cage with the other. 'You're going to take me to where he's hiding, and maybe... just maybe, we can reintroduce you to the other livestock.'

The gate opened and Nadan leant forward, as though preparing to climb out. 'Eno, too, otherwise no deal.' Nadan's hand reached back.

Mycol seethed over at me with a snarl. 'No, he stays with—'

His sentence was cut short by Nadan's knife, which had been stabbed into the side of Mycol's head.

Mycol's face scrunched. His whole body tensed. The monstrous hunchback toppled, colliding into the table on his way down. He was motionless. His flames were no more.

I shook my bars. 'Let me out, quick!'

Nadan, still in his cage, was in shock over his success. He snapped out of it and leapt out, before rushing over to Mycol's body. 'We don't have much time.'

'The guards?' I asked as Nadan forcibly wrenched his knife back out of Mycol's head.

He then rifled through the same pockets we had seen Mycol stash the key. Nadan found it and sprinted over to my cage. 'No, before he gets up again.' Once my cage was unlocked, Nadan offered his uninjured hand to mine. 'From now on, we stick together.'

I narrowed my eyes resolutely and grabbed hold. 'We *fight* together.'

As I was pulled out, Mycol's green fiery aura reignited around his entire body.

Nadan forced me across the room towards the stairs. 'Don't stop.'

'Silly children,' I heard a voice say from behind as we ran up the steps two at a time. 'A disciple cannot be killed so easily.'

The dim light of the dungeon was overpowered by green. The door above was open. I briefly glanced back to see Mycol sitting up again, completely healed and wreathed in fire.

Thirty-Three: Lost in Hate

Sacet

Noor, Malu and I tread up another dune. We had been travelling east-northeast since the attack yesterday, using Doron's cave in the Unclaimed Wastes as a starting point. Resting overnight under a colossal hanging cliff, we then resumed our journey at dawn. Now, the midday sun bore down on us again, cooking our necks and faces.

The unending dunes showed no signs of flattening their rhythmic rise and fall. Every time we scaled one, I would look to the farthest point on the horizon and open a portal to it, prioritising higher elevations like mountaintops. We'd then step through and repeat the process. I had easily done it a hundred times already and I was getting tired.

Our new robes, which we had found stashed in Doron's cave, lightly dragged along the sand. It was strange seeing the two of them dressed in nomadic clothes, but it was also quite liberating. The airy comfort was refreshing and knowing that we couldn't be tracked was a tremendous relief.

Although we had the setting sun on our backs for a second time, it had actually been *less* than a day of travelling. We were moving so fast with each jump that the sun was passing over us quicker than usual.

I still felt guilty for abandoning the city and its people, but with so many casualties, the survivors probably assumed we were among the dead, too. Knowing the Dominion and their obsession over me, I might have even saved lives by leaving.

Terel and Tarsus were still back there, and I trusted them. They'd do what was right to help everyone. It was probably still early morning in New Elysia, with everyone waking to the horror of their new reality. They were going to need their leadership.

As we travelled, I couldn't shake the sneaking suspicion that we were becoming progressively more lost. Additionally, another issue weighed heavily on my mind: Neva's words about Eno. I hadn't really had time to mull them over, seeming as we had been fighting pretty much since then. I wanted to believe he was still alive, but why would I trust anything *she* said? That wispy witch had probably been broken out of prison during the attack, too.

Noor pointed to the next mountain in the distance. 'There.'

'Got it,' I replied, focusing on it and opening another portal.

We stepped through, and I collapsed to my knees on the new dusty mountaintop. The view of the next desert valley—though naturally breathtaking, dotted with shrubs and hazy heatwaves—didn't inspire confidence that we were getting any closer to our destination.

I closed the portal and raised my hand up at them. 'I need another rest.'

Malu glanced back and shielded her eyes from the glare. 'How far do you think we've travelled?'

Noor scouted around again, attempting to recognise familiar landmarks and analyse the sun's position. 'New Elysia and MDC are on opposite sides of Seron, and Doron's cave was about the half-way point. So, maybe three quarters of the way? I'll know when we're getting close.'

The other two took a seat on some nearby rocks as they waited for me to recuperate. As I tried steadying my breathing, I gave a short chuckle.

Malu shrugged. 'What's so funny?'

'Nothing,' I replied, 'it's just that travelling like this with you two…

it reminds me of when I was travelling with my brother and Tau. Eno loved taunting her. He always acted like she was our prisoner but deep down I could see he cared about her... in his own way. She was like another sister for him, one that he could boss around.'

'And Tau,' I continued, 'she'd always be complaining about something. Usually the heat. She'd burn to a crisp in no time out here.'

Noor nodded. 'That definitely sounds like her.'

Malu smirked and looked up at the sky, also remembering. 'That felt like a lifetime ago now. Iya, Verre and I came to capture you. Remember that day?'

I nodded. 'Yeah. Looking back, I realise the three of you were going easy on me.'

Malu pointed at me and frowned. 'And you tried to kill me with a portal.'

I sniggered. 'Lucky for you I was no good back then.' We shared a smile, and I looked down. 'That was the last time I talked to Eno.'

Malu slowly stood and approached. 'He seemed like a nice kid.' She placed a hand on my shoulder and scrunched her lips. 'About yesterday...'

I looked up at her. 'It's okay, you don't have to—'

'No,' she interrupted. 'Let me say what I *need* to say.' She exhaled and bit her lip. 'I'm sorry. I didn't mean all of what I said. I... I *dislike* you sometimes but... you're still my friend. And... my mistakes are on me, not you.' She glanced to the horizon. 'And as for Eno and Tau, we'll find them this time. We won't stop until we do.'

I patted her hand still on my shoulder and stood. 'Thank you, and I'm sorry, too.' I leant forward and hugged her gently. She resisted at first but eventually gave in and hugged me back.

Noor was grinning at us from his rock. Malu and I let go and we all shared a quiet moment together listening to the howling wind.

I finally glanced at them both. 'Ready?'

They nodded and I focused on the next mountain peak. The portal opened and we trudged through.

Another great valley lay before us, this time filled with jungle, green as far as we could see. There were more mountain ranges in the distance, and it looked like the ocean was to the southeast.

All our eyes widened and gleamed.

Noor threw his arms wide. 'This is it. The jungles of Avarut.' He cheered and jumped on the spot, before pointing to the next mountain range. 'Those are the Caelum Mountains.' He then spied the distant ocean. 'And over there, that's Tuloch's Gulf.'

His excitement was infectious. We all smiled from ear to ear, laughed with joy, and hugged one another in celebration.

'I know *exactly* where we are,' Noor said.

I jumped into Noor's arms and kissed him. We enjoyed the moment and then relaxed, looking out at the view with our arms around each other's shoulders.

I pointed to the jungle. 'We'll set up camp and plan.'

Malu nudged Noor and smiled. 'Hey, tonight, we salute those that have fallen.'

He grinned back. 'And tomorrow, we avenge them.'

Starlight shone through the cave's mouth and illuminated the tiny patch of rock we claimed. The air was stale, mouldy, and cold—far removed from the comfort I had grown used to in New Elysia. A constant drip, drip, dripping echoed, not just in the cave but in my mind, eroding away my chance of a proper rest.

I was wedged between Noor and Malu on the sand bed I had hardened earlier. Our robes covered us well, but they offered little warmth. We weren't equipped to sleep in the cold, so after last night's freezing experience, we huddled closer to stave off the incessant shivering.

Malu was snoring quietly. It was amazing that she could fall asleep so easily after all that had happened.

As for me, my eyelids were heavy, but I just couldn't fall asleep. I was exhausted in every way that you could be. I stargazed and thought back to what the man had said: that he'd destroy everything and everyone, leaving me to last.

A single tear squeezed out and rolled onto my cheek, but Noor's warm thumb wiped it away. I stared deep into his star-reflecting eyes. He stared back in silence, before leaning in and planting a tender kiss on my forehead. His lips stayed there, and he put an arm around me.

'Tomorrow, we make them all pay,' I whispered.

Noor tightened his hug. I closed my eyes and nestled into his chest. There was a great warmth inside him. My second perception could see him frowning. He was worried about tomorrow, we all were.

As I finally drifted off, I felt the heat of the flames the man had wrought. All I could hear were cries for help before they were drowned out by laserfire. Everything burned. Everything faded. And then nothing. Just me standing there on an infinite white horizon, the last person alive, filled with guilt.

The next day

Outside the MDC limits

The distant city was tall, dark and shaped like an incomplete hemisphere. The outer walls reminded me of Tetsu's shield, except it was missing the top. Instead of covering the circular city with a roof, the highest points of the wall bristled with colossal metal spikes and barbed wire, like an impassable thornbush.

There was a considerable open expanse between us and the walls. Rubbish heaps and ruinous metal frames were strewn all about the large stretch of otherwise flat sand.

Ever since I used the Awakener back in New Elysia, my enhanced perception had maintained its extended range. Even from our safe position beyond the outskirts, ducked down in the jungle brush, I could sense inside most of the city on this side.

Our position's limited view belied the city's enormity. Inside the hemisphere, the city sank deep into the ground, like a colossal crater filled with towering, many-storied buildings. Everything on the far side was beyond my vision's reach. However, I suspected moving closer would be too risky.

I sensed automated machinery and haggard men attending them. Factories of smog and soot. Every building was industrious, yet bleak. Tank after tank dropped off conveyor belts, bathed in the flickering orange glow of the roaring forges. Small boys jumped from catwalks and balconies, hooking chains onto overhead wires to get around the labyrinthine mess of grey and black.

Pockmarked concrete streets were littered with trash. Great lumbering vehicles traversed them, some with wheels or tracks, others hovering above, each slow yet powerful. Thousands of shattered windows. Busted doors banged in the wind. Every surface was cold and hard. Filth abounds.

My enemy was a most sickly thing. I would pity them all were I not so angry.

I sat down behind a tree, crossed my legs, closed my eyes and inspected each and every major building I could find. Noor and Malu knelt down beside me, trying to stay out of view.

Noor pointed at the city. 'The Military Wing should be on the south side. The King's Palace will be in its centre. Do you see it?'

The building he was speaking of was the largest in the city, just like the Royal Citadel back in New Elysia.

'It's at my limit,' I said, 'but I see it.'

My perception flew through its corridors and chambers searching for the king. Each room was more lavish than the last. Guards were plentiful, but I couldn't see Tuloch anywhere. His throne was empty, as were his extravagant personal chambers.

'Can you see him?' Malu asked. 'The king? Or the big guy?'

I shook my head and furrowed my brow. 'No, neither yet.'

I randomly searched around the Military Wing, then around the rest of the city. There were far too many people and places to check.

'He's not in the Palace,' I surmised. 'I don't see Tau or Tetsu either.'

Noor brushed my shoulder. 'No Eno?'

I sighed and shook my head again. 'No. I need more time to search.'

Malu tapped me on the side, breaking my concentration. 'Every moment we spend here increases the chance of being discovered. We move onto Plan B, like we agreed.'

I nodded, pushed up from the tree and focused on a large patch of sand between the bushes. I pointed my palms at it and shifted the top sand away, gradually digging a pit. Over time, I compacted the bottom lower and wider until it was almost as hard as rock.

When it was deep enough to hide the three of us, we hopped down into it, and I raised my hands up again.

I pulled the excess sand above our heads in the shape of a dome, then solidified it as I had seen the sand acolytes do numerous times. I left a couple of windows and a door so that fresh air and light could still come through. The final result reminded me of the adobes that some nomads would build as a shelter.

'Let's begin,' I said.

Both Malu and Noor nodded and took strong stances. Malu wore a steadfast scowl, while Noor appeared more apprehensive, breathing quickly with slightly trembling hands.

During our attack on Vemos, I had opened portals to the munitions warehouse. I still remembered where the bombs were placed, as well as their sizes. I doubted anyone had moved them, given all the chaos in the last couple of days. I opened a tiny portal and peeked through, and sure enough, most were still there.

I sensed the sky above the Palace and opened another portal. Several of the largest bombs tumbled through. As they were still plummeting, I opened even more portals over their factories, labs and military compounds. They all came down at once. We could hear the faint whistling from here.

One explosion after another tore through the city, each blast a booming roar. It sounded like a beast smashing against the walls of a cave. The ground rumbled beneath the sheer force.

I sensed colossal flames erupting in every direction, devouring entire city blocks in an instant. The once-imposing Palace crumbled as I sent more and more bombs. Its decadent and oppressive walls obliterated as if they were made of paper. Building-sized chunks of stone and twisted metal were hurled skyward, raining down upon the city streets.

The labs were particularly volatile, their flames turned different colours as they ignited vats of gasses and chemicals. The factories exploded just as violently, with each of their massive mechanical projects tipping and falling into liquid fire. Soldiers and workers futilely scurried before melting into the floors alongside their evil inventions.

Streets were now filled with screaming citizens, gawking at the commotion from afar. I sent more bombs their way, too. All panicked, all scrambled away, desperate to preserve the lives my wrath hadn't yet reached. The fire surged through the streets like rivers, incinerating countless fleeing people.

I gritted my teeth. I remembered the man's threats once more. He was going to kill every last one of my people and leave me to last? No. I would kill every last one of *his* people and leave *him* to last.

More portals over the residential areas. More bombs. Another hailstorm of projectiles whistled down, their collective screech terrifying those below. The portal gobbled up every last bomb, as the fire did my enemies. The next wave of explosions rocked the city so hard that even the sand dome above our heads cracked. Their polluted skies were now red.

Now it was Noor's turn. I pictured multiple locations all around the city and opened as many portals as I could to those locations in front of Noor, grouped together in a circular cluster. Each one was tiny, and their destinations were placed in the sky above the areas. I stretched the destinations as wide as I could.

'Now?' Noor stammered.

'Kill them,' I said.

He threw his arms at the portal cluster. His red-hot laser blazed the portals and then poured through the numerous holes. Each beam split into the city, amplified in size and intensity. The at least thirty separate lasers sliced through enemies and structures as ably as Noor would on his own. I slowly tilted each destination portal, causing the lasers to trace across the streets and rooftops, cutting a swathe along each building and collapsing them.

Thirty-Four: Misery Eater

Eno

Earlier

Nadan and I burst through the rusty door at the top of the stairs and into the corridor, leaving Mycol and his dungeon behind. I had toured through this creepy corridor before, past all its macabre furniture and knick-knacks, so I was fairly confident I knew where the exit was.

I pointed left towards the huge, unsettling painting of Mycol in a field of bones. 'This way!'

We sprinted to it and around the corner. Another intersection, which way next? I had seen those disgusting jars before. Right.

Stomps behind us. 'That was a dirty... little trick you pulled, Nadan,' Mycol's voice bellowed as he reached the top of the basement stairs. Neither of us dared to look back.

Each piece of decor we passed was still familiar. I recognised that necrolisk shell hanging on the wall. Left here. As we ran, Nadan continued to fiddle with his collar, wedging his knife into wherever it would fit.

More stomps. The carpet shook. 'The longer you cling to life… the stronger the taste.'

Another corner and we halted. Three Terror Guards blocked the front entrance ahead. They stared us down through their emotionless skull masks. Their batons crackled with greenish-yellow electricity, causing me to jump in fear. This was the only exit I knew of.

I glanced back to see Mycol rounding the final corner, slowing from a panting, lumbering lurch to a calm stroll, arms behind his back, a smug, crooked grin on his face. 'Come closer… let me… *taste…* your fear.' His body ignited with green once more, and he stretched out to us while edging forward. I suddenly felt exhausted, like I couldn't go on.

Nadan's eyes darted between Mycol and the Terror Guards before he yanked me sideways. He clawed at the handle of the nearest door with his bad hand and ripped it open. We dashed through the door and bounded up the stairs.

'Get them!' Mycol commanded back in the corridor, and the guards pursued us in.

Now that I was away from Mycol's death aura, my jelly legs strengthened again. We ran up the cornered stairs so fast that we shouldered into multiple walls.

Sparks forked through the air and narrowly missed us. I briefly glanced over the railing to see a guard pointing his baton upwards. They had range!

Reaching the top, we burst into a dark, cage-filled room. These cages were large enough to stand in, and most contained downtrodden men, women, and even children. Almost all of them moaned in pain or cried in despair, and had contorted, misshapen bodies similar to Mycol's. Few even noticed our entrance.

Far side windows overlooked the courtyard three storeys below, where hundreds of men were currently running drills. On two rusted tables in the centre, a man and woman lay strapped down, their motionless bodies either unconscious or lifeless.

A young man with whitish-blue hair in a Terror Guard uniform, minus the mask, stood over them with eyes closed in concentration, likely another of Mycol's lackeys. His back glowed with light-blue fire, resembling Tau's healing power.

Nadan and I continued to run. As we passed the cages, I noticed a fully grown, muscular man weeping uncontrollably, and in the cage next to him was a toddler giving us a stern look.

'Hey… hey, kids!' the little boy chirped before groaning in pain. 'Get me out of here!'

It felt wrong. Unnatural. The child's eyes bore into me with something far too knowing for his age.

We reached the operating tables and stopped, realising there were no other exits.

'Are you ignoring me?' the toddler shouted after us. 'Open this cage, now!'

The blond healer's eyes sprung open and focused on us. 'What are you kids doing in here?' He backed away from us, confused and surprisingly afraid.

The guards caught up and rushed into the room behind us, banging their batons along the cage bars as they ran.

I signalled to Nadan—first at the window, then to the healer. 'Remember when I helped you bump into Ido?' I said, referring to when Nadan deliberately wanted me to tackle him.

It took him a moment, but he nodded back, and the two of us darted at the cowering healer.

'Ge-get back. Guards!'

It was too late, we both shoulder-charged into him and with our combined strength were able to barrel through him and the window. The glass shattered and sliced at all of us, but I felt no pain.

As we plummeted, we grabbed the man, desperate to cushion our fall. The wind whipped at our clothes.

In that moment of falling, I had no fear, but rather weightlessness. Even if the fall killed me, it was better than what I left behind.

We slammed into the courtyard pavement with a bloody splatter, then everything went dark.

Slowly, a face emerged from the inky black—Sacet. She watched me silently with sullen eyes, so sorrowfully that my chest tightened with guilt.

A brief, tingling sensation spread along my phantom limbs, and the blackness shifted. Other faces began to surface, warm and smiling: Tau, her long auburn hair swishing; Pilgrim, with his usual toothy grin; Turen, standing tall and granting an approving nod; and his son, Toroi, folding his arms and wearing a far more mischievous smirk.

Sacet's face softened when our friends arrived. They stood together and stared back at me with kindness.

The space expanded. More faces appeared. All the boys from the Feeble Fortress stepped out of the void, and the crowd grew larger. Nomads, hundreds of them robed in desert garb, appeared sporadically all around. Two figures caught my eye: my mother and father. They, too, smiled, full of quiet pride.

I stood in the centre, no longer surrounded by shadows. Their mouths didn't move, but their voices still flooded the air. *We fight together.* The words spread through me with warmth, melting away the guilt that had clung to me so tightly.

My eyes sprang open. Nadan also came to. We were both sprawled on top of the healer, and although there was a huge spray of blood on the concrete, any wounds we may have sustained had been healed, as I had hoped. Even Nadan's missing fingers had returned, and his scars were smooth skin once again.

'There!' a voice roared behind us. 'Bring them to me!'

It was Mycol. He stomped out of his facility entrance with a swarm of Terror Guards. He grunted with each stride, each more intense than the last, revelling in the hunt.

Nadan and I scrambled to our feet, leaving the still bewildered healer lying on his back. We continued to run across the courtyard. Now that we were out, I had no idea where to go next.

'Help us!' Nadan shouted to the training soldiers. 'Help! They're trying to kill us.'

Those that were training, muscle-bound giants all, paused to observe the commotion, but upon seeing the pursuing Terror Guard, fretfully turned their backs on us.

'Mycol, they saw the grafting chamber,' a timid man's voice said behind us.

'Get back inside!' Mycol screamed at the healer as he and his small army passed him. 'Before anyone else sees you, fool.'

The healer, still with his aura lit, grovelled with a bow, before cowering and retreating.

Nadan and I were running towards the courtyard's only exit, a huge archway that led into the city, but several more Terror Guard were coming from that direction as well. A few approached from the Feeble Fortress, and several more closed in from other angles.

We changed direction repeatedly to avoid them but were herded towards the courtyard's centre, where one of the sunken arena pits was. Several heads popped up along the pit's edge, all belonging to boys from the Feeble Fortress.

'Is that... Nadan?' Ido said.

'What? Where?' another boy added.

The other boys were our last chance. Would they risk themselves to help us though? We didn't have any other choice, so rushed over to the pit. The boys were all crowded beneath the edge, and Nadan and I jumped down to join them.

Keenu darted over. 'Eno? Nadan? What are you—'

'Mycol's coming,' Nadan said, immediately finding Mui and giving him a strong hug. 'We were right about everything. What they're doing in there...'

The boys quizzically murmured amongst themselves.

Mui had puffy eyes and blotchy cheeks. He squeezed Nadan tight. 'I told you not to say anything, stupid.'

I reached out to multiple boys, but each backed away. 'Please help, he's going to kill us.'

Nadan released his little brother and shifted to the centre of the group. 'Listen to us, we need to fight him. Otherwise—'

'No!' Ido interrupted, shoving me back to the wall. '*You're* the ones that pissed him off.' He turned to the others with a drooping, almost melting face. 'No one interfere, otherwise we'll be punished, too.'

Several Terror Guards appeared on the pit's lip and leered down. We all looked up at the dark silhouettes surrounding us, one by one casting more shadows into the arena. Nadan hurriedly went back to stabbing at his collar.

I shook my head and clenched my fists. 'Don't you get it? We're all Mycol's experiments. We can either fight him together now or die alone in his cages.'

A loud groan emanated from behind the guards. Mycol pushed through them and stood over the pit. 'You won't die, nor will you be alone.' He caught his breath and cackled, before pointing at his chest. 'Your brothers' strength is always within… me.'

All the boys, even Ido, stared at Mycol with a new kind of fear. Like me, they must have realised what we truly were to him. We collectively backed away from the edges and went back-to-back in the centre.

'Knock them out,' Mycol ordered his guards, and they all pointed their batons into the pit.

A momentary silence fell upon us, stealing our breath long before the inevitable poisonous gas would. But that silence was broken by a high-pitched whistling noise, quiet at first, then progressively louder and louder. All exchanged confused glances, until finally looking up.

With a blinding flash, an almighty boom rumbled through the air, many of us held our ears in response. One of the nearest facilities exploded as though a bomb had hit it, the shockwave so massive it took most of us off our feet.

A second explosion rocked a warehouse at the far end of the courtyard. Both the concrete and the air around us cracked. The sky above was set aflame, and waves of fire washed over the buildings of the Military Wing.

Distant men squealed and shrieked as they ran or leapt from windows like charred embers, each a lit torch to spread the fire farther.

'We're under attack,' Mycol gutturally shouted to cut through the chaotic noise. 'Don't just stand there, defensive positions! All of you, out of the pit, now!'

Almost everyone mobilised, heading for the nearest ladders. We boys also began to move.

'Not… you two,' Mycol said, pointing his gnarled finger at Nadan and I.

Nadan pushed his brother behind to shield him. The other boys froze, me included. The last of the Terror Guard disappeared from the pit's lip, into the surrounding miasma of glowing orange smoke.

Meanwhile, although the bombs were still falling and the fires still raged, Mycol remained unperturbed. He leapt into the pit and slammed down with a roaring, fiery display of power, fracturing more concrete and bolstering his already formidable aura.

'The rest of you… move.'

The boys of the Feeble Fortress, whether out of loyalty or sheer terror, hadn't moved another step. Even Keenu stepped in front of me. Our pack of rejects stared Mycol down with hesitance. I could tell from looking at them they all now understood; it was either him or us.

'Fine,' Mycol uttered as he raised his hands, 'this experiment is terminated… and so are all of you.'

Thirty-Five: Never Had A Choice

Tau

Our view of the world through the wide, panoramic windows would have been awe-inspiring under any other circumstances. We were so high above Seron that I could feel the distance; it stretched through me, further from everything I once was.

The entire planet, everything that I had ever known, hung outside that window. It wasn't until I saw it like this that I realised how barren it really was. There were patches of green, usually close to the small, sparse oceans, but most of the surface was brown and yellow. As though burning and dying, this eternal war had cooked our world. The snow I experienced as a sweet, innocent child was a distant memory for both me and Seron.

The Overwatch control room was filled with more enemies than I could count. Tetsu and I were sitting at the end of a long steel table, quietly waiting for all this to be over. I absentmindedly fiddled with the collar around my neck, partly thankful my detestable aura was contained. Tetsu, meanwhile, having a purely defensive power, was collar-free.

The table had an elegant purple tablecloth and lots of empty glasses, as though they were getting ready to celebrate. We were told everyone was anticipating the end of Sacet's Harrowing, something I still didn't quite understand.

Spies and acolytes of all sorts were throughout the room, most of whom I didn't recognise. Some were sitting at the table, others were spread around, having private conversations.

Midway down the table were most of Verre's former acolyte colonels. They were playing a game on the tabletop using a holographic display. There was a mix of red and blue dots shooting at one another.

The girls clenched at the air and somehow the game knew what they wanted to do. Korin was straining the hardest, she had lost every game so far. She was getting angrier with each loss while the others around her laughed.

'These Concordites are terrible,' she remarked. 'I'm taking MD next time.'

'Fine with us,' her opponent replied.

Another girl slapped Korin on the back. 'You just don't know how to command. I'll challenge winner.'

Was it really a game they were playing? Or were they commanding actual troops from up here?

There was a noise from behind as the control room door opened, and Tetsu and I glanced back. More guests?

Neva, the missing colonel strutted in. She raised her arms to stretch. 'Nice of all of you to just leave me rotting in that cell. I wasn't worth a rescue?'

'Get over it, Neva,' one girl said, still focused on the holographic dots. 'I'd *hardly* call a couple of days in prison "rotting".'

Neva flicked her hair and put her hands on her hips. 'That numpty necrolisk boy was more help than all of you. I had to convince one of Sacet's little helpers to execute me in the end.'

Neva noticed Tetsu and I and smirked. She strolled over, gently grabbed my shoulders from behind, and bent down to my ear. 'If it isn't the exalted *Queen of Light*? Nice of you to finally join the winning team.' She giggled, then thankfully left to join the other girls.

Farther down the table, Kalek was sitting in a custom chair, enlarged for his gargantuan frame. He clutched the armrests so tightly that they were beginning to rip.

Leaning against a wall to our right was Amiki. She was doing her best to avoid everyone, especially me. I occasionally noticed her grimacing at me with guilt, before she'd look away again.

It turned out she wasn't one of their spies after all. As she explained during her betrayal, it was all for the chance of seeing her family again, who weren't even on this space station. For now, she was a prisoner like us, without the privilege to wander freely.

Tuloch's command chair was empty at the end of the table. He was to my left on the far side of the chamber, monitoring at least fifty or so staff at their workstations.

Every row of desks had holographic displays and complex control panels. The displays showed all sorts of people and places on Seron. Occasionally, I'd notice a live feed of someone I knew.

They were also monitoring this space station, too. Almost every chamber I had seen had a dome-shaped camera in it, usually hanging in the corner.

I felt like such a fool looking at their setup. They had cameras and agents throughout every city on the planet. They also had hundreds of orbital cameras scanning the planet's surface non-stop. It was no wonder they were always a step ahead. We were so small in their grand scheme.

From what we had seen and overheard so far, Tarsus and Terel were now in command at New Elysia, currently trying to clean up the remains of our fledgling empire. Coleo had been released from prison and was assisting them. Based on the way they were being spied on, all three had thankfully always been on our side.

Because most of our city was in ruins, the nomads had constructed a refugee camp in the Royal Gardens for all those who had lost their homes. If anyone knew how to survive in dire situations, it was them.

Tuloch didn't care about any of that. All he wanted to know was where Sacet was. Every terminal operator was questioning their spies around the globe, trying to find out where my friends had gone, but no one had any answers. The furious, fake king was growing redder and redder with each passing moment.

Beyond the other end of the table, our most dangerous foe of all was still standing at the window with his arms behind his back, staring out into space. He hadn't moved since we got here, instead admiring the brilliant panorama.

'Look at them all,' I said quietly to Tetsu. '*Evil* people. If I had my powers, I'd kill each and every…' I reached up to my collar and pulled on it, before shaking my head and groaning. 'What am I saying?'

Tetsu leant closer. 'What's wrong?'

'I keep thinking these awful things,' I said, slumping against the table. 'I thought I was past all this. I've always tried to be a good person, but I knew the whole time I was bad.'

He reached out and grabbed my trembling hand. 'Don't say that. These past few days, in particular, have been tough on you. Before we came here, you had never even killed anyone before, but this place, these people…'

I pulled my hand from his grasp and sighed. 'The truth is: I *have* killed, back when I was a little sister.'

Tetsu's expression showed renewed concern. 'I'm… I'm sorry. You never told me.'

I averted my eyes. 'I never told *anyone*. I've been lying about it my whole life, pretending to be this… innocent paragon of virtue.'

Tetsu slowly nodded. 'I see. Well, I'm sure you had a good reason to kill, right? Defending yourself?'

I shook my head out of shame. The poor girl's dead face was burnt into my mind like a brand. 'Unlike me, she *was* just some innocent kid.' I glared over to Amiki. 'Only Amiki knew. She promised I'd *never* have to kill again. What a *childish* idea that was. I was born into this, so I never had a choice.'

'Never had a choice?' a voice said from behind and we both glanced back.

It was Iya. She circled around and sat next to me, opposite Tetsu. 'How about when you *chose* to strangle me to death? I would have happily brought you to this room, had you *asked* nicely.'

I scoffed. 'You people kidnapped us against our will. Do we have the choice to leave this place, Iya?'

She weighed my words for a moment. '*Hmm*, I guess not.' She looked around to make sure no one was listening. 'Would you believe… that *I*… didn't have a choice either?'

Tetsu shrugged. 'In being evil?'

She rolled her eyes. 'In *all* of it. I can't go home until I've finished the job.'

I pointed back at her. 'It was *your* choice to be cruel to us.'

Iya shrugged. 'You thought *that* was cruel? Try meeting my parents. Anyway, it was my job. That's what this Harrowing is all about.' She leaned in closer and lowered her voice. 'Between you and me: I *hate* this place. I *hate* getting orders. I *hate* all these people. And I *hate* how much of a fuss we're all making over Sacet.'

Tetsu gestured at us. 'If you hate them so much, then why aren't you on *our* side?'

She shook her head. 'Because even with all the choices you want, your side *isn't* going to win.'

As she stood, I grabbed onto her wrist to stop her. 'If more people like you chose to do the right thing, then good would at least stand a chance.' I let go of her and frowned, realising the hypocrisy of my own words.

'*Good*? Evil?' she said with a raised eyebrow. 'We're *all* monsters, Tau. Some of us just haven't accepted that yet.' She turned and headed farther down the table, leaving us to silently contemplate.

After a short while, Tetsu pulled his chair closer to me and grabbed my hand again. 'Listen, all of this has made me realise that I was wrong for pushing you to be more… aggressive. I wanted to say that I… I'm sorry.'

'You were right to say those things.'

He raised his free hand. 'No. You should choose to be who you *want* to be, and not what everyone else tries to turn you into. What *I* was trying to turn you into. I thought I was helping you become a tougher queen, but…'

I stared into his eyes. 'But what?'

He grinned. 'You were perfect just the way you were.'

My cheeks warmed. 'Well, I… wouldn't say… I don't think I'm *perfect*. But thank you.' I sighed. 'So, what do we do now? Just sit here and wait?'

His expression softened. 'What do you *want* to do?'

I pondered the question for a moment, remembering Iya's cynicism. 'I want to *choose* to be good. I want to help my friends.'

Tetsu nodded with another smile. 'Then that's what we'll do. We'll help our friends.'

I instantly felt a massive weight lift off me: the world's expectations, the pressure of the entire war on my shoulders, gone. Win or lose, it didn't matter. I would be the best that only I could be, and I'd no longer gorge myself on regret, guilt and selfishness.

'Am I getting a promotion or what?' Neva asked loudly. She looked around at everyone. 'I'm pretty sure that thing I found was *extremely* valuable. Where is it, anyway?'

What was she talking about? What thing? Everyone went silent.

'The artefact is already in transit to Aster,' Tuloch called out from the control panels. 'And next time you ask for a promotion, I'll demote you instead.' He went back to concentrating on all the displays.

Kalek shot up from his seat, breaking it. '*Ahhh*! I'm *tired* of waiting!'

Korin looked up from her game. 'Calm down you giant oaf.'

'No! I'm sick of doing nothing.' He glared over at Tetsu and I and stomped around the table towards us.

We both stood and backed away. Why was no one trying to stop this?

He reached Tetsu first, grabbed him by the throat and lifted him into the air. 'You two *know* where she is, don't you?'

'Stop it!' I shouted. 'Leave him alone!'

Tetsu spat into his Kalek's face. Kalek reeled back, wiped it away with his free hand and scowled. He raised his hand, preparing to strike.

'You little *sh*—'

'Kalek!' Tuloch yelled, walking away from the control panels and over to us. 'Put him down, now!'

Kalek's fist stopped in front of Tetsu's face. He slowly lowered and released him.

'I've told you before,' Tuloch continued, 'we're in space, in a *very* delicate container, and a lummox like you could blast a hole just by sneezing, so show some self-control.'

'Sorry, Sir,' Kalek mumbled, before backing away. 'But they know something, Sir, I'm sure of it.'

'How could they?' Iya interrupted from the far end of the table. 'They were captured before any of the *real* fighting began.'

Korin sneered at me. 'Yeah, and let's be honest, they're not exactly the brightest bunch.'

'Bright enough to evade Overwatch,' Tuloch said, looking back at the equipment and shaking his head. 'Perhaps I should put an end to this Harrowing. We can't torture her if we don't know where she is.'

'Sir, we have something,' one of the surveillance operators said from their control panel. 'MDC is under attack as we speak.'

'What?' Tuloch yelled, storming back over to them.

The other spies and acolytes stood and went over with him. Kalek rushed over excitedly, causing the floor to shake with each stride. Even Amiki showed a little enthusiasm, pushing off against the wall, walking around the back of my chair and joining the others.

The invincible man at the window continued to stare out, indifferent to the rest.

The operator flicked her screens through images of the attack. 'MDC is being bombed. Sacet's portals are showing up all over the city.'

The screen showed the city's streets and countless men running from the destruction. Everyone watching the screens stood with their mouths agape.

'And… looks like reports of Noor's laser tearing up the place, too.'

Tuloch shook his head. 'I should have never spared that boy.'

'Sir, you'll want to see this. It's—'

'My palace!' Tuloch yelled in disbelief. He leant over the control panel to get a closer look. 'Where is she?'

'I'm having a little trouble with that, Sir,' a different operator said. He hastily battered the controls. The display cycled through different cameras. 'Scanners aren't picking them up in the city.'

Tuloch slammed his fist down on the panel, causing the operator to jump in fright. 'They won't *be* in the city.'

'I found them,' the first operator said. Her display zoomed in on the desert outside the city. 'They're in a… sand building? Of some kind?'

The satellite feed showed what appeared to be a sandy circle, maybe a dome. The scanners showed heat signatures rising from it.

Get out of there, Sacet, what are you doing?

'Get to your drop pods,' Tuloch ordered. 'It's time for this game to end. Kill her and her little friends.'

The others exchanged looks. The spies and acolytes turned to the control room's exit.

'No,' the man by the window said in a deep, strong voice.

Everyone stopped and looked over at him.

'What is it, Caelum?' Tuloch asked.

There was an awkward silence in the room as they all waited for him to speak.

He slowly turned and looked at all of us. 'The Harrow will continue. Leave her to me. All the men… to the city, for crowd control.'

The male spies and acolytes nodded without question.

Tuloch pointed to the exit. 'Go, now!'

They complied, turning and sprinting for the door. Many passed the table. Kalek stomped by with an overjoyed grin. They all ran into the corridor and out of sight.

'The rest of you stay,' Caelum commanded.

The women frowned, then returned and sank into their seats. Iya put her feet up. Korin shrugged and led the others back to the game they were playing.

Caelum finally moved away from the window and floated through the control room. As he glided over the table and my head, he glared down, before silently disappearing into the corridor with the others.

Tuloch glanced to the far corner of the room. 'Verre, escort those two to their rooms. Make sure they're locked in.'

Verre, the former illusory queen herself, had been sitting in the shadows, celebrating early with a glowing green drink. With an audible groan, she abandoned her quiet table and approached us. 'Iya, Amiki, care to assist me?'

Amiki nodded but still avoided looking at me.

Tuloch and Iya both exchanged a seething glower before she eventually complied.

'Fine!' she snapped, standing and joining us.

Verre gestured Tetsu and I to the door. 'Shall we?'

We stood and followed Verre out of the control room into the corridor. While Verre led, Amiki and Iya trailed behind, both looking like they didn't want to be there.

Tetsu and I had traversed these corridors several times now, having been escorted back and forth to our tiny, separate sleeping quarters. As usual, none of our escorts were paying us much mind, confident we weren't a threat.

I needed to warn my friends about what was coming. Even if I didn't get there in time, I had to help them somehow.

There was a bend in the corridor coming up where no cameras could see, a blind spot. It was now or never, all we had to do was overpower two acolytes and a martial arts specialist. Hmm, no. Maybe there was another option?

I glanced back at the dawdling girls. 'You know, after I first met you, Iya, I remember hoping we were going to be friends.'

Her eyes widened before she huffed and averted her gaze. 'I don't *do* friends anymore.'

Verre chuckled from the front. 'Indeed, there's a very good reason for that.'

Iya gave the same spiteful look to her as she had given Tuloch. I didn't know why she was so hate-filled, but I certainly felt it. She was clearly hurting in a way that healing couldn't help.

I looked down at my shuffling feet and shrugged. 'Well, I think everyone needs friends.' I then turned to Amiki. 'Have you spoken to your parents yet?'

She halted for a moment, then caught up again. 'I… I thought… you and I would be with them by now. I'm… sor—'

'Don't torture her, Tau,' Verre called. 'You and your Concordites left her no choice.'

'I wasn't torturing her,' I replied. 'What she did… is done. I just wanted to know if any good came out of it.'

Both the girls looked even more dejected than before.

We had reached the blind spot. I gave Tetsu a subtle gesture towards Verre. As if instinctively knowing what I was thinking, he responded with a knowing nod. This was it.

'And one more thing,' I added as Tetsu lined an unaware Verre up with the nearest wall, 'there's *always* a choice.'

Tetsu scrunched up his face and charged, raising his shield at the last moment. Verre didn't even see him coming. The edge of his shield smacked into Verre's back and drove her into the wall with a crushing, fleshy squish.

The other two didn't know how to react at first. After a few moments, they broke out of their shock and took fighting stances.

Pinned and bleeding from her lips and ears, Verre was motionless and possibly dead. As quickly as he had attacked, Tetsu ran over to envelop me with his shield, before staring the girls down. Verre's body slumped to the floor behind us. Iya took a step back and raised her fingers, as though ready to pinch an invisible object hanging in front of her face.

I put up my hands. 'Wait! Everyone, stop. Please, listen!'

They all paused and glanced at one another.

I pointed up at the ceiling. 'There are no cameras here. Just listen.' I took a few calm steps forward, out of Tetsu's shield.

'Tau?' he blurted.

'It's okay,' I assured him, before looking back at the girls. 'None of us want to fight each other.'

Iya and Amiki nervously eyed each other once more, remaining in their stances. Tetsu begrudgingly brought down his shield and joined my side.

I lowered my head. 'I *know* we have already lost. Even still, all I want to do is go down to the planet to help my friends. Can you just… let us go?'

Iya shook her head. 'I have orders, Tau.'

Tetsu motioned back the way we came. 'The orders of those you hate. Why don't you break free of them? *We* did.'

Iya continued to shake her head and furrowed her brow. I reached out to her, but she pulled away with wide eyes. I offered a small bow instead. 'I'm sorry for strangling you. That was me… at my lowest point, making the wrong choice.'

She stared at me for the longest time, eventually relaxing her stance with a sigh. She gave a slight nod, her lips pressed into a thin line. 'I guess I might've done something similar.'

My smile spread. 'Instead of being on the winning side, wouldn't you rather be on the right one, with a friend?'

She looked down, and her eyes darted from side to side in thought. I then turned to Amiki, whose stance faltered and broke as she shook with guilt.

Her jaw quivered in fear. 'Tau, *please* don't ask me to do this. When

I got here, they told me that if I didn't follow orders, instead of letting me see my parents, they'd *kill* them again.' She nervously glanced at Verre's body, then to Iya. 'What are your orders, Ma'am?'

Iya remained silent.

I gave a long, drawn-out sigh. It was cruel of them to use her family against her like this. At the same time, I was disheartened by how far my friend had fallen.

After not receiving a response, Amiki approached Tetsu and I. 'Knock me out or… or kill me. I can't help, but this way I can at least say—'

Amiki suddenly rocketed upwards, and her head hit the ceiling so hard, that we all heard a loud snap. Her body remained there for a moment, limp and hanging like a ragdoll, before dropping back down in a thudding heap.

Standing behind her was Iya, her fingers in front of her eyes again. She slowly lowered her hands, then signalled over her shoulder with a nod. 'This way.'

Tetsu and I exchanged a bewildered look.

Iya turned on the spot and marched in the other direction. 'Hurry up, before I change my mind.'

Tetsu and I dashed to catch up and strode down the corridor with her.

'You chose good in the end,' I said.

Iya curled her lips in disgust. 'Maybe. Or maybe I just want to do my own thing.'

Tetsu was checking corners and doorways as we walked. 'Aren't *you* worried what they'll do if they find out?'

Iya snorted as we turned another corner. 'I'm not afraid of them. I'm *untouchable*.'

Unsure of what she meant, Tetsu and I didn't question further.

We reached the end of the corridor and entered a room labelled as the "Pod Bay". It was filled with small alcoves where mechanical drop pods would normally go, but most were empty. Iya spotted one nearby and led us to it.

There were technicians here, too. Three men approached us and procured their sidearms.

'What are you doing in here?' one asked, aiming his weapon at us. 'Aren't those the prisoners?'

Iya stomped up to him and prodded his chest with her finger. 'I am Princess Iya, daughter of Emperor Avarut and Empress Suralia. I will do *whatever* I want, *whenever* I want. And if *any* of you degenerates get in my way, I'll have you permanently executed! Understand?'

All three men were shaking. They lowered their sidearms and fearfully nodded, unable to speak.

'Now drop your weapons!' Iya added and the men complied. The pistols clattered on the steel floor. Iya pointed at the drop pod. 'Open it!'

One of the men rushed over to the pod and fiddled with the controls. A door on the pod's side whooshed open, revealing two seats inside.

Iya turned to me. 'Wait.' She picked up the sidearm from the grated floor and fiddled with buttons on the side of it. 'Tau, come here.'

I went over and she brought the pistol to my collar. She discharged the device at its lowest setting. I felt the searing heat on my neck. It was cooking my skin.

'*Ahhhhh!*'

'Stop whining,' Iya said. 'You'll heal it in a moment.'

It eventually cut through the collar, and she chucked it to the ground.

A familiar, tingling sensation spread around my neck. I felt it with my hand and noticed the burnt skin was already healed.

'See?' Iya said. She pointed at the technicians again. 'Strap them in!'

Tetsu and I were corralled into the same two-person pod. We laid back in the seats and watched as the technicians buckled our straps.

'Where are we... we sending them, Princess?'

Iya passed me the pistol and nodded. 'The same as the others.'

I grinned back. 'Thank you.'

She smirked. 'Don't take *too* long to lose. Oh, and Tau?'

'Yeah?'

'Make sure you tell Sacet what I did.'

The technicians backed out and the pod door whooshed closed. The buttons and lights in the pod's interior blinked and shone. Mechanical noises whirred and buzzed. A holographic map appeared showing MDC.

I reached out and to hold Tetsu's hand. He reached back and gripped it.

There was a winding noise from below our feet, and suddenly the pod plummeted.

Thirty-Six: Make Them Suffer

Sacet

'Keep firing!' I yelled to Noor over the deafening laser. 'Don't give up!'

He nodded back enthusiastically, but he seemed to be struggling to maintain his attack for this long. He was drenched in sweat and his arms were shaking.

Our sandy dome outside the MDC city limits was surprisingly still holding strong. I wondered how long it would take for them to find us.

Malu was standing by with a determined stare. 'Make them suffer like they made *us* suffer.'

The bombings had brought down many of the larger structures throughout the city. The burning buildings were crumbling onto the now-dead enemy bodies.

'Is the Palace still standing?' Noor yelled over the screeching laser.

I smiled. 'Not anymore. That was the first to go. I've bombed the barracks, factories, labs... pretty much the whole city is on fire.'

Noor glanced at me while straining. 'Wait, I thought we were only attacking the evil ones? You know, the soldiers and the scientists? The king?'

'No, I meant *all* of them.'

He stopped firing his laser, lowered his arms and turned. 'Now hold on, I didn't want to kill innocent civilians. That's not justice, Sacet.'

I closed the cluster of portals in front of him. 'But Noor, they've killed so *many* of our people. Don't you hate them? Their people are complicit in all of this!'

Malu folded her arms and narrowed her gaze at Noor. 'That's right. This is vengeance. It's time for them to pay for what they did.'

Noor closed his eyes and shook his head. 'Then we're just as bad as them, killing indiscriminately. Don't you see?'

Malu scoffed and stormed up to him. 'That's funny, coming from you. A mass murderer that killed hundreds of women indiscriminately.'

He gritted his teeth and shoved her back. 'That's not me anymore. And how do *you* get off lecturing me on morality?'

I got between them and raised my palms. 'Both of you, stop. We don't have time for this. We... we...'

Noor grabbed my arm. 'Sacet, I know I said I shared your anger; I do. But trust me when I say this is only going to make things worse!'

Malu noticed how distracted I had suddenly become. 'What is it?'

I sensed fiery streaks in the sky. Missiles... no. Drop pods like before, hurtling down from the upper reaches of the atmosphere.

'They're here,' I said.

Noor's anger faded. He became focused again. 'From the sky?'

'Then we should leave,' Malu suggested. She waited for me to react, but I didn't. 'Sacet? Attack from the shadows, remember? We need to go so we can strike again later.'

I looked down. 'But I haven't found Tau or Tetsu yet. What if they're still here somewhere?'

'And what if they're not?' she replied.

I sighed. 'I need more time.'

Malu groaned. 'I say we attack another city.'

Noor shrugged and turned to me. 'Maybe you can call on reinforcements?'

He reminded me of when Marid, Noor and I were recently in the briefing room in the Military Quad. Marid had said that if I made a portal in that room, alarms would go off throughout the facility and soldiers would come.

I looked away. 'Marid…'

The drop pods plummeted through the sky. Strangely, they weren't coming directly for us but at the city instead. The capsules clustered together in groups. Most were headed to the demolished palace.

I focused on a few empty, intact rooms near the Palace landing sites and opened portals at each location. The destination of each was located inside the briefing room back in New Elysia. I saw the alarms going off through my own portals.

'Hopefully, those who are still alive will answer the call,' I said.

Malu put a hand on her hip. 'So, we're going with plan C, then? Fight to the death?'

I nodded. 'We fight until we find them.'

The pods descended into the city. Each capsule used its boosters to slow and land safely. Their doors opened one after another.

'They've landed in the city,' I explained.

Noor wandered over to a window and peered out. 'They don't know we're here?'

Malu joined him and smiled. 'They're looking in the wrong place.'

Kalek was the first one I saw. He leapt out of his capsule, grinning ecstatically. He surveyed his ruined surroundings. I opened a portal behind him, jettisoning him into space for the second time. He must *really* hate me by now. Who was next?

High above the city in the upper reaches of my perception, another projectile was falling through the sky. A man.

'It's him,' I said.

Noor and Malu turned and narrowed their eyes. They didn't need to ask; they knew who I meant.

The man rocketed down, again much faster than the capsules. He was coming straight for us.

'Keep him guessing,' Malu suggested. 'Put us in a different position.'

I nodded and the two of them joined my side. I sensed a nearby desert cliff. There was nothing but sand above it. The cliff overlooked everything, the city and the jungle below. I opened a portal under our feet and transported us to the clifftop.

Malu's face lit up, admiring the destruction we had wrought. Noor, however, lowered his head in shame. Pillars of black smoke streaked the sky.

Far above we all saw the invincible man whiz down to our previous location. He smashed into the dome. A cloud of sand erupted in all directions. All the trees in the area fell from the shockwave.

Malu tapped me on the shoulder and went in front of me. 'Like we practised.'

I nodded. 'Good luck.'

Noor and I took a few steps back. I pointed my hands at the sand under Malu's feet and caused her to sink underground. I separated the sand to leave her enough oxygen, then closed the top up and solidified it all.

Realising we had moved, the man shot back up into the sky, examined the desert in all directions and quickly caught sight of us.

Noor took a strong position in the sand and raised his arms again, ready to fire.

'Wait for it,' I instructed.

The man flew towards us at breakneck speed. We heard a sonic boom in his wake. Noor fired, and the man didn't bother avoiding it. He landed on the cliff's precipice, maybe 30 paces away from us, then smiled, completely ignoring Noor's beam.

Noor realised his attack was doing nothing again, so the two of us backed away. The man hovered closer.

'Now… don't give up so easily this time,' he said.

That's it, just a little farther.

He scowled. 'What are you waiting for? Attack me!'

He passed Malu's concealed position.

'Now!' I shouted at Noor, and he fired again.

I pointed my hands at Malu's hiding spot and did an uppercut, launching her out of the ground and into the air. A cloud of sand exploded. The man was too busy being unimpressed with Noor's laser again to notice her.

Malu did an aerial flip and twist as she came back down to land on his back. The man's eyes widened. Malu grabbed both sides of his head and strained. But there was no burst of water like we were expecting.

'*Arrrrrrrgghhh*!' he shouted.

What at first I thought was a profuse amount of sweat coming from the man's cheeks was actually water. Malu's power was working, but it was terribly slow against him. She gritted her teeth and strained harder.

The man grabbed her wrists and peeled her off, before whipping her whole body over his own and smacking her to the ground. He had thrown her so hard that her head now slumped to the side. Her eyes stared into the distance at nothing. She was dead.

The man's cheeks were bleeding, having had the first layers of skin liquefied. He looked livid. I didn't know what to do next, we didn't have a backup plan for this.

'Noor, fire again!'

I opened a portal in front of Noor's beam with the exit above the man's head pointing down. Noor's heatwave went forward, through and down over him. It incinerated Malu's body but did not affect the man.

I stretched the exit so wide that its radius almost reached us. Like a blinding flash, Noor's vertical beam filled my sight. The laser bathed the entire area in heat and destruction. The force of the beam was so great, it took both Noor and I off our feet and threw us backwards onto the sand. The cliffside quaked, beginning to crumble.

My skin sizzled from the burning. Smoke was rising from the sand. Noor and I slowly brought ourselves up and waited for the haze to clear.

The ground in front of us was gone, replaced by a gaping hole, a new cliffside. The hole went deep, deep into the ground below. The sides of the gaping tunnel glowed red.

The man was floating in the same place he was when the laser had first hit him. He hadn't moved and his expression hadn't changed, if anything he was calmer.

Noor threw his hands forward again, but in the time it took to blink, the man barrelled towards him, stopped short, grasped Noor's neck and lifted him. He glanced over at me to make sure I was paying attention.

'Stop! Don't kill him!' I screamed.

He stared at me as Noor floundered and kicked at his stomach to no avail.

'So, you're... the one in charge,' Noor said through choked breaths. 'I'm... going... to kill...'

Snap!

While still looking at me, the man broke Noor's neck. 'Hush now,' he said, before casually tossing Noor's body towards me.

His body sailed through the air, crashed into the sand and slid until it stopped just short of me.

I fell to my knees and placed my hands on him, hoping that he would wake up. I tried shaking him awake. My hands trembled and I closed my eyes.

'What will you do now?' the man inquired as he floated across the sands towards me. 'I just killed your little boyfriend.'

I got up and stumbled back. 'Stay away from me!'

He continued to slowly float in my direction. 'Make me.'

He was baiting me. Every time I used my powers, he attacked. He was too powerful for me, and he knew it.

'I asked you something,' he said, getting closer. 'What will you do?'

I knelt back into the sand again. 'Nothing,' I said, bending over and placing my hands flat on the ground.

The man stopped in his tracks in front of me. 'What did you say?'

I stared at the ground. 'I'm going to do nothing.'

'I could kill you in the blink of an eye.'

I looked back up at him. 'I know. You should do it because I'm not fighting anymore.'

'Get up and fight back!'

'No.'

The man lowered his eyebrows, a look of confusion spreading across his usual stoic guise. I locked my gaze with his.

He smiled and then his face went blank again. 'We have *all* of your friends,' he said, landing on the sand. 'I have enjoyed torturing them, *especially* Tau.'

I gritted my teeth. 'Why? Why are you doing this?'

'Your parents, if you could call them that, are long-time favourites of mine, too,' he continued, placing his hands behind his back. 'We've made them suffer for many long cycles.'

'You're lying,' I yelled.

He smiled again. 'But I have a new favourite now. Your brother, Eno. I torture him as if he were you, and he *begs* for mercy daily. He begs for *you* to save him, but you never come.'

My hands were shaking with rage, I could barely contain myself. I hated him so much. I would make everyone he had *ever* cared about suffer. I'd start with every remaining person in the MDC.

My soldiers had started piling in through the portals to help us, so I closed them, cutting off any further reinforcements. Those already through could be resurrected later. His people needed to suffer right now. *He* needed to suffer. I would break him!

I peered up at the sun. No distance was too great for me. If I could see it, then I could teleport to it.

'I like to let him bleed out, then we resurrect him and start over. And when I'm done with you, I'm going back for *him* again, one more time.'

'Enough!' I shot up.

I threw my hand to the city and a portal opened above the tallest buildings. Its opening was small at first, but my rage fuelled my power, and I stretched it larger than any portal I had ever created, with a diameter of multiple city blocks.

The sun's intense light poured through and washed over the horizon in all directions. Its radiation surged and the city turned red. My portal to the star's atmosphere began to boil the already burning wasteland.

Thirty-Seven: Not In Pain Anymore

Eno

Earlier

The bombs had stopped falling, now replaced with giant, red spinning lasers slicing through distant skyscrapers. Here in the pit, we had been unaffected by the explosions and lasers overhead. Instead, we had a much bigger problem in front of us – Mycol.

It was like he didn't even care that the city was under attack, he only had eyes for Nadan and I. He stared us down and breathed heavily like a savage animal. His green flames somehow caught on the ground, spreading hate along the concrete.

Thankfully the boys of the Feeble Fortress were now united. They shifted uncomfortably whenever Mycol made the slightest twitch. I didn't like our chances.

Ateity, the nearest boy to Mycol, charged him, flinging weak, ineffective sparks into his face. Though the eldest of us, Ateity was tiny compared to the flaming monster. In response, Mycol formed a tiny ball of fire in his hand and turfed it his way, engulfing him in green death.

The teenager screamed in agony, quickly dealt with as easy as that. It was such a horrendous way to go. Before he hit the ground, Mycol expelled the poor boy's soul and sucked it into his mouth.

He stomped forward and cackled. 'Feels good… to clean house.' He laid eyes on Nadan and went directly for him with a snarl.

I ran to the nearest boy and frantically pointed at my collar. 'Help me get this off!'

Terrified as the rest of them, he shook his head. 'I… I can't? My power can't do that.'

Arbol and Mannox, the next two boys nearest to Mycol, lunged at him, the first with bony, sword-like spikes protruding from his palms and the other with a flashing body, producing mildly annoying bursts of light. Mycol quickly dispatched the latter with a backhand, knocking him out cold.

I collided with another boy and begged him to help with my collar but received no help.

Keenu stepped forward, whole body shaking. 'I'll… I'll stop him… somehow.'

I looked up and noticed one of the Terror Guard's batons teetering over the pit's lip, almost about to fall in. He must have dropped it after the explosions hit. I started climbing the ladder nearest to it.

Arbol managed to stab Mycol in the side, but the man guffawed and pinned the boy's arm down. He couldn't escape! Mycol grinned, for the proximity to his aura was slowly killing the boy, who quickly went limp and fell to the ground.

'Another ready for consumption.'

'That's enough, Mycol!' Keenu shouted. 'S-s-stop this!'

Mycol's larger eye widened. 'Oh? No "Mycol, Sir"?' He trudged toward Keenu, dragging the now unconscious boy with him. 'I thought I taught you better respect than that, Keenu, you snivelling little weakling.'

Keenu backed away, but he was too slow. When Mycol reached him, he continued stomping through his intangible body. Although unable to touch, Keenu was also knocked out by Mycol's aura.

Some of the boys were crying, their previous bravery only temporary.

The ladder climb was taking too long, so only halfway up, I

instead leapt along the pit's edge to where the baton was and only just managed to grab it.

I landed back in the pit, pointed the terror stick at our oppressor and pressed the biggest button on the handle all the way down. Yellowish-green gas puffed out in projectile form, and shortly after the baton electrified it. The shocking gas reached Mycol, and as his body manically vibrated, he involuntarily dropped Arbol on the ground.

Alas, after the shock was over, Mycol was still left standing and staring me down. He breathed in what was left of the gas on purpose. 'If only sleep… could come that easy for me.'

'Got it!' Nadan yelled, finally able to crack open his collar and throw it away with Mui's help.

Mycol focused on him and his eyes widened, showing a glimmer of fear. He roared, threw his arms up and summoned an enormous fireball as large as he was. He held nothing back.

Nadan smirked, grit his teeth, locked eyes with the brute, and stabbed himself in the bicep. He had no doubt given himself tremendous pain, but he didn't break his fiery gaze.

In an instant, it was as if Mycol had suffered a heart attack. His fireball dissipated; each lick of flame harmlessly snuffed out. He clutched his torso and let out a terrible groan. Blood spurted from his nose, and he doubled over in pain.

The boys all cheered, perhaps prematurely, for Mycol only required a short moment to compose himself. He stood back up again and reignited his aura.

The cautiously optimistic smile faded from Ido's face. 'It didn't work.' He and the remaining boys continued to back away.

Mui, white eyes flickering, joined his brother's side. 'No, it did. You killed one of the people trapped inside of him. Hit him again!'

With that, Nadan ripped the large knife out of his arm, tearing along the muscle. He screeched and opened his blackened eyes, refusing to take them off Mycol, who also reeled back.

This time Mycol was brought to his knees, and he spewed green vapours of energy, which floated up and faded away. He raised his hand to his engorged chest again, which appeared a bit smaller than before. His face was shrinking, too.

He cried out and then continued to crawl towards Nadan. His hands were still engulfed in fire. We all backed away from him.

Blood was still flowing from Nadan's arm at a dangerous rate. As Mycol was bringing himself to his feet again, Nadan took a deep breath and stabbed down into his own thigh. The knife pierced deep. He screamed and stared at Mycol yet again. 'We… will never… be a part of you!'

Mycol staggered and almost toppled, but this time he managed to stay up. His body shrunk again as more energy left it. He was almost upon us. He reached out to Nadan, causing small green streams to leech away from him.

Nadan panicked, wrenched the knife out and plunged it into his stomach instead. As he stared at Mycol, his eyes had turned completely black and empty, and he fell to the ground.

Without any shrieks of pain this time, Mycol fell, too, and the two of them collapsed onto the ground in a heap. Mycol's fiery hands extinguished, and his open eyes remained still, staring at the side of the pit. His body, now regular-sized and an emaciated, thin husk, convulsed, then finally came to rest.

Nadan hadn't fared much better; he was writhing in pain with his knife still protruding from his guts. A pool of blood had formed around them both.

Mui knelt beside his brother and hugged him, as though able to see him clearly. 'Nadan, you did it. I can't see him anymore. He's dead.'

Keenu got up, too, and the two of us came over as well. Arbol and Mannox were also prodded awake and brought to their feet. All the surviving boys huddled around Nadan.

'I can't… open… my eyes,' Nadan said, each word a battle for him. 'Otherwise… I might… kill you, too.'

'It's okay, don't open them,' Mui replied, crying. 'You're going to be okay.'

'Don't be… dumb,' Nadan said, enduring wave after wave of pain. 'Little bro, go with them.' He pointed in a seemingly random direction. 'You guys just… get out of here.'

'What? I can't leave you,' Mui responded.

'Eno… Eno?' Nadan called.

I knelt beside him, too. 'I'm here.'

'We fought together, right?'

I smiled and nodded. 'Yeah, although I didn't do much.'

He latched onto me and pulled me close. 'Then you can… *argh…* pay me back. Be my brother's eyes, okay? Look after him.'

I grabbed hold of his wrist and shook it. 'Okay, I will. I promise.'

Keenu slapped his forehead. 'We've *killed* the Patriarch, we're as good as dead.'

'No,' I said. 'The city is under attack, so let's escape *now*.'

Mui's tear-filled eyes closed. 'I said I'm not leaving him.'

Nadan had gone silent and still. Mui looked back at his brother and gasped. 'I can't see him! Are his eyes open? Is he moving?'

'He's gone,' Ido said. 'He's not in pain anymore.'

'No, he's not dead!' Mui screamed, bending down and embracing his dead brother. Mui's tears streamed down his cheeks and down onto Nadan.

The lasers in the sky had stopped, and although the city still burned, the distant citizens still screamed, and the ground still rumbled from collapsing buildings, the boys of the Feeble Fortress took a moment to mourn our friend, our *hero*, Nadan.

Another explosion rocked the ground, this time from Mycol's building. The boys initially made fearful noises, but once we realised we weren't in immediate danger, we all turned and gladly watched the building—the symbol of our terror—burn.

Mycol's facility, his dungeon and all his experiments had been purged in flame. It wasn't a bomb this time, rather the spreading inferno must have ignited something quite flammable inside. I felt sorry for all the unlucky souls who had been "grafted", but at least they weren't in pain anymore. If only we could have saved them, too.

'What's that?' one boy yelled, pointing up in the sky.

Several projectiles were hurtling down towards us from the sky. Bombs? No, they had little jets coming out the bottom to slow their speed. They were going to land nearby.

Keenu gestured to the ladders. 'I think… we should get out of here, right now.'

'Where do we go?' Ido asked.

'Anywhere is better than here,' I replied, grabbing hold of a still-crying Mui's elbow and heaving him away from his dead brother.

We all made for the ladders and climbed out of the pit. I stayed by Mui's side, just as Nadan had asked. Now up on the pit's edge, we could all see the aftermath of the attack.

The metal courtyard was blackened with ash, and bits of soldiers were scattered about. I spotted a pair of legs still on fire without a torso.

The soldiers who were still alive were all yelling and running for their lives. Most were horribly burned. They were all fleeing to the main gates to join the city proper. There weren't any soldiers in the guard towers or patrolling on the walls, and that meant there was no one to stop us from leaving.

Our group stood in silence, stunned by the absolute carnage around us.

Mui swivelled in all directions, observing the path of destruction in his own way. 'I can see the shape of the city.'

The metal containers from the sky dropped into the neighbouring city areas, and a few landed at the far end of this courtyard. Were these the attackers? The Female Dominion?

Keenu was hyperventilating. 'We... need... weapons!'

'We *are* weapons,' I shouted. I took a few steps forward with Mui. 'They've treated us like outcasts, like freaks. But *we* will be the ones to survive this. Come on!'

The boys ran with me through the courtyard, heading towards the large entrance archway, in the opposite direction to the attackers. We reached the central pathway, and our group merged with the other fleeing soldiers who paid no attention to us.

Another loud noise boomed above. A metal rocket blazed through the sky, heading straight for us. Everyone scattered, trying to clear out of the way by diving into the nearby sparring pits and trenches to our sides. I grabbed Mui by the shoulders, and we leapt into the nearest pit as well.

The rocket fired out from underneath and slowed. It landed gently in front of the gate on the fractured courtyard surface, blocking our path. Its boosters finally ceased. We boys peeked out from our pits. The soldiers fled in every other direction, leaving us children with the metal container.

'Shouldn't we run away, too?' Keenu called.

Ido climbed out and raised his hands, preparing for combat. 'We take down anyone that gets in our way.'

The capsule's door hissed with air and shifted to the side, revealing two figures in the bright interior. They weren't wearing Dominion armour but instead were clad in odd grey fatigues. They were holding hands, and one appeared to have a weapon. Both undid their straps and reached for the door's edge.

'Get ready!' Ido yelled as the other boys clambered out of their holes, too.

The two figures, a man and a woman, climbed out of their vehicle and jumped down, landing on the pathway. I recognised the woman, the realisation nearly causing me to fall back into the pit.

'Wait!' I shouted to the others. 'Tau?'

I let go of Mui's wrist, sprang out of the pit, and bolted forward. When I reached the circle of other boys, I shoved them aside and kept running toward her. She smiled, leaning down to embrace me tightly.

'Eno,' she exclaimed. 'It's really you, isn't it? I *knew* we would find you.'

I eyed the grinning dark-skinned man with confusion. '*We*? If you're not with the Female Dominion, then... who's attacking?'

'Your sister is leading the attack,' Tau replied, letting go of me. 'We need to help her.'

I felt my eyes fill with tears. 'Sacet's alive?'

'Is that... Officer Tetsu?' one of the boys said.

I didn't recognise the man with Tau, but he smiled at all the boys.

'He's a legend!' Mannox said before running up to him. 'You'll protect us with your shield, won't you, Sir?'

'Is Noor with you?' another asked.

The others all rushed over, starstruck. Each voiced similar questions. Mui came over, too, guided by our voices.

Tetsu, as he was called, raised his hands for calm. 'Stick with me and you will have my shield.' This brought grins to their faces. 'We need to get to the desert on the western side. Can you help us?'

'Outside the city?' Keenu said. 'We'll help! We were headed there anyway.'

Ido raised a hand. 'Now hold on a second. Why are you helping a woman, Sir? Who is she?'

Tau looked at him and smiled proudly. 'I'm… I'm just a healer. And we're here to finally end this war.'

Something caught Tau's eye in the distance, and I followed her gaze. Coming down the central pathway of the courtyard was a contingent of marching soldiers. There were at least a hundred men. Most wore regular soldier attire and were armed with rifles.

Leading them were ten or so men wearing the same clothing as Tau and Tetsu.

'Agents,' Tau said under her breath. 'All of you, get behind us.'

Keenu agreeably darted behind Tetsu, but the others held their ground.

I looked up at Tau. 'They're our enemies?' She nodded, so I shook my head. 'No. We'll fight, too.'

I glanced at the other boys, who were already nodding in agreement.

'In that case,' Tau said, aiming her pistol at my neck, 'let's take this collar off.'

'W-wait!'

She fired, and although I felt extreme heat and sparks flew up near my eyes, the collar's latch melted and broke off. I fell to the ground in pain, severely burned on my neck.

'Hey!' Mui said. 'You could have killed him!'

This sparked more protests from the other boys.

I couldn't help but cry. 'It hurts… it hurts… oww.'

Tau breathed in and out quickly, psyching herself up. 'Don't worry, boys. I'm not done yet.' Her entire body, including her hair, glowed with an aura of light blue, far larger than the other healer. Silvery flames exploded out from her back and all around her.

The glow spread to the others in our group. We all looked down at our hands and bodies as a warm, tingling sensation overcame us. My neck instantly felt better, in fact I felt no pain at all. I was completely reenergised, ready to fight again.

Tau leant over and reached out her hand to me with a warm smile. She helped me stand, and I smiled back.

One of the strange men leading the soldiers had thick, red mist leaking out of his nostrils. He raised his hand, and the marching soldiers stopped.

'What are you two doing down here?' he called.

'Helping my friends,' Tau called back.

Every time I had used my powers, I was focused on my fear, my own survival. Every time except one, when I had been focused on saving my friends. In Pilgrim's old village, I saved the other prisoners by directing my power in an arc. I felt a similar way about my friends here, I wanted all of us to be free.

'I feel… invincible,' one boy said.

'Me, too!' another boy cried out.

Mui was staring into my eyes. 'I can see you guys. I can see everyone.'

Something had awakened inside each of us. The terror Mycol had instilled in us did not make us powerful, nor did the promise of vengeance. We weren't feeble or broken freaks; we had just been focused on the wrong things in life.

Ido stepped forward, transforming his body into a far taller and more muscular version of himself, looking even stronger than those who trained in the courtyard. He positioned himself in between us and the soldiers. All the others except for Keenu and Mui joined by his side. I took a deep breath and joined the line, too.

Tetsu stood next to Tau and brought his hands to the sides. A large, dome-like shield of white summoned around them both.

The agents showed off their powers, too. The first man exhaled a cloud of the toxic-looking gas. He controlled it and kept it away from his allies.

Another man threw his hands towards the walkway. Metal sheets ripped up from it and surrounded his body like armour. Yet another man began to glow, even brighter than Tau. His whole body shone, which reflected off all the metallic surfaces. Other men summoned fire at their fingertips or turned their arms into long spears.

A larger man stepped away from the others, turned brown and appeared to be melting. Spikes protruded out from all over his body like a thornbush, and he let out a monstrous moan. As his body grew and grew, his armour ripped and burst. He slowly transformed into a giant necrolisk-like creature, which roared into the open sky.

'Those guys there?' Keenu said. 'They are *terrifying*.'

'They're more terrifying than the Terror Guard,' another boy stated.

We were terrified, yes, but again we all stood firm.

Tau looked at the confident boys in front of her and nodded. 'With our powers protecting you, you have *nothing* to fear.'

The toxic acolyte smirked. 'I don't normally kill kids.' He pointed at Tau. 'From what I hear, *you're* the expert.'

The men at the front all laughed together. Even the necrolisk chattered its jaws as if it was joining in. What were they talking about? Tau would never do something like that.

She simply shrugged and smiled back at them. 'You can't get to me anymore. This Harrowing is over.'

They stopped laughing and the man's grin faded.

'Kill them,' he ordered.

The men launched their onslaught in unison, shooting a bevy of both acolyte and laser projectiles. Each attack landed on us boys, but they were either deflected or absorbed by our shared glowing aura. We looked at one another and cheered, realising we were indeed invincible.

One of the fireballs made its way over and hit me right in the face. It was like a strong gust of air had breezed past my cheeks. Still no pain.

The roaring necrolisk stormed forward. It brought one of its massive pincers down into our group, and those who weren't quick enough to dodge were smacked onto the ground underneath it. The strike fractured the concrete under us even further, but the boys remained unharmed, instead crawling out from under the claw and standing again.

I threw my hands towards the monster, sending a focused shockwave at its abdomen. It blasted the creature into the air and over the heads of the other acolytes. It crashed and rolled into one of the far sparring arenas, howling on the way down.

The boys charged into enemy lines. Arbol regrew his palm spikes and somehow fired one like a projectile into an enemy soldier's neck. He inspected his hand with glee as it regrew yet again and then continued to fire into the oncoming pack.

With a glint in his eye, Keenu bolted past me toward the man with spears for arms. Shockingly, all the projectiles phased through Keenu's unhindered body. As the man stabbed forward, his spears predictably went right through Keenu as though he weren't there.

Keenu continued to run through the man, reached for his sidearm on his belt, and somehow grabbed it. He pressed it against the shocked man's face and shot him point-blank. Then, Keenu aimed at the others, continuing his killing spree, completely untouchable.

Tau and Tetsu slowly moved up with us. The constant barrage of projectiles could not breach Tetsu's shield. He defended her, and she, in turn, protected all of us with her aura of invincibility.

Ido was pummelling his enemies with reckless abandon, emboldened by the aura. A few soldiers tried tackling him from behind, and Ido's back formed impaling spikes, perhaps as a reflex.

The toxic acolyte sent a large, floating cloud over the battlefield. Many of the soldiers began to choke on their own ally's power and quickly dropped dead, but it had no effect on us.

I received another projectile to the face and returned it with a shockwave of my own, sending the glittering, bright acolyte to the other side of the courtyard. I threw my power sometimes so strongly that it shattered men's armour and contorted their bodies in midair.

Mui had wandered out of Tetsu's shield and into the middle of the fight. He seemed to understand where everyone was. One of the soldiers, a massive, hulking brute, charged him from the side. The man bowled Mui over, picked him up off the ground by the neck and punched the small child's face with a flurry of intense blows. Mui took each hit, unable to move and unable to strike back.

I had to save him. I fired a blast towards the brute, which sent them both into a nearby sparring pit. They separated in the air and eventually rolled to a stop.

I could see the frustration build inside of Mui. As he got to his feet, his eyes changed from white to pure black. He had the same empty gaze that his brother had. Mui stared over at the man, and they locked eyes. The burly man then fell to the ground, grabbing his head and shouting in agony. Mui's face was filled with loathing. The man writhed in unending pain.

As I fired more shockwaves, I noticed that we were being ambushed by a large force from behind. It was a team of fully armoured Female Dominion soldiers, at least a hundred of them.

Instead of firing on us or Tetsu's shield, they sprinted to be in line with it. They all jumped into the various sparring pits for cover and fired back at the MD soldiers. Tau pointed her fingers to her soldiers and spread her aura to them as well, an invincible army.

Most of the enemy acolytes who weren't already dead regrouped farther down the courtyard. The necrolisk had climbed out of the pit and joined them. Overwhelmed, they began their retreat, leaving all their soldiers behind.

The toxic acolyte had frozen in place. Something in the sky had drawn his attention. I followed his gaze and saw it. Behind us, far above the buildings was a giant maelstrom of fire. The blinding great circle grew over the city and a wave of heat washed over us. It was so bright, that everyone avert their eyes.

The courtyard was filled with even more screaming than before; all our enemies cried out as they caught fire. I looked over at Tau and the others. We were unaffected, still protected by her aura.

The enemies screamed the same way Ateity had when he was burnt to death. They turned bright orange. Their bodies smouldered and fumes vented from their cavities. The distant necrolisk howled once more as its numerous limbs fell off its torso. Its jaw peeled off and onto the ground, sizzling. The creature collapsed and melted into char like the others.

The entire environment around us had changed; everything now had a blinding red hue about it. The sky was literally fire. The wind had picked up, too, and the ashes of the bodies flew towards the circle of fire above.

We all gathered around Tau again, including the female soldiers. Tetsu dropped his shield so that we could all huddle closer. Some of us were covered in blood, others shook in fear, unable to process what had happened.

'It's Sacet,' Tau yelled to us with a solemn expression. 'What is she doing?'

'That thing is massive,' Keenu said. 'It's going to kill everyone!'

I tugged on Tau's arm. 'We need to find her.'

Thirty-Eight: A Great Truth

Sacet

The scorching portal hung over the city, threatening to consume everything and everyone. Even from here, I could feel the air pressure change and the heat spike. With a mere lowering of my hands, I could bring the tear in reality crashing down onto them.

Even from here, outside the city limits, my perception sensed that most of the damage had already been done. The sunlight incinerated anyone left outside. The countless people hiding indoors couldn't escape the intense heat either. Flames billowed through every corridor and tunnel. Only those deeper underground were still alive. It appeared even all the electrical equipment had been disabled, too.

I looked away from the cliffside, over to Noor's body lying on the sand, and then at his killer in front of me. The man basked in the stunning flare of the star and the destruction it wrought.

A wide smile spread upon his face. 'Impressive.' He folded his arms and looked back at me to nod approvingly.

'If you don't release my family and friends, I'll destroy the whole city!'

His smile persisted. 'Is that so?'

He disappeared and I felt the wind whip behind me. He wrapped his arm around my neck and the other around my chest, gripping me tightly. I choked and wheezed.

He chuckled and bent closer to my ear. 'Is that the best you can threaten me with?'

I struggled against his hold but kept my arms up to maintain the portal. 'I'll do it.'

'Go ahead. Kill them all. I *want* you to. You really think I affiliate myself with any of *them*?'

'But… it's *your* city?'

He laughed and his chest heaved into my back. 'You *still* think I'm a Male Dominion soldier, don't you?'

'I don't know *what* you are.'

'It doesn't matter. In a moment, I'm going to snap your neck like I did to your annoying friend over there. And then it will all be over.' We floated up off the ground. 'But before that happens, how about we make this interesting? Destroy the city and I'll leave your brother alone.'

I could still sense thousands of survivors. But I didn't see evil faces filled with malicious intent anymore. I saw screaming children. Tears in adult men's eyes. I saw the fear. Just as scared and confused as anyone else would be. They huddled in their shelters, watching the ceilings rumble, out of options.

I didn't feel anger for them anymore. This man would callously discard their lives just as he would my people. They were manipulated like I was. What had I done? I had destroyed so much and killed *so* many. I was just as much a monster as he was.

He shook me in his arms. 'I'm growing impatient. Kill them!'

'They are not the enemy,' I whispered to myself. 'You are.'

Focusing on the sun, I released the portal above the city. It disappeared with a shockwave that rippled through the surrounding desert. A new portal opened from behind and I pulled it over the two of us tightly like a cloak.

We both floated in the star's atmosphere. The portal closed. Could not think. So bright. Burning. It was finally over.

There was a familiar tingling sensation. It was warm. I was alive.

I sat up on the cold, metal table. 'Tau?'

A moustachioed young man was standing over me. Like Tau, he had similar silvery-blue flames coming off his palms and wrists, but they appeared far weaker than hers normally would.

I shoved him away and hopped off the table. The room was small, with only one closed door. A large mirror was next to it.

My eyes were still blurrily adjusting, but I saw that my body had been completely reformed. I knew that because my coloured streaks were gone.

The man sighed. 'It will be over soon.' He turned to the door and approached it. It opened for him, and he left.

I felt a hand on my shoulder and jumped. It was Noor. He frowned. 'We lost.'

Malu was leaning against the wall behind him. We all had collars around our necks and wore the same simple grey outfits.

I leaned into Noor and hugged him. 'I couldn't do it.'

He hugged back, but his arms were limp.

'I killed *so* many people,' I continued, rubbing my face on his chest.

A voice cleared from behind and I turned.

Standing by the door was Marid. She wore similar clothing to us but had no collar. She stepped into the room and the door closed behind her.

'Marid! They brought you back...' I said, releasing Noor and darting around the steel table towards her.

She remained still, staring at me. Her lip trembled. She looked away from me and winced.

'What is it?' I asked. 'Marid...?'

'I'm sorry. They let *me* be the one to come speak to you. To tell you everything.'

'What are you talking about?' I asked.

Malu pushed off the wall and pointed at her. 'She's one of *them*.'

I stepped back and shook my head at Marid. 'No. No. Not you, too? Tell me she's wrong.'

Marid raised her hands. 'Please, hear me out.'

I fell against the table, continuing to shake my head in disbelief.

She closed her eyes. 'You all deserve the truth.' She sighed and walked over to the other side of the table. 'Seron is a farm. The acolytes are its crops. The war and suffering are the sun and rain.

'They made you children in batches, just as you would when making weapons of war. Each batch, or squad, had the same father and mother, but each squad was unique, with a different combination of acolyte parents. Sacet, Tau wasn't just your squad-sister growing up. She is your *real* sister.'

My lips quivered and I looked down at the floor.

Marid had a tear in her eye. 'As for your parents, acolytes have a better chance of having acolyte children... so...' She looked apprehensive, taking a deep breath. 'I am your *real* mother, and the man you've been fighting against, Caelum, is your father.'

I felt like I was going to throw up. I pushed away from the table. Noor grabbed me from behind and helped keep me from collapsing to the ground.

Marid gripped the table. 'All of this has repeated for *many* cycles, all to make more and more acolytes. Acolytes are the most valuable commodity that the Asterian Empire has. They use them for everything, and so they *must* keep growing them. There are other planet farms like Seron, each a different experiment. Most have wars between people divided up into random factions. Others are just prisons...'

She wandered around the table to get closer. '*This* planet used to belong to the nomads that *you* know today. But we invaded, enslaved them, assimilated them into our people, practically destroyed their planet's surface and built new cities upon it. Some of the nomads had their minds wiped and were left here as part of the experiment.'

Malu sobbed. Noor's mouth was agape. I backed into the wall. My knees wobbled so I slunk down.

Marid wiped her eyes before continuing. 'And as for why they focused on *you* so much, well... there are some extremely rare acolytes that *theoretically* never stop growing more powerful. Your father is one of them. They are immune to psychic control, which is why the scientists couldn't assimilate you. This is how they *knew* you were one of them.

'These special cases are supposed to have a particularly awful gestation period, known as the Harrow, or Harrowing. When they first discover their powers, they are treated cruelly, otherwise, they'd be weaker in the long run. Since their discovery, our species has only managed to grow six of them, including you.'

Malu's crying was getting worse. Noor brought both hands to his face and paced from side to side. I stared ahead, realising that everything I had done in my life had helped them. We remained in silence for what seemed an eternity.

'*Please* don't be angry with me,' Marid continued, focusing on me. 'When I was a little girl, my family and I fought and lost to the empire. I was brought to this world as a criminal, a prisoner. My sentence was to live my entire life here. They wiped my memory. It was a prison that I wasn't even *aware* of.'

She came even closer again. 'When I first met *you*, I was angry.' She smiled. 'I guess I was *always* angry. They had one last use for me though, to train you. They realised you were special not long after we started. So, they brought me up here and they returned my memory. *Everything* came back.'

She knelt to be at my level. 'They told me my sentence would be over if I did as I was told. It didn't seem so bad. All I had to do was hold this angry little portal girl's hand and make her stronger. But everything went out of control and the things they did to you... and then I got to know you.'

She reached out to my wrist and brushed it. 'So, I stayed with you and tried to help you avoid their traps.' She gave a solemn grin. 'But you never listened. You just... kept fighting it. Fighting them. Doing *exactly* what they wanted you to do.'

She slowly stood and backed away. 'I was told to bring you all to them when I was done.' She went to the door and rapped on it.

The door opened and several armed guards marched in. I could see even more of them outside the door.

I stared into her eyes. 'Why didn't you tell me?' My barely audible voice cracked.

Even more guards came through. They took Noor and Malu by the arms and dragged them out the door.

'I wanted to, so badly,' Marid replied. 'But I wanted my daughter's torture to end sooner, not prolong it.'

Two guards grabbed me, forced me up and hauled me towards the door.

She closed her eyes again. 'I'm sorry that I failed you in your first life, but I promise… I'll help you find happiness in your second.'

I stopped in front of the double doors and looked back at the others. Noor and Malu were behind me. Marid was by my side. The guards prodded me again.

I swallowed my breath, clenched my fists and walked forward. The doors parted and I was greeted by an odd sight. The large room was filled with all my enemies, many crowded around the door on the other side. They all smiled, cheered and clapped.

Verre's old colonels were in front.

'Here she is,' Korin said.

Neva slapped me on the back as I walked in. 'Congratulations!'

'You finally graduated, well done,' Korin added.

'Your Harrowing is over,' Aki said. 'Breathe!'

Several others praised me as I passed.

Kalek was standing at the near end of a long table in the centre of the control room. 'About time. Come sit over here.' He chuckled and pointed at the seat at the closest end. 'You're our guest of honour.'

I saw both Verre and Siph already seated at the table, as well as many others I didn't recognise. There were rows of equipment on the far-left side of the room. Many technicians got up from their seats and applauded. Everyone's smiles disturbed me.

The room had been decorated with colourful lights and hangings. The table had an elegant purple tablecloth atop it. There were snacks and swirling drinks laid out along it, too.

I walked forward and sat in the seat that Kalek was pulling out for me. With no other seats left, Malu and Noor stopped behind me. The room was packed with people all crowding around the table, staring at me. Marid avoided the others, instead slinking off to the side where the technicians were.

At the other end of the long table was the Male Dominion King, Tuloch. He, too, smiled at me, and I felt sick. For the past cycle, his face was what haunted me, the one pulling all the strings.

There was a wide window beyond the table. My jaw dropped when I saw what was outside. It was our planet. Staring out the window was my father, Caelum. He turned to look at me, holding his hands behind his back. He didn't smile like the others.

Tuloch picked up a drink and raised it. 'Welcome to Sacet. Her Harrowing is finally over.'

Everyone raised glowing, colourful drinks of their own and cheered in unison.

'Welcome to reality,' Verre said, leaning over and patting me on the shoulder. 'You're a *real* person now.'

Tuloch glanced over to Marid. 'Has she been filled in?'

Marid nodded back before leaning against one of the control panels.

Tuloch looked back at me. 'Good, good, then we can move forward from all the ugliness. Sacet, we sincerely apologise for everything we have done to you. It was a… *necessary* step for awakening your true potential. That being said, we hope it was a truly *horrendous* Harrowing we gave you.'

'Here, here!' a few people said at once.

Others around the room laughed and nodded in agreement.

'What are you going to do with us?' I asked, and some of them continued to chortle, shaking their heads at my naivety.

Tuloch laughed, too. 'You need to *relax* now. As we said, it's over.'

I gestured to the collar around my neck. 'If that's true, then why do I still have *this*?'

The others looked back at Tuloch to hear his response.

He took a sip of his drink and put the glass down. 'Let's be realistic here. If we brought you here *without* that, while your tensions are still high, you and your two friends would try to wreck the whole place. No, what needed to be done was for us to have some time to explain things to you. And after, when we take you home to Aster and you've calmed down, we'll remove it.'

I looked over at my mother. She wasn't smiling. She averted her eyes from me.

'Where's my brother?' I asked.

Tuloch glanced over to the side of the table.

There was a grotesque, misshapen, bulbous man. Based on his odd proportions, he reminded me of the one that ambushed us in the desert. Another man next to him had small puffs of red coming from his nostrils every time he exhaled.

'Last I heard,' Tuloch began, 'your brother was alive in MDC.'

The two men nodded.

My heart skipped a beat. Eno was okay. 'And our friends? What have you done with Tau and Tetsu?'

Tuloch glared at Verre. 'They are back on the surface with your brother. And they *shouldn't* be. They were *supposed* to be here to help you celebrate.'

Verre bowed her head in shame.

Tuloch stroked his moustache and looked over my shoulder. 'As for *these* friends, I suppose they can come with you if it puts you at ease. We know how much you like Noor, after all.'

The room burst into laughter again. Caelum continued to stare out the window in silence.

Noor's fists were shaking by his sides. 'I'll kill you, old man.'

Tuloch smashed his fist on the table and stood. 'You be silent, boy!' He pointed at both Noor and Malu. 'The only reason *you* two are here is as a courtesy to *her*.'

He slowly sat back down and reached for his drink.

'What about the others?' I asked as he took another sip, trying to divert him from Noor.

Tuloch put down the glass. 'The others? Everyone else on the planet will have a *different* fate. We will bring *some* with us, but now that we've let your little adventure run its course and reaped the profits, we need to reset the planet back to the way it was. We'll have to bring in a team of psychics from off-world to start reassigning everyone new lives.'

'You're going to start the war again?' I asked.

'Yes, *my* job here isn't done.' He gestured at everyone else in the room. 'And the same goes for the rest of the agents here.'

I shrugged and leant back. 'So, everything I've ever done was for nothing.'

Marid's gaze focused back on me. Her eyes darted about. She slowly walked over to one of the workstations.

Tuloch shook his head. 'It wasn't for nothing; look how powerful you've become.' He gestured back at Caelum. 'Of course, you're still no match for your father.'

I glanced around. 'Is power *all* that matters to you people? Don't you feel at least a *little* bit guilty for making people suffer for it?'

Korin scoffed. 'You're only saying that because you were raised without resurrection. *Everyone* who dies on Seron gets taken back to the homeworld.'

Kalek shrugged. 'Yeah. Maybe thousands of cycles ago, when death was still permanent, we feared it.'

Tuloch brought his fingers together and rested his elbows on the table. 'But now with resurrection, suffering is only temporary. Our species has *thrived* because of it. It is *all* for the greater good. Without death, we can make great advances in every field of study. Can't you at least see the positive side to all of this?'

Suddenly, I felt my powers return. My reawakened second perception spun in circles trying to adjust. While continuing to look back at Tuloch, I sensed over to Marid. She was quietly tapping keys on the machine as the others spoke, and when she finished, she looked over at me.

'You will be rich, powerful and famous when you return,' Tuloch continued.

Marid cupped both her hands and slowly brought them together, forming the shape of a sphere. Even though I was focused on Tuloch, she knew I could see her, right? What was she trying to… wait. I understood what she meant now.

'You will want for nothing.'

Both Noor and Malu shifted uncomfortably. They looked around nervously, then down at me. Did they feel their powers return, too?

'And you will be permitted to live for millennia,' Tuloch continued. 'Far longer than anyone else in this room. Your father here is over 1800 cycles old. You have practically an eternity to be… whatever you *want* to be.'

I could sense the entire space station now. There were empty prison cells on the far side, laboratories where healers were resurrecting the dead, and a launching bay with lines of pods and missiles. The station was filled with hundreds of personnel.

Tuloch and the others were still looking at me. They hadn't noticed yet.

'Well?' Tuloch said. 'What do you say to that?'

I shook my head. 'I only see the negatives.'

I thought about the desert just outside New Elysia.

'Unlike all of you, I was taught compassion.'

My perception focused on the entirety of the space station.

'I had a mother who was always there for me,' I said, looking over at Marid. 'She taught me right from wrong. And a father who cared about me.' I looked at Caelum. 'I wasn't just a *weapon* that could be improved. I was his daughter.'

Caelum floated closer. He scowled and pointed at me. 'I have *thousands* of children. Do you really think I have time for *all* of you? Don't kid yourself, the only reason you have the privilege of *knowing* me is because of your power!'

I shook my head again. 'I'm not a person to you, just an object you can exploit. You're a *terrible* father.'

I stood up from my seat, leaned forward and grabbed the glass in front of me. It had cold pink and white liquid inside, endlessly swirling. I took a sip. It was sweet, full of flavour.

Noor's fists clenched again. Did he know what I was about to do?

A large portal, big enough to envelop the entire space station began to open underneath it. As I started shifting it up, I put the glass back down and stared at Tuloch again.

'Thanks for the party in my honour, but we can't stay. Like you, we have a job to do.' I glanced back at Noor and nodded.

He didn't hesitate, he flung his arms forward and fired at Tuloch. The laser melted through his chest, his chair and into the window behind him, puncturing a hole into space.

Before anyone could react, I teleported Noor, Malu, Marid and I back to the planet's surface, just outside New Elysia.

The three of them jumped back in shock when we landed on the sand. I looked up into the sky and saw the bottom of the space station beginning to thread through the portal. I increased the speed the portal was swallowing it, and when it had reached the top, I closed it off.

The gargantuan structure fell towards the surface with loud metal groans and creaks. The four of us watched as it plummeted, hopefully at a safe distance.

The satellite impacted, sending a deluge of sand into the sky. The collision broke the various elongated pieces off the structure. A fiery column swelled. The ensuing explosion devastated the frame, sending building-sized pieces of wreckage over our heads.

I opened a portal in front of us like a shield. Millions of metal shards rained down on us with trails of flame in their wake. Many pieces whooshed through the portal, back into the sky elsewhere. A giant, hazy cloud burgeoned upwards: a mix of smoke, sand and fire.

Shooting up from the wreckage was an infuriated Caelum. The explosive force from his launch sent pieces of debris high into the sky, far above what the explosion had caused. He was seething red. His face had contorted to the extreme, the most emotion I had ever seen him show. A large, throbbing vein protruded from his neck and his eyes bulged. He closed his eyes and roared.

Now was the time. I created two portals to his sides while he was distracted by rage. Finally understanding what Marid was trying to tell me, I bent their shape into two hemispheres and clasped them around him. The loop was complete, a perfect, translucent sphere, distorting the view of the sky like a warped lens.

Inside I could sense Caelum flying through the edge of the sphere and immediately looping back on the other side of the sphere's interior. Without any light going in, it was completely dark. But *if* he could see anything, it would be his own endless, twisted reflection in all directions.

'You did it!' Marid yelled.

'Is he…?' Malu asked.

'He's trapped!' Noor said. 'Yes!'

As the others cheered and celebrated, I got my arms in a more comfortable position to hold the portals longer. While keeping them together, I floated the portals towards us.

I sensed two aircraft rise from New Elysia heading in this direction. They were filled with our troops.

Marid approached and smiled. 'That was *exactly* what I meant. I'm so proud of—'

'You're not off the hook yet... *mother*.'

Noor joined my side and pointed to the sphere. 'I guess now he can know the *privilege* of his own company.'

'But wait,' Malu began. 'Sacet, how long can you sustain that portal?'

The others noticed the aircraft in the distance.

I gestured to them with my chin. 'It'll be okay. We'll get a lift to the inhibitor cells.'

'And then we kill him?' Malu suggested.

The sphere had reached us and was floating by our side.

I shook my head. 'No, he must *not* die. We will keep him alive for as long as we can. Otherwise, he might return as the others did.'

The two aircraft glided over our position to survey the destruction. Malu and Noor waved at them with both arms to get their attention.

Marid pointed over to the burning satellite wreckage. 'Don't look now, but another one survived.'

It was Kalek, sprinting through the sand towards us and angrily shouting.

I smirked. 'I can't afford to lose concentration on Caelum. Kalek can chill out in space again.'

Thirty-Nine: Hope Is A Choice

The next day

New Elysia Prison Quad

There was no one in the corridor with me. I was finally alone. A moment without watching Caelum in his cell, without others around to judge me or call on me for aid.

I collapsed against the corridor wall, slid down to the floor, and bawled, closing my eyes.

How could I live with myself after all that I had done? After everything they put me through, I had grown so accustomed to taking lives. I had become the very thing I hated most in life. All those families were torn apart because of me. All those innocent people murdered because it had to be done *my* way. All that hate now directed at my actions.

'Commander Sacet?' I heard a voice say.

I wiped my eyes and shook myself back to my surroundings. I searched for the source but saw no one in the corridor.

'Commander, do you read?' the voice repeated through the headset.

I pressed a button on it. 'I'm here. Who is this?'

'It's… Coleo,' she replied.

I exhaled. 'Coleo, it's good to hear your voice. I'm glad I was wrong about you. I'm sorry.'

'That's okay, everything worked out, so…' she continued. 'More spies could still be out there, so stay alert.'

'I will.'

'We have incoming,' she continued. 'I've directed them to land by the Citadel entrance. You should come see them.'

I pushed against the wall and stood. 'Who is it?'

'You'll see. Coleo out.'

I panted for a moment, going over the possibilities. I thought back to the great golden doors of the Royal Citadel and opened a portal to my side. I stepped through and was met by the gleaming sunlight reflecting off the golden tower.

The path at my feet was clear to the Residential Rim. The city's flames had finally been put out. To the sides of the path, thousands of tents filled the Royal Gardens. Tens of thousands of our displaced citizens wandered between them.

People were making merriment over what little they had. Laughing and smiling. Sharing food and dancing together.

I sensed a Male Dominion aircraft in the sky. It was already circling the tower. All those in the gardens looked up and watched as it descended. It homed in on the path in front of me.

I could already sense the people inside it. There was Tau, Tetsu and fourteen young boys strapped into the seats. There were a few Male Dominion soldiers, too. Sitting amongst the boys was Eno.

I put a hand over my mouth and cried out. Tears instantly welled all over again, but this time for joy. I wandered closer. My shaking legs were about to give.

The craft landed on the path and a ramp lowered. The door in the fuselage opened and Tau came out first. She and I locked eyes. She smiled and moved to the side.

Eno squeezed past, jumped down the ramp and sprinted towards me. I wobbled forward but fell to my knees. I cried and reached both hands towards him. He leapt into my arms and hugged me back.

'I'm so sorry,' I said, crying into his shoulder. 'I should have *never* sent you so far away.'

He squeezed tighter. 'I never stopped thinking about you. I thought you died.'

'And I thought *you* died.'

Tau and the other passengers had disembarked and approached as well. The engines shut down.

A crowd of others had wandered over from the campsites and surrounded the craft for a better look. I spotted many familiar faces among them. I noticed Urias and Commander Terel walking together.

I stood while keeping an arm around Eno. I smiled again at Tau and gave a little bow. 'It is good to see you again, my Queen.'

She laughed. 'How about just sister?' She waited for my confused reaction. 'Coleo told us.'

'You know that... you and I...?'

She came over and hugged me, too. 'Somehow, I think I *always* knew. We didn't call each other squad-sisters for nothing, did we?'

When she released me, I looked down at Eno. 'And you know, too?'

He shrugged. 'That you're not *really* my sister? I didn't know but... I *should* have. The way Grandpa treated you differently. That and... you look *nothing* like Mum and Dad.'

We giggled for a moment.

I shook my head. 'And that doesn't bother you?'

'Of course not,' he said. 'You're my big sister, Sas, and you *always* will be.' He glanced back at the other smiling boys. 'Family doesn't just mean blood.'

Each boy nodded and watched on.

I smiled, leaned down and hugged Eno again. I looked over at the Male Dominion soldiers, and then at Tau.

She raised a hand to calm me. She turned and noticed the crowd of people that had gathered around us. 'Everyone, I am glad to be back,' she shouted. 'Things will be different this time. I have good news. I have secured a ceasefire. Soon, the whole world will be at peace. The war is over!'

The crowd erupted in cheers. The MD soldiers took off their helmets and discarded them. They looked out at the crowd of women and nomads. They smiled and pumped their fists in the air like the crowd did, before wandering over to join them in celebration.

The thirteen other young boys also cheered and playfully ran about. In their number, I spotted two smiling, black-haired brothers. The older one was trying to guide the younger, as though he were injured, but the small boy held up his hand, indicating he could walk on his own. They, too, happily joined the others.

'Eno!' a deep voice bellowed from the crowd.

It was Pilgrim. He pushed through the line and dashed towards us.

'Pilgrim!' Eno yelled back.

Eno left my grasp and ran to him. When they met, Pilgrim grabbed Eno under the armpits and lifted him high into the air. The two of them laughed, cried and cheered. Pilgrim regaled Eno about his own tales and led him to the others. Sabikah was there, too, and Pilgrim reintroduced Eno to her.

I reached out towards them. 'Eno?'

Tau put a hand on my shoulder. 'Let him go.'

'But I only *just* got him back?'

She put an arm around me. 'There will be plenty of time to reconnect. And anyway, something tells me you're not the only one that's looking out for him now.'

Tetsu wandered over to our side. 'Congratulations on your victory… Commander.'

Tau smirked at us both. 'Let's do away with the titles altogether, I think.'

I nodded. 'I agree. All this power just corrupts everything.'

Tau gestured out at the crowd. 'Let's just be people helping people.'

The three of us looked out at them for a moment.

Tau pointed over at Eno. 'You know, Eno's not the same goofy little kid we used to know. He's quite the warrior now. His powers are impressive.'

I stared at Tau with my mouth open. 'He's an acolyte?'

Tetsu laughed. 'Sure is. A powerful one.'

The smile disappeared from Tau's face, and she turned to me. 'Speaking of powerful acolytes, it's time I see our father.'

I nodded and thought back to the Prison Quadrant. I opened a portal to where I had left Noor, Malu and Marid last. Tau and Tetsu entered it first and I followed onto the catwalk on the other side.

'Tetsu!' Noor yelled.

The boys immediately ran towards each other and collided, embracing tightly. They laughed and celebrated just as the others had before.

Tau ran to Malu and hugged her.

As usual, Malu was taken off guard by the act of love, but she eventually accepted it and hugged back. 'It's good to see you again.'

'Where have you been, brother?' Noor asked Tetsu. 'I needed your shield plenty of times out there.'

Tetsu glanced over his shoulder at Tau. 'There was someone else who needed it a little more.'

Tau noticed Marid and nodded. 'Mother.'

Malu and Tau released as Marid cautiously approached.

'Welcome back, Tau,' Marid began before pausing. She looked between Tau and I, ashamed. 'Can you ever forgive me?'

Tau leant forward without hesitation and hugged her, too. 'Only if you continue to advise me.'

Marid happily embraced her. 'Always, daughter.'

Both turned to me.

I shook my head. 'You're going to have to do more to *earn* my trust back.'

'Sacet,' Tau said, reaching out her hand to me. 'Trust me. We can't live our lives never putting faith in others.'

I stared at her hand for a moment. I took it and she pulled me closer to Marid. Marid gave an earnest smile and raised her arms for another hug.

I sighed and closed my eyes. 'Alright.'

Marid put her arms around me. I didn't move at first but begrudgingly hugged her back.

A long, deep chuckle sounded from below. We all looked over the edge of the catwalk and down into the inhibitor cells. Caelum was where I had left him, sitting cross-legged in the centre of his cell, looking up and laughing at us.

'Even after *all* I've done to you,' he said, 'you *still* have hope. I have... failed.'

Tau gripped the railing and shook her head at him. 'Hope is a choice we all make. It is something that you, even with all your power, can't control in others.'

'When I get out of here, there will be no more games. No more chances. I will kill you *all* in an instant. We'll see how long your hope lasts then.'

Tau shrugged. 'Until that day comes, you will stay locked away here. Alone and forgotten, so that maybe a little joy can come into the world for once.'

Forty: The Greed of an Empire

Neva

18 days later

Far away, on the planet Aster

I confidently strode down the seemingly endless blue rug towards the throne, dragging my shimmering golden dress with me. I hoped the empress would appreciate its beauty as much as I did. More importantly, I hoped they both adored the gift I had brought them.

The four court servants brought it up the rear in a large case, one on each corner. The imbeciles had better be careful to not step on my dress. Easy now, Neva. Compose yourself. Best behaviour.

As they had suggested, it was best I didn't make sudden movements. Some of the empire's deadliest assassins and acolytes lurked in the upper rafters. They were peering down from their shadowy ledges, watching for the slightest mistake. Anything even *close* to aggression would be punished brutally.

At the end of the darkened chamber sat the empire's glorious rulers, Emperor Avarut and Empress Suralia. Their thrones were immense,

J.B. VILLINGER

made from pure gold and platinum. Luxuriously furnished, too. I imagined they'd feel the most lavish of comfort.

Another old man stood to the side of the chamber, and I recognised him instantly. It was Raumanu, the most famous Chosen of them all. He was the eldest, the wisest and arguably the most powerful.

His eyes were closed and most of his weight was supported by his signature tungsten cane. He was balding, with tufts of white hair coming out the sides. He had a white beard and moustache, too.

I could see now why others spoke often of his advanced age. He had withered to such an extreme that it was a wonder resurrection and age rejuvenation could *still* keep him alive. Being two and a half millennia old would certainly do that to a person.

The emperor and empress shared this fate, too. It was known by all and said by none. Being the oldest people in the empire had its drawbacks. Their skin drooped, their eyes were sullen, and their bodies were frail and brittle. I'd rather be dead than as hideous as them. They, on the other hand, were too stubborn to die.

Conversely, their robes were magnificent, cut from the finest materials, with edges laced finer still. They glowed splendidly.

I led my entourage down the aisle and as we reached the large, carpeted square in front of their thrones, we stopped and bowed.

'Emperor and Empress, praise be to your immortal gloriousness.'

I averted my gaze, awaiting their approval. It felt like the longest and tensest moment of my life. Did I say it right? What if I insulted them somehow?

'Rise,' the emperor said gruffly, uninterested.

The empress leant off the edge of her seat. 'My, my, what a beautiful dress. And so young, too.' She smiled, which caused her loose cheeks to stretch oddly.

I raised my head and smiled. 'Thank you, Empress. It is a part of my body. I bring news of the Harrowing.' I stood and approached closer.

'You have word of Sacet?' the emperor asked, sitting up in his chair. Every word he uttered was like a menacing bite. I wasn't sure if it was involuntary.

'Correct, Sire. The Overwatch operation *severely* underestimated her. Along with her friends, their powers, and even more so, their resolve.'

The empress looked over to her lifelong lover, examining his reaction. He quietly seethed but gestured for me to continue.

'They destroyed our station, killing almost every agent on board. I evacuated so that I could return word to you.'

The emperor's face screwed up in a furious contortion. I half expected him to give the order for my permanent execution on the spot for delivering such heinous news.

He was shaking, barely able to contain himself. 'I *thought* we sent Caelum there?'

'You did, Sire, and he was able to awaken the Chosen, but Sacet… captured him.'

The emperor, struggling to understand the concept of failure, looked at his own shaking fists. 'You're telling us the most *powerful* Chosen in the known universe was unable to defeat her?'

I nodded. 'That is correct. *But*, I believe this to be a *good* thing. It means another powerful Chosen can join the others.'

'*If* we manage to capture her,' the emperor added.

The empress brandished her long, red fingernails in front of her for examination. 'What is the state of the harvest world in question?'

'I'm afraid all control has been relinquished. With no senior agents left, the planet has achieved… peace. They *all* know the truth now.'

The emperor was deep in thought and the chamber went silent.

I performed a curtsy. 'Glorious ones, if I may, I… have also brought a gift for the empire, for you.' I gestured back at the servants.

The empress scoffed. 'There is *no* gift I don't *already* have. I doubt you could impress *me*.'

The court servants lifted the case past me and gently placed it on the floor in front of the thrones. They busted the latches and opened it. Inside sat the seemingly innocuous metal shard. It was still glowing and produced a minor hum.

'What is this?' the emperor asked, peering closer but then leaning back in his seat, unamused.

'It is an object that grants acolyte power,' I explained.

Both of their faces lit up in surprise. Even Raumanu moved away from the wall and hobbled closer with his cane to get a better look.

'It gives power?' the empress asked.

'Yes,' I replied. 'I stole it while spying on Sacet. I insisted I deliver it to you personally. While in transit, our scientists have already begun to analyse it, and they can verify its limitless power.'

'How does it work?' the empress asked, staring at it and tilting her head in uncertainty.

'Anyone who touches it is given the temporary use of a specific power – in *this* case, the ability to control sand.'

I nodded at the servants. One was holding a jar of sand for demonstration. I gracefully waved my hands up and down at the jar and soon the grains sifted out and into the air. I gently lowered it back down and looked back at the captivated rulers.

I smiled back at the emperor as he stood up from his throne. 'I am already an acolyte with a *different* power. But touching the shard grants me another. And it works on those without powers, too. Would your Grace care to try?'

'Bring it closer,' he rasped, struggling to make his way down the steps.

I shot a stern look at the servants and gestured towards him. They sprung forward, picked up the case, brought it to him and held it up for him to reach.

'I just… touch it?' he asked.

'Yes, Sire.' I raised a hand in caution. 'But be warned, it can be discomforting at first.'

A malevolent grin spread across his worn face. He held his hands out hesitantly before diving forward and grabbing hold. As the object glowed brightly, he gritted his teeth and groaned in pain. The flare intensified and white veins appeared on his withered thin arms. I raised my hand to shield my face until it was over.

I could hear him laughing and so I looked back with relief. He threw his hands at the jar, and it exploded in all directions, sending sand far down the blue carpeting and glass shards into the servant's faces. I felt my body shift apart, too. I strained it back into place.

'This is incredible!' he yelled, his words echoing throughout the chamber. 'I feel *young* again.'

The empress smiled at her husband, then back at me. '*How* did it come to be?'

'That is still a mystery, I'm afraid,' I replied.

'I want *more*,' the emperor said, placing his hands gently onto the artefact's case. 'We must find *more* of these.'

The empress' smile stretched again. 'I was wrong about your gift, young lady. It has *pleased* me greatly.' She turned back to the emperor. 'Now, how are we to deal with this rebellious Chosen?'

The emperor snarled. 'Too much time and effort have been spent trying to bring her here. Now that she has been created, we have what we need from that harvest world.' He glanced at Raumanu. 'I want *you* to go there and end it.'

Raumanu almost lost his balance. 'Sire?'

'Wipe it clean,' the emperor reiterated. '*Destroy* the whole planet.'

Raumanu attempted a short bow with only his head. 'Very well, Sire.'

'And you,' the emperor said, looking back at me as he slowly shuffled up the steps. 'You will also go back. That was the planet I sent my daughter to, was it not?'

He meant Iya. That spoilt little princess allowed Tau and Tetsu to escape. Should I tell him the truth? No, I could use this against her later.

'It was, Sire,' I replied. 'Iya was… *instrumental* in Sacet's Harrowing.'

'Good, then tell her the banishment is over,' he said, sitting down on his throne. 'Bring her home to us.'

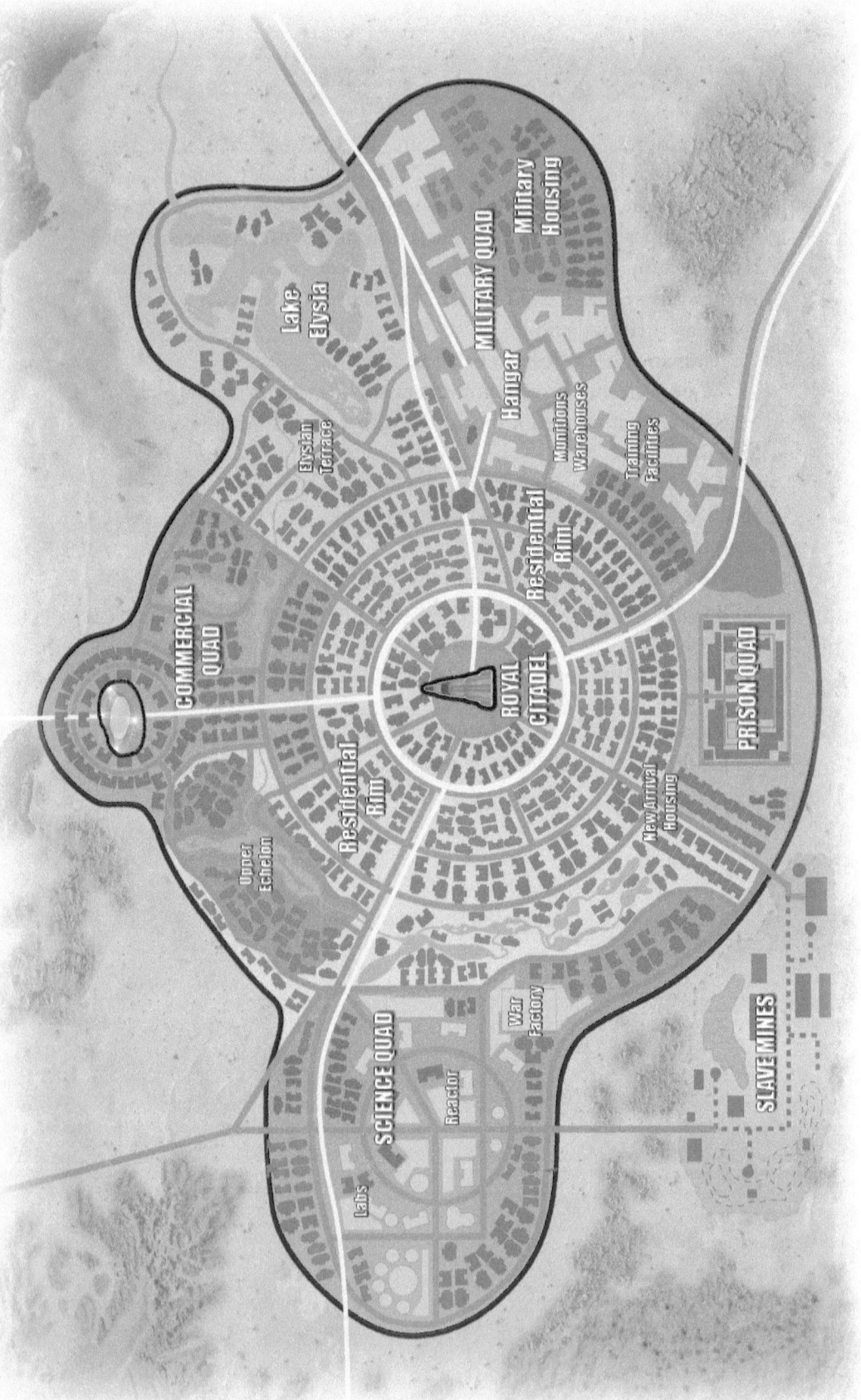

Streak Colour

White - Science
Blue - Soldier
Red - Support
Green - Special Ops
Yellow - Air Force
Purple - Acolyte

Tip Colour

White - Initiate
Blue - Trooper
Red - Corporal
Green - Officer
Yellow - Colonel
Black - Commander

Destruction
Main Combat Forces

King Tuloch

Havoc
Shock Troops

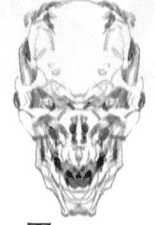

Terror
Psychological Warfare

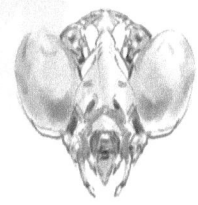

TDC
(Terror Division Control)
Acolyte Containment Specialists

Corruption
Espionage

Note from the Author

I often think about what it means to be happy. Is it having a loving family and a good job? Is it a full life of distractions, or does happiness come from accumulating more and more wealth? How about fame? Is ignorance truly bliss, or should my learning forever expand my horizons? Maybe happiness will fall into my lap when I least suspect it. Or maybe I'm overthinking it and I should feel happy I'm even alive.

One thing is for certain: back when I wrote this book, I wasn't happy. I was constantly searching for happiness, so much so that I forgot to live my life along the way. I often blamed the world for anything negative it threw at me, however small. I was a sad, bitter man who sometimes overlooked the little things that brought joy. I wasted so much time feeling sorry for myself when I could have been living, not caring what people thought or what material possessions I had.

I learned that others can help you to be happy, but ultimately happiness is something you *choose*, just like with hope and purpose. It might take years until you realise it's been staring you right in the face this whole time. And when you've found it, even when hard times persist, nothing can ever harm you again.

For more happy content and hopeful updates from J.B. Villinger's works, contact him directly at jvillinger@live.com.au, or you can also find him on Wattpad @ JamesVillinger.